The Best AMERICAN SHORT STORIES 2005

GUEST EDITORS OF
THE BEST AMERICAN SHORT STORIES

1978 TED SOLOTAROFF
1979 JOYCE CAROL OATES
1980 STANLEY ELKIN
1981 HORTENSE CALISHER
1982 JOHN GARDNER
1983 ANNE TYLER
1984 JOHN UPDIKE
1985 GAIL GODWIN
1986 RAYMOND CARVER
1987 ANN BEATTIE
1988 MARK HELPRIN
1989 MARGARET ATWOOD
1990 RICHARD FORD
1991 ALICE ADAMS
1992 ROBERT STONE
1993 LOUISE ERDRICH
1994 TOBIAS WOLFF
1995 JANE SMILEY
1996 JOHN EDGAR WIDEMAN
1997 E. ANNIE PROULX
1998 GARRISON KEILLOR
1999 AMY TAN
2000 E. L. DOCTOROW
2001 BARBARA KINGSOLVER
2002 SUE MILLER
2003 WALTER MOSLEY
2004 LORRIE MOORE
2005 MICHAEL CHABON

The Best AMERICAN SHORT STORIES® 2005

Selected from
U.S. and Canadian Magazines
by MICHAEL CHABON
with KATRINA KENISON

With an Introduction by Michael Chabon

HOUGHTON MIFFLIN COMPANY
BOSTON • NEW YORK 2005

Visit our Web site: www.houghtonmifflinbooks.com.

ISSN: 0067-6233
ISBN-13: 978-0-618-42349-1 ISBN-10: 0-618-42349-4
ISBN-13: 978-0-618-42705-5 (pbk.) ISBN-10: 0-618-42705-8 (pbk.)

Printed in the United States of America

MP 10 9 8 7 6 5 4 3 2 1

Contents

Foreword

I AM A PERSON who grew up, as they used to say, "with her nose in a book," and who now reads for a living, some three thousand short stories a year, as well as various manuscripts for friends and acquaintances. Getting paid for what one loves to do is a great blessing of course, but it is also a fact that turning your avocation into your job can have its drawbacks. Like the chef who stops cooking at home, I face my own occupational hazard — losing the joy of reading just for the fun of it. After a day of required reading, I don't always reach for the half-finished novel or story collection on my bedside table. Sometimes, the line between business and pleasure is hard to discern.

I happen to live, however, with two adolescent boys who read voraciously and widely for the sheer delight of wallowing, like hedonists, in stories. Reading is how they relax, jump-start their imaginations, learn about the world, fill solitary hours, reward themselves after a long school day, a tough basketball game, a test survived. They choose to begin their days, and end them, reading. When you're a teenager enthralled by books, real life, with all its attendant difficulties, can seem like something of an intrusion; the world on the page is far more compelling than the quotidian realities of seventh-grade math or tenth-grade lunchroom dynamics.

Early mornings find my younger son propped on pillows, stealing an hour of reading before having to race to get ready for school. At night, it is always a battle to get the books put away, the lights turned off. Riding in the car, it is often the kids who demand silence, I who want to sing along with the radio. "Mom," they protest, "we're *reading!*"

Entertainment may indeed have a bad name among serious people, as Michael Chabon suggests in his trenchant introduction to this volume, but to a couple of teenage boys, being entertained is what life is all about. Given the myriad entertainment options available these days, it's a wonder that books hold sway at all. And yet, mysteriously, remarkably, for those lucky individuals who choose to latch on to the printed word and drink deeply thereof, books seem to offer a degree of nourishment and unadulterated satisfaction that no other medium can begin to match. Without the benefit of batteries, chips, bells, or whistles, they transport us. They demand our engagement with words and images, depend upon our ability to imagine, comprehend, and project ourselves into the hearts and minds of others unlike ourselves. If my sons wish to escape into alternate realities for hours each day, they could be doing worse; there is something hallowed, still, about the printed page (even the yellowed printed page of an old, used mass-market paperback) that a computer or TV screen cannot begin to approach.

For anyone who doesn't happen to share a home with boys at the moment, a cursory list of the current and recent favorites in our house will give some idea of where they seek their pleasures: Robert Jordan's Wheel of Time trilogy, *Conan the Barbarian* (many volumes read in no particular order), *Jaws, Mad About the Seventies* (compiled by *Mad* magazine), *The Andromeda Strain, The Curious Incident of the Dog in the Night-time,* Ken Burns's *History of Jazz, Reversing the Curse,* Michael Crichton's *Timeline* and *State of Fear, The Everything Cartooning Book, The Highwayman, And There Was Light* (a memoir by a blind hero of the French Resistance), Stephen King's *It* (my younger son) and King and Stewart O'Nan's chronicle of the 2004 Red Sox season, *Faithful* (my older son). . . . It is an undulating sea of literature which I know better than to critique or quantify. They chart their own course.

However, at thirteen, Jack is much taken with the notion of "bests." The Academy Awards are of great interest, as is the *New York Times* bestseller list. He and his friends passionately compile lists of best movies, best songs, actors, foods, teachers, sports teams, and, especially, best books. The top-ten list is always in flux but always ready to be rattled off to any interested party. The other day, Jack was fantasizing about creating his own book award, imagining just how satisfying it would be to call up Peter Benchley, thirty years after he scared a nation of swimmers out of the water, to let him know that, in his opinion, *Jaws* was the best book ever written, and that he, Mr. Benchley, could in fact come to a ceremony to receive his prize — a trophy that Jack envisioned as a huge golden statue of a book, lying open, with a golden page caught in mid-turn.

In a way, I get to live out Jack's fantasy each year when I call the authors of the stories included in *The Best American Short Stories* to let them know that their works have been selected as among "the best" of the year — not by a thirteen-year-old, but by a distinguished peer and fellow author. The task of letting a writer know that his or her words have been read, appreciated, and, ultimately, chosen to appear in this volume is certainly a joyous one. It would be lovely to offer each of them a golden book trophy as well, but inclusion in the anthology seems to bring its own measure of satisfaction. Joy Williams observed some years ago that "a significant story is always greater than the writer writing it." Surely even the most experienced author can't really know, until a work goes out into the world and finds its readers, just what has been wrought.

The stories in this year's *BASS* originally appeared online and in thirteen different publications. They vary widely in genre, style, tone, and substance, but they have something in common, too. Each is, in its own way, significant, simply by virtue of the fact that it has already succeeded in reaching out to readers and making contact. Most of us aren't blessed with schedules that allow for four or five hours of recreational reading a day; only particular interstices of life — youth, convalescence, unemployment, long vacations, old age, perhaps — seem to offer such leisure. And yet, we do turn, even in the midst of our harried and overscheduled lives, to stories for sustenance and for diversion. Those stories that seem to express and nurture our highest aspirations satisfy a certain hunger in the soul. And those that fearlessly embrace the baser realities of the human condition feed us equally well, for they give us courage to see the truth, to make our peace with what is, to carry on the heroic work of survival, growth, and change.

After fifteen years as annual editor of *The Best American Short Stories,* and thousands upon thousands of stories, I do still read, above all, for the fun of it. If the experience of meeting another mind on the page ever begins to feel like work, then I will know, for sure, it's time to stop. Meanwhile, I need only glance at my own two sons to be reminded, on a daily basis, of the alchemy that occurs when a story finds its audience, when writer and reader connect, when a good tale offered is gratefully received.

Michael Chabon cast a wide net as guest editor this year, reading even more stories than I sent him, even though I actually ended up sending him more than the usual 120. It was a year of unusual abundance, and he did an extraordinary job of making sure that the stories published in 2004 got their due, reading across genres and through several intimidating piles in his quest. Authors and readers alike can be grateful for his willingness to read above and beyond the call of duty. My thanks to Debbie Johnston, who proved herself an excellent first reader, and to Ryan Mann at Houghton Mifflin, for making my job easier in many small but significant ways. And thanks, especially, to the editors of those magazines that continue to publish fiction, in the belief that the stories of our time are worth reading, sharing, and preserving.

The stories chosen for this anthology were originally published between January 2004 and January 2005. The qualifications for selection are (1) original publication in nationally distributed American or Canadian periodicals; (2) publication in English by writers who are American or Canadian, or who have made the United States or Canada their home; (3) original publication as short stories (excerpts of novels are not knowingly considered). A list of magazines consulted for this volume appears at the back of the book. Editors who wish their short fiction to be considered for next year's edition should send their publications to Katrina Kenison, c/o The Best American Short Stories, Houghton Mifflin Company, 222 Berkeley Street, Boston, MA 02116.

K.K.

Introduction

ENTERTAINMENT HAS A BAD NAME. Serious people, some of whom write short stories, learn to mistrust and even to revile it. The word wears spandex, pasties, a leisure suit studded with blinking lights. It gives off a whiff of Coppertone and dripping Creamsicle, the fake-butter miasma of a movie-house lobby, of karaoke and Jagermeister, Jerry Bruckheimer movies, a Street Fighter machine grunting solipsistically in the corner of an ice-rink arcade, bread and circuses, the *Weekly World News*. Entertainment trades in cliché and product placement. It sells action figures and denture adhesive. It engages regions of the brain far from the centers of discernment, critical thinking, ontological speculation. It skirts the black heart of life and drowns life's lambency in a halogen glare. Intelligent people must keep a certain distance from its productions. They must handle the things that entertain them with gloves of irony and postmodern tongs. Entertainment, in short, means junk, and too much junk is bad for you — bad for your heart, your arteries, your mind, your soul.

But maybe these intelligent and serious people, my faithful straw men, are wrong. Maybe the reason for the junkiness of so much of what pretends to entertain us is that we have accepted — indeed, we have helped to articulate — such a narrow, debased concept of entertainment. The brain is an organ of entertainment, sensitive at any depth and over a wide spectrum. But we have learned to mistrust and despise our human aptitude for being entertained, and in that sense we get the entertainment we deserve.

I'd like to believe that, because I read for entertainment, and I write to entertain. Period. Oh, I could decoct a brew of other, more impressive motivations and explanations. I could uncork some stuff about reader response theory, or the Lacanian *parole.* I could go on — God knows I've done it elsewhere — about the storytelling impulse and the need to make sense of experience through story. A spritz of Jung might scent the air. I could adduce Kafka's formula, as the brilliant Lorrie Moore did in this space last year, of a book as an axe for the frozen sea within. I could go down to the café at the local mega-bookstore and take some wise words of Abelard or Koestler, about the power of literature, off a mug. But in the end — here's my point — it would still all boil down to *entertainment,* and its suave henchman, pleasure. Because when the axe bites the ice, you feel an answering throb of delight all the way from your hands to your shoulders, and the blade tolls like a bell for miles.

Therefore I would like to propose expanding our definition of entertainment to encompass everything pleasurable that arises from the encounter of an attentive mind with a page of literature. In so doing I will only be codifying what has, all my life, been my operating definition.

Here is a sample, chosen at random from my career as a reader, of encounters that would be covered under my new definition of entertainment: the engagement of the interior ear by the rhythm and pitch of an original prose style; the dawning awareness that giant mutant rat people dwell in the walls of a ruined abbey in England; two hours spent bushwhacking through a densely packed argument about the structures of power as embodied in nineteenth-century prison architecture; the consummation of a great love aboard a lost Amazonian riverboat or in Elizabethan slang; the intricate fractal patterning of motif and metaphor in Nabokov and Neil Gaiman; stories of pirates, zeppelins, sinister children; a thousand-word-long sentence comparing homosexuals to the Jews in a page of Proust; a duel to the death with broadswords on the seacoast of ancient Zingara; the outrageousness of whale slaughter or mule slaughter in Melville or Cormac McCarthy; the outrageousness of Dr. Charles Bovary's clubfoot-correcting device; the outrageousness of outrage in a page of Philip Roth; words written in smoke across the London sky on a day in June 1923; a momentary gain in my own sense of shared despair, shared nullity, shared rapture, shared loneliness, shared brokenhearted glee; the recounting of a portentous birth, a disastrous wedding, or a midnight death-watch on the Neva.

The original sense of the word *entertainment* is a lovely one of mutual support through intertwining, like a pair of trees grown together, each sustaining and bearing up the other. It suggests a kind of midair transfer of strength, contact across a void, like the tangling of cable and steel between two lonely bridgeheads. I can't think of a better approximation of the relation between reader and writer. Derived senses of fruitful exchange, of reciprocal sustenance, of welcome offered, of grasp and interrelationship, of a slender span of bilateral attention along which things are given and received, still animate the word in its verb form: we entertain visitors, guests, ideas, prospects, theories, doubts, and grudges.

At some point, inevitably, as generations of hosts entertained generations of guests with banquets and feasts and displays of artifice, the idea of pleasure seeped into the pores of the word. And along with pleasure (just as inevitably, I suppose) came disapproval, a sense of hollowness and hangover, the saturnine doubtfulness that attaches to delight and artifice and show — to pleasure, that ambiguous gift. It's partly the doubtfulness of pleasure that taints the name of entertainment. Pleasure is unreliable and transient. Pleasure is Lucy with the football. It is the roguish boyfriend who upends your heart with promises, touches you for twenty bucks, and then blows town. Pleasure is easily synthesized, mass-produced, individually wrapped. Its benefits do not endure, and so we come to mistrust them, or our taste for them.

The other taint is that of passivity. At some point in its history, the idea of entertainment lost its sense of mutuality, of exchange. One either entertains or is entertained, is the actor or the fan. As with all one-way relationships, grave imbalances accrue. The entertainer balloons with a dangerous need for approval, validation, love, and box office; while the one entertained sinks into a passive spectactorship, vacantly munching great big salty handfuls right from the foil bag. We can't take pleasure in a work of art, not in good conscience, without accepting the implicit intention of the artist to please us. But somewhere along the course of the past century or so, as the great machinery of pleasure came online, turning out products that, however pleasurable, suffer increasingly from the ills of mass manufacture — spurious innovation, inferior materials, alienated labor, and an excess of market research — that intention came to seem suspect, unworthy, and somehow cold and hungry at its core, like the eyes of a brilliant comedian. Lunch counters, muffler shops, dinner theaters, they aim to please; but *writers*? No self-respecting literary genius, even an occasional maker of avowed entertainments like Graham Greene, would ever describe himself as primarily an "entertainer." An entertainer is a man in a sequined dinner jacket, singing "She's a Lady" to a hall filled with women rubber-banding their underpants up onto the stage.

Yet entertainment — as I define it, pleasure and all — remains the only sure means we have of bridging, or at least of feeling as if we have bridged, the gulf of consciousness that separates each of us from everybody else. The best response to those who would cheapen and exploit it is not to disparage or repudiate but to reclaim entertainment as a job fit for artists and for audiences, a two-way exchange of attention, experience, and the universal hunger for connection.

The short story maps the most efficient path for spanning the chasm between two human skulls. Cartographers employ different types of maps — political, topographic, dot — to emphasize different kinds of information. These different types are complementary; taken together they increase our understanding. In other introductions to other collections of short stories, I have argued for the commonsense proposition that, in constructing our fictional maps, we ought not to restrict ourselves to one type or category. Science fiction, fantasy, crime fiction — all these genres and others have rich traditions in the American short story, reaching straight back to Poe and Hawthorne, our first great practitioners of the form. One of the pioneers of the modern "psychological" short story as we now generally understand it, Henry James, wrote so many out-and-out ghost stories that they fill an entire book. But the same process of commercialization and mass appeal that discredited entertainment, or the idea of literature as entertainment, also devastated our notion of the kinds of short stories that belong in college syllabi, prestigious magazines, or yearly anthologies of the best American short stories (another victory, in my view, for the enemies of pleasure, in their corporate or ivory towers). In spite of this general neglect by the literary mainstream, however, those other traditional genres remain viable and lively and powerful models of the short story, whether in the hands of a daring soul like Kelly Link or those of a crime novelist, like Dennis Lehane, who takes a brilliant chance on the form that brought us some of the best work that Hammett and Chandler ever did.

I guess that in the end all this talk of pleasure and entertainment is by way of acknowledging the obvious: I have no idea if these are the twenty best short stories published in the United States during 2004, or not. And neither do you. Or rather, you may feel very strongly that they are not, or that some of the stories here deserve the honor and some don't. But as you make your assessment — as you judge the product of my judgment — you will be relying, whether consciously, unconsciously, or in full-blown denial, on the same fundamental criterion as that on which I relied: the degree to which each of these stories catches hold of you, banishes everything but the interplay of your imagination and the author's, your ear and the author's, your solitude and the author's. That's entertainment. Short stories entertain; they aim to please. These are the twenty stories that pleased me best.

MICHAEL CHABON

TOM PERROTTA

The Smile on Happy Chang's Face

FROM POST ROAD

THE SUPERIOR WALLCOVERINGS WILDCATS were playing in the Little League championship game, and I wanted them to lose. I wanted the Town Pizza Ravens and their star pitcher, Lori Chang, to humiliate them, to run up the score and taunt them mercilessly from the first-base dugout. I know this isn't an admirable thing for a grown man to admit — especially a grown man who has agreed to serve as home-plate umpire — but there are feelings you can't hide from yourself, even if you'd just as soon chop off your hand as admit them to anyone else.

I had nothing against the Wildcat players. It was their coach I didn't like, my next-door neighbor, Carl DiSalvo, the Kitchen Kabinet King of Northern New Jersey. I stood behind the backstop, feeling huge and bloated in my cushiony chest protector, and watched him hit infield practice. A shamelessly vain man, Carl had ripped the sleeves off his sweatshirt, the better to display the rippling muscles he worked for like a dog down at Bally's. I knew all about his rippling muscles. Our driveways were adjacent, and Carl always seemed to be returning from an exhilarating session at the gym just as I was trudging off to work in the morning, my head still foggy from another rotten night's sleep.

"I'm getting pretty buff," he would tell me, proudly rubbing his pecs or biceps. "Wish I'd been built like this when I was younger."

Fuck you, I invariably thought, but I always said something polite, like "Keep it up" or "I gotta start working out myself."

Carl and I had known each other forever. In high school we

played football together — I was a starter, a second-team All-County linebacker, while Carl barely dirtied his uniform — and hung out in the same athletic crowd. When he and Marie bought the Detmeyers' house nine years ago, it had seemed like a lucky break for both of us, a chance to renew a friendship that had died of natural causes when we graduated and went our separate ways — me to college and into the management sector, Carl into his father's remodeling business. I helped him with the move, and when we finished, we sat on my patio with our wives, drinking beer and laughing as the summer light faded and our kids played tag on the grass. We called each other "neighbor" and imagined barbecues and block parties stretching far into the future.

"Nice pickup, Trevor," he called to his third baseman. "But let's keep working on that throw, okay, pal?"

So many things had happened since then. I was still living in the same house, but Jeanie and the kids were gone. And I had come to despise Carl, even though he'd done nothing to deserve it except live his own happy life right next to my sad one, where I had no choice but to witness it all the time and pretend not to mind.

Go fuck yourself, I thought. *Okay, pal?*

"Jackie *boy.*" Tim Tolbert, the first-base umpire and president of the Little League, pummeled my chest protector as though it were a punching bag. "Championship *game.*" He looked happier than a grown man has a right to be. "*Very* exciting."

As usual, I wanted to grab him by the collar and ask what the hell he had to be so cheerful about. He was a baby-faced, prematurely bald man who sold satellite dishes all day, then came home to his wife, a scrawny exercise freak obsessed with her son's peanut allergy. She'd made a big stink about it when the kid entered kindergarten, and now the school cafeteria wasn't allowed to serve PB&J sandwiches anymore.

"Very exciting," I agreed. "Two best teams in the league."

"Not to mention the two best umps," he said, giving me a brotherly squeeze on the shoulder.

This much I owed to Tim — he was the guy who convinced me to volunteer as an umpire. He must have known how isolated I was feeling, alone in my house, my wife and kids living with my mother-in-law, nothing to do at night but stare at the TV and stuff my face with sandwich cream cookies. I resisted at first, not wanting to give people a new opportunity to whisper about me, but he kept at it until finally I gave in.

And I loved it. Crouching behind the catcher, peering through the horizontal bars of my mask, my whole being focused on the crucial, necessary difference between a ball and a strike, I felt clear-headed and almost serene, free of the bitterness and shame that were my constant companions during the rest of my life.

"Two best umps?" I glanced around in mock confusion. "Me and who else?"

An errant throw rolled against the backstop, and Carl jogged over to retrieve it. He grabbed the ball and straightened up, turning to Tim and me as if we'd asked for his opinion.

"Kids are wound tight," he said. "I keep telling 'em it doesn't matter if you win or lose, but I don't think they believe me."

Carl grinned, letting us know he didn't believe it, either. Like me, he was in his midforties, but he was carrying it off with a little more panache than I was. He had thick gray hair that made for a striking contrast with his still-youthful body, and a gap between his front teeth that women supposedly found irresistible (at least that's what Jeanie used to tell me). His thick gold necklace glinted in the evening sun, spelling his name to the world.

"You're modeling the proper attitude," Tim told him. "That's all you can do."

The previous fall, a guy named Joe Funkhauser, the father of one of our high school football players, got into an argument with an opposing player's father in the parking lot after a bitterly contested game. Funkhauser beat the guy into a coma and was later charged with attempted murder. The Funkhauser Incident, as the papers called it, attracted a lot of unfavorable attention to our town and triggered a painful round of soul-searching among people concerned with youth sports. In response to the crisis, Tim had organized a workshop for Little League coaches and parents, trying to get them to focus on fun rather than competition, but it takes more than a two-hour seminar to change people's attitudes about something as basic as the difference between winning and losing.

"I don't blame your team for being spooked," I said. "Not after what Lori did to them last time. Didn't she set some kind of league record for strikeouts?"

Carl's grin disappeared. "I've been meaning to talk to you about that, Jack. The strike zone's down here. Not up here." He illustrated this point by slicing imaginary lines across his stomach and throat.

"Right," I said. "And it's six points for a touchdown."

"I don't mean to be a jerk about it," he continued, "but I thought you were making some questionable judgments."

"Funny," I said. "They're only questionable when they don't go your way."

"Just watch the high strikes, that's all I'm saying."

Tim kept smiling stiffly throughout this exchange, as if it were all just friendly banter, but he seemed visibly relieved by the sight of Ray Santelli, the Ravens' manager, returning from the snack bar with a hot dog in each hand.

"Just got outta work," he said, by way of explanation. "Traffic was a bitch on the Parkway."

Ray was a dumpy guy with an inexplicably beautiful Russian wife. A lot of people assumed she was mail order, despite Ray's repeated claims that he'd met her at his cousin's wedding. He ran a livery business with his brother and sometimes kept a white stretch limo parked in the driveway of his modest Cape Cod on Dunellen Street. The car was like the wife, a little too glamorous for its humble surroundings.

"It's those damn toll plazas," observed Tim. "They were supposed to be gone twenty years ago."

Before anyone could chime in with the ritual agreement, our attention was diverted by the appearance of Mikey Fellner wielding his video camera. A mildly retarded guy in his early twenties, Mikey was a familiar figure at local sporting events, graduations, carnivals, and political meetings. He videotaped everything and saved the tapes, which he labeled and shelved in chronological order in his parents' garage. This was apparently part of the syndrome he had — it wasn't Down's but something more exotic, I forget the name — some compulsion to keep everything fanatically organized. He trained the camera on me, then got a few seconds of Santelli wiping mustard off his chin.

"You guys hear?" Carl asked. "Mikey says they're gonna show the game on cable access next week."

Mikey panned over to Tim, holding the camera just a couple of inches from his face. He wasn't big on respecting other people's boundaries, especially when he was working. Tim didn't seem to mind, though.

"Championship *game,*" he said, giving a double thumbs-up to the viewing audience. "*Very* exciting."

Little League is a big deal in our town. You could tell that just by looking at our stadium. We've got dugouts, a big electronic scoreboard, and a padded outfield fence covered with ads for local businesses, just like the pro teams (that's how we paid for the scoreboard). We play the national anthem over a really good sound system, nothing like the scratchy loudspeaker they used when I was a kid. The bleachers were packed for the championship game, and not just with the families of the players. It was a bona fide local event.

The Wildcats were up first, and Carl was right: his team had a bad case of the jitters. The leadoff hitter, Justin O'Malley, stepped up to the plate white-knuckled and expecting the worst, as if Lori Chang were Roger Clemens. He planted himself as far away from the plate as possible, stood like a statue for three called strikes, and seemed relieved to return to the bench. The second batter, Mark Rigato, swung blindly at three bad pitches, including a high and tight third strike that almost took his head off. His delayed evasive action, combined with the momentum of his premature swing, caused him to pirouette so violently that he lost his balance and ended up face down in the dirt.

"Strike three," I said, taking care to keep my voice flat and matter-of-fact. I wasn't one of those showoff umps who said *Stee-rike!* and did a big song and dance behind the plate. "Batter's out."

The words were barely out of my mouth when Carl came bounding out of the third-base dugout. He had his bare arms spread wide, as if volunteering for a crucifixion.

"Goddamn it, Jack! That was a bean ball!"

I wasn't fooled by his theatrics. By that point, just six pitches into the first inning, it was already clear that Lori Chang was operating at the top of her game, and you didn't need Tim McCarver to tell you that Carl was trying to mess with her head. I should've ordered him back to the dugout and called for play to resume, but there was just enough of a taste in my mouth from our earlier encounter that I took the bait. I removed my mask and took a few steps in his direction.

"Please watch your language, Coach. You know better than that."

"She's throwing at their heads!" Carl was yelling now, for the benefit of the spectators. "She's gonna kill someone!"

"The batter swung," I reminded him.

"He was trying to protect himself. You gotta warn her, Jack. That's your job."

"You do your job, Carl. I'll take care of mine."

I had just pulled my mask back over my head when Tim came jogging across the infield to back me up. We umpires made it a point to present a unified front whenever a dispute arose.

"It's okay," I told him. "Let's play ball."

He gave me one of those subtle headshakes, the kind you wouldn't have noticed if he hadn't been standing six inches in front of you.

"He's right, Jack. You should talk to her."

"You're playing right into his hands."

"Maybe so," he admitted. "But this is the championship. Let's keep it under control."

He was forcing me into an awkward position. I didn't want to be Carl's puppet, but I also didn't want to argue with Tim right there in the middle of the infield. As it was, I could feel my authority draining away by the second. Someone on the Ravens' side yelled for us to stop yapping and get on with the game. A Wildcats fan suggested we'd been bought and paid for by Town Pizza.

"We gotta be careful here." Tim gestured toward the Wildcats' dugout, where Mikey had his video camera set up on a tripod. "This is gonna be on TV."

Lori Chang smiled quizzically as I approached the mound, as if she couldn't possibly imagine why I was paying her a social visit in the middle of the game.

"Is something wrong?" she asked, sounding a little more worried than she looked.

Lori was one of only three girls playing in our Little League that season. I know it's politically incorrect to say so, but the other two, Allie Regan and Steph Murkowski, were tomboys — husky, tough-talking jockettes you could easily imagine playing college rugby and marching in Gay Pride parades later in their lives.

Lori Chang, on the other hand, didn't even look like an athlete. She was petite, with a round, serious face and lustrous hair that she wore in a ponytail threaded through the back of her baseball cap. Unlike Allie and Steph, both of whom were fully developed in a chunky, none-too-feminine way, Lori had not yet reached puberty. She was lithe and curveless, her chest as flat as a boy's beneath the stretchy fabric of her Ravens jersey. And yet — I hope it's okay for me to talk like this, because it's true — there was something undeniably sexual about her presence on the baseball field. She wore lipstick and nail polish, giggled frequently for no reason, and blushed when her teammates complimented her performance. She was always tugging down her jersey in the back, as if she suspected the shortstop and third baseman of paying a little too much attention to her ass. In short, she was completely adorable. If I'd been twelve, I would've had a hopeless crush on her.

Which is why it was always such a shock when she let loose with the high, hard one. Unlike other pitchers her age, who struggled just to put the ball over the plate, Lori actually had a strategy, a potent combination of control, misdirection, patience, and outright intimidation. She tended to jam batters early in the count and occasionally brushed them back, though to my knowledge, she'd never actually hit anyone. Midcount, she often switched to change-ups and breaking balls, working on the outside corner. Once she had the batter appropriately spooked and thoroughly off balance, she liked to rear back and finish him off with a sizzler right down the pipe. These two-strike fastballs hopped and dived so unpredictably that it was easy to lose track of them. Some of the batters didn't even realize the ball had crossed the plate until they heard the slap of leather against leather and turned in angry amazement to see a small but decisive puff of dust rising from the catcher's mitt.

I had no idea where she learned to pitch like that. Lori was a newcomer to our town, one of those high-achieving Asian kids who've flocked here in the past decade (every year, it seems, the valedictorian of our high school has a Chinese or Korean or Indian last name). In just a few months, she'd established herself as an excellent student, a gifted violinist, and a powerhouse on the baseball diamond, despite the fact that she could usually be found waiting tables and filling napkin dispensers at Happy Wok #2, the restaurant her parents had opened on Grand Avenue.

"There's nothing wrong," I told her. "Just keep right on doing what you're doing."

Her eyes narrowed with suspicion. "You came all the way out here to tell me that?"

"It's really not that far," I said, raising my mask just high enough so she could see that I was smiling.

By the end of the third inning, Lori had struck out eight of the first nine batters she'd faced. The only Wildcat to even make contact with the ball was Ricky DiSalvo, Carl's youngest son and the league leader in home runs and RBIs, who got handcuffed by a fastball and dinged a feeble check-swing groundout to second.

Lori's father, Happy Chang, was sitting by himself in the third-base bleachers, surrounded by Wildcats fans. Despite his nickname, Mr. Chang was a grim, unfriendly man who wore the same dirty beige windbreaker no matter how hot or cold it was and always seemed to need a shave. Unlike the other Asian fathers in our town — most of them were doctors, computer scientists, and businessmen who played golf and made small talk in perfect English — Happy Chang had a rough edge, a just-off-the-boat quality that reminded me of those guys you often saw milling around on Canal Street in the city, making disgusting noises and spitting on the sidewalk. I kept glancing at him as the game progressed, waiting for him to crack a smile or offer a word of encouragement, but he remained stone-faced, as if he wished he were back at his restaurant, keeping an eye on the lazy cooks instead of watching his amazing daughter dominate the Wildcats in front of the whole town on a lovely summer evening.

Maybe it's a Chinese thing, I thought. Maybe they don't like to show emotion in public. Or maybe — I had no idea, but it didn't keep me from speculating — he wished he had a son instead of a daughter (as far as I could tell, Lori was an only child). Like everybody else, I knew about the Chinese preference for boys over girls. One of my coworkers, a single woman in her late thirties, had recently traveled to Shanghai to adopt a baby girl abandoned by her parents. She said the orphanages were full of them.

But if Happy Chang didn't love his daughter, how come he came to every game? For that matter, why did he let her play at all? My best guess — based on my own experience as a father — was that he simply didn't know what to make of her. In China, girls didn't play baseball. So what did it mean that Lori played the game as well or better than any American boy? Maybe he was divided in his own mind between admiring her talent and seeing it as kind of a curse, a symbol of everything that separated him from his own past. Maybe that was why he faithfully attended her games but always sat scowling on the wrong side of the field, as if he were rooting for her opponents. Maybe his daughter was as unfathomable to him as my own son had been to me.

Like most men, I'd wanted a son who reminded me of myself as a kid, a boy who lived for sports, collected baseball cards, and hung pennants on his bedroom walls. I wanted a son who played tackle football down at the schoolyard with the other neighborhood kids and came home with ripped pants and skinned knees. I wanted a son I could take to the ballpark and play catch with in the backyard.

But Jason was an artistic, dreamy kid with long eyelashes and delicate features. He loved music and drew elaborate pictures of castles and clouds and fairy princesses. He enjoyed playing with his sisters' dolls and exhibited what I thought was an unhealthy interest in my wife's jewelry and high heels. When he was seven years old, he insisted on going out trick-or-treating dressed as Pocahontas. Everywhere he went, people kept telling him how beautiful he was, and it was impossible not to see how happy this made him.

Jeanie did her best to convince me that it wasn't a problem; she cut out magazine articles that said he was simply engaged in harmless "gender play" and recommended that we let him follow his heart and find his own way in the world. She scolded me for using words like *sissy* and *wimp* and for trying to enforce supposedly outdated standards of masculinity. I tried to get with the program, but it was hard. I was embarrassed to be seen in public with my own son, as if he somehow made me less of a man.

It didn't help that Carl had three normal boys living right next door. They were always in the backyard kicking a soccer ball, tossing a football, or beating the crap out of one another. Sometimes they included my son in their games, but it wasn't much fun for any of them.

Jason didn't want to play Little League, but I made him. I thought putting on a uniform might transform him into the kind of kid I would recognize as my own. Despite the evidence in front of my face, I refused to believe you could be an American boy and not love baseball and not want to impress your father with your athletic prowess.

It's easy to say you should just let a kid follow his heart. But what if his heart takes him places you don't want to go? What if your ten-year-old son wants to take tap-dancing lessons in a class full of girls? What if he's good at it? What if he tells you when he's fourteen that he's made it onto the chorus of *Guys and Dolls* and expects you to be happy about this? What if when he's fifteen he tells you he's joined the Gay and Lesbian Alliance at his progressive suburban high school? What if this same progressive school has a separate prom for boys who want to go with boys and girls who want to go with girls? Are you supposed to say, *Okay, fine, follow your heart, go to the prom with Gerald, just don't stay out too late?*

I only hit him that once. He said something that shocked me and I slapped him across the face. He was the one who threw the first punch, a feeble right cross that landed on the side of my head. Later, when I had time to think about it, I was proud of him for fighting back. But at the time, it just made me crazy. I couldn't believe the little faggot had hit me. The punch I threw in return is the one thing in my life I'll regret forever. I broke his nose, and Jeanie called the cops. I was taken from my house in handcuffs, the cries of my wife and children echoing in my ears. As I ducked into the patrol car, I looked up and saw Carl watching me from his front stoop, shaking his head and trying to comfort Marie, who for some reason was sobbing audibly in the darkness, like it was her own child whose face I'd bloodied in a moment of thoughtless rage.

Lori Chang kept her perfect game going all the way into the top of the fifth, when Pete Gonzalez, the Wildcats' all-star shortstop, ripped a two-out single to center. A raucous cheer erupted from the third-base dugout and bleachers, both of which had lapsed into a funereal silence over the past couple of innings. It was an electrifying sound, a collective whoop of relief, celebration, and resurgent hope.

On a psychological level, that one hit changed everything. It was as if the whole ballpark suddenly woke up to two very important facts: (1) Lori Chang was not, in fact, invincible, and (2) the Wildcats could actually still win. The score was only 1–0 in favor of the Ravens, a margin that had seemed insurmountable a moment ago but that suddenly looked a whole lot slimmer now that the tying run was standing on first with a lopsided grin on his face, shifting his weight from leg to leg like he needed to go to the bathroom.

The only person who didn't seem to notice that the calculus of the game had changed was Lori Chang herself. She stood on the mound with her usual poker face, an expression that suggested profound boredom more than it did killer concentration, and waited for Trevor Mancini to make the sign of the cross and knock imaginary mud off his cleats. Once he got himself settled, she nodded to the catcher and began her wind-up, bringing her arms overhead and lowering them with the painstaking deliberation of a tai chi master. Then she kicked high and whipped a fastball right at Trevor, a guided missile that thudded into his leg with a muffled *whump,* the sound of a broomstick smacking a rug.

"Aaah, shit!" Trevor flipped his bat in the air and began hopping around on one foot, rubbing frantically at his leg. "Shit! Shit! Shit!"

I stepped out from behind the catcher and asked if he was okay. Trevor gritted his teeth and performed what appeared to be an involuntary bow. When he straightened up, he looked more embarrassed than hurt.

"Stings," he explained.

I told him to take his base and he hobbled off, still massaging the sore spot. A chorus of boos had risen from the third-base side, and I wasn't surprised to see that Carl was already out of the dugout, walking toward me with what could only be described as an amused expression.

"Well?" he said. "What're you gonna do about it?"

"The batter was hit by a pitch. It's part of the game."

"Are you kidding me? She threw right at him."

Right on schedule, Tim came trotting over to join us, followed immediately by Ray Santelli, who approached us with his distinctive potbellied swagger, radiating an odd confidence that made you forget that he was just a middle-aged chauffeur with a comb-over.

"What's up?" he inquired. "Somebody got a problem?"

"Yeah, me," Carl told him. "I got a problem with your sweet little pitcher throwing bean balls at my players."

"That was no bean ball," I pointed out. "It hit him in the leg."

"So that's okay?" Carl was one of those guys who smiled when he was pissed off. "It's okay to hit my players in the leg?"

"She didn't do it on purpose," Santelli assured him. "Lori wouldn't do that."

"I don't know," Tim piped in. "It looked pretty deliberate from where I was standing."

"How would you know?" Santelli demanded, an uncharacteristic edge creeping into his voice. "Are you some kind of mind reader?"

"I'm just telling you what it looked like," Tim replied.

"Big deal," said Santelli. "That's just your subjective opinion."

"I'm an umpire," Tim reminded him. "My subjective opinion is all I have."

"Really?" Santelli scratched his head, feigning confusion. "I thought you guys were supposed to be objective. When did they change the job description?"

"All right," said Tim. "Whatever. It's my objective opinion, okay?"

"Look," I said. "We're doing the best we can."

"I sure as hell hope not," Carl shot back. "Or else we're in big trouble."

Sensing an opportunity, Santelli cupped his hands around his mouth and called out, "Hey, Lori, did you hit that kid on purpose?"

Lori seemed shocked by the question. Her mouth dropped open and she shook her head back and forth, as if nothing could have been further from the truth.

"It slipped," she said. "I'm really sorry."

"See?" Santelli turned back to Tim with an air of vindication. "It was an accident."

"Jack?" Carl's expression was a mixture of astonishment and disgust. "You really gonna let this slide?"

I glanced at Tim for moral support, but his face was blank, pointedly devoid of sympathy. I wished I could have thought of something more decisive to do than shrug.

"What do you want from me?" There was a pleading note in my voice that was unbecoming in an umpire. "She said it slipped."

"Now wait a minute —" Tim began, but Carl didn't let him finish.

"Fine," he said. "The hell with it. If that's the way it's gonna be, that's the way it's gonna be. Let's play ball."

Carl stormed off, leaving the three of us standing by the plate, staring at his back as he descended into the dugout.

"You can't know what's in another person's heart." Santelli shook his head, as if saddened by this observation. "You just can't."

"Why don't you shut up," Tim told him.

Lori quickly regained her composure when play resumed. With runners on first and second, she calmly and methodically struck out Antoine Frye to retire the side. On her way to the dugout she stopped and apologized to Trevor Mancini, resting her hand tenderly on his shoulder. It was a classy move. Trevor blushed and told her to forget about it.

Ricky DiSalvo was on the mound for the Wildcats, and though he had nowhere near Lori's talent, he was pitching a solid and effective game. A sidearmer plagued by control problems and a lack of emotional maturity — I had once seen him burst into tears after walking five straight batters — Ricky had wisely decided that night to make his opponents hit the ball. All game long, he'd dropped one fat pitch after another right over the meatiest part of the plate.

The Ravens, a mediocre hitting team on the best of days, had eked out a lucky run in the second on a single, a stolen base, an overthrow, and an easy fly ball to right field that had popped out of Mark Diedrich's glove, but they'd been shut out ever since. Ricky's confidence had grown with each successive inning, and he was throwing harder and more skillfully than he had all game by the time Lori Chang stepped up to the plate with two outs in the bottom of the fifth.

I guess I should have seen what was coming. When I watched the game on cable access a week later, it all seemed painfully clear in retrospect, almost inevitable. But at the time, I didn't sense any danger. We'd had some unpleasantness the previous inning, but it had passed when Lori apologized to Trevor. The game had moved forward, slipping past the trouble as easily as water flowing around a rock.

I did notice that Lori Chang looked a little nervous in the batter's box, but that was nothing unusual. As bold and powerful as she was on the mound, Lori was a surprisingly timid hitter. She tucked herself into an extreme crouch, shrinking the strike zone down to a few inches, and tried to wait out a walk. She rarely swung and was widely, and fairly, considered to be an easy out.

For some reason, though, Ricky seemed oddly tentative with his first couple of pitches. Ball one kicked up dirt about ten feet from the plate. Ball two was a mile outside.

"Come on," Carl called impatiently from the dugout. "Just do it."

Lori tapped the fat end of her bat on the plate. I checked my clicker and squatted into position. Ricky glanced at his father and started into his herky-jerky wind-up.

On TV it all looks so fast and clean — Lori gets beaned and she goes down. But on the field it felt slow and jumbled, my brain lagging a beat behind the action. Before I can process the fact that the ball's rocketing toward her head, Lori's already said, "Ooof!" Her helmet's in the air before I register the sickening crack of impact, and by then she's already crumpled on the ground. On TV, it looks as though I move quickly, rolling her onto her back and coming in close to check her breathing, but in my memory it's as if I'm paralyzed, as if the world has stopped and all I can do is stare at the bareheaded girl lying motionless at my feet.

Then the quiet bursts into commotion. Tim's right beside me, shouting, "Is she okay? Is she okay?" Ricky's moving toward us from the mound, his glove pressed to his mouth, his eyes stricken with terror and remorse.

"Did I hurt her?" he asks. "I didn't mean to hurt her."

"I think you killed her," I tell him, because as far as I can tell, Lori's not breathing.

Ricky stumbles backward, as if someone's pushed him. He turns in the direction of his father, who's just stepped out of the dugout.

"You shouldn't have made me do that!" Ricky yells.

"Oh, my God," says Carl. He looks pale and panicky.

At that same moment, Happy Chang's scaling the third-base fence and sprinting across the infield to check on his daughter's condition. At least that's what I think he's doing, right up to the moment when he veers suddenly toward Carl, emitting a cry of guttural rage, and tackles him savagely to the ground.

Happy Chang is a small man, no bigger than some of our Little Leaguers, and Carl is tall and bulked up from years of religious weightlifting, but it's no contest. Within seconds, Happy's straddling Carl's chest and punching him repeatedly in the face, all the while shouting what must be very angry things in Chinese. Carl doesn't even try to defend himself, not even when Happy Chang reaches for his throat.

Luckily for Carl, two of our local policemen, Officers Freylinghausen and Hughes — oddly enough, the same two who'd arrested me for domestic battery — are present at the game, and before Happy Chang can finish throttling Carl, they've rushed the field and broken up the fight. They take Happy Chang into custody with a surprising amount of force — with me they were oddly polite — Freylinghausen grinding his face into the dirt while Hughes slaps on the cuffs. I'm so engrossed by the spectacle that I don't even realize that Lori's regained consciousness until I hear her voice.

"Daddy?" She says the word quietly, and for a second I think she's talking to me.

My whole life fell apart after I broke my son's nose. By the time I got out on bail the next morning, Jeanie had already taken the kids to her mother's house and slapped me with a restraining order. The day after that she started divorce proceedings.

In the year that had passed since then, nothing much had changed. I had tried apologizing in a thousand different ways, but it didn't seem to matter. As far as Jeanie was concerned, I'd crossed some unforgivable line and was beyond redemption.

I accepted the loss of my wife as a fair punishment for what I'd done, but it was harder to accept the loss of my kids. I had some visiting rights, but they were severely restricted. Basically, I took my daughters — they were eleven and thirteen — to the movies or the mall every other Saturday, then to a restaurant, and then back to their grandmother's. They weren't allowed to stay overnight with me. It killed me to walk past their empty rooms at night, to not find them asleep and safe, and to be fairly sure I never would.

Once in a while Jason joined us on our Saturday excursions, but usually he was too busy with his plays. He had just finished his junior year in high school, capping it off with a starring role in the spring musical, *Joseph and the Amazing Technicolor Dreamcoat.* People kept telling me how great he was, and I kept agreeing, embarrassed to confess that I hadn't seen the show. My son had asked me not to come, and I'd respected his wishes.

A year on my own had given me a lot of time to think, to come to terms with what had happened, and to accept my own responsibility for it. It also gave me a lot of time to stew in my own anger, to indulge the conviction that I was a victim too, every bit as much as my wife and son. I wrote Jeanie and my kids a lot of letters trying to outline my complicated position on these matters, but no one ever responded to them. It was like my side of the story had disappeared into some kind of void.

That's why I wanted so badly for my family to watch the championship game on cable access. I had e-mailed them all separately, telling them when it would be broadcast and asking them to please tune in. I called them the day it aired and left a message reminding them to be sure to stick it out all the way to the end.

What I wanted them to see was the top of the sixth and final inning, the amazing sequence of events that took place immediately following the bean-ball fiasco, after both Carl and Ricky DiSalvo had been ejected from the game and Happy Chang had been hauled off to the police station.

Despite the fact that she'd been knocked unconscious just a few minutes earlier, Lori was back on the mound for the Ravens. She'd been examined and given a clean bill of health by Sharon Nelson, whose son, Daniel, played second base for the Wildcats. Dr. Nelson assured us that Lori hadn't suffered a concussion and was free to continue playing if she felt up to it.

She started out strong, striking out Jeb Partridge and retiring Hiro Tamanaki on an easy infield fly. But then something happened. Maybe the blow to the head had affected her more seriously than she'd let on, or maybe she'd been traumatized by her father's arrest. Whatever the reason, she fell apart. With only one out remaining in the game, she walked three straight batters to load the bases.

I'd always admired Lori's regal detachment, her ability to remain calm and focused no matter what was going on, but now she just looked scared. She cast a desperate glance at the first-base dugout, silently pleading with her coach to take her out of the game, but Santelli ignored her. No matter how badly she was pitching, she was still his ace. And besides, the next batter was Mark Diedrich, the Wildcats' pudgy right fielder, one of the weakest hitters in the league.

"Just settle down," Santelli told her. "Strike this guy out and we can all go home."

Lori nodded skeptically and got herself set on the mound. Mark Diedrich greeted me with a polite nod as he stepped into the batter's box. He was a nice kid, a former preschool classmate of my youngest daughter.

"I wish I was home in bed," he told me.

The first pitch was low. Then came a strike, the liveliest breaking ball Lori had thrown all inning, but it was followed by two outside fastballs (Ricky's bean ball had clearly done the trick; Lori wasn't throwing anywhere near the inside corner). The next pitch, low and away, should have been ball four, but inexplicably, Mark lunged at it, barely nicking it foul.

"Oh, Jesus," he whimpered. "Why did I do that?"

So there we were. Full count, bases loaded, two out. Championship game. A score of 1–0. The whole season narrowing down to a single pitch. If the circumstances had been a little different, it would have been a beautiful moment, an umpire's dream.

But for me, the game barely existed. All I could think of just then was the smile on Happy Chang's dirty face as the cops led him off the field. I was kneeling on the ground, trying to comfort Lori, when Happy turned in our direction and said something low and gentle in Chinese, maybe asking if she was all right or telling her not to worry. Lori said something back, maybe that she was fine or that she loved him.

"Easy now," Santelli called from the dugout. "Right down the middle."

Lori tugged her shirt down in the back and squinted at the catcher. Mark Diedrich's face was beet red, as if something terribly embarrassing were about to happen.

"Please, God," I heard him mutter as Lori began her wind-up. "Don't let me strike out."

I should have been watching the ball, but instead I was thinking about Happy Chang and everything he must have been going through at the police station, the fingerprinting, the mug shot, the tiny holding cell. But mainly it was the look on his face that haunted me, the proud and defiant smile of a man at peace with what he'd done and willing to accept the consequences.

The ball smacked into the catcher's mitt, waking me from my reverie. Mark hadn't swung. As far as I could determine after the fact, the pitch appeared to have crossed the plate near the outside corner, though possibly a bit on the high side. I honestly didn't know if it was a ball or a strike.

I guess I could have lied. I could have called strike three and given the game to the Ravens, to Lori Chang and Ray Santelli. I could have sent Mark Diedrich sobbing back to the dugout, probably scarred for life. But instead I pulled off my mask.

"Jack?" Tim was standing between first and second with his palms open to the sky. "You gonna call it?"

"I can't," I told him. "I didn't see it."

There was a freedom in admitting it that I hadn't anticipated, and I dropped my mask to the ground. Then I slipped my arms through the straps of my chest protector and let that fall, too.

"What happened?" Mark Diedrich asked in a quavery voice. "Did I strike out?"

"I don't know," I told him.

Boos and angry cries rose from the bleachers as I made my way toward the pitcher's mound. I wanted to tell Lori Chang that I envied her father, but I had a feeling she wouldn't understand. She seemed relieved when I walked past her without saying a word. Mikey Fellner was out of the dugout and videotaping me as I walked past second base and onto the grass. He followed me all the way across center field, until I climbed the fence over the ad for the Prima Ballerina School of Dance and left the ballpark.

That's what I wanted my ex-wife and children to see — an umpire walking away from a baseball game, a man who had the courage to admit that he'd failed, who understood that there were times when you had no right to judge, responsibilities you were no longer qualified to exercise. I hoped they might learn something new about me, something I hadn't been able to make clear to them in my letters and phone calls.

But of course I was disappointed. What's in your heart sometimes remains hidden, even when you most desperately want it to be revealed. I remembered my long walk across the outfield as a dignified, silent journey, but on TV I seem almost to be jogging. I look sweaty and confused, a little out of breath as I mumble a string of barely audible excuses and apologies for my strange behavior. If Jeanie and the kids had been watching, all they would have seen was an unhappy man they already knew too well, fleeing from the latest mess he'd made: just me, still trying to explain.

DENNIS LEHANE

Until Gwen

FROM THE ATLANTIC MONTHLY

YOUR FATHER PICKS YOU UP FROM PRISON in a stolen Dodge Neon, with an 8-ball of coke in the glove compartment and a hooker named Mandy in the back seat. Two minutes into the ride, the prison still hanging tilted in the rearview, Mandy tells you that she only hooks part-time. The rest of the time she does light secretarial for an independent video chain and tends bar, two Sundays a month, at the local VFW. But she feels her calling — her true calling in life — is to write.

You go, "Books?"

"Books." She snorts, half out of amusement, half to shoot a line off your fist and up her left nostril. "Screenplays!" She shouts it at the dome light for some reason. "You know — movies."

"Tell him the one about the psycho saint guy." Your father winks at you in the rearview, like he's driving the two of you to the prom. "Go ahead. Tell him."

"Okay, okay." She turns on the seat to face you, and your knees touch, and you think of Gwen, a look she gave you once, nothing special, just looking back at you as she stood at the front door, asking if you'd seen her keys. A forgettable moment if ever there was one, but you spent four years in prison remembering it.

". . . so at his canonization," Mandy is saying, "something, like, happens? And his spirit comes *back* and goes into the body of this priest. But, like, the priest? He has a brain tumor. He doesn't know it or nothing, but *he* does, and it's fucking up his, um —"

"Brain?" you try.

"Thoughts," Mandy says. "So he gets this saint in him and that *does it,* because, like, even though the guy was a saint, his spirit has become evil, because his soul is gone. So this priest? He spends the rest of the movie trying to kill the pope."

"Why?"

"Just listen," your father says. "It gets good."

You look out the window. A car sits empty along the shoulder. It's beige, and someone has painted gold wings on the sides, fanning out from the front bumper and across the doors. A sign is affixed to the roof with some words on it, but you've passed it by the time you think to wonder what it says.

"See, there's this secret group that works for the Vatican? They're like a, like a . . ."

"A hit squad," your father says.

"Exactly," Mandy says, and presses her finger to your nose. "And the lead guy, the, like, head agent? He's the hero. He lost his wife and daughter in a terrorist attack on the Vatican a few years back, so he's a little fucked up, but —"

You say, "Terrorists attacked the Vatican?"

"Huh?"

You look at her, waiting. She has a small face, eyes too close to her nose.

"In the *movie,*" Mandy says. "Not in real life."

"Oh. I just — you know, four years inside, you assume you missed a couple of headlines, but . . ."

"Right." Her face is dark and squally now. "Can I finish?"

"I'm just saying," you say and snort another line off your fist, "even the guys on death row would have heard about that one."

"Just go with it," your father says. "It's not, like, real life."

You look out the window, see a guy in a chicken suit carrying a can of gas in the breakdown lane, think how real life isn't like real life. Probably more like this poor dumb bastard running out of gas in a car with wings painted on it. Wondering how the hell he ever got here. Wondering who he'd pissed off in that previous real life.

Your father has rented two rooms at an Econo Lodge so that you and Mandy can have some privacy, but you send Mandy home after she twice interrupts the sex to pontificate on the merits of Michael Bay films.

You sit in the blue-wash flicker of ESPN and eat peanuts from a plastic bag you got out of a vending machine and drink plastic cupfuls of Jim Beam from a bottle your father presented when you reached the motel parking lot. You think of the time you've lost, and how nice it is to sit alone on a double bed and watch TV, and you think of Gwen, can taste her tongue for just a moment, and you think about the road that's led you here to this motel room on this night after forty-seven months in prison, and how a lot of people would say it was a twisted road, a weird one, filled with curves, but you just think of it as a road like any other. You drive down it on faith, or because you have no other choice, and you find out what it's like by the driving of it, find out what the end looks like only by reaching it.

Late the next morning your father wakes you, tells you he drove Mandy home and you've got things to do, people to see.

Here's what you know about your father above all else: people have a way of vanishing in his company.

He's a professional thief, a consummate con man, an expert in his field — and yet something far beyond professionalism is at his core, something unreasonably arbitrary. Something he keeps within himself like a story he heard once, laughed at maybe, yet swore never to repeat.

"She was with you last night?" you say.

"You didn't want her. Somebody had to prop her ego back up. Poor girl like that."

"But you drove her home," you say.

"I'm speaking Czech?"

You hold his eyes for a bit. They're big and bland, with the heartless innocence of a newborn's. Nothing moves in them, nothing breathes, and after a while you say, "Let me take a shower."

"Fuck the shower," he says. "Throw on a baseball cap and let's get."

You take the shower anyway, just to feel it, another of those things you would have realized you'd miss if you'd given it any thought ahead of time — standing under the spray, no one near you, all the hot water you want for as long as you want it, shampoo that doesn't smell like factory smoke.

Drying your hair and brushing your teeth, you can hear the old man flicking through channels, never pausing on one for more than thirty seconds: Home Shopping Network — zap. Springer — zap. Oprah — zap. Soap-opera voices, soap-opera music — zap. Monster-truck show — pause. Commercial — zap, zap, zap.

You come back into the room, steam trailing you, pick your jeans up off the bed, and put them on.

The old man says, "Afraid you'd drowned. Worried I'd have to take a plunger to the drain, suck you back up."

You say, "Where we going?"

"Take a drive." Your father shrugs, flicking past a cartoon.

"Last time you said that, I got shot twice."

Your father looks back over his shoulder at you, eyes big and soft. "Wasn't the car that shot you, was it?"

You go out to Gwen's place, but she isn't there anymore. A couple of black kids are playing in the front yard, black mother coming out on the porch to look at the strange car idling in front of her house.

"You didn't leave it here?" your father says.

"Not that I recall."

"Think."

"I'm thinking."

"So you didn't?"

"I told you — not that I recall."

"So you're sure."

"Pretty much."

"You had a bullet in your head."

"Two."

"I thought one glanced off."

You say, "Two bullets hit your fucking head, old man, you don't get hung up on the particulars."

"That how it works?" Your father pulls away from the curb as the woman comes down the steps.

The first shot came through the back window, and Gentleman Pete flinched. He jammed the wheel to the right and drove the car straight into the highway exit barrier, air bags exploding, water barrels exploding, something in the back of your head exploding, glass pebbles filling your shirt, Gwen going, "What happened? Jesus. What happened?"

You pulled her with you out the back door — Gwen, your Gwen — and you crossed the exit ramp and ran into the woods and the second shot hit you there but you kept going, not sure how, not sure why, the blood pouring down your face, your head on fire, burning so bright and so hard that not even the rain could cool it off.

"And you don't remember nothing else?" your father says. You've driven all over town, every street, every dirt road, every hollow you can stumble across in Sumner, West Virginia.

"Not till she dropped me off at the hospital."

"Dumb goddamn move if ever there was one."

"I seem to remember I was puking blood by that point, talking all funny."

"Oh, you remember that. Sure."

"You're telling me in all this time you never talked to Gwen?"

"Like I told you three years back, that girl got gone."

You know Gwen. You love Gwen. This part of it is hard to take. You remember Gwen in your car and Gwen in the cornstalks and Gwen in her mother's bed in the hour just before noon, naked and soft. You watched a drop of sweat appear from her hairline and slide down the side of her neck as she snored against your shoulder blade, and the arch of her foot was pressed over the top of yours, and you watched her sleep, and you were so awake.

"So it's with her," you say.

"No," the old man says, a bit of anger creeping into his puppy-fur voice. "You called me. That night."

"I did?"

"Shit, boy. You called me from the pay phone outside the hospital."

"What'd I say?"

"You said, 'I hid it. It's safe. No one knows where but me.'"

"Wow," you say. "I said all that? Then what'd I say?"

The old man shakes his head. "Cops were pulling up by then, calling you 'motherfucker,' telling you to drop the phone. You hung up."

The old man pulls up outside a low red-brick building behind a tire dealership on Oak Street. He kills the engine and gets out of the car, and you follow. The building is two stories. Facing the street are the office of a bail bondsman, a hardware store, a Chinese takeout place with greasy walls the color of an old dog's teeth, and a hair salon called Girlfriend Hooked Me Up that's filled with black women. Around the back, past the whitewashed windows of what was once a dry cleaner, is a small black door with the words TRUE-LINE EFFICIENCY EXPERTS CORP. stenciled on the frosted glass.

The old man unlocks the door and leads you into a ten-by-ten room that smells of roast chicken and varnish. He pulls the string of a bare light bulb, and you look around at a floor strewn with envelopes and paper, the only piece of furniture a broken-down desk probably left behind by the previous tenant.

Your father crab-walks across the floor, picking up envelopes that have come through the mail slot, kicking his way through the paper. You pick up one of the pieces of paper and read it.

Dear Sirs,

Please find enclosed my check for $50. I look forward to receiving the information packet we discussed as well as the sample test. I have enclosed a SASE to help facilitate this process. I hope to see you someday at the airport!

Sincerely,
Jackson A. Willis

You let it drop to the floor and pick up another one.

To Whom It May Concern:

Two months ago, I sent a money order in the amount of fifty dollars to your company in order that I may receive an information packet and sample test so that I could take the US government test and become a security handler and fulfill my patriotic duty against the al Qadas. I have not received my information packet as yet and no one answers when I call your phone. Please send me that information packet so I can get that job.

Yours truly,
Edwin Voeguarde
12 Hinckley Street
Youngstown, OH 44502

You drop this one to the floor too and watch your father sit on the corner of the desk and open his fresh pile of envelopes with a penknife. He reads some, pauses only long enough with others to shake the checks free and drop the rest to the floor.

You let yourself out, go to the Chinese place and buy a cup of Coke, go into the hardware store and buy a knife and a couple of tubes of Krazy Glue, stop at the car for a minute, and then go back into your father's office.

"What're you selling this time?" you say.

"Airport security jobs," he says, still opening envelopes. "It's a booming market. Everyone wants in. Stop them bad guys before they get on the plane, make the papers, serve your country, and maybe be lucky enough to get posted near one of them Starbucks kiosks. Hell."

"How much you made?"

Your father shrugs, though you're certain he knows the figure right down to the last penny.

"I've done all right. Hell else am I going to do, back in this shit town for three months, waiting on you? 'Bout time to shut this down, though." He holds up a stack of about sixty checks. "Deposit these and cash out the account. First two months, though? I was getting a thousand, fifteen hundred checks a week. Thank the good Lord for being selective with the brain tissue, you know?"

"Why?" you say.

"Why what?"

"Why you been hanging around for three months?"

Your father looks up from the stack of checks, squints. "To prepare a proper welcome for you."

"A bottle of whiskey and a hooker who gives lousy head? That took you three months?"

Your father squints a little more, and you see a shaft of gray between the two of you, not quite what you'd call light, just a shaft of air or atmosphere or something, swimming with motes, your father on the other side of it looking at you like he can't quite believe you're related.

After a minute or so your father says, "Yeah."

Your father told you once you'd been born in New Jersey. Another time he said New Mexico. Then Idaho. Drunk as a skunk a few months before you got shot, he said, "No, no. I'll tell you the truth. You were born in Las Vegas. That's in Nevada."

You went on the Internet to look yourself up but never did find anything.

Your mother died when you were seven. You've sat up at night occasionally and tried to picture her face. Some nights you can't see her at all. Some nights you'll get a quick glimpse of her eyes or her jawline, see her standing by the foot of her bed, rolling her stockings on, and suddenly she'll appear whole cloth, whole human, and you can smell her.

Most times, though, it's somewhere in between. You see a smile she gave you, and then she'll vanish. See a spatula she held turning pancakes, her eyes burning for some reason, her mouth an O, and then her face is gone and all you can see is the wallpaper. And the spatula.

You asked your father once why he had no pictures of her. Why hadn't he taken a picture of her? Just one lousy picture?

He said, "You think it'd bring her back? No, I mean, do you? Wow," he said, and rubbed his chin. "Wouldn't that be cool."

You said, "Forget it."

"Maybe if we had a whole album of pictures?" your father said. "She'd, like, pop out from time to time, make us breakfast."

Now that you've been in prison, you've been documented, but even they'd had to make it up, take your name as much on faith as you. You have no Social Security number or birth certificate, no passport. You've never held a job.

Gwen said to you once, "You don't have anyone to tell you who you are, so you don't *need* anyone to tell you. You just are who you are. You're beautiful."

And with Gwen that was usually enough. You didn't need to be defined — by your father, your mother, a place of birth, a name on a credit card or a driver's license or the upper left corner of a check. As long as her definition of you was something she could live with, then you could too.

You find yourself standing in a Nebraska wheat field. You're seventeen years old. You learned to drive five years earlier. You were in school once, for two months when you were eight, but you read well and you can multiply three-digit numbers in your head faster than a calculator, and you've seen the country with the old man. You've learned people aren't that smart. You've learned how to pull lottery-ticket scams and asphalt-paving scams and get free meals with a slight upturn of your brown eyes. You've learned that if you hold ten dollars in front of a stranger, he'll pay twenty to get his hands on it if you play him right. You've learned that every good lie is threaded with truth and every accepted truth leaks lies.

You're seventeen years old in that wheat field. The night breeze smells of wood smoke and feels like dry fingers as it lifts your bangs off your forehead. You remember everything about that night because it is the night you met Gwen. You are two years away from prison, and you feel like someone has finally given you permission to live.

This is what few people know about Sumner, West Virginia: every now and then someone finds a diamond. Some dealers were in a plane that went down in a storm in '51, already blown well off course, flying a crate of Israeli stones down the eastern seaboard toward Miami. Plane went down near an open mineshaft, took some swing-shift miners with it. The government showed up, along with members of an international gem consortium, got the bodies out of there, and went to work looking for the diamonds. Found most of them, or so they claimed, but for decades afterward rumors persisted, occasionally given credence by the sight of a miner, still grimed brown by the shafts, tooling around town in an Audi.

You'd been in Sumner peddling hurricane insurance in trailer parks when word got around that someone had found a diamond as big as a casino chip. Miner by the name of George Brunda, suddenly buying drinks, talking to his travel agent. You and Gwen shot pool with him one night, and you could see his dread in the bulges under his eyes, the way his laughter exploded too high and too fast.

He didn't have much time, old George, and he knew it, but he had a mother in a rest home, and he was making the arrangements to get her transferred. George was a fleshy guy, triple-chinned, and dreams he'd probably forgotten he'd ever had were rediscovered and weighted in his face, jangling and pulling the flesh.

"Probably hasn't been laid in twenty years," Gwen said when George went to the bathroom. "It's sad. Poor sad George. Never knew love."

Her pool stick pressed against your chest as she kissed you, and you could taste the tequila, the salt, and the lime on her tongue.

"Never knew love," she whispered in your ear, an ache in the whisper.

"What about the fairground?" your father says as you leave the office of True-Line Efficiency Experts Corp. "Maybe you hid it there. You always had a fondness for that place."

You feel a small hitch. In your leg, let's say. Just a tiny clutching sensation in the back of your right calf. But you walk through it, and it goes away.

You say to your father as you reach the car, "You really drive her home this morning?"

"Who?"

"Mandy?"

"Who's . . . ?" Your father opens his door, looks at you over it. "Oh, the whore?"

"Yeah."

"Did I drive her home?"

"Yeah."

Your father pats the top of the door, the cuff of his denim jacket flapping around his wrist, his eyes on you. You feel, as you always have, reflected in them, even when you aren't, couldn't be, wouldn't be.

"Did I drive her home?" A smile bounces in the rubber of your father's face.

"Did you drive her home?" you say.

That smile's all over the place now — the eyebrows, too. "Define home."

You say, "I wouldn't know, would I?"

"You're still pissed at me because I killed Fat Boy."

"George."

"What?"

"His name was George."

"He would have ratted."

"To who? It wasn't like he could file a claim. Wasn't a fucking lottery ticket."

Your father shrugs, looks off down the street.

"I just want to know if you drove her home."

"I drove her home," your father says.

"Yeah?"

"Oh, sure."

"Where'd she live?"

"Home," he says, and gets behind the wheel, starts the ignition.

You never figured George Brunda for smart, and only after a full day in his house, going through everything down to the point of removing the drywall and putting it back, resealing it, touching up the paint, did Gwen say, "Where's the mother stay again?"

That took uniforms, Gwen as a nurse, you as an orderly, Gentleman Pete out in the car while your father kept watch on George's mine entrance and monitored police activity over a scanner.

The old lady said, "You're new here, and quite pretty," as Gwen shot her up with phenobarbital and Valium and you went to work on the room.

This was the glitch: You'd watched George drive to work, watched him enter the mine. No one saw him come back out again, because no one was looking on the other side of the hill, at the exit of a completely different shaft. So while your father watched the front, George took off out the back, drove over to check on his investment, walked into the room just as you pulled the rock from the back of the mother's radio, George looking politely surprised, as if he'd stepped into the wrong room.

He smiled at you and Gwen, held up a hand in apology, and backed out of the room.

Gwen looked at the door, looked at you.

You looked at Gwen, looked at the window, looked at the rock filling the center of your palm, the entire center of your palm. Looked at the door.

Gwen said, "Maybe we —"

And George came through the door again, nothing polite in his face, a gun in his hand. And not any regular gun — a motherfucking six-shooter, like they carried in westerns, long, thin barrel, a family heirloom maybe, passed down from a great-great-great-grandfather, not even a trigger guard, just the trigger, and crazy fat George the lonely unloved pulling back on it and squeezing off two rounds, the first of which went out the window, the second of which hit metal somewhere in the room and then bounced off that. The old lady went *"Ooof,"* even though she was doped up and passed out, and it sounded to you like she'd eaten something that didn't agree with her. You could picture her sitting in a restaurant, halfway through coffee, placing a hand to her belly, saying it: *"Ooof."* And George would come around to her chair and say, "Is everything okay, Mama?"

But he wasn't doing that now, because the old lady went ass-end-up out of the bed and hit the floor, and George dropped the gun and stared at her and said, "You shot my mother."

And you said, "*You* shot your mother," your entire body jetting sweat through the pores all at once.

"No, you did. No, you did."

You said, "Who was holding the fucking gun?"

But George didn't hear you. George jogged three steps and dropped to his knees. The old lady was on her side, and you could see blood staining the back of her white johnny.

George cradled her face, looked into it, and said, "Mother. Oh, Mother, oh, Mother, oh, Mother."

And you and Gwen ran right the fuck out of that room.

In the car Gwen said, "You saw it, right? He shot his own mother."

"He did?"

"He did," she said. "Baby, she's not going to die from that."

"Maybe. She's old."

"She's old, yeah. The fall from the bed was worse."

"We shot an old lady."

"We didn't shoot her."

"In the ass."

"We didn't shoot anyone. He had the gun."

"That's how it'll play, though. You know that. An old lady. Christ."

Gwen's eyes were the size of that diamond as she looked at you, and then she said, *"Ooof."*

"Don't start," you said.

"I can't help it, Bobby. Jesus."

She said your name. That's your name — Bobby. You loved hearing her say it.

Sirens were coming up the road behind you now, and you were looking at her and thinking, This isn't funny, it isn't, it's fucking sad, that poor old lady, and thinking, Okay, it's sad, but God, Gwen, I will never, ever live without you. I just can't imagine it anymore. I want to . . . What?

Wind was pouring into the car, and the sirens were growing louder, an army of them, and Gwen's face was an inch from yours, her hair falling from behind her ear and whipping across her mouth, and she was looking at you, she was seeing you — really *seeing* you. Nobody'd ever done that, nobody. She was tuned to you like a radio tower out on the edge of the unbroken fields of wheat, blinking red under a dark-blue sky, and that night breeze lifting your bangs was her, for Christ's sake, her, and she was laughing, her hair in her teeth, laughing because the old lady had fallen out of the bed and it wasn't funny, it wasn't, and you said the first part in your head, the "I want to" part, but you said the second part aloud: "Dissolve into you."

And Gentleman Pete, up there at the wheel, on this dark country road, said, "What?"

But Gwen said, "I know, baby. I know." And her voice broke around the words, broke in the middle of her laughter and her fear and her guilt, and she took your face in her hands as Pete drove up on the interstate, and you saw all those siren lights washing across the back window like Fourth of July ice cream. Then the window came down like yanked netting and chucked glass pebbles into your shirt, and you felt something in your head go all shifty and loose and hot as a cigarette coal.

The fairground is empty, and you and your father walk around for a bit. The tarps over some of the booths have come undone at the corners, and they rustle and flap, caught between the wind and the wood, and your father watches you, waiting for you to remember, and you say, "It's coming back to me. A little."

Your father says, "Yeah?"

You hold up your hand, tip it from side to side.

Out behind the cages where, in summer, they set up the dunking machine and the bearded lady's chair and the fast-pitch machines, you see a fresh square of dirt, recently tilled, and you stand over it until your old man stops beside you, and you say, "Mandy?"

The old man chuckles softly, scuffs at the dirt with his shoe, looks off at the horizon.

"I held it in my hand, you know," you say.

"I'd figure," the old man says.

It's quiet, the land flat and metal-blue and empty for miles in every direction, and you can hear the rustle of the tarps and nothing else, and you know that the old man has brought you here to kill you. Picked you up from prison to kill you. Brought you into the world, probably, so eventually he could kill you.

"Covered the center of my palm."

"Big, huh?"

"Big enough."

"Running out of patience, boy," your father says.

You nod. "I'd guess you would be."

"Never my strong suit."

"No."

"This has been nice," your father says, and sniffs the air. "Like old times, reconnecting and all that."

"I told her that night to just go, just put as much country as she could between you and her until I got out. I told her to trust no one. I told her you'd stay hot on her trail even when all logic said you'd quit. I told her even if I told you I had it, you'd have to cover your bets — you'd have to come looking for her."

Your father looks at his watch, looks off at the sky again.

"I told her if you ever caught up to her, to take you to the fairground."

"Who's this we're talking about?"

"Gwen." Saying her name to the air, to the flapping tarps, to the cold.

"You don't say." Your father's gun comes out now. He taps it against his outer knee.

"Told her to tell you that's all she knew. I'd hid it here. Somewhere here."

"Lotta ground."

You nod.

Your father turns so you are facing, his hands crossed over his groin, the gun there, waiting.

"The kinda money that stone'll bring," your father says, "a man could retire."

"To what?" you say.

"Mexico."

"To what, though?" you say. "Mean old man like you? What else you got, you ain't stealing something, killing somebody, making sure no one alive has a good fucking day?"

The old man shrugs, and you watch his brain go to work, something bugging him finally, something he hasn't considered until now.

"It just come to me," he says.

"What's that?"

"You've known for, what, three years now that Gwen is no more?"

"Dead."

"If you like," your father says. "Dead."

"Yeah."

"Three years," your father says. "Lotta time to think."

You nod.

"Plan."

You give him another nod.

Your father looks down at the gun in his hand. "This going to fire?"

You shake your head.

Your father says, "It's loaded. I can feel the mag weight."

"Jack the slide," you say.

He gives it a few seconds and then tries. He yanks back hard, bending over a bit, but the slide is stone.

"Krazy Glue," you say. "Filled the barrel, too."

You pull your hand from your pocket, open up the knife. You're very talented with a knife. Your father knows this. He's seen you win money this way, throwing knives at targets, dancing blades between your fingers in a blur.

You say, "Wherever you buried her, you're digging her out."

The old man nods. "I got a shovel in the trunk."

You shake your head. "With your hands."

Dawn is coming up, the sky bronzed with it along the lower reaches, when you let the old man use the shovel. His nails are gone, blood crusted black all over the older cuts, red seeping out of the newer ones. The old man broke down crying once. Another time he got mean, told you you weren't his anyway, some whore's kid he found in a barrel, decided might come in useful on a missing-baby scam they were running back then.

You say, "Was this in Las Vegas? Or Idaho?"

When the shovel hits bone, you say, "Toss it back up here," and step back as the old man throws the shovel out of the grave.

The sun is up now, and you watch the old man claw away the dirt for a while, and then there she is, all black and rotted, bones exposed in some places, her rib cage reminding you of the scales of a large fish you saw dead on a beach once in Oregon.

The old man says, "Now what?" and tears flee his eyes and drip off his chin.

"What'd you do with her clothes?"

"Burned 'em."

"I mean, why'd you take 'em off in the first place?"

The old man looks back at the bones, says nothing.

"Look closer," you say. "Where her stomach used to be."

The old man squats, peering, and you pick up the shovel.

Until Gwen, you had no idea who you were. None. During Gwen, you knew. After Gwen, you're back to wondering.

You wait. The old man keeps cocking and re-cocking his head to get a better angle, and finally, finally, he sees it.

"Well," he says, "I'll be damned."

You hit him in the head with the shovel, and the old man says, "Now, hold on," and you hit him again, seeing her face, the mole on her left breast, her laughing once with a mouth full of popcorn. The third swing makes the old man's head tilt funny on his neck, and you swing once more to be sure and then sit down, feet dangling into the grave.

You look at the blackened, shriveled thing lying below your father, and you see her face with the wind coming through the car and her hair in her teeth and her eyes seeing you and taking you into her like food, like blood, like what she needed to breathe, and you say, "I wish . . ." and sit there for a long time with the sun beginning to warm the ground and warm your back and the breeze returning to make those tarps flutter again, desperate and soft.

"I wish I'd taken your picture," you say finally. "Just once."

And you sit there until it's almost noon and weep for not protecting her, and weep for not being able to know her ever again, and weep for not knowing what your real name is, because whatever it is or could have been is buried with her, beneath your father, beneath the dirt you begin throwing back in.

LYNNE SHARON SCHWARTZ

A Taste of Dust

FROM NINTH LETTER

DRIVING UP FROM THE CITY, Violet had imagined the house as substantial but hadn't envisioned this bay-windowed, white mansion in miniature set far back from the curving suburban street. Large elms shaded the lawn; the hedges were expertly trimmed; too late for many flowers in October, but lots of shrubs. Definitely a hired gardener, or else Cindy had an unusually green thumb. Little in that line could be expected of Seth, unless he'd changed drastically and become a devotee of the Home Depot in the mall a few miles back. An SUV loomed in the broad driveway; she pulled up behind it. There would be a dog too, she guessed, a big one. Any minute it might come bounding across the lawn. She steeled herself. She'd pat it and not shrink from the paws clawing at her slate-blue silk suit, bought especially for the occasion, to show off her undefeated body and long legs.

An instant after she rang, as if he'd been waiting behind the door, there was Seth, restraining the dog by its collar. Violet fussed over the animal to give herself more time. A white and amber collie, prototypical faithful Lassie, it sniffed her with cordial interest. A contented dog.

"Violet! It's been so long. You look marvelous!"

She forced herself to look up. "Thank you." She couldn't say the same, even to be polite. It would be too blatant a lie. What she had managed to stave off these sixteen years had conquered him. He had passed the threshold of the country of the old, gone soft, and begun to shrink and stoop. His face was pouchy. His jaw had lost its clean, firm line. His lips were thinner, tighter. At his age, one either crossed that border abruptly — overnight — or was granted, by luck or genes or time spent at the gym, a few more years of being presentable. Seth, never athletic, wasn't one of the lucky ones. His clothes were still good, expensive and pressed, though they couldn't hang with the same grace. They would have suited him better had they been wrinkled. The shirt was deep blue, always his best color, though Violet couldn't help imagining the flesh beneath, sagging, folding on itself, with a pale, lifeless tinge.

He bent down to kiss her cheek and hug her awkwardly. She sympathized: how do you hug an ex-wife? She'd anticipated this moment and wondered if the mere brush of bodies could revive years of intimacy. It could. He was the naked man who had bent over her night after night, until he stopped. The inimitable scent and feel of ancient sex embalmed hit like a rush of stale hot air on her skin. She drew back as soon as she decently could.

Behind Seth, Cindy, once the secret girlfriend and now the anointed wife, waited in the spacious foyer, uncertain what to do with her arms. They were opened — bare, taut, and pink — but not quite wide enough to hug, ready for whatever Violet was ready for. Packed snugly in her beige slacks and shirt, Cindy served her time at the gym, no doubt about that. Violet had seen her only in snapshots that the children, bitter and out of sorts after their weekend visits years ago, used to thrust in front of her, inviting her disdain, which she refused to give. They showed a curly-haired, rosy, rounded Cindy. Cute. Violet had never been cute or cuddly. Sleek and smooth and dark. Elegant when young, and now becoming stately as well.

Today's Cindy had outgrown cuteness. Violet's interest was purely clinical by now, yet maybe in the course of the afternoon she'd spot something that would make it all clear, some feature in Cindy notably lacking in herself. Youth and cuteness didn't seem enough to account for so much devastation. Cindy's hair was the color fortyish women often chose, somewhere between chestnut and gold, and there was a bit too much of it, Violet thought. She could also go easier on the makeup; the impression was altogether too bright, too much wattage. Violet ignored the half-spread arms and extended a hand. There were no prescribed words for this sort of meeting, but fortunately the dog made lots of noise. He was excited by the visitor and for no apparent reason seemed to take a shine to Violet.

"Come meet Lisa and Jenny." Obeying Cindy's wave, the teenage girls sidled up, more Seth's than their mother's, at least in appearance — lanky, olive-skinned, in tight jeans and bare midriffs. Nothing much to say. Well, what could they say? Their father's first wife? Opposite of a stepmother — a negative quantity, no word in the language for what she was to them. Could they even believe their father had once been married to her, a doctor, they'd surely been told, with shiny black hair gathered in a knot at her neck, green eyes — tiger eyes, Seth used to say — and of all things, a designer suit for a family dinner? Yet it was their admiration she would have liked, more than Cindy's. To her chagrin, Violet was wishing they could find her in every way more awesome and glamorous than their mother, unattainably glamorous. A futile wish, she knew, for their idea of glamour would be a bared navel studded with a rhinestone.

Drinks and snacks appeared. Five minutes later Grace was at the door, exuberant even after the four-hour drive from Boston, rushing over to Violet first. "Mom, it's so great to see you! I've missed you! I took two days off so I can stay with you."

Violet lapsed into easeful pleasure, a kind of melting from within. Her daughter brought a change of weather, light breaking through smog. Next came the guests of honor, the reason for this reunion: Evan, returning home after two years in Prague, with a wife, a new baby, and mounds of luggage. Her son had gone away a boy, she thought with a lump in her throat, and come back a man. Embraces, clamor, everyone happy and beautiful. So happy, so beautiful, that Violet was stunned to be feeling joy here in Seth's house. She could almost ignore Cindy's high-pitched, restless voice. In fact if Cindy and her sulky girls would be considerate enough to disappear, this would be her family, her loved ones assembled, blooming, thriving. She would have had time to watch Seth grow old and his decline would not be so appalling.

Not that she wanted him back. God, no. She was no longer the woman who could contort herself to fit his erratic moods. She just wanted to pretend, for one Sunday afternoon, that all the banal ugliness of his leaving had never taken place, the mutual rants, accusations, recriminations. And when they stopped, the dialogues that kept fomenting in her head, with her supplying Seth's half, brutally parsing her every failing, social, sexual, culinary, political, parental . . . until she'd exhausted her imagination. The whole ordeal was like some dreadful disaster cliché — earthquake, volcano, hurricane — and in its aftermath she had set about rebuilding. But so many disaster areas never regain their former luster.

After his bottle, the four-month-old baby was passed around. Violet could have swept him off to a private room and held him in her arms all day, but she didn't prolong her turn. There would be plenty of time to revel. She simply recorded the soft, compact feel of him, a memory to return to later, as she used to record the feel of Seth's caresses to summon up the next morning when her patients arrived with their woes, their cataracts, their ripped corneas and detached retinas.

When Seth's turn came he cradled the baby awkwardly, letting the head loll backward over the crook of his elbow as the small torso threatened to slip from his grasp. Violet held her breath.

"Not like that!" Cindy darted over to settle the bundle securely in his arms. "With Lisa and Jenny, I was always afraid he'd drop them on their heads; he had such a weird way of holding them."

Seth shot a glance at Violet. His myopic eyes, narrowed behind the frameless, octagonal glasses, were duller than she remembered. She used to write his prescriptions. He might need a change; he was squinting, though it could have been from anger. If she'd ever spoken that way in public, which was inconceivable, he would have been enraged. Anyway, he'd held their babies just fine.

The message in his face — unmistakably a message — was complex and would have to be decoded at leisure. But even this quick glance, like a glance at a patient, told something. Embarrassment, along with a cavalier disregard for it: we know each other so well, Violet, I can afford to let you see my embarrassment. Depletion. Maybe self-pity. All so unlike what she'd imagined. All these years, as she glided over the even surface of her life — her work, her succession of men, her friends — she'd pictured Seth as the doting husband and father, and as being doted on in turn, basking in fond attention. Years ago Violet would have loved the taste of this moment; now it soured her mouth.

Suddenly Seth began bouncing the baby in the air. Encased in its terrycloth, the child gurgled and giggled.

He's just been fed, Violet thought. If you keep that up he'll spit all over you.

She was prophetic. From the baby's lips, parted in glee, popped a gob of clotted milk that formed a spreading island on the front of Seth's blue shirt.

"Oh, I'm so sorry." Carla, the new daughter-in-law, rushed over with a wad of tissues, dabbing furiously at the shirt, then at the baby's glistening chin.

Cindy shook her head. "I had a feeling that would happen." She looked at Violet for confirmation: we mothers know, don't we? Violet couldn't bring herself to grin in complicity. She hadn't forgotten Grace and Evan's teenage reports on Cindy, offered along with the photos. Grace: She doesn't like me using her shampoo. She watches how I do the dishes. I tie up the phone too long. Evan: She says I'm a sloppy eater. She didn't want me taking the car. . . . Violet had counseled patience. Soon they'd be grown and none of it would matter. For herself, though, long after she was able to think of Seth without anger, the shampoo and the forbidden car still rankled.

Cindy had barely spoken when Lisa and Jenny moaned in unison like a Greek chorus. "Yuck. You smell all cheesy, Dad."

More stooped than before, Seth trudged upstairs and reappeared in an old tan sweater. His sparse graying hair was slightly mussed like a boy's, as if his mother had tousled it affectionately. That must have happened when he pulled the sweater over his head and didn't think to repair the damage. He looked more boyish now — a boy afflicted by premature aging — than he had in his youth.

"Dinner!" Cindy announced brightly. Seth circled the table pouring wine (a less than steady hand, Violet noted — anxiety or Parkinson's?) while Cindy carried platters out from the kitchen. Be sure to say something, Violet reminded herself. Give credit where it's due. She probably couldn't have managed a dinner on such a grand scale. She was long out of the habit, just a meal now and then for a few women friends, or for Philip, her occasional lover of the past three years.

"Dad, you passed me by," Lisa, the fifteen-year-old, complained. "Don't I get any wine?"

"Well, I don't think . . ."

"Come on, it's a special occasion."

He poured her half an inch.

"Me too, then," wailed Jenny.

"Uh-uh. Thirteen is too young."

"What on earth are you doing?" said Cindy, entering with a bowl of rice. "Wine? You know it's not allowed. Lisa, put that down this minute. What is the matter with you, Seth?"

"A few drops won't do any harm."

She snatched the glass away and poured the contents into her own.

"Well, I'm definitely old enough and I'd love some, Dad." That was Grace the good, extending her glass to salvage the moment. Seth didn't seem to hear her. He was staring at Violet again with some kind of appeal in his face. But what could she do? She couldn't even fix his rumpled hair.

"This roast beef is marvelous, Cindy. And the green rice. How did you do that?"

By frying it lightly first and using plenty of parsley, Cindy disclosed. She'd be glad to share the recipe. It was the least she could do, thought Violet, and leaned down to stroke the dog, who'd parked himself beside her chair.

An appeal for what? Rescue? He must know it was too late for rescue. They were both too sensible, too adult — too old! — for any impulsive return of the prodigal husband. An appeal nonetheless. For pity? Forgiveness? She could hardly even muster regret anymore. There was just the desiccation of the post-volcanic terrain.

"So, Evan, tell us about Prague." Grace again, determined to keep the chatter going. "It's not still the new Paris, is it? Was it ever, really?"

Well, yes, it had quieted down, but they should have seen it a couple of years ago . . . "We were constantly meeting people we knew on the streets. If you can't make it in New York, try Prague. That was the mantra." He turned to his half-sisters. "We got some really good stuff coming through for a while. The Orient Express, the Original Oregano Head Trip."

"The Orient Express?" said Seth. "I thought they discontinued that. And what the hell is the Original Oregano — whatever?"

Oh, stop, Violet urged mutely. Keep still and wait.

"They're groups, Dad," said Lisa with a contempt made sharper by its restraint. Seth's pouring her the wine evidently hadn't won him any points. Jenny tittered, and both girls rolled their eyes.

"Oh. Groups," he echoed uncertainly.

Everyone but Violet burst out laughing. Carla clapped her hand over her mouth and looked around as if for guidance: is it okay to laugh? Even the dog barked with what seemed like amusement, and again Violet stroked it.

In his confusion Seth was gazing at Violet.

"You know, rock bands," she murmured.

"Oh, right." He smiled wanly, trying to join in the merriment, but it was too late.

"By the way, Dad," Evan said, "you'll like this. I used to see Vaclav Havel sometimes in one of the local cafés. People just went right up and spoke to him."

Seth had admired Havel from the time he was a dissident playwright in blue jeans. Speak up, Violet beamed in his direction. Take your rightful place. But he just nodded and bent absorbedly over his plate. Food, she'd learned way back in her internship, is the last best pleasure of the old.

There wasn't much lingering after the fruit salad. Lisa and Jenny vanished and pounding music came from upstairs; Carla excused herself to tend to the baby. Evan went out to admire Grace's new car while Seth helped Violet on with her coat. He'd always done that, even though she would have preferred to do it herself. But she was too civil to rebuff any well-meant impulse. How careful she'd been, in so many ways, and what had it gotten her? Cindy wasn't careful. Cindy had a free hand. Seth wasn't going anywhere, surely not now. And Cindy was fed up. Her prosperous, sexy wheeler-dealer would soon be retiring, doddering around the house day and night, underfoot. More trouble than the dog. Who would have dreamed she could be the instrument of the revenge Violet once craved? No, be kind to him, Violet wanted to tell her in farewell, but that would never do. She might have said it to the girls — she no longer cared what they thought of her — but that would only make things worse.

He gave her the look again as she said goodbye. This time his face was overlaid with misery. Regret. She would have been patient, the look said. He wouldn't have been the butt of jokes, with her. She would have been gracious, indulgent with his mishaps, keeping him well informed. Those were the rewards a faithful husband reaps after a lifetime of decent behavior. And now . . .

But you would have had to tolerate me, Violet thought, and you didn't love me. She'd wasted hours pondering why she'd become unloved and still didn't know; maybe no one ever did. All she knew was that he couldn't give up his bliss in those solid pink arms.

Those pink arms were clasping the dog, as Cindy knelt down in a lavish spasm of affection that was also a restraining embrace, so the eager creature wouldn't leap on Violet to protest her leaving. "Kootchy kootchy poochy-woochy," Cindy kept repeating in little-girl squeals, letting the dog lick her face till it shone.

That was how it must have been, kootchy kootchy, pink and smoochy. That was what he had craved and bought at so high a price. For that she had had to suffer. It was no more just or rational than the arbitrary blows of disease, the failures of vision she dealt with every day, and it could hardly be called a surprise. Even the devastation and the calm aftermath seemed inevitable now, the detachment hollowed out inside her like a crater. And yet seeing it so clearly brought a jolt.

She tried to telegraph back the kindly message he wanted: I'm sorry it turned out this way. I would help you if I could. But as the door shut behind her, her face showed envy, not sorrow. He owned all the misery his risks had earned; he was in the thicket of his mistakes, impaled, fending off an excess of feeling, even if it was remorse. His life was dense and palpitating. She was clean and dry as old bones.

THOMAS McGUANE

Old Friends

FROM THE NEW YORKER

JOHN BRIGGS WAS MADE AWARE OF THE FACT that some sort of problem existed for his friend and former schoolmate Erik Faucher by the sheer accident of a request for information from their former class secretary, Everett Hoyt, who in the thirty years since they'd graduated from Yale had hardly set foot out of New Haven. With ancestors buried at the old Center Church, in spitting distance of both the regicide Dixwell and Benedict Arnold's wife, Hoyt was paralyzed by a sense of generational permanence. People said that if he hadn't got into Yale, he wouldn't have gone to college at all but would have remained at home, waiting to bury his parents. Now, in place of any real social life, he edited the alumni newsletter, often accompanying his requests for official items with small indiscretions.(He called these tidbits, which he delivered with a certain giddiness, "Entre News"; they generally concerned marital failures or business malfeasances, and they almost never made it into the alumni letter.)

Hoyt phoned Briggs at his summer home, in Montana, on a nondescript piece of prairie that Briggs had inherited from a farmer uncle, and, while pretending to hunt up class news, insinuated that Faucher, having embezzled a fortune from a bank in Boston, had gone into hiding. "I've heard through private sources that our class scofflaw is now headed your way," he said.

Briggs waited for Hoyt's giggle to subside. "I hope so," he snapped. "I've missed Erik." But once he'd hung up the phone he began to worry that Faucher might actually come.

*

Faucher's ex-wife, Carol, having declined to account for the time difference between Montana and the East Coast, called at five the next morning. "So very nice to hear your voice," Briggs said. "How are you?"

"I'm calling about Erik. He has not been behaving sensibly at all."

Briggs absorbed this in silence. He knew that if he said anything at all he'd have to stand up for Faucher, and he wasn't sure that he wanted to.

"Carol, you've been divorced a long time," he said finally.

"We have mutual interests. I don't know what sort of plan he has in place. And there's Elizabeth." Elizabeth was their daughter.

"I'm sure he's made a very sensible plan."

"I don't want Elizabeth to wind up sleeping in her car. Or me, either, for that matter."

"I don't think your argument is with me." This was in response to her tone.

"Did I say it was? I'm just saying, 'Help.' I'm saying, 'It's about time you did.'"

When Briggs failed to reply, she added, "I know where he's going and who to put on his trail."

Briggs's friendship with Faucher had been long and intermittent. Arbitrarily assigned as roommates at the boarding school they'd attended before Yale — a place built with iron-ore and taconite dollars and modeled on English public schools — the boys had grown up believing that America was a British fantasy and that the true work of the nation was undertaken by pencil-wristed Episcopalians who sang their babies to sleep with Blake's "Jerusalem" and uttered mild orotundities like "great good fortune" and "safe as houses." They had also been sold the notion of loyalty, much as the credulous are sold the far-fetched basics of religion.

Briggs and Faucher had become lifelong friends without ever quite getting past the fact that their discomfort with each other occasionally boiled over into active detestation. After college, each had been in the other's wedding, and they had lived, for a short time, in the same neighborhood in New Haven while they tried to launch their careers. As Briggs began to travel more and more, and Faucher relocated to Boston, their relationship had been reduced, for the most part, to memories, and not ones that either man particularly enjoyed revisiting — though they continued to make sentimental phone calls on holidays and to perform euphoric re-enactments of soccer triumphs on the rare occasions when they were actually together. In the subsequent quarter-century, although they had spent quite a bit of time begrudging each other's successes and savoring the failures, thanks to that burdensome code of loyalty, each had done the other a favor. When Briggs was in his twenties and had sunk everything he had into a small mining company in Alberta with ruinous short-term expenses, Faucher had rescued him from bankruptcy by finding a buyer. And when Faucher, on assignment as part of a Boston Congregationalists' outreach to hungry Guatemalans, was pulled from the second story of a burning whorehouse, Briggs had called every classmate and pal in journalism in a desperate stand to keep the news out of the papers.

For decades, Briggs and Faucher had each been searching for an unforgivable trait in the other that would relieve him of this abhorrent, possibly lifelong burden. But now that they had years of history and continuity to contend with, it had become harder and harder to imagine a liberating offense.

Faucher turned up one evening while Briggs was preparing his notes for a company stalemate in Delaware, for which he was serving as an independent negotiator. It surprised Briggs that Faucher had managed to find him at all, having ventured forth from the Hertz counter at the Billings airport with nothing but a state map. He arrived with a girl he'd picked up on the way, whose feral screeches in the upstairs guest room were soon clearly audible to Briggs. Her name was Marjorie, Faucher said — "Marge, short for margarine, the cheap spread." This was not the sort of remark that Briggs appreciated and was therefore exactly in the style to which Faucher had gravitated over the years. Around midnight, Faucher reeled downstairs to inquire, with a hitch of his head, "Do you want some of this?"

"Oh, no," Briggs said. "All for you."

Thereafter, Marjorie, who seemed an attractive and reasonable girl once she started sobering up, came downstairs to complain that Faucher had asked her to brush his teeth for him. Briggs advised her to be patient — Faucher would soon realize that he had to brush his own teeth and would then go to sleep. Briggs offered her the rollout on the sun porch, but she returned to Faucher wearily, having first gone to the front window to cast a longing eye at the rental car. She wore a negligee that just reached her hips and, as she slowly climbed the stairs, presented a view that was somewhat veterinary in quality. The aroma of gin trailed her. When Briggs went to bed, he thought, I don't know anyone who drinks gin anymore. He couldn't understand why this fact annoyed him. A full moon showing through the blinds left bands of cool light on the walls. The CD of Segovia that he'd put on at minimum volume to help him sleep cycled on — "Recuerdos de la Alhambra," again and again.

He hadn't been asleep for long when he was awakened by noises. In the kitchen there were intruders. Briggs heard them thumping around and opening cupboards and speaking in muffled tones. He wondered for a moment if he had forgotten that he was expecting someone. Once out of bed, he slipped into his closet, where his twelve-gauge resided on parallel coat hooks for just such a time as this. Briggs quietly chambered two shells and lifted the barrels until the lock closed.

In the living room, he knelt behind the big floral wing chair that faced the fireplace and its still dying embers. From here, he could see the intruders as silhouettes, moving around the kitchen, briefly illuminated by the refrigerator light. He lifted the gun and, resting it on the back of the chair, leveled it at the closest figure. Only then did he recognize the man as his nearest neighbor, with whom he shared a water right from the irrigation ditch and a relationship that strained to be pleasant; the other intruder was the man's wife, a snappish, leanly attractive farm woman, who was less diplomatic in concealing her distaste for Briggs. Listening to their conversation, Briggs understood that they had expected him to be out of town and that they were raiding his refrigerator for beer. On reflection, he decided that confronting them would create waves of difficulty for him in the future and that this episode would be best forgotten or set aside for use another time. So he put the gun away and crept back to bed. The neighbors departed a short time later with a farewell fling of beer cans into his roses.

Faucher's voice came from the top of the stairs. "Were those people looking for me?" he demanded.

"No, Erik. Go back to sleep. They've gone," Briggs replied.

*

Marjorie was the first up: she had a remedial geometry class to teach at the high school. "Always a challenge after a long night," she explained to Briggs. She wore a pleated blue skirt and a pale-green sweater that buttoned at the throat. Her hair was drawn back from a prettily modeled forehead. She was at the stove, one hand on a hip, the other managing a spatula. "Potatoes O'Brien and eggs. Then I've got to run."

"You don't have to cook."

"Oh, I can't have a day with missing pieces." She cast a brilliant smile his way and held it just long enough to suggest that he'd missed the boat. Erik wouldn't be getting up for breakfast, because, Marjorie explained, he had an upset tummy. She held the spatula in the air while she said this, suggesting with a quoting motion that she was only repeating the facts as they'd been given to her. Then she made an upset-tummy face. Marjorie reminded Briggs of teachers he'd had — punctilious, too ready to use physical gestures to explain the obvious, a hint of the scold. They ate together with the unexpected comfort of strangers at a diner. She paid absolute attention to her food, looking up at him intermittently. She raised a forefinger.

"First thing he said to me was 'You're amazing.' I have learned that when they tell you you're amazing, it's over before it starts."

"Just as well. Neither of you was feeling any pain."

"I never have any idea what will happen when I get drunk. But why would you get drunk if you knew what was going to happen?" she said. "You probably get off just watching other people make mistakes. That's not a nice trait, Mr. Briggs!"

She smoothed her skirt and checked it for crumbs. "I'm out of here," she said as she stood up. "What's the weather like?" She went to the window and craned to see the sky. "Not too bad. Okay, bye."

When Briggs heard the shower start upstairs, he went outside and smelled the new morning wind coming through the fields. There were a few small white clouds gathering in the east, and a quarter mile off he could see a harrier working its way just over the surface of the hills. From time to time, it swung up to pivot on a wingtip, and then resumed its sweep. The window of the upstairs bathroom opened and a wisp of steam came out, followed by the head of Erik Faucher. "John! What a morning!" Briggs was filled with a sudden, unexpected fondness for Faucher. This feeling lasted only until Faucher began singing in the shower, and Briggs found his presence insufferable again.

Faucher appeared in the yard in light-colored pleated pants, a hemp belt, and a long-sleeved blue cotton shirt. Though his hair was gunmetal gray, he still had the vigorous black eyebrows that Briggs associated with his French blood. Raising them, he told Briggs that he'd flown in from Boston, following an itinerary that was slightly less convenient than a trip to Kazakhstan, now that centralized air-routing had made Montana oddly more remote. He didn't seem tired or hung over, and his frame looked well exercised. "I see Marge made off with the rental car," he said.

Briggs made him some coffee and a piece of toast, which he nibbled cautiously while reading the obituaries in a week-old Billings *Gazette.* "One of these Indians dies, they list every relative in the world. This one has three columns of kinfolk — Falls Down, Bird in Ground, Spotted Bear, Tall Enemy, Pretty on Top. Where does it end? And all their affiliations! The True Cross Evangelical Church, the Whistling Water Clan, the Bad War Deeds Clan. All I ever belonged to was Skull and Bones, and I ain't too proud of that! So please don't list it when I go. I'm no Indian!"

Briggs eyed the bright prairie sun that was working its way across the window behind the sink. He treasured his solitary spells in this house, as infrequent as they were, and he tended to waste very few minutes of them. This one, it seemed, was doomed.

"Look at us, John, two lonely middle-aged guys."

"Filled with hope."

"Not me, John. But I'm expecting that Montana will change all that. One of my great regrets," Faucher said solemnly, "is that when we were young, married, and almost always drunk we didn't take a little time out to fuck each other's beautiful wives."

"That time has come and gone," Briggs said.

"A fellow should smell the roses once in a while. Now those two are servicing others. Perhaps in intimate moments they tell their new men how unsatisfactory we were."

"Very plausible."

Their wives had despised each other. Carol was a classic, now extinct type from Cold Spring Harbor, New York. Having attended Mount Holyoke, she had felt it her mission to carry forward to new generations the Mount Holyoke worldview. When their daughter,

Elizabeth, was expelled from the college for drug use, Faucher's suggestion that there were other, possibly more forgiving institutions had placed him permanently outside the wall that sheltered his wife and child. When, even with certified rehabilitation, Elizabeth failed to be reinstated at Mount Holyoke, she lost interest in college altogether and joined the navy, where she was immediately happy as a machinist's mate. Faucher was bankrupt by then, a result of habitual overextension, and his inability to support Carol in the style to which she had been accustomed led to divorce and to Carol's current position as a receptionist at a hearing-aid outlet on Route 90 between Boston and Natick. Relatively few years had brought them to this point and neither quite understood how.

Briggs had always been quite uncomfortable with Carol, and he had been greatly relieved when it was no longer necessary for the two of them to speak. His own wife, Irena, had been a beauty, a big-eyed, russet-haired trilingual girl from Ljubljana whom he'd met at a trade conference in Milan, where she was translating and he was negotiating for a Yugoslav-American businessman whose family's property had been nationalized by the Communists. John and Irena were married for only a few years — long enough for her to come to know and loathe the Fauchers. Briggs wasn't sure what else had gone wrong, except that she'd never much liked America and had been continually exasperated by Americans' assumption that Briggs had somehow rescued her. In the end, aroused by the independence of Slovenia, she grew homesick and left, but not before remarking that Carol was a pig and Erik was a goat.

All of which lent Faucher's wife-swapping lament its own particular comedy.

"Don't worry about me overstaying my welcome," Faucher said. "I'm quite considerate that way."

"Farthest thing from my mind," Briggs said. "Let's go for a walk."

"Do you have an answering machine?"

"Yes, and I've turned it on."

"A walk would be good," Faucher said. "We'll teach those fools to wait for the beep."

"I want you to see the homestead cemetery. It's been fenced off for eighty years and still has all the old prairie flowers that are gone everywhere else. I have some forebears there."

They followed a seasonal creek toward the low hills in the west where the late-morning sun illuminated towering white clouds. The air was so clear that their shadows could be seen on the grass hillsides like birthmarks. Faucher seemed happier.

"I'm so glad to get out of Boston," he said. "It was unbelievably muggy. There was a four-day teachers' demonstration across from my apartment — you know, where they go, 'Hey, hey, ho, ho, we don't want to . . .' whatever. Four days. Sweating and listening to those turds chant."

Briggs could see the grove of ash and alders at the cemetery just emerging from the horizon as they hiked. About twice a summer, very old people with California or Washington plates came, mowed the grass, and otherwise tended the few graves: most homesteaders had been starved out before they'd had time to die. These were the witnesses.

As they came over a slight rise, a sheet of standing rainwater was revealed in an old buffalo wallow; a coyote lit out across the water with unbelievable acceleration, leaving fifteen yards of pluming rooster tails behind him. Faucher gazed for a moment, then said, "That was no dog. You could run a hundred of them by me and I'd never say it was a dog. Not me."

At the little graveyard, Briggs said, "All screwed by the government." He was standing in front of his family graves, which were just like the others — names, dates, nothing else. "Cattle haven't been able to get in here since the thirties. The plants are here, the old heritage flowers and grasses. Surely you think that's interesting."

"I'm going to have to take your word for it."

"Erik, look at what's in front of you," Briggs said, more sharply than he'd intended, but Faucher just stared off into the distance, not seeming to hear him.

Needle and thread, buffalo, and orchard grass spread like a billowing counterpane around the small headstones. Shining through were shooting stars, pasqueflowers, prairie smoke, arrowleaf balsamroot, and wild roses, amid small clouds of bees and darting blue butterflies. A huge cottonwood sheltered it all. Off to one side was a vigorous bull thistle that had passed unnoticed by the people in battered sedans, hard old people who didn't talk, taking turns with the scythe. They looked into cellar holes and said, "We grew up here." No sense in conveying any of this to Faucher, who was mooning by the old fence.

"I could stand a nap," he said.

"Then that's what you shall have. But in the meantime please try to get something out of these surroundings. It's tiresome just towing you around."

"I was imagining laying my weary bones among these dead. In the words of Chief Joseph, 'From here I will fight no more forever.' Who was in the house last night?"

"That was my neighbor and his wife. They stopped by for a beer."

"Well, I guess you know your own society. That would seem very strange in Boston."

From the alcove off his bedroom, which served as an office, Briggs could look through the old glass windows with their bubbles and imperfections and see Faucher sitting on the lawn, arms propped behind him, face angled into the sun like a girl in a Coppertone ad. Briggs was negotiating for a tiny community in Delaware that was being blackmailed by a flag manufacturer for tax millage against purported operating costs, absent which the manufacturer threatened to close the plant and strand 251 minimum-wage workers. A North Carolina village that had lost its pulp mill wanted the flag company, and even if Briggs worked as hard as he could, one town would die.

He explained this to Faucher as they drove to town for dinner. Faucher made a waving movement with his hand and said *"Hasta la vista"* to whichever town it was that had to disappear. But it was otherwise a nice ride down the valley, mountains emerging below fair-weather altocumulus clouds, small ranches on either side at the heads of sparkling creeks. A self-propelled swather followed by ravens moved down a field, pivoting nimbly at the end of each row, while in the next meadow, already gleaned, a wheel-line sprinkler emitted a low fog on the regrowth. A boy in a straw hat stood at a concrete headgate and, turning a wheel, let a flood of irrigation water race down a dusty ditch.

Town was three churches, a row of bars, a hotel with a restaurant, and a filling station. Each church had a framed announcement board standing in front, the Catholic with Mass schedules, the Lutheran with a passage from the Bible, and the Evangelical with a warning. The bars, likewise, had bright signs inviting ranchers, families, sportsmen, and motorcyclists, respectively. Entirely different kinds of vehicles were parked in front of each: old sedans in front of the ranchers' bar, pickup trucks in front of the local video-gaming youth-cult stop, and in front of the hotel some foreign models from Bozeman and Livingston. The clouds were moving fast now, and when Briggs got out of the car, the hotel towering over him looked like the prow of a ship crossing a pale-blue ocean.

Faucher scanned his menu vigorously. "My God, this all looks good," he said. "And it'll look even better after a stunning bourbon-and-ditch." He was like a vampire coming to life at sundown; pale flames arose beneath his skin with each cocktail.

They ordered their dinner from a ruddy-faced girl who seemed excited by every choice they made. She had a Fritz the Cat tattoo on her upper arm, which Faucher peered at over the top of his menu. Briggs asked for a bottle of Bandol as well, and, when the candles had been lit, he assumed that it was time for Faucher to make himself plain.

But then the mayor came to the table, with the vibrant, merry hustle with which he generally drew attention to himself. Briggs introduced him to Faucher, who smiled patiently and stared at the man's fringed vest. Following the local convention, the mayor asked Briggs when he'd got back.

"I've been back about five times this summer," Briggs said. "From Tanzania, Berlin, Denver, Surinam." He was always exasperated at being asked this question. The mayor held his head in his hands.

"Surinam! Never heard of it! Denver I've heard of! What's in Surinam?"

"Bauxite."

"Baux —"

"Pal," Faucher said. "Give it a rest. We're trying to eat." He made a shooing motion and the mayor left. Faucher raised his eyebrows as he asked Briggs, "How can we miss him if he won't go away?"

The last time Briggs had seen Faucher, he had been insuring marine cargo out of a nice office on Old Colony Avenue in Boston and doing rather well, especially in the early days when Everett Hoyt had tipped him off to opportunities with former classmates. Now, Faucher said, he was an investment adviser at a tiny merchant bank in Boston. He liked to meet his clients in St. Louis Square on warm spring days (he had a key) to lay out the year's strategy — clients who were charmed by his arrival on a Raleigh ten-speed. He kept a hunter-jumper at Beverly and dropped into equestrian talk to baffle the credulous, using terms like *levade* and *piaffe* and *volte* to describe the commonplace trades he made, or comparing a sustained investment strategy to such esoterica as Raimondo D'Inzeo's taking the Irish Bank at Aachen on the great Merano. His own equestrian activities, he admitted, consisted of jumping obstacles that would scarcely weary a poodle, in the company of eight- and nine-year-old girls, under the tutelage of the roaring Madame Schacter, a tyrant in jodhpurs. Still, for his clientele, horses and yachts were reassuring entities, things to which one could turn one's attention when times were good.

Current times, however, were not at all good. Once, Faucher had been able to make cavalier decisions about his clients' investments; lately, they trusted him less and obliged him to chase obscure indices across the moonscape of foreign equities.

The dining room was full, and the neighboring bar nearly so. Briggs spotted Marjorie at the bar but thought it best not to mention it.

Faucher said, "John, I've got to tell you, I'm burning out. Nothing makes me happy anymore. I need new work. I want to be more like you. I need a gimmick. You get the time-zone watch from Sharper Image, and the rest is a walk in the park. Whereas my job is to reassure people who are afraid to lose what they have because they don't know how they got it in the first place. John, it's not that I mind lying, but I like variety and I'm not getting it." His face was mottled with an emotion that Briggs found difficult to fathom. "I desperately wish to be a cowboy," Faucher concluded.

"That family" — he added, pointing conspicuously at a nearby table where a rancher, his wife, and their three nearly grown children were at their meal — "have been here for an hour and haven't spoken to each other once. Don't these people know how to have fun?" The family heard this, the father glaring into the space just over his plate, his wife grinning in fear at a mustard jar. "We do that when we hate people," Faucher said.

"I don't think they hate each other, Erik."

"Well, it sure looks like it! I've never seen such depressing people."

Marjorie proceeded from the bar with a tall, colorful drink. She was wearing a red tunic with military buttons over a short skirt and boots, her hair pulled tight and tied straight atop her head with a silver ribbon. Briggs was glad to see her: she looked full of life. She said, "May I?"

Briggs quickly got to his feet and pulled out a chair, steadying her arm as she sat. Faucher looked glum. He said in an unconvincing monotone, "Sorry I missed you this morning. I understand you cooked a marvelous breakfast."

"It filled us up, didn't it?" she said to Briggs.

"All we could eat and no leftovers," Briggs agreed.

"What'd you do with the rental car?" Faucher barked.

"In front of the bank, keys under the seat."

Faucher lost interest in the car. "Not like I'll need it," he said with a moan.

The ranch family stood without looking at one another, an action that obliged at least two of them to survey the crown molding on the walls. The father glared at Faucher and dribbled some coins to the table from a huge paw while his waitress scowled from across the room. Karaoke had started at the bar, and a beaming wheat farmer was singing "That's Amore."

"Can I get a menu?" Marjorie asked, craning around the room.

"Has it possibly occurred to you that we're having a private conversation?" Faucher said.

Marjorie stopped all animation for a moment. "Oh, I'm so sorry." She looked crushed as she arose. Briggs tried to smile and opened his hands helplessly. She gave him a little wave, paused uncertainly, picked up her drink, then turned toward the bar and was gone. Briggs's face was red. He practically shouted, "I'm surprised you have any friends at all!"

"I only have one: you."

"Well, don't count on that, if you continue in this vein."

"I suppose it made sense for me to change planes twice and rent a car to have you address me with such loftiness," Faucher wailed. "I came to you in need, but your ascent to the frowning classes must make that unclear."

After dinner, they had a glass of brandy. Marjorie appeared on the karaoke floor and managed to raise the volume as she belted out "Another Somebody Done Somebody Wrong Song," followed immediately by a ghastly imitation of Cher, all pursed lips and slumberous eyes, doing "I Got You Babe." She directed various Frug moves and Vegas gestures Faucher's way. Feeling under attack, Faucher urged Briggs to call for the bill and pay it promptly. "I can't believe how quickly things have gone downhill," he said, hunched over as if under mortar fire.

Marjorie followed them out of the bar. She was so angry she moved in jerks. She walked straight over to Briggs and said, "You think you're above all this, don't you?" Then she slapped him across the face, so astonishing him that he neither raised a protective hand nor averted the now stinging cheek. "You want another one?" she inquired, lips flattened against her teeth.

"I think I'll hold off," Briggs said.

"Ask yourself what Jesus would do," Faucher suggested.

Marjorie whirled on him, and Briggs hurried away toward the boarded-up mercantile store where he'd parked; Faucher joined him. When they got to the car, they looked back to see Marjorie's friends restraining her theatrically by the arms. A cowboy with a goatee and a jet-black Stetson stared ominously as they were forced to pass close to him in order to get out of the lot.

"Don't drive next to them, for Chrissakes!" Faucher said. "The big one is about to come out of the bag!"

Faucher mused as they drove south into the piney hills and grassland. "People have become addicted to hidden causes. That's why you were the one to get slapped. They've been trained to mistrust anything that's right in front of their eyes. Oh, John, my path has been uneven. I've made so many enemies. Some of them intend to hunt me with dogs."

"Outlast them." Briggs listlessly watched the road for deer, vaguely hoping that whoever happened to be hunting Faucher with dogs would be lucky enough to catch him.

"I hope I can. Really, I've come here because you never quite give up on me, do you?"

"We are old friends," Briggs droned.

"Perhaps once I'm a cowboy you'll invest your remarks with greater meaning. Anyway, to continue my saga: I knew the noose was tightening, but I had been so diligent over the years at helping my clients improperly state assets for death taxes that I expected them to drop all complaints against me."

It seemed that Faucher had lost important inhibitions, however; he'd crossed the line, running afoul of the law at several points, including attempted blackmail. When one of his clients, with whom he had reached a mutually satisfactory agreement trading forgiveness for secrecy, died, snoopy children arrived in Faucher's world, followed by investigators, and, "*Net-net,* I'm on the run."

*

Just before sunrise, Briggs heard Faucher calling to him. He climbed the stairs, pulling on a sweatshirt and shorts, and entered the guest room. He found Faucher kneeling next to the window, curtains pulled back slightly, gesturing for Briggs to join him.

In the yard below, two men stood smoking next to a vehicle with government plates. "They're here for me, John," Faucher said. "I can't believe you did this. Now I'm going to jail."

"You know perfectly well that I didn't do this," Briggs said. But nothing could prevent him from feeling unreasonably guilty.

"Judas Iscariot — that's how I shall always know you."

They carried Faucher away. Briggs ran alongside in an L. L. Bean bathrobe pouring out offers of help, but Faucher waved him off like a man shooing flies.

The weather began to change, and the high white clouds moved across the horizon, leaving ghostly streaks in their place. One quiet afternoon, while Briggs was going over the casework he'd take on after the demise of the town in Delaware — mine mitigation in Manitoba, bike paths, a public swimming pool, a library wing given in exchange for ground permanently poisoned by cyanide — the phone rang. It was Carol. She brought him the news that Faucher was going to prison. He had been ruinously disagreeable in court, inflating the sentences to which his crimes had already given rise. She aired this as yet another grievance, as though little good could be extracted from Faucher now. "You were with him, John. Why didn't you help him?"

"I didn't know how to help him. We were just spending time together."

"You were just spending time together?"

"I'm afraid that's it. I feel I wasn't very perceptive."

"You have my agreement on that," Carol said. "He left you literally eager for imprisonment. You had a chance to put him back on his feet and you let him fall."

"Well, I don't know the facts. I —"

"You don't need to know the facts. You need to listen to what I'm telling you."

"Carol, I don't think you understand how tiresome you've become."

"Is that your way of commiserating with me?"

"Yes," Briggs said simply. "Yes, Carol, it is."

At times, Briggs worried that there *was* something he should have done. The whole experience had been like missing a catch on the high trapeze: the acrobat is pulling away from you, falling into the distance. Or perhaps the acrobat is pulling you off your own trapeze. Neither thought was pleasant.

It was inevitable that Briggs would get worked over once again for the newsletter. Hoyt wanted to know how Briggs had found Faucher. "Breathing," Briggs said.

"You've got good air out there," Hoyt said. "I'll give you that."

That November, while on his way to the town in North Carolina that he had saved from oblivion, Briggs stopped in Boston, rented a car, and drove to the prison at Walpole. Faucher refused to see him. In the pale-green visitors' room, Briggs rose slowly to acknowledge the uniformed custodian who bore the rejection. He was furious.

But once he was seated on the plane, drink in hand, looking out onto the runway at men pushing carts, a forklift wheeling along a train of red lights, a neighboring jet pushing back, he felt a little better. His second drink was delivered reluctantly by a harried stewardess — and only because Briggs told her that he was on his way to his mother's funeral. At this point, a glow seemed to form around Briggs's seatmate, and Briggs struck up a conversation with him, ordering drinks for both of them as soon as the plane was airborne. The seatmate, an unfriendly black man who worked for Prudential Insurance, actually was going to a funeral, the funeral of a friend, and this revelation triggered a slightly euphoric summary of Briggs's friendship with Faucher, delivered in remarkable detail, considering that Briggs's companion was trying to read. Briggs concluded his description of his visit to the prison and Faucher's refusal to see him by raising his arms in the air and crying, "Hallelujah!," a gesture that made him realize, instantly, that he had had enough to drink. The seatmate narrowed his eyes, and when Briggs explained that, at long last, that chapter of his life was over, the man, turning back to his open book, said wearily, "Do you actually believe that?"

J. ROBERT LENNON

Eight Pieces for the Left Hand

FROM GRANTA

One

AUTUMN, ONCE THE MOST POPULAR SEASON in this town of tall trees, is now regarded with dread, thanks to the bitter athletic rivalry between our two local high schools. The school in the neighborhood commonly called the Flats is attended by the children of the working class, who are employed by the town's restaurants, motels, gas stations, and factories and who live in those low-lying areas most frequently plagued by pollution, flood, and crime. The school in the Heights, on the other hand, is populated by the children of academics who live on wooded hillside lots that offer panoramic views of our valley. Students at the Flats consider students at the Heights to be prissy, pampered, trust-fund half-wits, while Heights students regard Flats students as mustachioed, inbred gas huffers. Historically, these class tensions were brought to bear in the annual football game, played at our university's enormous stadium the last weekend in October.

Five years ago, however, some Heights players spray-painted ethnic slurs on the dusty American sedans of several Flats team members, and the Flats players retaliated by flinging bricks through the windows of the shiny, leased sports coupes of their rivals. Four years ago, a massive melee at a fast-food restaurant landed players from both teams in the hospital. Three years ago, the much-painted Seniors' Rock in front of Flats High was rolled into a nearby creek, and the brand-new Sciences Wing of Heights High was set on fire. Two years ago, each coach was kidnapped by still unidentified members of the opposing team and traded on Friendship Bridge at midnight of game day; and last year the Flats' beloved mascot, the Marauding Goat, was disemboweled before the war memorial in Peters Park, while not a mile away the starting quarterback for the Heights was partially paralyzed in a hit-and-run incident outside a drive-up bank. The subsequent game was canceled.

This year's game has also been canceled, but for a different reason entirely. A steep drop in the population of our town has made the existence of both high schools fiscally untenable, and beginning with the fall semester the two will be combined into a single entity, to be called Area High. It remains unclear how the rivalry will play itself out, but many seem convinced that the solution lies in targeting a common enemy, such as the students of nearby Valley High, thought by all to be buck-toothed hicks, or those of faraway City Regional, who, everyone knows, are greasy-haired gangbangers. Meanwhile the peace here in our town remains uneasy, and we await with trepidation the turning of the leaves.

Two

A local poet of considerable national fame completed a new collection of poems that had, due to a painful and scandalous series of personal problems, been delayed in editing and publication for some years. When the revisions were finally finished, the poet typed up a clean copy of the manuscript and got into his car to bring it to the copy shop for reproduction.

On the way, however, the poet was pulled over for running a red light and was subsequently found to be drunk. Due to a new and unforgiving drunk-driving law in our state, his car was taken from his possession and his license revoked.

Upon regaining sobriety, the poet realized that his poetry manuscript was still in the car and asked the police to return it to him. The police, however, maintained that the contents of the car no longer belonged to him and refused. Their refusal resulted in a protracted legal battle, during which our beloved poet died, leaving uncertain the fate of the manuscript.

But the poet's publisher, eager to issue a posthumous volume, struck a bargain with the police department: if someone at the station would read the finished poems over the phone, an editor could transcribe them and issue them in book form without the manuscript's changing hands. After all, the publisher argued, even if the manuscript legally belonged to the city, its contents did not, as they were devised outside the poet's car. The police agreed to this scheme, the phone recitation took place, and the book was issued to great acclaim, assuring the poet a place in the literary canon that he had not enjoyed in life.

Eventually, however, the poet's estate won its legal battle against the city, and the original manuscript was recovered. All were shocked to learn that it bore little resemblance to the published book.

It was not long before a city policeman confessed to having improvised much of the manuscript during its telephone transcription. His only explanation was that he saw room for improvement and could not resist making a few changes here and there. Almost immediately, the policeman was asked to leave the force, and the acclaimed book was completely discredited. The true manuscript was published in its entirety, to tepid reviews.

The policeman has continued to write poetry. Most agree that it is excellent, but few will publish the work of someone known to be so dishonest.

Three

A farmer who lives on our road had lost three mailboxes in as many weeks to the drunken antics of some local youths, who had taken to driving past late at night and smashing the mailboxes with a baseball bat. Because the police had been uncooperative in apprehending the youths, the farmer devised a solution to the problem: he bought two mailboxes — a gigantic, industrial-strength one, and a small aluminium one — and arranged the boxes one inside the other, with a layer of cement between the two. He mounted this monstrous mega-box on a length of eight-inch steel pipe, which was set into a four-foot post hole and stabilized there with thirty additional gallons of cement.

The following weekend the youths sped past in their convertible, and T., the captain of the high school baseball team and a local slugger of some renown, swung at the box from a standing position in the back seat. With the bat moving at more than seventy-five miles per hour relative to the car, and the car itself traveling nearly as fast, the combined velocity of the impact was approximately 150 miles per hour. It was at this speed that the bat ricocheted and struck the head of J., a seventeen-year-old girl sitting in the car, killing her instantly.

A series of criminal charges and civil suits followed. T. was tried as an adult and convicted of involuntary manslaughter. The driver of the car was sentenced to community service on charges of vandalism and reckless endangerment. The farmer was also convicted of reckless endangerment and fined; in response he sued the police department for failing to address the problem beforehand. The parents of the dead girl lobbied to have all the car's living occupants, five in all, expelled from school; they also sued T., the driver, and the farmer for several million dollars. They even tried, and failed, to sue the hardware store where the farmer had bought his cement-mailbox supplies, arguing that the store's employees ought to have figured out what the farmer was doing and stopped him. In a peripheral case, T.'s parents sued the hospital where he was treated for a broken arm; apparently the doctors there had set the break improperly, resulting in a painful resetting that was likely to ruin T.'s chances to play baseball in the major leagues. Their lawyers demanded a percentage of T.'s projected future salary.

In the end, all charges were reversed on appeal. It seemed that everyone involved was to blame, which the courts determined was no different from no one being to blame. All that remains, apart from the many legal debts incurred by the litigants and the accused, is the cement mailbox, which has proven too costly and cumbersome to remove.

Four

One night, while our cat was curled up on my lap, placidly purring, I noticed that his collar was somewhat crooked, and in the process of righting it I happened to catch a glimpse of the identification tag that hung from it. The tag, a worn, stamped-metal disc, told me that the cat's name was Fluffy.

Our cat, however, was named Horace. Reading further, I discovered that the tag bore an address on our old street in a faraway town we had lived in temporarily and not our permanent address.

I gave the matter some thought and concluded that there were two possible explanations. One was that while we were living in the faraway town, our cat's collar was switched with another cat's, perhaps as some kind of prank. The other was that we had accidentally gotten hold of someone else's cat and abandoned our own.

Initially I dismissed the second possibility, as it had been five years since we lived in that town, and this cat had very much come to seem like ours, and the town we lived in permanently his rightful home. But as I reflected, I realized how very unlikely a prank the switching of collars was; and simultaneously I began to recall changes in our cat's personality around the time of our move, which, quite naturally, we assumed to be consequences of the move itself but which now suddenly seemed like the consequences of our having taken possession of an entirely different cat.

On impulse, I got up and called the phone number printed on the tag. A woman answered. I asked her if she had lost a cat named Fluffy, and after a long pause she replied that yes, she had, many years ago, and did I have some information about him? I told her that I had found his collar, unconnected to any cat. Did she want me to send it to her? After a dramatic pause, the woman told me to go ahead and do so, and I did, the next day. I also ordered, through a pet-supply catalogue, a new tag with the name Horace printed on it. Though I no longer consider this to have been a cowardly act, I went through several weeks of self-doubt at the time. As for now, I can only hope that the original Horace was taken in by a kind family.

Five

At a bend in a winding country road outside our town, there once lived a family whose only child, a girl, was born deaf. When the girl grew old enough to play outside on her own, the family had the county erect a yellow sign near the house, which read DEAF CHILD AREA. The idea was that motorists would drive more slowly, knowing that a nearby child could not hear their approach.

By the time I was a boy, the deaf child had become a teenager and after a while left town for college. She returned occasionally to visit but for the most part was no longer around. Eventually she married and settled in a faraway city. Her parents, aware of the sign's superfluity, wrote a letter asking the county to come and take it down; but though the county promised to see to the matter, no workmen ever arrived.

At about the time I myself married, the deaf child's parents retired and decided to move away to someplace warmer. They sold their house, and it was promptly bought by a local professor. The professor, however, was soon offered a position at another university, which he was obliged to occupy immediately. With no time to sell the house he had just bought, the professor hired a property management company to offer the house for rent. At this point it caught my attention. My wife was pregnant with our first child, and we had begun to worry that our small apartment would be unsuitable for raising a family. After a look at the house in the country, we decided to rent it and soon moved in.

For several months we ignored the sign, which had grown old and battered and at any rate had nothing to do with us. But as winter approached and my wife's due date drew near, I noticed that her eyes lingered on the sign whenever we pulled into the driveway, and more than once I caught her staring out at it from our future child's bedroom, which we had furnished and filled with colorful toys. One night, as we lay awake in bed, my wife turned to me and asked if I might remove the sign somehow. She realized she was being irrational but nonetheless feared the sign might bring some harm to our baby, and she didn't think she could sleep until the sign was gone.

This seemed perfectly reasonable. I got out of bed and dressed, then brought a box of tools out to the roadside, where I examined the sign. I saw that it had been bolted onto a metal post and that I could simply remove the sign and leave the post where it stood in the ground. I did this quickly and prepared to go inside.

But something compelled me to go out behind the house and find a shovel, which I used to dig the post out of the ground. The ground was cold, and the work slow going. When I finished, I took the sign and post and put them in the back of the car and drove down to the lake, where I threw them out as far as I could into the water. They splashed onto the surface and sunk out of sight.

When I returned home, my wife didn't ask me where I'd driven. After that we slept comfortably and did so every night until our child was born without illness or defect.

Six

There were six students in our school play: Jason, Heather, Kevin, Carol, Matt, and me. But in the script, which our teachers had obtained from a catalogue, our characters were given other names: Scott, Jenny, Robert, Melissa, Bill, and Larry. Since the oldest of us was seven, we had never before been in a play, and the difficulty of memorizing our lines was compounded by the necessity of learning new names for both ourselves and the others. For weeks we struggled through rehearsals, slowly gaining ground. Then, at the last minute, our teachers, fearing a debacle, told us to forget the stage names and simply use our own.

But our teachers had acted at the very height of our put-upon duality, and their command effected a desperate confusion, which manifested itself onstage that night as complete theatrical anarchy. We addressed one another by whatever names happened to pop into our heads and forgot almost every scripted line, leaving our audience with only the vaguest notion of the drama's direction. The performance ended in chaos and tears, with our baffled parents applauding politely and our teachers holding their shocked faces in their hands.

Sadly, the confusion didn't end there. For weeks, we were distracted during classes, failing to respond to our teachers' direct enquiries, and were moody and unresponsive at home. When we met in the halls or on the playground, we greeted each other with incorrect names or none at all.

Most of us recovered, but Jason has married seven times, and Heather, from whom no one has heard in twenty years, is rumored to have gone mad. One lonely fall afternoon I called our local mental hospital in search of her but was told that no patient by that name was in residence.

Seven

A local professor was honored, and a national newspaper ran a photograph of him writing on a chalkboard before a classroom full of students. Not long afterward, the professor was asked to speak at the annual meeting of a club for left-handed persons. In his letter, the club's president explained that he had seen the photo and noticed the professor's left-handedness; he believed the professor was a credit to "lefties" and would make an inspiring and enlightening guest. Included with the letter was a booklet listing the accomplishments of left-handed people, photocopied articles asserting the creative and intellectual superiority of lefties, and a catalogue of whimsical products for the left-handed, including special coffee mugs, pens, and eating utensils with pro-left-hand messages printed on them.

The professor agreed to speak to the club and was given a large honorarium, free transportation, and a lavish hotel suite complete with mini-gym and sauna. When at last he stood before the assembled lefties, he thanked them for their invitation, then proceeded to berate them for their smugness and stupidity. He pointed out that he was, in fact, right-handed and only appeared left-handed in the photo because the newspaper had reversed the negative; if they had looked a little more closely, he said, they would have noticed that the writing on the chalkboard was backward. He told them that they should honor others for their achievements and not their genetic circumstances, and then, only minutes into his speech, stepped down from the dais and caught a cab to the airport.

When, years later, the professor lost his right arm in a highway crash, he was unsurprised to receive a flood of congratulatory letters and the first in an endless stream of free "lefty" gift items that have appeared almost daily on his doorstep ever since. Far from being angry, he views this unfortunate turn of events as a kind of poetic justice and even tried to apologize to the lefties' club in a kind letter to its president. However, his speech had cut too deeply, and the lefties continue to bombard him with junk.

Meanwhile, the professor has learned to play a variety of left-hand pieces on the piano and is said to be as dexterous with his left hand alone as he once was with both. He has also joined a national organization of people who have lost the use of one or more limbs and is scheduled to speak at its next annual meeting.

Eight

A local novelist spent ten years writing a book about our region and its inhabitants, which, when completed, added up to more than

1,000 pages. Exhausted by her effort, she at last sent it off to a publisher, only to be told that it would have to be cut by nearly half. Though daunted by the work ahead of her, the novelist was encouraged by the publisher's interest and spent more than a year excising material.

But by the time she reached the requested length, the novelist found it difficult to stop. In the early days of her editing, she would struggle for hours to remove words from a sentence, only to discover that its paragraph was better off without it. Soon she discovered that removing sentences from a paragraph was rarely as effective as cutting entire paragraphs, nor was selectively erasing paragraphs from a chapter as satisfying as eliminating chapters entirely. After another year, she had whittled the book down into a short story, which she sent to magazines.

Multiple rejections, however, drove her back to the chopping block, where she reduced her story to a vignette, the vignette to an anecdote, the anecdote to an aphorism, and the aphorism, at last, to this haiku:

Tiny upstate town
Undergoes many changes
Nonetheless endures

Unfortunately, no magazine would publish the haiku. The novelist has printed it on note cards, which she can be found giving away to passers-by in our town park, where she is also known sometimes to sleep, except when the police, whose thuggish tactics she so neatly parodied in her original manuscript, bring her in on charges of vagrancy. I have a copy of the haiku pinned above my desk, its note card grimy and furred along the edges from multiple profferings, and I read it frequently, sometimes with pity but always with awe.

KELLY LINK

Stone Animals

FROM CONJUNCTIONS

HENRY ASKED A QUESTION. He was joking.

"As a matter of fact," the real estate agent snapped, "it is."

It was not a question she had expected to be asked. She gave Henry a goofy, appeasing smile and yanked at the hem of the skirt of her pink linen suit, which seemed as if it might, at any moment, go rolling up her knees like a window shade. She was younger than Henry and sold houses that she couldn't afford to buy.

"It's reflected in the asking price, of course," she said. "Like you said."

Henry stared at her. She blushed.

"I've never seen anything," she said. "But there are stories. Not stories that I know. I just know there are stories. If you believe that sort of thing."

"I don't," Henry said. When he looked over to see if Catherine had heard, she had her head up the tiled fireplace, as if she were trying it on, to see whether it fit. Catherine was six months pregnant. Nothing fit her except for Henry's baseball caps, his sweatpants, his T-shirts. But she liked the fireplace.

Carleton was running up and down the staircase, slapping his heels down hard, keeping his head down and his hands folded around the banister. Carleton was serious about how he played. Tilly sat on the landing, reading a book, legs poking out through the railings. Whenever Carleton ran past, he thumped her on the head, but Tilly never said a word. Carleton would be sorry later and never even know why.

Catherine took her head out of the fireplace. "Guys," she said.

"Carleton, Tilly. Slow down a minute and tell me what you think. Think King Spanky will be okay out here?"

"King Spanky is a cat, Mom," Tilly said. "Maybe we should get a dog, you know, to help protect us." She could tell by looking at her mother that they were going to move. She didn't know how she felt about this, except she had plans for the yard. A yard like that needed a dog.

"I don't like big dogs," said Carleton, six years old and small for his age. "I don't like this staircase. It's too big."

"Carleton," Henry said. "Come here. I need a hug."

Carleton came down the stairs. He lay down on his stomach on the floor and rolled, noisily, floppily, slowly, over to where Henry stood with the real estate agent. He curled like a dead snake around Henry's ankles. "I don't like those dogs outside," he said.

"I know it looks like we're out in the middle of nothing, but if you go down through the backyard, cut through that stand of trees, there's this little path. It takes you straight down to the train station. Ten-minute bike ride," the agent said. Nobody ever remembered her name, which was why she had to wear too-tight skirts. She was, as it happened, writing a romance novel, and she spent a lot of time making up pseudonyms, just in case she ever finished it. Ophelia Pink. Matilde Hightower. LaLa Treeble. Or maybe she'd write gothics. Ghost stories. But not about people like these. "Another ten minutes on that path and you're in town."

"What dogs, Carleton?" Henry said.

"I think they're lions, Carleton," said Catherine. "You mean the stone ones beside the door? Just like the lions at the library. You love those lions, Carleton. Patience and Fortitude?"

"I've always thought they were rabbits," the real estate agent said. "You know, because of the ears. They have big ears." She flopped her hands and then tugged at her skirt, which would not stay down. "I think they're pretty valuable. The guy who built the house had a gallery in New York. He knew a lot of sculptors."

Henry was struck by that. He didn't think he knew a single sculptor.

"I don't like the rabbits," Carleton said. "I don't like the staircase. I don't like this room. It's too big. I don't like *her.*"

"Carleton," Henry said. He smiled at the real estate agent.

"I don't like the house," Carleton said, clinging to Henry's ankles. "I don't like houses. I don't want to live in a house."

"Then we'll build you a tepee out on the lawn," Catherine said. She sat on the stairs beside Tilly, who shifted her weight, almost imperceptibly, toward Catherine. Catherine sat as still as possible. Tilly was in fourth grade and difficult in a way that girls weren't supposed to be. Mostly she refused to be cuddled or babied. But she sat there, leaning on Catherine's arm, emanating saintly fragrances: peacefulness, placidness, goodness. *I want this house,* Catherine said, moving her lips like a silent-movie heroine, to Henry, so that neither Carleton nor the agent, who had bent over to inspect a piece of dust on the floor, could see. "You can live in your tepee, and we'll invite you to come over for lunch. You like lunch, don't you? Peanut butter sandwiches?"

"I don't," Carleton said, and sobbed once.

But they bought the house anyway. The real estate agent got her commission. Tilly rubbed the waxy stone ears of the rabbits on the way out, pretending that they already belonged to her. They were as tall as she was, but that wouldn't always be true. Carleton had a peanut butter sandwich.

The rabbits sat on either side of the front door. Two stone animals sitting on cracked, mossy haunches. They were shapeless, lumpish, patient in a way that seemed not worn down, but perhaps never really finished in the first place. There was something about them that reminded Henry of Stonehenge. Catherine thought of topiary shapes, *The Velveteen Rabbit,* soldiers who stand guard in front of palaces and never even twitch their noses. Maybe they could be donated to a museum. Or broken up with jackhammers. They didn't suit the house at all.

"So what's the house like?" said Henry's boss. She was carefully stretching rubber bands around her rubber-band ball. By now the rubber-band ball was so big, she had to get special extra-large rubber bands from the art department. She claimed it helped her think. She had tried knitting for a while, but it turned out that knitting was too utilitarian, too feminine. Making an enormous ball out of rubber bands struck the right note. It was something a man might do.

It took up half of her desk. Under the fluorescent office lights it had a peeled red liveliness. You almost expected it to shoot forward and out the door. The larger it got, the more it looked like some kind of eyeless, hairless, legless animal. Maybe a dog. A Carleton-sized dog, Henry thought, although not a Carleton-sized rubber-band ball.

Catherine joked sometimes about using the carleton as a measure of unit.

"Big," Henry said. "Haunted."

"Really?" his boss said. "So's this rubber band." She aimed a rubber band at Henry and shot him in the elbow. This was meant to suggest that she and Henry were good friends and just goofing around, the way good friends did. But what it really meant was that she was angry at him. "Don't leave me," she said.

"I'm only two hours away." Henry put up his hand to ward off rubber bands. "Quit it. We talk on the phone, we use e-mail. I come back to town when you need me in the office."

"You're sure this is a good idea?" his boss said. She fixed her reptilian, watery gaze on him. She had problematical tear ducts. Though she could have had a minor surgical procedure to fix this, she'd chosen not to. It was a tactical advantage, the way it spooked people.

It didn't really matter that Henry remained immune to rubber bands and crocodile tears. She had backup strategies. She thought about which would be most effective while Henry pitched his stupid idea all over again.

Henry had the movers' phone number in his pocket, like a talisman. He wanted to take it out, wave it at the Crocodile, say, Look at this! Instead he said, "For nine years, we've lived in an apartment next door to a building that smells like urine. Like someone built an entire building out of bricks made of compressed red pee. Someone spit on Catherine in the street last week. This old Russian lady in a fur coat. A kid rang our doorbell the other day and tried to sell us gas masks. Door-to-door gas-mask salesman. Catherine bought one. When she told me about it she burst into tears. She said she couldn't figure out if she was feeling guilty because she'd bought a gas mask, or if it was because she hadn't bought enough for everyone."

"Good Chinese food," his boss said. "Good movies. Good bookstores. Good dry cleaners. Good conversation."

"Tree houses," Henry said. "I had a tree house when I was a kid."

"You were never a kid," his boss said.

"Three bathrooms. Crown moldings. We can't even see our nearest neighbor's house. I get up in the morning, have coffee, put Carleton and Tilly on the bus, and go to work in my pajamas."

"What about Catherine?" The Crocodile put her head down on her rubber-band ball. Possibly this was a gesture of defeat.

"There was that thing. Catherine's whole department is leaving. Like rats deserting a sinking ship. Anyway, Catherine needs a change. And so do I," Henry said. "We've got another kid on the way. We're going to garden. Catherine'll teach ESL, find a book group, write her book. Teach the kids how to play bridge. You've got to start them early."

He picked a rubber band off the floor and offered it to his boss. "You should come out and visit some weekend."

"I never go upstate," the Crocodile said. She held on to her rubber-band ball. "Too many ghosts."

"Are you going to miss this? Living here?" Catherine said. She couldn't stand the way her stomach poked out. She couldn't see past it. She held up her left foot to make sure it was still there and pulled the sheet off Henry.

"I love the house," Henry said.

"Me too," Catherine said. She was biting her fingernails. Henry could hear her teeth going click, click. Now she had both feet up in the air. She wiggled them around. Hello, feet.

"What are you doing?"

She put them down again. On the street outside, cars came and went, pushing smears of light along the ceiling, slow and fast at the same time. The baby was wriggling around inside her, kicking out with both feet like it was swimming across the English Channel, the Pacific. Kicking all the way to China. "Did you buy that story about the former owners moving to France?"

"I don't believe in France," Henry said. *"Je ne crois pas en France."*

"Neither do I," Catherine said. "Henry?"

"What?"

"Do you love the house?"

"I love the house."

"I love it more than you do," Catherine said, although Henry hated it when she said things like that. "What do you love best?"

"That room in the front," Henry said. "With the windows. Our bedroom. Those weird rabbit statues."

"Me too," Catherine said, although she didn't. "I love those rabbits."

Then she said, "Do you ever worry about Carleton and Tilly?"

"What do you mean?" Henry said. He looked at the alarm clock: it was 4:00 A.M. "Why are we awake right now?"

"Sometimes I worry that I love one of them better," Catherine said. "Like I might love Tilly better. Because she used to wet the bed. Because she's always so angry. Or Carleton, because he was so sick when he was little."

"I love them both the same," Henry said.

He didn't even know he was lying. Catherine knew, though. She knew he was lying, and she knew he didn't even know it. Most of the time she thought that it was okay. As long as he thought he loved them both the same and acted as if he did, that was good enough.

"Well, do you ever worry that you love them more than me?" she said. "Or that I love them more than I love you?"

"Do you?" Henry said.

"Of course," Catherine said. "I have to. It's my job."

She found the gas mask in a box of wineglasses, and also six recent issues of *The New Yorker,* which she still might get a chance to read someday. She put the gas mask under the sink and *The New Yorker*s in the sink. Why not? It was her sink. She could put anything she wanted into it. She took the magazines out again and put them into the refrigerator, just for fun.

Henry came into the kitchen, holding silver candlesticks and a stuffed armadillo, which someone had made into a purse. It had a shoulder strap made out of its own skin. You opened its mouth and put things inside it, lipstick and subway tokens. It had pink gimlet eyes and smelled strongly of vinegar. It belonged to Tilly, although how it had come into her possession was unclear. Tilly claimed she'd won it at school in a contest involving doughnuts. Catherine thought it more likely Tilly had either stolen it or (slightly preferable) found it in someone's trash. Now Tilly kept her most valuable belongings inside the purse to keep them safe from Carleton, who was covetous of the previous things — because they were small and because they belonged to Tilly — but afraid of the armadillo.

"I've already told her she can't take it to school for at least the first two weeks. Then we'll see." She took the purse from Henry and put it under the sink with the gas mask.

"What are they doing?" Henry said. Framed in the kitchen window, Carleton and Tilly hunched over the lawn. They had a pair of scissors and a notebook and a stapler.

"They're collecting grass." Catherine took dishes out of a box, put the bubble wrap aside for Tilly to stomp, and stowed the dishes in a cabinet. The baby kicked like it knew all about bubble wrap. "Whoa, Fireplace," she said. "We don't have a dancing license in there."

Henry put out his hand, rapped on Catherine's stomach. *Knock, knock.* It was Tilly's joke. Catherine would say, "Who's there?" and Tilly would say, "Candlestick's here." "Fat Man's here." Box. Hammer. Milkshake. Clarinet. Mousetrap. Fiddlestick. Tilly had a whole list of names for the baby. The real estate agent would have approved.

"Where's King Spanky?" Henry said.

"Under our bed," Catherine said. "He's up in the box frame."

"Have we unpacked the alarm clock?" Henry said.

"Poor King Spanky," Catherine said. "Nobody to love except an alarm clock. Come upstairs and let's see if we can shake him out of the bed. I've got a present for you."

The present was in a U-Haul box exactly like all the other boxes in the bedroom, except that Catherine had written HENRY'S PRESENT on it instead of LARGE FRONT BEDROOM. Inside the box were Styrofoam peanuts and then a smaller box from Takashimaya. The Takashimaya box was fastened with a silver ribbon. The tissue paper inside was dull gold, and inside the tissue paper was a green silk robe with orange sleeves and heraldic animals in orange and gold thread. "Lions," Henry said.

"Rabbits," Catherine said.

"I didn't get you anything," Henry said.

Catherine smiled nobly. She liked giving presents better than getting presents. She'd never told Henry because it seemed to her that it must be selfish in some way she'd never bothered to figure out. Catherine was grateful to be married to Henry, who accepted all presents as his due; who looked good in the clothes she bought him; who was vain, in an easygoing way, about his good looks. Buying clothes for Henry was especially satisfying now, while she was pregnant and couldn't buy them for herself.

She said, "If you don't like it, then I'll keep it. Look at you, look at those sleeves. You look like the emperor of Japan."

They had already colonized the bedroom, making it full of things that belonged to them. There was Catherine's mirror on the wall, and their mahogany wardrobe, their first real piece of furniture, a wedding present from Catherine's great-aunt. There was their serviceable queen-size bed with King Spanky lodged up inside it, and there was Henry, spinning his arms in the wide orange sleeves, like an embroidered windmill. Henry could see all of these things in the mirror, and behind him, their lawn and Tilly and Carleton, stapling grass into their notebook. He saw all of these things and he found them good. But he couldn't see Catherine. When he turned around, she stood in the doorway, frowning at him. She had the alarm clock in her hand.

"Look at you," she said again. It worried her, the way something, someone, *Henry,* could suddenly look like a place she'd never been before. The alarm began to ring and King Spanky came out from under the bed, trotting over to Catherine. She bent over, awkwardly — ungraceful, ungainly, so clumsy, so fucking awkward; being pregnant was like wearing a fucking suitcase strapped across your middle — put the alarm clock down on the ground, and King Spanky hunkered down in front of it, his nose against the ringing glass face. And that made her laugh again. Henry loved Catherine's laugh. Downstairs, their children slammed a door open, ran through the house, carrying scissors, both Catherine and Henry knew, and slammed another door open and were outside again, leaving behind the smell of grass. There was a store in New York where you could buy a perfume that smelled like that.

Catherine and Carleton and Tilly came back from the grocery store with a tire, a rope to hang it from, and a box of pancake mix for dinner. Henry was online, looking at a JPEG of a rubber-band ball. There was a message, too. The Crocodile needed him to come into the office. It would be just a few days. Someone was setting fires, and there was no one smart enough to see how to put them out except for him. They were his accounts. He had to come in and save them. She knew Catherine and Henry's apartment hadn't sold; she'd checked with their listing agent. So surely it wouldn't be impossible, not impossible, only inconvenient.

He went downstairs to tell Catherine. "That *witch,*" she said, and then bit her lip. "She called the listing agent? I'm sorry. We talked about this. Never mind. Just give me a moment."

Catherine inhaled. Exhaled. Inhaled. If she were Carleton, she would hold her breath until her face turned red and Henry agreed to stay home, but then again, it never worked for Carleton. "We ran into our new neighbors in the grocery store. She's about the same age as me. Liz and Marcus. One kid, older, a girl, um, I think her name was Alison, maybe from a first marriage — potential babysitter, which is really good news. Liz is a lawyer. Gorgeous. Reads Oprah books. He likes to cook."

"So do I," Henry said.

"You're better looking," Catherine said. "So do you have to go back tonight, or can you take the train in the morning?"

"The morning is fine," Henry said, wanting to seem agreeable.

Carleton appeared in the kitchen, his arms pinned around King Spanky's middle. The cat's front legs stuck straight out, as if Carleton were dowsing. King Spanky's eyes were closed. His whiskers twitched Morse code. "What are you wearing?" Carleton said.

"My new uniform," Henry said. "I wear it to work."

"Where do you work?" Carleton said, testing.

"I work at home," Henry said. Catherine snorted.

"He looks like the king of rabbits, doesn't he? The emperor of Rabbitaly," she said, no longer sounding particularly pleased about this.

"He looks like a princess," Carleton said, now pointing King Spanky at Henry like a gun.

"Where's your grass collection?" Henry said. "Can I see it?"

"No," Carleton said. He put King Spanky on the floor, and the cat slunk out of the kitchen, heading for the staircase, the bedroom, the safety of the bedsprings, the beloved alarm clock, the beloved. The beloved may be treacherous, greasy-headed, and given to evil habits, or else it can be a man in his late forties who works too much, or it can be an alarm clock.

"After dinner," Henry said, trying again, "we could go out and find a tree for your tire swing."

"No," Carleton said regretfully. He lingered in the kitchen, hoping to be asked a question to which he could say yes.

"Where's your sister?" Henry said.

"Watching television," Carleton said. "I don't like the television here."

"It's too big," Henry said, but Catherine didn't laugh.

Henry dreams he is the king of the real estate agents. Henry loves his job. He tries to sell a house to a young couple with twitchy noses and big dark eyes. Why does he always dream that he's trying to sell things?

The couple stare at him nervously. He leans toward them as if he's going to whisper something in their silly, expectant ears. It's a secret he's never told anyone before. It's a secret he didn't even know that he knew. "Let's stop fooling," he says. "You can't afford to buy this house. You don't have any money. You're rabbits."

"Where do you work?" Carleton said in the morning when Henry called from Grand Central.

"I work at home," Henry said. "Home where we live now, where you are. Eventually. Just not today. Are you getting ready for school?"

Carleton put the phone down. Henry could hear him saying something to Catherine. "He says he's not nervous about school," she said. "He's a brave kid."

"I kissed you this morning," Henry said, "but you didn't wake up. There were all these rabbits on the lawn. They were huge. King Spanky–sized. They were just sitting there like they were waiting for the sun to come up. It was funny, like some kind of art installation. But it was kind of creepy, too. Think they'd been there all night?"

"Rabbits? Can they have rabies? I saw them this morning when I got up," Catherine said. "Carleton didn't want to brush his teeth this morning. He says something's wrong with his toothbrush."

"Maybe he dropped it in the toilet, and he doesn't want to tell you," Henry said.

"Maybe you could buy a new toothbrush and bring it home," Catherine said. "He doesn't want one from the drugstore here. He wants one from New York."

"Where's Tilly?" Henry said.

"She says she's trying to figure out what's wrong with Carleton's toothbrush. She's still in the bathroom," Catherine said.

"Can I talk to her for a second?" Henry said.

"Tell her she needs to get dressed and eat her Cheerios,"

Catherine said. "After I drive them to school, Liz is coming over for coffee. Then we're going to go out for lunch. I'm not unpacking another box until you get home. Here's Tilly."

"Hi," Tilly said. She sounded as if she was asking a question.

Tilly never liked talking to people on the telephone. How were you supposed to know if they were really who they said they were? And even if they were who they claimed to be, they didn't know whether you were who you said you were. You could be someone else. They might give away information about you and not even know it. There were no protocols. No precautions.

She said, "Did you brush your teeth this morning?"

"Good morning, Tilly," her father (if it was her father) said. "My toothbrush was fine. Perfectly normal."

"That's good," Tilly said. "I let Carleton use mine."

"That was very generous," Henry said.

"No problem," Tilly said. Sharing things with Carleton wasn't like having to share things with other people. It wasn't really like sharing things at all. Carleton belonged to her, like the toothbrush. "Mom says that when we get home today, we can draw on the walls in our rooms if we want to, while we decide what color we want to paint them."

"Sounds like fun," Henry said. "Can I draw on them, too?"

"Maybe," Tilly said. She had already said too much. "Gotta go. Gotta eat breakfast."

"Don't be worried about school," Henry said.

"I'm not worried about school," Tilly said.

"I love you," Henry said.

"I'm real concerned about this toothbrush," Tilly said.

He closed his eyes only for a minute. Just for a minute. When he woke up, it was dark and he didn't know where he was. He stood up and went over to the door, almost tripping over something. It sailed away from him in an exuberant, rollicking sweep.

According to the clock on his desk, it was 4:00 A.M. Why was it always 4:00 A.M.? There were four messages on his cell phone, all from Catherine.

He went online and checked train schedules. Then he sent Catherine a fast e-mail: "Fell asleep @ midnight? Mssed trains. Awake now, going to keep on working. Pttng out fires. Take the train home early afternoon? Still lv me?" Before he went back to work, he kicked the rubber-band ball back down the hall toward the Crocodile's door.

Catherine called him at 8:45.

"I'm sorry," Henry said.

"I bet you are," Catherine said.

"I can't find my razor. I think the Crocodile had some kind of tantrum and tossed my stuff."

"Carleton will love that," Catherine said. "Maybe you should sneak in the house and shave before dinner. He had a hard day at school yesterday."

"Maybe I should grow a beard," Henry said. "He can't be afraid of everything all the time. Tell me about the first day of school."

"We'll talk about it later," Catherine said. "Liz just drove up. I'm going to be her guest at the gym. Just make it home for dinner."

At 6:00 P.M. Henry e-mailed Catherine again. "Srry. Accidentally startd avalanche while puttng out fires. Wait up for me? How ws second day of school?" She didn't write him back. He called and no one picked up the phone. She didn't call.

He took the last train home. By the time they reached the station, he was the only one left in his car. He unchained his bicycle and rode it home in the dark. Rabbits pelted across the footpath in front of his bike. There were rabbits foraging on his lawn. They froze as he dismounted and pushed the bicycle across the grass. The lawn was rumpled; the bike went up and down over invisible depressions that he supposed were rabbit holes. There were two short, fat men standing in the dark on either side of the front door, waiting for him, but when he came closer, he remembered that they were stone rabbits. "Knock, knock," he said.

The real rabbits on the lawn tipped their ears at him. The stone rabbits waited for the punch line, but they were just stone rabbits. They had nothing better to do.

The front door wasn't locked. He walked through the downstairs rooms, putting his hands on the backs and tops of furniture. In the kitchen, cut-down boxes leaned in stacks against the wall, waiting to be recycled or remade into cardboard houses and spaceships and tunnels for Carleton and Tilly.

Catherine had unpacked Carleton's room. Night-lights in the shapes of bears and geese and cats were plugged into every floor outlet. There were little low-watt table lamps as well — hippo, robot, gorilla, pirate ship. Everything was soaked in a tender, peaceable light, translating Carleton's room into something more than a bedroom: something luminous, numinous, a cartoony midnight church of sleep.

Tilly was sleeping in the other bed.

Tilly would never admit that she sleepwalked, the same way that she would never admit that she sometimes still wet the bed. But she refused to make friends. Making friends would have meant spending the night in strange houses. Tomorrow morning she would insist that Henry or Catherine must have carried her from her room, put her to bed in Carleton's room for reasons of their own.

Henry knelt down between the two beds and kissed Carleton on the forehead. He kissed Tilly, smoothed her hair. How could he not love Tilly better? He'd known her longer. She was so brave, so angry.

On the walls of Carleton's bedroom, Henry's children had drawn a house. A cat nearly as big as the house. There was a crown on the cat's head. Trees or flowers with pairs of leaves that pointed straight up, still bigger, and a stick figure on a stick bicycle, riding past the trees. When he looked closer, he thought that maybe the trees were actually rabbits. The wall smelled like Froot Loops. Someone had written HENRY IS A RAT FINK! HA HA! He recognized his wife's handwriting.

"Scented markers," Catherine said. She stood in the door, holding a pillow against her stomach. "I was sleeping downstairs on the sofa. You walked right past and didn't see me."

"The front door was unlocked," Henry said.

"Liz says nobody ever locks their doors out here," Catherine said. "Are you coming to bed, or were you just stopping by to see how we were?"

"I have to go back in tomorrow," Henry said. He pulled a toothbrush out of his pocket and showed it to her. "There's a box of Krispy Kreme doughnuts on the kitchen counter."

"Delete the doughnuts," Catherine said. "I'm not that easy." She took a step toward him and accidentally kicked King Spanky. The cat yowled. Carleton woke up. He said, "Who's there? Who's there?"

"It's me," Henry said. He knelt beside Carleton's bed in the light of the Winnie-the-Pooh lamp. "I brought you a new toothbrush."

Carleton whimpered.

"What's wrong, spaceman?" Henry said. "It's just a toothbrush." He leaned toward Carleton and Carleton scooted back. He began to scream.

In the other bed, Tilly was dreaming about rabbits. When she'd come home from school, she and Carleton had seen rabbits sitting on the lawn as if they had kept watch over the house all the time that Tilly had been gone. In her dream they were still there. She dreamed she was creeping up on them. They opened their mouths, wide enough to reach inside like she was some kind of rabbit dentist, and so she did. She put her hand around something small and cold and hard. Maybe it was a ring, a diamond ring. Or a. Or. It was a. She couldn't wait to show Carleton. Her arm was inside the rabbit all the way to her shoulder. Someone put their hand around her wrist and yanked. Somewhere her mother was talking. She said —

"It's the beard."

Catherine couldn't decide whether to laugh or cry or scream like Carleton. That would surprise Carleton, if she started screaming, too. "Shoo! Shoo, Henry — go shave and come back as quick as you can, or else he'll never go back to sleep."

"Carleton, honey," she was saying as Henry left the room, "it's your dad. It's not Santa Claus. It's not the big bad wolf. It's your dad. Your dad just forgot. Why don't you tell me a story? Or do you want to go watch your daddy shave?"

Catherine's hot-water bottle was draped over the tub. Towels were heaped on the floor. Henry's things had been put away behind the mirror. It made him feel tired, thinking of all the other things that still had to be put away. He washed his hands, then looked at the bar of soap. It didn't feel right. He put it back on the sink, bent over and sniffed it, and then tore off a piece of toilet paper, used the toilet paper to pick up the soap. He threw it in the trash and unwrapped a new bar of soap. There was nothing wrong with the new soap. There was nothing wrong with the old soap either. He was just tired. He washed his hands and lathered up his face, shaved off his beard, and watched the little bristles of hair wash down the sink. When he went to show Carleton his brand-new face, Catherine was curled up in bed beside Carleton. They were both asleep. They were still asleep when he left the house at five-thirty the next morning.

*

"Where are you?" Catherine said.

"I'm on my way home. I'm on the train." The train was still in the station. They would be leaving any minute. They had been leaving any minute for the last hour or so, and before that, they had had to get off the train twice, and then back on again. They had been assured there was nothing to worry about. There was no bomb threat. There was no bomb. The delay was only temporary. The people on the train looked at each other, trying to seem as if they were not looking. Everyone had their cell phones out.

"The rabbits are out on the lawn again," Catherine said. "There must be at least fifty or sixty. I've never counted rabbits before. Tilly keeps trying to go outside to make friends with them, but as soon as she's outside, they all go bouncing away like beach balls. I talked to a lawn specialist today. He says we need to do something about it, which is what Liz was saying. Rabbits can be a big problem out here. They've probably got tunnels and warrens all through the yard. It could be a problem. Like living on top of a sinkhole. But Tilly is never going to forgive us. She knows something's up. She says she doesn't want a dog anymore. It would scare away the rabbits. Do you think we should get a dog?"

"So what do they do? Put out poison? Dig up the yard?" Henry said. The man in the seat in front of him got up. He took his bags out of the luggage rack and left the train. Everyone watched him go, pretending they were not.

"He was telling me they have these devices, kind of like ultrasound equipment. They plot out the tunnels, close them up, and then gas the rabbits. It sounds gruesome," Catherine said. "And this kid, this baby has been kicking the daylights out of me. All day long it's kick, kick, jump, kick, like some kind of martial artist. He's going to be an angry kid, Henry. Just like his sister. Her sister. Or maybe I'm going to give birth to rabbits."

"As long as they have your eyes and my chin," Henry said.

"I've gotta go," Catherine said. "I have to pee again. All day long it's the kid jumping, me peeing, Tilly getting her heart broken because she can't make friends with the rabbits, me worrying because she doesn't want to make friends with other kids, just with rabbits, Carleton asking if today he has to go to school, does he have to go to school tomorrow, why am I making him go to school when everybody there is bigger than him, why is my stomach so big and fat, why does his teacher tell him to act like a big boy? Henry, why are we doing this again? Why am I pregnant? And where are you? Why aren't you here? What about our deal? Don't you want to be here?"

"I'm sorry," Henry said. "I'll talk to the Crocodile. We'll work something out."

"I thought you wanted this, too, Henry. Don't you?"

"Of course," Henry said. "Of course I want this."

"I've gotta go," Catherine said again. "Liz is bringing some women over. We're finally starting that book club. We're going to read *Fight Club.* Her stepdaughter, Alison, is going to look after Tilly and Carleton for me. I've already talked to Tilly. She promises she won't bite or hit or make Alison cry."

"What's the trade? A few hours of bonus TV?"

"No," Catherine said. "Something's up with the TV."

"What's wrong with the TV?"

"I don't know," Catherine said. "It's working fine. But the kids won't go near it. Isn't that great? It's the same thing as the toothbrush. You'll see when you get home. I mean, it's not just the kids. I was watching the news earlier, and then I had to turn it off. It wasn't the news. It was the TV."

"So it's the downstairs bathroom and the coffee maker and Carleton's toothbrush and now the TV?"

"There's some other stuff as well, since this morning. Your office, apparently. Everything in it — your desk, your bookshelves, your chair, even the paper clips."

"That's probably a good thing, right? I mean, that way they'll stay out of there."

"I guess," Catherine said. "The thing is, I went and stood in there for a while and it gave me the creeps, too. So now I can't pick up e-mail. And I had to throw out more soap. And King Spanky doesn't love the alarm clock anymore. He won't come out from under the bed when I set it off."

"The alarm clock, too?"

"It does sound different," Catherine said. "Just a little bit different. Or maybe I'm insane. This morning, Carleton told me that he knew where our house was. He said we were living in a secret part of Central Park. He said he recognizes the trees. He thinks that if he walks down that little path, he'll get mugged. I've really got to go, Henry, or I'm going to wet my pants, and I don't have time to change again before everyone gets here."

"I love you," Henry said.

"Then why aren't you here?" Catherine said victoriously. She hung up and ran down the hallway toward the downstairs bathroom. But when she got there, she turned around. She went racing up the stairs, pulling down her pants as she went, and barely got to the master bedroom bathroom in time. All day long she'd gone up and down the stairs, feeling extremely silly. There was nothing wrong with the downstairs bathroom. It was just the fixtures. When you flushed the toilet or ran water in the sink. She didn't like the sound the water made.

Several times now, Henry had come home and found Catherine painting rooms, which was a problem. The problem was that Henry kept going away. If he didn't keep going away, he wouldn't have to keep coming home. That was Catherine's point. Henry's point was that Catherine wasn't supposed to be painting rooms while she was pregnant. Pregnant women were supposed to stay away from paint fumes. Catherine had solved this problem by wearing the gas mask while she painted. She had known the gas mask would come in handy. She told Henry she promised to stop painting as soon as he started working at home, which was the plan. Meanwhile, she couldn't decide on colors. She and Carleton and Tilly spent hours looking at paint strips with colors that had names like Sangria, Peat Bog, Tulip, Tantrum, Planetarium, Galactica, Tea Leaf, Egg Yolk, Tinker Toy, Gauguin, Susan, Envy, Aztec, Utopia, Wax Apple, Rice Bowl, Cry Baby, Fat Lip, Green Banana, Trampoline, Fingernail. It was a wonderful way to spend time. They went off to school, and when they got home, the living room would be Harp Seal instead of Full Moon. They'd spend some time with that color, getting to know it, ignoring the television, which was haunted (*haunted* wasn't the right word, of course, but Catherine couldn't think what the right word was), and then a couple of days later, Catherine would go buy some more primer and start again. Carleton and Tilly loved this. They begged her to repaint their bedrooms. She did.

She wished she could eat paint. Whenever she opened a can of paint, her mouth filled with saliva. When she'd been pregnant with Carleton, she hadn't been able to eat anything except olives and hearts of palm and dry toast. When she'd been pregnant with Tilly, she'd eaten dirt once in Central Park. Tilly thought they should name the baby after a paint color — Chalk, or Dilly Dilly, or Keelhauled. Lapis Lazulily. Knock, Knock.

Catherine kept meaning to ask Henry to take the television and put it in the garage. Nobody ever watched it now. They'd had to stop using the microwave as well, and a colander, some of the flatware, and she was keeping an eye on the toaster. She had a premonition, or an intuition. It didn't feel wrong, not yet, but she had a feeling about it. There was a gorgeous pair of earrings that Henry had given her — how was it possible to be spooked by a pair of diamond earrings? — and yet. Carleton wouldn't play with his Lincoln Logs, and so they were going to the Salvation Army, and Tilly's armadillo purse had disappeared. Tilly hadn't said anything about it, and Catherine hadn't wanted to ask.

Sometimes, if Henry wasn't coming home, Catherine painted after Carleton and Tilly went to bed. Sometimes Tilly would walk into the room where Catherine was working, Tilly's eyes closed, her mouth open, a tourist-somnambulist. She'd stand there with her head cocked toward Catherine. If Catherine spoke to her, she didn't answer, and if Catherine took her hand, she would follow Catherine back to her own bed and lie down again. But sometimes Catherine let Tilly stand there and keep her company. Tilly was never so attentive, so *present,* when she was awake. Eventually she would turn and leave the room and Catherine would listen to her climb back up the stairs. Then Catherine would be alone again.

Catherine dreams about colors. It turns out her marriage was the same color she had just painted the foyer. Velveteen Fade. Leonard Felter, who had had an ongoing affair with two of his graduate students, several adjuncts, two tenured faculty members, brought down Catherine's entire department, and saved Catherine's marriage, would make a good lipstick or nail polish. Peach Nooky. There's the Crocodile, a particularly bilious Eau de Vil, a color that tastes bad when you say it. Her mother, who had always been disappointed by Catherine's choices, turned out to have been a beautiful, rich, deep chocolate. Why hadn't Catherine ever seen that before? Too late, too late. It made her want to cry.

Liz and she are drinking paint, thick and pale as cream. "Have some more paint," Catherine says. "Do you want sugar?"

"Yes, lots," Liz says. "What color are you going to paint the rabbits?"

Catherine passes her the sugar. She hasn't even thought about the rabbits, except which rabbits does Liz mean, the stone rabbits or the real rabbits? How do you make them hold still?

"I got something for you," Liz says. She's got Tilly's armadillo purse. It's full of paint strips. Catherine's mouth fills with water.

Henry dreams he has an appointment with the exterminator. "You've got to take care of this," he says. "We have two small children. These things could be rabid. They might carry plague."

"See what I can do," the exterminator says, sounding glum. He stands next to Henry. He's an odd-looking, twitchy guy. He has big ears. They contemplate the skyscrapers that poke out of the grass like obelisks. The lawn is teeming with skyscrapers. "Never seen anything like this before. Never wanted to see anything like this. But if you want my opinion, it's the house that's the real problem —"

"Never mind about my wife," Henry says. He squats down beside a knee-high art deco skyscraper and peers into a window. A little man looks back at him and shakes his fists, screaming something obscene. Henry flicks a finger at the window, almost hard enough to break it. He feels hot all over. He's never felt this angry before in his life, not even when Catherine told him that she'd accidentally slept with Leonard Felter. The little bastard is going to regret what he just said, whatever it was. He lifts his foot.

The exterminator says, "I wouldn't do that if I were you. You have to dig them up, get the roots. Otherwise, they just grow back. Like your house. Which is really just the tip of the iceberg lettuce, so to speak. You've probably got seventy, eighty stories underground. You gone down on the elevator yet? Talked to the people living down there? It's your house, and you're just going to let them live there rent-free? Mess with your things like that?"

"What?" Henry says, and then he hears helicopters, fighter planes the size of hummingbirds. "Is this really necessary?" he says to the exterminator.

The exterminator nods. "You have to catch them off guard."

"Maybe we're being hasty," Henry says. He has to yell to be heard above the noise of the tiny, tinny, furious planes. "Maybe we can settle this peacefully."

"Hemree," the interrogator says, shaking his head. "You called me in because I'm the expert, and you knew you needed help."

Henry wants to say, "You're saying my name wrong." But he doesn't want to hurt the undertaker's feelings.

The alligator keeps on talking. "Listen up, Hemreeee, and shut up about negotiations and such, because if we don't take care of this right away, it may be too late. This isn't about home ownership, or lawn care, Hemreeeeee, this is war. The lives of your children are at stake. The happiness of your family. Be brave. Be strong. Just hang on to your rabbit and fire when you see delight in their eyes."

He woke up. "Catherine," he whispered. "Are you awake? I was having this dream."

Catherine laughed. "That's the phone, Liz," she said. "It's probably Henry, saying he'll be late."

"Catherine," Henry said. "Who are you talking to?"

"Are you mad at me, Henry?" Catherine said. "Is that why you won't come home?"

"I'm right here," Henry said.

"You take your rabbits and your crocodiles and get out of here," Catherine said. "And then come straight home again."

She sat up in bed and pointed her finger. "I am sick and tired of being spied on by rabbits!"

When Henry looked, something stood beside the bed, rocking back and forth on its heels. He fumbled for the light, got it on, and saw Tilly, her mouth open, her eyes closed. She looked larger than she ever did when she was awake. "It's just Tilly," he said to Catherine, but Catherine lay back down again. She put her pillow over her head. When he picked Tilly up, to carry her back to bed, she was warm and sweaty, her heart racing as if she had been running through all the rooms of the house.

He walked through the house. He rapped on walls, testing. He put his ear against the floor. No elevator. No secret rooms, no hidden passageways.

There wasn't even a basement.

Tilly has divided the yard in half. Carleton is not allowed in her half, unless she gives permission.

From the bottom of her half of the yard, where the trees run beside the driveway, Tilly can barely see the house. She's decided to name the yard Matilda's Rabbit Kingdom. Tilly loves naming things. When the new baby is born, her mother has promised that she can help pick out the real names, although there will only be two real names, a first one and a middle. Tilly doesn't understand why there can only be two. *Oishii* means delicious in Japanese. That would make a good name, either for the baby or for the yard, because of the grass. She knows the yard isn't as big as Central Park, but it's just as good, even if there aren't any pagodas or castles or carriages or people on roller skates. There's plenty of grass. There are hundreds of rabbits. They live in an enormous underground city, maybe a city just like New York. Maybe her dad can stop working in New York and come work under the lawn instead. She could help him, go to work with him. She could be a biologist, like Jane Goodall, and go and live underground with the rabbits. Last year her ambition had been to go and live secretly in the Metropolitan Museum of Art, but someone has already done that, even if it's only in a book. Tilly feels sorry for Carleton. Everything he ever does, she'll have already been there. She'll already have done that.

Tilly has left her armadillo purse sticking out of a rabbit hole. First she made the hole bigger, then she packed the dirt back in around the armadillo so that only the shiny, peeled snout poked out. Carleton digs it out again with his stick. Maybe Tilly meant him to find it. Maybe it was a present for the rabbits, except what is it doing here, in his half of the yard? When he lived in the apartment, he was afraid of the armadillo purse, but there are better things to be afraid of out here. But be careful, Carleton. Might as well be careful. The armadillo purse says don't touch me. So he doesn't. He uses his stick to pry open the snap mouth, dumps out Tilly's most valuable things, and with his stick pushes them one by one down the hole. Then he puts his ear to the rabbit hole so that he can hear the rabbits say thank you. Saying thank you is polite. But the rabbits say nothing. They're holding their breath, waiting for him to go away. Carleton waits, too. Tilly's armadillo, empty and smelly and haunted, makes his eyes water.

Someone comes up and stands behind him. "I didn't do it," he says. "They fell."

But when he turns around, it's the girl who lives next door. Alison. The sun is behind her and makes her shine. He squints. "You can come over to my house if you want to," she says. "Your mom says. She's going to pay me fifteen bucks an hour, which is way too much. Are your parents really rich or something? What's that?"

"It's Tilly's," he says. "But I don't think she wants it anymore."

She picks up Tilly's armadillo. "Pretty cool," she says. "Maybe I'll keep it for her."

Deep underground, the rabbits stamp their feet in rage.

Catherine loves the house. She loves her new life. She's never understood people who get stuck, become unhappy, can't change, adapt. So she's out of a job. So what? She'll find something else to do. So Henry can't leave his job yet, won't leave his job yet. So the house is haunted. That's okay. They'll work through it. She buys some books on gardening. She plants a rosebush and a climbing vine in a pot. Tilly helps. The rabbits eat off all the leaves. They bite through the vine.

"Shit," Catherine says, when she sees what they've done. She shakes her fists at the rabbits on the lawn. The rabbits flick their ears at her. They're laughing, she knows it. She's too big to chase after them.

"Henry, wake up. Wake up."

"I'm awake," he said, and then he was. Catherine was crying. Noisy, wet, ugly sobs. He put his hand out and touched her face. Her nose was running.

"Stop crying," he said. "I'm awake. Why are you crying?"

"Because you weren't here," she said. "And then I woke up and you were here, but when I wake up tomorrow morning you'll be gone again. I miss you. Don't you miss me?"

"I'm sorry," he said. "I'm sorry I'm not here. I'm here now. Come here."

"No," she said. She stopped crying, but her nose still leaked. "And now the dishwasher is haunted. We have to get a new dishwasher before I have this baby. You can't have a baby and not have a dishwasher. And you have to live here with us. Because I'm going to need some help this time. Remember Carleton, how fucking hard that was."

"He was one cranky baby," Henry said. When Carleton was three months old, Henry had realized that they'd misunderstood something. Babies weren't babies, they were land mines, bear traps, wasp nests. They were a noise, which was sometimes even not a noise, but merely a listening for a noise; they were a damp, chalky smell; they were the heaving, jerky, sticky manifestation of not-sleep. Once Henry had stood and watched Carleton in his crib, sleeping peacefully. He had not done what he wanted to do. He had not bent over and yelled in Carleton's ear. Henry still hadn't forgiven Carleton, not yet, not entirely, not for making him feel that way.

"Why do you have to love your job so much?" Catherine said.

"I don't know," Henry said. "I don't love it."

"Don't lie to me," Catherine said.

"I love you better," Henry said. He does, he does, he does love Catherine better. He's already made that decision. But she isn't even listening.

"Remember when Carleton was little and you would get up in the morning and go to work and leave me all alone with them?" Catherine poked him in the side. "I used to hate you. You'd come home with takeout, and I'd forget I hated you, but then I'd remember again, and I'd hate you even more because it was so easy for you to trick me, to make things okay again, just because for an hour I could sit in the bathtub and eat Chinese food and wash my hair."

"You used to carry an extra shirt with you, when you went out," Henry said. He put his hand down inside her T-shirt, on her fat, full breast. "In case you leaked."

"You can't touch that breast," Catherine said. "It's haunted." She blew her nose on the sheets.

Catherine's friend Lucy owns an online boutique, Nice Clothes for Fat People. There's a woman in Tarrytown who knits stretchy, sexy argyle sweaters exclusively for NCFP, and Lucy has an appointment with her. She wants to stop off and see Catherine afterward, before she has to drive back to the city again. Catherine gives her directions and then begins to clean house, feeling out of sorts. She's not sure she wants to see Lucy right now. Carleton has always been afraid of Lucy, which is embarrassing. And Catherine doesn't want to talk about Henry. She doesn't want to explain about the downstairs bathroom. She had planned to spend the day painting the wood trim in the dining room, but now she'll have to wait.

The doorbell rings, but when Catherine goes to answer it, no one is there. Later on, after Tilly and Carleton have come home, it rings again, but no one is there. It rings and rings, as if Lucy is standing outside, pressing the bell over and over again. Finally Catherine pulls out the wire. She tries calling Lucy's cell phone but can't get through. Then Henry calls. He says that he's going to be late.

Liz opens the front door, yells, "Hello, anyone home?! You've got to see your rabbits, there must be thousands of them. Catherine, is something wrong with your doorbell?"

Henry's bike, so far, was okay. He wondered what they'd do if the Toyota suddenly became haunted. Would Catherine want to sell it? Would resale value be affected? The car and Catherine and the kids were gone when he got home, so he put on a pair of work gloves and went through the house with a cardboard box, collecting all the things that felt haunted. A hairbrush in Tilly's room, an old pair of Catherine's tennis shoes. A pair of Catherine's underwear that he found at the foot of the bed. When he picked them up he felt a sudden shock of longing for Catherine, like he'd been hit by some kind of spooky lightning. It hit him in the pit of the stomach, like a cramp. He dropped the underwear in the box.

The silk kimono from Takashimaya. Two of Carleton's night-lights. He opened the door to his office, put the box inside. All the hair on his arms stood up. He closed the door.

Then he went downstairs and cleaned paintbrushes. If the paintbrushes were becoming haunted, if Catherine was throwing them out and buying new ones, she wasn't saying. Maybe he should check the Visa bill. How much were they spending on paint anyway?

Catherine came into the kitchen and gave him a hug. "I'm glad you're home," she said. He pressed his nose into her neck and inhaled. "I left the car running — I've got to pee. Would you go pick up the kids for me?"

"Where are they?" Henry said.

"They're over at Liz's. Alison is babysitting them. Do you have money on you?"

"You mean I'll meet some neighbors?"

"Wow, sure," Catherine said. "If you think you're ready. Are you ready? Do you know where they live?"

"They're our neighbors, right?"

"Take a left out of the driveway, go about a quarter of a mile, and they're the red house with all the trees in front."

But when he drove up to the red house and went and rang the doorbell, no one answered. He heard a child come running down a flight of stairs and then stop and stand in front of the door. "Carleton? Alison?" he said. "Excuse me, this is Catherine's husband, Henry. Carleton and Tilly's dad." The whispering stopped. He waited for a bit. When he crouched down and lifted the flap of the mail slot, he thought he saw someone's feet, the hem of a coat, something furry? A dog? Someone standing very still, just to the right of the door? Carleton, playing games. "I see you," he said, and wiggled his fingers through the mail slot. Then he thought maybe it wasn't Carleton after all. He got up quickly and went back to the car. He drove into town and bought more soap.

Tilly was standing in the driveway when he got home, her hands on her hips. "Hi, Dad," she said. "I'm looking for King Spanky. He got outside. Look what Alison found."

She held out a tiny toy bow strung with what looked like dental floss, an arrow the size of a needle.

"Be careful with that," Henry said. "It looks sharp. Archery Barbie, right? So did you guys have a good time with Alison?"

"Alison's okay," Tilly said. She belched. "'Scuse me. I don't feel very good."

"What's wrong?" Henry said.

"My stomach is funny," Tilly said. She looked up at him, frowned, and then vomited all over his shirt, his pants.

"Tilly!" he said. He yanked off his shirt, used a sleeve to wipe her mouth. The vomit was foamy and green.

"It tastes horrible," she said. She sounded surprised. "Why does it always taste so bad when you throw up?"

"So that you won't go around doing it for fun," he said. "Are you going to do it again?"

"I don't think so," she said, making a face.

"Then I'm going to go wash up and change clothes. What were you eating, anyway?"

"Grass," Tilly said.

"Well, no wonder," Henry said. "I thought you were smarter than that, Tilly. Don't do that anymore."

"I wasn't planning to," Tilly said. She spit in the grass.

When Henry opened the front door, he could hear Catherine talking in the kitchen. "The funny thing is," she said, "none of it was true. It was just made up, just like something Carleton would do. Just to get attention."

"Dad," Carleton said. He was jumping up and down on one foot. "Want to hear a song?"

"I was looking for you," Henry said. "Did Alison bring you home? Do you need to go to the bathroom?"

"Why aren't you wearing any clothes?" Carleton said.

Someone in the kitchen laughed, as if they had heard this.

"I had an accident," Henry said, whispering. "But you're right, Carleton, I should go change." He took a shower, rinsed and wrung out his shirt, put on clean clothes, but by the time he got downstairs, Catherine and Carleton and Tilly were eating Cheerios for dinner. They were using paper bowls, plastic spoons, as if it was a picnic. "Liz was here, and Alison, but they were going to a movie," Catherine said. "They said they'd meet you some other day. It was awful — when they came in the door, King Spanky went rushing outside. He's been watching the rabbits all day. If he catches one, Tilly is going to be so upset."

"Tilly's been eating grass," Henry said.

Tilly rolled her eyes. As if.

"Not again!" Catherine said. "Tilly, real people don't eat grass. Oh, look, fantastic, there's King Spanky. Who let him in? What's he got in his mouth?"

King Spanky sits with his back to them. He coughs and something drops to the floor, maybe a frog, or a baby rabbit. It goes scrabbling across the floor, half-leaping, dragging one leg. King Spanky just sits there, watching as it disappears under the sofa. Carleton freaks out. Tilly is shouting, "Bad King Spanky! Bad cat!" When Henry and Catherine push the sofa back, it's too late, there's just King Spanky and a little blob of sticky blood on the floor.

Catherine would like to write a novel. She'd like to write a novel with no children in it. The problem with novels with children in them is that bad things will happen either to the children or else to the parents. She wants to write something funny, something romantic.

It isn't very comfortable to sit down now that she's so big. She's started writing on the walls. She writes in pencil. She names her characters after paint colors. She imagines them leading beautiful, happy, useful lives. No haunted toasters. No mothers no children no crocodiles no photocopy machines no Leonard Felters. She writes for two or three hours, and then she paints the walls again before anyone gets home. That's always the best part.

"I need you next weekend," the Crocodile said. Her rubber-band ball sat on the floor beside her desk. She had her feet up on it, in an attempt to show it who was boss. The rubber-band ball was getting too big for its britches. Someone was going to have to teach it a lesson, send it a memo.

She looked tired. Henry said, "You don't need me."

"I do," the Crocodile said, yawning. "I *do.* The clients want to take you out to dinner at the Four Seasons when they come in to town. They want to go see musicals with you. *Rent. Phantom of the Lion Cabaret.* They want to go to Coney Island with you and eat hot dogs. They want to go out to trendy bars and clubs and pick up strippers and publicists and performance artists. They want to talk about poetry, philosophy, sports, politics, their lousy relationships with their fathers. They want to ask you for advice about their love lives. They want you to come to the weddings of their children and make toasts. You're indispensable, honey. I hope you know that."

"Catherine and I are having some problems with rabbits," Henry said. The rabbits were easier to explain than the other thing. "They've taken over the yard. Things are a little crazy."

"I don't know anything about rabbits," the Crocodile said, digging her pointy heels into the flesh of the rubber-band ball until she could feel the red rubber blood come running out. She pinned Henry with her beautiful, watery eyes.

"Henry." She said his name so quietly that he had to lean forward to hear what she was saying.

She said, "You have the best of both worlds. A wife and children who adore you, a beautiful house in the country, a secure job at a company that depends on you, a boss who appreciates your talents, clients who think you're the shit. You *are* the shit, Henry, and the thing is, you're probably thinking that no one deserves to have all this. You think you have to make a choice. You think you have to give up something. But you don't have to give up anything, Henry, and anyone who tells you otherwise is a fucking rabbit. Don't listen to them. You can have it all. You *deserve* to have it all. You love your job. Do you love your job?"

"I love my job," Henry says. The Crocodile smiles at him tearily.

It's true. He loves his job.

When Henry came home, it must have been after midnight, because he never got home before midnight. He found Catherine standing on a ladder in the kitchen, one foot resting on the sink. She was wearing her gas mask, a black cotton sports bra, and a pair of black sweatpants rolled down so far that he could see she wasn't wearing any underwear. Her stomach stuck out so far she had to hold her arms at a funny angle to run the roller up and down the wall in front of her. Up and down in a V. Then fill the V in. She had painted the kitchen ceiling a shade of purple so dark, it almost looked black. Midnight Eggplant.

Catherine had recently begun buying paints from a specialty catalogue. All the colors were named after famous books — *Madame Bovary, Forever Amber, Fahrenheit 451, The Tin Drum, A Curtain of Green, 20,000 Leagues Under the Sea.* She was painting the walls *Catch-22*, a novel she'd taught over and over again to undergraduates. It had gone over pretty well. The paint color was nice, too. She couldn't decide if she missed teaching. The thing about teaching and having children was that you always ended up treating your children like undergraduates and your undergraduates like children. There was a particular tone of voice. She'd even used it on Henry a few times, just to see if it worked.

All the cabinets were fenced around with masking tape, like a crime scene. The room stank of new paint.

Catherine took off the gas mask and said, "Tilly picked it out. What do you think?" Her hands were on her hips. Her stomach poked out at Henry. The gas mask had left a ring of white and red around her eyes and chin.

Henry said, "How was the dinner party?"

"We had fettuccine. Liz and Marcus stayed and helped me do the dishes."

("Is something wrong with your dishwasher?" "No. I mean, yes. We're getting a new one.")

She had had a feeling. It had been a feeling like déjà vu, or being drunk, or falling in love. Like teaching. She had imagined an audience of rabbits out on the lawn, watching her dinner party. A classroom of rabbits, watching a documentary. Rabbit television. Her skin had felt electric.

"So she's a lawyer?" Henry said.

"You haven't even met them yet," Catherine said, suddenly feeling possessive. "But I like them. I really, really like them. They wanted to know all about us. You. I think they think that either we're having marriage problems or that you're imaginary. Finally I took Liz upstairs and showed her your stuff in the closet. I pulled out the wedding album and showed them photos."

"Maybe we could invite them over on Sunday? For a cookout?" Henry said.

"They're away next weekend," Catherine said. "They're going up to the mountains on Friday. They have a house up there. They've invited us. To come along."

"I can't," Henry said. "I have to take care of some clients next weekend. Some big shots. We're having some cash-flow problems. Besides, are you allowed to go away? Did you check with your doctor — what's his name again, Dr. Marks?"

"You mean, did I get my permission slip signed?" Catherine said. Henry put his hand on her leg and held on. "Dr. Marks said I'm shipshape. That was his exact word. Or maybe he said tiptop. It was something alliterative."

"Well, I guess you ought to go then," Henry said. He rested his head against her stomach. She let him. He looked so tired. "Before Golf Cart shows up. Or what is Tilly calling the baby now?"

"She's around here somewhere," Catherine said. "I keep putting her back in her bed and she keeps getting out again. Maybe she's looking for you."

"Did you get my e-mail?" Henry said. He was listening to Catherine's stomach. He wasn't going to stop touching her unless she told him to.

"You know I can't check e-mail on your computer anymore," Catherine said.

"This is so stupid," Henry said. "This house isn't haunted. There isn't any such thing as a haunted house."

"It isn't the house," Catherine said. "It's the stuff we brought with us. Except for the downstairs bathroom, and that might just be a draft, or an electrical problem. The house is fine. I love the house."

"Our stuff is fine," Henry said. "I love our stuff."

"If you really think our stuff is fine," Catherine said, "then why did you buy a new alarm clock? Why do you keep throwing out the soap?"

"It's the move," Henry said. "It was a hard move."

"King Spanky hasn't eaten his food in three days," Catherine said. "At first I thought it was the food, and I bought new food and he came down and ate it and I realized it wasn't the food, it was King Spanky. I couldn't sleep all night, knowing he was up under the bed. Poor spooky guy. I don't know what to do. Take him to the vet? What do I say? Excuse me, but I think my cat is haunted? Anyway, I can't get him out of the bed. Not even with the old alarm clock, the haunted one."

"I'll try," Henry said. "Let me try and see if I can get him out." But he didn't move. Catherine tugged at a piece of his hair and he put up his hand. She gave him her roller. He popped off the cylinder and bagged it and put it in the freezer, which was full of paintbrushes and other rollers. He helped Catherine down from the ladder. "I wish you would stop painting."

"I can't," she said. "It has to be perfect. If I can just get it right, then everything will go back to normal and stop being haunted and the rabbits won't tunnel under the house and make it fall down, and you'll come home and stay home, and our neighbors will finally get to meet you and they'll like you and you'll like them, and Carleton will stop being afraid of everything, and Tilly will fall asleep in her own bed, and stay there, and —"

"Hey," Henry said. "It's all going to work out. It's all good. I really like this color."

"I don't know," Catherine said. She yawned. "You don't think it looks too old-fashioned?"

They went upstairs and Catherine took a bath while Henry tried to coax King Spanky out of the bed. But King Spanky wouldn't come out. When Henry got down on his hands and knees and stuck the flashlight under the bed, he could see King Spanky's eyes, his tail hanging down from the box frame.

Out on the lawn the rabbits were perfectly still. Then they sprang up in the air, turning and dropping and landing and then freezing again. Catherine stood at the window of the bathroom, toweling her hair. She turned the bathroom light off, so that she could see them better. The moonlight picked out their shining eyes, the moon-colored fur, each hair tipped in paint. They were playing some rabbit game like leapfrog. Or they were dancing the quadrille. Fighting a rabbit war. Did rabbits fight wars? Catherine didn't know. They ran at each other and then turned and darted back, jumping and crouching and rising up on their back legs. A pair of rabbits took off in tandem, like racehorses, sailing through the air and over a long curled shape in the grass. Then back over again. She put her face against the window. It was Tilly, stretched out against the grass, Tilly's legs and feet bare and white.

"Tilly," she said, and ran out of the bathroom, wearing only the towel around her hair.

"What is it?" Henry said as Catherine darted past him and down the stairs. He ran after her, and by the time she had opened the front door, was kneeling beside Tilly, the wet grass tickling her thighs and her belly, Henry was there, too, and he picked up Tilly and carried her back into the house. They wrapped her in a blanket and put her in her bed, and because neither of them wanted to sleep in the bed where King Spanky was hiding, they lay down on the sofa in the family room, curled up against each other. When they woke up in the morning, Tilly was asleep in a ball at their feet.

For a minute or two last year, Catherine thought she had it figured out. She was married to a man whose specialty was solving problems, salvaging bad situations. If she did something dramatic enough, if she fucked up badly enough, it would save her marriage. And it did, except that once the problem was solved and the marriage was saved and the baby was conceived and the house was bought, then Henry went back to work.

She stands at the window in the bedroom and looks out at all the trees. For a minute she imagines that Carleton is right, and they are living in Central Park and Fifth Avenue is just right over there.

Henry's office is just a few blocks away. All those rabbits are just tourists.

Henry wakes up in the middle of the night. There are people downstairs. He can hear women talking, laughing, and he realizes Catherine's book club must have come over. He gets out of bed. It's dark. What time is it anyway? But the alarm clock is haunted again. He unplugs it. As he comes down the stairs, a voice says, "Well, will you look at that!" and then "Right under his nose the whole time!"

Henry walks through the house, turning on lights. Tilly stands in the middle of the kitchen. "May I ask who's calling?" she says. She's got Henry's cell phone tucked between her shoulder and her face. She's holding it upside down. Her eyes are open, but she's asleep.

"Who are you talking to?" Henry says.

"The rabbits," Tilly says. She tilts her head, listening. Then she laughs. "Call back later," she says. "He doesn't want to talk to you. Yeah. Okay." She hands Henry his phone. "They said it's no one you know."

"Are you awake?" Henry says.

"Yes," Tilly says, still asleep. He carries her back upstairs. He makes a bed out of pillows in the hall closet and lays her down across them. He tucks a blanket around her. If she refuses to wake up in the same bed that she goes to sleep in, then maybe they should make it a game. If you can't beat them, join them.

Catherine hadn't had an affair with Leonard Felter. She hadn't even slept with him. She had just said she had, because she was so mad at Henry. She could have slept with Leonard Felter. The opportunity had been there. And he had been magical somehow: the only member of the department who could make the photocopier make copies, and he was nice to all of the secretaries. Too nice, as it turned out. And then, when it turned out that Leonard Felter had been fucking everyone, Catherine had felt she couldn't take it back. So she and Henry had gone to therapy together. Henry had taken some time off work. They'd taken the kids to Disney World. They'd gotten pregnant. She'd been remorseful for something she hadn't done. Henry had forgiven her. Really, she'd saved their marriage. But it had been the sort of thing you could only do once.

If someone had to save the marriage a second time, it would have to be Henry.

Henry went looking for King Spanky. They were going to see the vet: he had the cat cage in the car, but no King Spanky. It was early afternoon, and the rabbits were out on the lawn. Up above, a bird hung, motionless, on a hook of air. Henry craned his head, looking up. It was a big bird, a hawk maybe? It circled, once, twice, again, and then dropped like a stone toward the rabbits. The rabbits didn't move. There was something about the way they waited, as if this was all a game. The bird cut through the air, folded like a knife, and then it jerked, tumbled, fell, the wings loose. The bird smashed into the grass and feathers flew up. The rabbits moved closer, as if investigating.

Henry went to see for himself. The rabbits scattered, and the lawn was empty. No rabbits, no bird. But there, down in the trees, beside the bike path, Henry saw something move. King Spanky swung his tail angrily, slunk into the woods.

When Henry came out of the woods, the rabbits were back guarding the lawn again and Catherine was calling his name. "Where were you?" she said. She was wearing her gas mask around her neck, and there was a smear of paint on her arm. Whiskey Horse. She'd been painting the linen closet.

"King Spanky took off," Henry said. "I couldn't catch him. I saw the weirdest thing — this bird was going after the rabbits, and then it fell —"

"Marcus came by," Catherine said. Her cheeks were flushed. He knew that if he touched her, her skin would be hot. "He stopped by to see if you wanted to go play golf."

"Who wants to play golf?" Henry said. "I want to go upstairs with you. Where are the kids?"

"Alison took them in to town, to see a movie," Catherine said. "I'm going to pick them up at three."

Henry lifted the gas mask off her neck, fitted it around her face. He unbuttoned her shirt, undid the clasp of her bra. "Better take this off," he said. "Better take all your clothes off. I think they're haunted."

"You know what would make a great paint color? Can't believe no one has done this yet. Yellow Sticky. What about King Spanky?" Catherine said. She sounded like Darth Vader, maybe on purpose, and Henry thought it was sexy: Darth Vader, pregnant with his child. She put her hand against his chest and shoved. Not too hard, but harder than she meant to. It turned out that painting had given her some serious muscle. That will be a good thing when she has another kid to haul around.

"Yellow Sticky. That's great. Forget King Spanky," Henry said. "He's great."

Catherine was painting Tilly's room Lavender Fist. It was going to be a surprise. But when Tilly saw it, she burst into tears. "Why can't you just leave it alone?" she said. "I liked it the way it was."

"I thought you liked purple," Catherine said, astounded. She took off her gas mask.

"I hate purple," Tilly said. "And I hate you. You're so fat. Even Carleton thinks so."

"Tilly!" Catherine said. She laughed. "I'm pregnant, remember?"

"That's what you think," Tilly said. She ran out of the room and across the hall. There were crashing noises, the sounds of things breaking.

"Tilly!" Catherine said.

Tilly stood in the middle of Carleton's room. All around her lay broken night-lights, lamps, broken light bulbs. The carpet was dusted in glass. Tilly's feet were bare and Catherine looked down, realized that she wasn't wearing shoes either. "Don't move, Tilly," she said.

"They were haunted," Tilly said and began to cry.

"So how come your dad's never home?" Alison said.

"I don't know," Carleton said. "Guess what? Tilly broke all my night-lights."

"Yeah," Alison said. "You must be pretty mad."

"No, it's good that she did," Carleton said, explaining. "They were haunted. Tilly didn't want me to be afraid."

"But aren't you afraid of the dark?" Alison said.

"Tilly said I shouldn't be," Carleton said. "She said the rabbits stay awake all night, that they make sure everything is okay, even when it's dark. Tilly slept outside once, and the rabbits protected her."

"So you're going to stay with us this weekend," Alison said.

"Yes," Carleton said.

"But your dad isn't coming," Alison said.

"No," Carleton said. "I don't know."

"Want to go higher?" Alison said. She pushed the swing and sent him soaring.

When Henry puts his hand against the wall in the living room, it gives a little, as if the wall is pregnant. The paint under the paint is wet. He walks around the house, running his hands along the walls. Catherine has been painting a mural in the foyer. She's painted trees and trees and trees. Golden trees with brown leaves and green leaves and red leaves, and reddish trees with purple leaves and yellow leaves and pink leaves. She's even painted some leaves on the wooden floor, as if the trees are dropping them. "Catherine," he says. "You have got to stop painting the damn walls. The rooms are getting smaller."

Nobody says anything back. Catherine and Tilly and Carleton aren't home. It's the first time Henry has spent the night alone in his house. He can't sleep. There's no television to watch. Henry throws out all of Catherine's paintbrushes. But when Catherine gets home, she'll just buy new ones.

He sleeps on the couch, and during the night someone comes and stands and watches him sleep. Tilly. Then he wakes up and remembers that Tilly isn't there.

The rabbits watch the house all night long. It's their job.

Tilly is talking to the rabbits. It's cold outside, and she's lost her gloves. "What's your name?" she says. "Oh, you beauty. You beauty." She's on her hands and knees. Carleton watches from his side of the yard.

"Can I come over?" he says. "Can I please come over?"

Tilly ignores him. She gets down on her hands and knees, moving even closer to the rabbits. There are three, one of them almost close enough to touch. If she moves her hand slowly, maybe she can grab one by the ears. Maybe she can catch one and train it to live inside. They need a pet rabbit. King Spanky is haunted. He spends most of his time outside. Her parents keep their bedroom door shut so that King Spanky can't get in.

"Good rabbit," Tilly says. "Just stay still. Stay still."

The rabbits flick their ears. Carleton begins to sing a song Alison has taught them, a skipping song. Carleton is such a girl. Tilly puts out her hand. There's something tangled around the rabbit's neck, like a piece of string or a leash. She wiggles closer, holding out her hand. She stares and stares and can hardly believe her eyes. There's a person, a little man, sitting behind the rabbit's ears, holding on to the rabbit's fur and the piece of knotted string with one hand. His other hand is cocked back, like he's going to throw something. He's looking right at her — his hand flies forward and something hits her hand. She pulls her hand back, astounded. "Hey!" she says, and she falls over on her side and watches the rabbits go springing away. "Hey, you! Come back!"

"What?" Carleton yells. He's frantic. "What are you doing? Why won't you let me come over?"

She closes her eyes, just for a second. Shut up, Carleton. Just shut up. Her hand is throbbing and she lies down, holds her hand up to her face. Shut. Up.

Wake up. Wake *up*. When she wakes up, Carleton is sitting beside her. "What are you doing on my side?" she says, and he shrugs.

"What are you doing?" he says. He rocks back and forth on his knees. "Why did you fall over?"

"None of your business," she says. She can't remember what she was doing. Everything looks funny. Especially Carleton. "What's wrong with you?"

"Nothing's wrong with me," Carleton says, but something is wrong. She studies his face and begins to feel sick, as if she's been eating grass. Those sneaky rabbits! They've been distracting her, and now, while she wasn't paying attention, Carleton's become haunted.

"Oh, yes it is," Tilly says, forgetting to be afraid, forgetting her hand hurts, getting angry instead. She's not the one to blame. This is her mother's fault, her father's fault, and it's Carleton's fault, too. How could he have let this happen? "You just don't know it's wrong. I'm going to tell Mom."

Haunted Carleton is still a Carleton who can be bossed around. "Don't tell," he begs.

Tilly pretends to think about this, although she's already made up her mind. Because what can she say? Either her mother will notice that something's wrong or else she won't. Better to wait and see. "Just stay away from me," she tells Carleton. "You give me the creeps."

Carleton begins to cry, but Tilly is firm. He turns around, walks slowly back to his half of the yard, still crying. For the rest of the afternoon, he sits beneath the azalea bush at the edge of his side of the yard and cries. It gives Tilly the creeps. Her hand throbs where something has stung it. The rabbits are all hiding underground. King Spanky has gone hunting.

"What's up with Carleton?" Henry said, coming downstairs. He couldn't stop yawning. It wasn't that he was tired, although he was tired. He hadn't given Carleton a good-night kiss, just in case it turned out he was coming down with a cold. He didn't want Carleton to catch it. But it looked like Carleton, too, was already coming down with something.

Catherine shrugged. Paint samples were balanced across her stomach like she'd been playing solitaire. All weekend long, away from the house, she'd thought about repainting Henry's office. She'd never painted a haunted room before. Maybe if you mixed the paint with a little bit of holy water? She wasn't sure: what was holy water anyway? Could you buy it? "Tilly's being mean to him," she said. "I wish they would make some friends out here. He keeps talking about the new baby, about how he'll take care of it. He says it can sleep in his room. I've been trying to explain babies to him, about how all they do is sleep and eat and cry."

"And get bigger," Henry said.

"That, too," Catherine said. "So did he go to sleep okay?"

"Eventually," Henry said. "He's just acting really weird."

"How is that different from usual?" Catherine said. She yawned. "Is Tilly finished with her homework?"

"I don't know," Henry said. "You know, just weird. Different weird. Maybe he's going through a weird spell. Tilly wanted me to help her with her math, but I couldn't get it to come out right. So what's up with my office?"

"I cleared it out," Catherine said. "Alison and Liz came over and helped. I told them we were going to redecorate. Why is it that we're the only ones who notice everything is fucking haunted around here?"

"So where'd you put my stuff?" Henry said. "What's up?"

"You're not working here now," Catherine pointed out. She didn't sound angry, just tired. "Besides, it's all haunted, right? So I took your computer in to the shop, so they could have a look at it. I don't know, maybe they can unhaunt it."

"Well," Henry said. "Okay. Is that what you told them? It's haunted?"

"Don't be ridiculous," Catherine said. She discarded a paint strip. Too lemony. "So I heard about the bomb scare on the radio."

"Yeah," Henry said. "The subways were full of kids with crewcuts and machine guns. And they evacuated our building for about an hour. We all went and stood outside, holding on to our laptops like idiots, just in case. The Crocodile carried out her rubber-band ball, which must weigh about thirty pounds. It kind of freaked people out, even the firemen. I thought the bomb squad was going to blow it up. So tell me about your weekend."

"Tell me about yours," Catherine said.

"You know," Henry said. "Those clients are assholes. But they don't know they're assholes, so it's kind of okay. You just have to feel sorry for them. They don't get it. You have to explain how to have fun, and then they get anxious, so they drink a lot and so you have to drink, too. Even the Crocodile got drunk. She did this weird wriggly dance to a Pete Seeger song. So what's their place like?"

"It's nice," Catherine said. "You know, really nice."

"So you had a good weekend? Carleton and Tilly had a good time?"

"It was really nice," Catherine said. "No, really, it was great. I had a fucking great time. So you're sure you can make it home for dinner on Thursday."

It wasn't a question.

"Carleton looks like he might be coming down with something," Henry said. "Here. Do you think I feel hot? Or is it cold in here?"

Catherine said, "You're fine. It's going to be Liz and Marcus and some of the women from the book group and their husbands, and what's her name, the real estate agent. I invited her, too. Did you know she's written a book? I was going to do that! I'm getting the new dishwasher tomorrow. No more paper plates. And the lawn-care specialist is coming on Monday to take care of the rabbits. I thought I'd drop off King Spanky at the vet, take Tilly and Carleton back to the city, stay with Lucy for two or three days — did you know she tried to find this place and got lost? She's supposed to come up for dinner, too — just in case the poison doesn't go away right away, you know, or in case we end up with piles of dead rabbits on the lawn. Your job is to make sure there are no dead rabbits when I bring Tilly and Carleton back."

"I guess I can do that," Henry said.

"You'd better," Catherine said. She stood up, with some difficulty, and came and leaned over his chair. Her stomach bumped into his shoulder. Her breath was hot. Her hands were full of strips of color. "Sometimes I wish that instead of working for the Crocodile, you were having an affair with her. I mean, that way you'd come home when you're supposed to. You wouldn't want me to be suspicious."

"I don't have any time to have affairs," Henry said. He sounded put out. Maybe he was thinking about Leonard Felter. Or maybe he was picturing the Crocodile naked. The Crocodile wearing stretchy red rubber sex gear. Catherine imagined telling Henry the truth about Leonard Felter. I didn't have an affair. Did not. Is that a problem?

"That's exactly what I mean," Catherine said. "You'd better be here for dinner. You live here, Henry. You're my husband. I want you to meet our friends. I want you to be here when I have this baby. I want you to fix what's wrong with the downstairs bathroom. I want you to talk to Tilly. She's having a rough time. She won't talk to me about it."

"Tilly's fine," Henry said. "We had a long talk tonight. She said she's sorry she broke all of Carleton's night-lights. I like the trees, by the way. You're not going to paint over them, are you?"

"I had all this leftover paint," Catherine said. "I was getting tired of just painting with the rollers. I wanted to do something fancier."

"You could paint some trees in my office, when you paint my office."

"Maybe," Catherine said. "Ooof, this baby won't stop kicking me." She lay down on the floor in front of Henry and lifted her feet into his lap. "Rub my feet. I've still got so much fucking paint. But once your office is done, I'm done with the painting. Tilly told me to stop it or else. She keeps hiding my gas mask. Will you be here for dinner?"

"I'll be here for dinner," Henry said, rubbing her feet. He really meant it. He was thinking about the exterminator, about rabbit corpses scattered all across the lawn, like a war zone. Poor rabbits. What a mess.

After they went to see the therapist, after they went to Disney World and came home again, Henry said to Catherine, "I don't want to talk about it anymore. I don't want to talk about it ever again. Can we not talk about it?"

"Talk about what?" Catherine said. But she had almost been sorry. It had been so much work. She'd had to invent so many details that eventually it began to seem as if she hadn't made it up after all. It was too strange, too confusing, to pretend it had never happened, when, after all, it *had* never happened.

Catherine is dressing for dinner. When she looks in the mirror, she's as big as a cruise ship. A water tower. She doesn't look like herself at all. The baby kicks her right under the ribs.

"Stop that," she says. She's sure the baby is going to be a girl. Tilly won't be pleased. Tilly has been extra good all day. She helped make the salad. She set the table. She put on a nice dress.

Tilly is hiding from Carleton under a table in the foyer. If Carleton finds her, Tilly will scream. Carleton is haunted, and nobody has noticed. Nobody cares except Tilly. Tilly says names for the baby, under her breath. Dollop. Shampool. Custard. Knock, Knock. The rabbits are out on the lawn, and King Spanky has gotten into the bed again, and he won't come out, not for a million haunted alarm clocks.

Her mother has painted trees all along the wall under the staircase. They don't look like real trees. They aren't real colors. It doesn't look like Central Park at all. In among the trees, her mother has painted a little door. It isn't a real door, except that when Tilly goes over to look at it, it is real. There's a doorknob, and when Tilly turns it, the door opens. Underneath the stairs, there's another set of stairs, little dirt stairs, going down. On the third stair, there's a rabbit sitting there, looking up at Tilly. It hops down, one step, and then another. Then another.

"Rumpelstiltskin!" Tilly says to the rabbit. "Lipstick!"

Catherine goes to the closet to get out Henry's pink shirt. What's the name of that real estate agent? Why can't she ever remember? She lays the shirt on the bed and then stands there for a moment, stunned. It's too much. The pink shirt is haunted. She pulls out all of Henry's suits, his shirts, his ties. All haunted. Every fucking thing is haunted. Even the fucking shoes. When she pulls out the drawers, socks, underwear, handkerchiefs, everything, it's all spoiled. All haunted. Henry doesn't have a thing to wear. She goes downstairs, gets trash bags, and goes back upstairs again. She begins to dump clothes into the trash bags.

She can see Carleton framed in the bedroom window. He's chasing the rabbits with a stick. She hoists open the window, leans out, yells, "Stay away from those fucking rabbits, Carleton! Do you hear me?"

She doesn't recognize her own voice.

Tilly is running around downstairs somewhere. She's yelling, too, but her voice gets farther and farther away, fainter and fainter. She's yelling, "Hairbrush! Zeppelin! Torpedo! Marmalade!"

The doorbell rings.

The Crocodile started laughing. "Okay, Henry. Calm down."

He fired off another rubber band. "I mean it," he said. "I'm late. I'll be late. She's going to kill me."

"Tell her it's my fault," the Crocodile said. "So they started dinner without you. Big deal."

"I tried calling," Henry said. "Nobody answered." He had an idea that the phone was haunted now. That's why Catherine wasn't answering. They'd have to get a new phone. Maybe the lawn specialist would know a house specialist. Maybe somebody could do something about this. "I should go home," he said. "I should go home right now." But he didn't get up. "I think we've gotten ourselves into a mess, me and Catherine. I don't think things are good right now."

"Tell someone who cares," the Crocodile suggested. She wiped at her eyes. "Get out of here. Go catch your train. Have a great weekend. See you on Monday."

So Henry goes home, he has to go home, but of course he's late, it's too late. The train is haunted. The closer they get to his station, the more haunted the train gets. None of the other passengers seem to notice. It makes Henry sick to his stomach. And, of course, his bike turns out to be haunted, too. It's too much. He can't ride it home. He leaves it at the station and he walks home in the dark, down the bike path. Something follows him home. Maybe it's King Spanky.

Here's the yard, and here's his house. He loves his house, how it's all lit up. You can see right through the windows, you can see the living room, which Catherine has painted Ghost Crab. The trim is Rat Fink. Catherine has worked so hard. The driveway is full of cars, and inside, people are eating dinner. They're admiring Catherine's trees. They haven't waited for him, and that's fine. His neighbors: he loves his neighbors. He's going to love them as soon as he meets them. His wife is going to have a baby any day now. His daughter will stop walking in her sleep. His son isn't haunted. The moon shines down and paints the world a color he's never seen before. Oh, Catherine, wait till you see this. Shining lawn, shining rabbits, shining world. The rabbits are out on the lawn. They've been waiting for him, all this time, they've been waiting. Here's his rabbit, his very own rabbit. Who needs a bike? He sits on his rabbit, legs pressed against the warm, silky, shining flanks, one hand holding on to the rabbit's fur, the knotted string around its neck. He has something in his other hand, and when he looks, he sees it's a spear. All around him, the others are sitting on their rabbits, waiting patiently, quietly. They've been waiting for a long time, but the waiting is almost over. In a little while, the dinner party will be over and the war will begin.

NATHANIEL BELLOWS

First Four Measures

FROM THE PARIS REVIEW

IT WAS COLD OUT, AND I WAS EARLY. The door was locked, so I sat on the front steps of the church, listening to the woman who took her piano lesson before me. She was good, better than I was, and the music she played was complicated, flourished. I thought of my teacher and where he was while the woman played — leaning back in his chair near the windows or sitting next to her on the bench with his hand covering her face?

I wondered where Mrs. Spence was — probably at home, rattling around in the kitchen, waiting for me to get back. My parents had found her ad in the local newspaper, offering her services as a house sitter, and had hired her to stay with me while they were away.

I had tried to tell them that a house sitter normally takes care of an empty house. But they told me that a single individual — especially a fourteen-year-old — staying alone in a large house like ours actually makes the house seem emptier than with no one there at all.

"It's an issue of scale," said my father, who was an architect and was delighted to find, once again, how his profession informed almost every conversation.

"And perspective," said my mother, who was a medical researcher but had always loved the arts.

A week later, Mrs. Spence arrived carrying an old-looking suitcase and a hatbox.

"Isn't that funny?" my mother whispered to me in the front hall, handing me Mrs. Spence's coat to hang up.

"What?" I said.

"The hatbox," she smiled. "It's so *antiquated.* Do you think there's actually a hat in there?"

Mrs. Spence stayed in the second-floor guest bedroom. It had a large bathroom with velvet wallpaper and a tin soak tub. My room was on the third floor, but I could hear her through the air vents, scuffing about, running the taps, singing under her breath. She had been hired to stay a month. Otherwise, I found out, she lived in Oak Village, a retirement community made up of mustard-colored condos, about ten minutes away, just off the interstate.

The morning after my parents left, when I came downstairs to leave for school, I noticed a strange mixture of smells in the house — cleaning solvents and cooking meat. Mrs. Spence was in the kitchen, wearing a light blue uniform, frying pink rectangles of canned ham that threw beads of fat into the air.

"Did my parents ask you to wear that dress?" I asked her.

"Good morning to you," she said, smiling. "And this is a uniform, not a dress," she said. She looked down at herself and frowned slightly. "I guess it does look like a dress. But no, they didn't ask me to wear it. I brought it with me."

She had a round, ruddy face that was lined, but not heavily. Her hair was long and silver, which she wore down her back in a low ponytail, tied with a ribbon that looked like it belonged on a wreath. She didn't look like the other elderly people I saw at the grocery store or the mall — staggering along with their walkers or sitting on benches, looking around at the passing world, amazed and disappointed.

"I'm wearing this because I don't want to wear my nice clothes while I cook," she said.

"Do you wear it at home when you cook?" I asked.

"I don't cook at home," she said. "Where I live everyone goes out to eat. We have a shuttle bus to take us to any restaurant in the area that we want."

She flipped the hissing ham with a rubber spatula, which had been singed along its edge. The grease from the pan released a puff of dark smoke into the air.

"I'm worried you might start a fire with that ham," I said. I put on my backpack and walked out of the room.

"Where are you going?" she said. "Aren't you going to eat breakfast?"

"No," I said.

"Well then, I'll pick you up after school!" she called out. "Out front!"

"I take the bus!" I called back.

I could hear her behind me, hurrying to the front hall to catch me before I got onto the front porch.

"You don't have to take a ride home from me," she said, a little winded, resting against the banister. "But I'll be there in front of your school at three o'clock, if you want one."

After school, she was out front, just like she said she would be. As we drove home, I gripped the seat belt across my chest and kept my eyes closed.

"Will you stay on the road, please?" I said.

"I'm on the road!" she said. "I'm a very good driver!" She kneaded her thigh with her left hand and steered with her right. "Ooo," she moaned. "I've got lots of knots in my legs today."

"I should have taken the bus," I said into my lap.

"The bus is unsafe."

"This is unsafe! How is the bus unsafe?"

"All those children? In the hands of a stranger?"

"You're a stranger," I said.

"Besides, a bus is much bigger than a car," she said. "And harder to control."

"Like you'd know."

We sat in silence. I watched the trees flicker past the windows in smears of green and gold.

"I made some brownies today," she said. "You can have some when we get home."

"*If* we get home."

"Oh, shut it."

I waited for the church bells to toll out the hour. I knew then the woman who had her lesson before me would come out the door, and I could go inside. High above me, the steeple, with a gold cross at its point, jutted into the sky, puncturing the passing clouds, which seemed full of flurries.

My old piano teacher, Mrs. Clark, had moved away. She had

heard of Mr. Nichols, who gave lessons at the church, and recommended him to me before she left.

Mrs. Clark always had me play pieces that were slightly below what I thought I could play — once I had an idea of my abilities. She had a tendency to praise me in a high-pitched voice, which sounded both supportive and impatient. She was a good teacher, but an easy one — she was never harsh with me when I hadn't practiced or when I got lazy. But when I played well, she squeezed my shoulder warmly and said that she was proud of me. And this was something my mother didn't even do — on any occasion. And neither would my father.

At my first lesson with Mr. Nichols, I was nervous. The church auditorium was large and echoing, with two grand pianos, a darkened stage with heavy velvet curtains, and a side room where mechanical floor polishers and cleaning supplies were stored. There were two small lamps, one on each piano, providing small pockets of light above the keys. All along the walls of the auditorium hung children's drawings of lambs and doves and people with joined hands, united in a circle.

For the entire hour of my first lesson, I played the pieces that I'd learned with Mrs. Clark. Mr. Nichols sat in a chair beside his piano and looked out the windows. When I finished one piece, I just moved on to another, because he didn't say anything. Sometimes he would glance over at me and nod expectantly. When I was done with them all, I sat back on the bench, and he got up from his chair and took his place at his piano. He played a piece of music that was so haunting and sad, it seemed to fill the vast space of the dark auditorium.

"This is what you'll learn with me," he said when he was finished. His voice was slightly nasal, and he looked at me directly through the smudged square lenses of his glasses.

"What you've learned so far is below you," he said. "You've been underestimated."

He stood up and stretched, so his cardigan hiked up to reveal the striped edge of his boxer shorts ballooning over his waistband.

"So," he said. "Would you say that piece was more beautiful than anything you've learned so far?"

"Definitely," I said. "Who wrote it? I'm sure my parents would like to know."

"Not that it's any of their business," he said. "But it's Schubert. It's the second movement of his Sonata in B-flat Major."

"Oh," I said. The information had no meaning for me, but the music still lingered in my head, so I attempted to memorize the words for the sake of merely knowing them.

"We'll start with this, and perhaps later we'll consider the other movements." He looked at me directly. "This should be a challenge," he said. "But I have confidence in you."

"Thank you," I said.

"Yes," he said, smiling, brushing his sparse hair across his forehead. "You should thank me." He took the folder of music I had worked on with Mrs. Clark, walked over to the wastebasket, and dropped it in.

On the first weekend together, I reminded Mrs. Spence that she was allowed to do what she wanted and that staying with me every minute of the day was not necessary.

"You probably have a life outside of my house, right?" I said. "A life you'll want to get back to?"

Even when I took lessons from Mrs. Clark, I was never able to practice with anyone in the house. Practicing alone was all I was ever used to. My parents had a very regimented schedule, which I adapted to my own: I would play the piano in the afternoons when I got home from school, and by the time they came home in the early evening, I would be at the dining-room table, doing my homework.

"What about you?" said Mrs. Spence. "Don't you have a life outside this house?"

"I have piano lessons," I said, not wanting to get into a discussion of how I fit into the social order of my school, or, rather, how I didn't. "Next week."

"I didn't know that," she said, impressed. "I've never heard you play."

"That doesn't mean I don't have lessons," I said. "I practice at school."

"Why, when you have a great big piano in the other room?"

"Because it's out of tune," I lied.

"Well, I wouldn't know much about that," she said. "In tune, out of tune, it can't be all that different. It would be nice to hear a little music in this place." She looked down at me where I lay reading on the couch. "I would love to hear you play sometime."

"Maybe," I said.

"If not now, then perhaps sometime soon?"

"I said maybe."

She looked out the window, into the backyard, where fragments of sun were shifting around the lawn.

"It's nice out, you know," she said. "The weather in late autumn. I'd like to be out in the fresh air."

"Be my guest."

"Wouldn't you rather be outside?" she said. "Come on, let's go outside. We could go for a drive."

"No, thank you," I said. "I cherish my life."

"Don't start. I'll be good, you'll see." She laughed. "Just don't make me nervous, and you won't have to worry."

"How do I make you nervous?"

"You don't understand," she said, carefully.

"I don't understand what?"

"I'm trying to take care of you," she said.

"No," I said. "You don't understand. I don't need to be taken care of."

"Well," she said. "I'm trying to be your friend."

She looked at me, and I couldn't tell if she was angry or upset. She sat down in a chair beside the couch and kneaded her legs with her fingers, grimacing.

"Fine," I said. "We can go, if you want. Just please try to drive like a sane person."

"Of course! And you know what?"

"What?"

"I'll take you to meet Candy."

"Who's Candy?" I asked.

"Candy's my dog," she said. "My companion." She put her hand on my shoulder as we walked into the kitchen to get our coats. "That is, when I'm not here."

On the day of my second lesson, it was freezing out, and I walked the whole way to the church from school. Inside, I could hear someone playing the piano. I looked through the glass panels of the auditorium doors and saw a woman playing the piano I usually played. Mr. Nichols was sitting in his chair, looking off dreamily, and after she finished her piece, he dismissed her without getting up.

I opened the door and Mr. Nichols waved me over to the radiator. He told me to lay my gloves and jacket over the pipes. He took my hands in his hands and rubbed them vigorously. Then he held my hands and kept them there, clutched, staring down at the knot of our entangled fingers.

"Should I —" I began.

"No talking," he said, and slowly rubbed my knuckles and palms. "Be quiet." After a minute he said, "Okay, go and sit down."

He went over to his bag and removed a sheaf of papers, then sat at his keyboard and played the piece he had played for me before. The eerie music filled the room, and I imagined how the music would sound being played in my house. How the whole place would be filled with what I was producing from my hands — this music that I was trusted and talented enough to learn. I pictured the empty rooms filling like a flood, the house drowned in my accomplishment.

Mr. Nichols walked over to my piano and placed the sheets on the music tray before me.

"Play the right hand," he said. "First four measures."

I played the measures with my right hand, slowly and cautiously. After a few times, it sounded okay, but not great.

"Now play the left hand," he said. "Same four measures."

I did, and after a few times, it was relatively comfortable. Though his standing so close to me was not.

"Now together," he said. "Both hands."

I played them together, slowly, painfully, trying to merge the two separate groups of notes. I leaned toward the music, scrutinizing the page. It sounded terrible.

"I'm sorry," I said.

"Try it again," he said. "First four measures. Both hands."

I played the first four measures again and again, until I could get through them without it sounding too bad. Finally, when it was beginning to sound fluid, he said, "Okay."

He sat down on the bench next to me. He took the music and turned it upside down.

"Same four measures," he said. "Both hands."

"What?" I said. "It's too hard as it is."

"Nonsense," he said, moving even closer to me.

I stared at the bottom of the page, trying to reassemble the notes in my head. It was impossible. But I tried, mostly by memory and by sound.

"Again," he said, each time I stumbled to the end.

Finally, I got through it without too many problems, though my eyes were swimming, and my head had begun to ache.

"Jeez," I said, exhausted.

"Very nice," he laughed, and turned toward me.

He put the palm of his hand on my lower back, right above my belt. I immediately jolted upright when I felt it press firmly against my spine. He moved closer and put his other hand over my eyes. His rough fingertips scratched against my cheek and forehead, as he pressed his hand firmly against the bridge of my nose. With my eyes open, I could see through the cracks in his fingers — a jumble of notes, irreconcilable. His hand smelled like soil, and like dust, and the cuff of his sweater had a slight tinge of mothballs.

Before I could pull away, he held me tighter and said, "Again. First four measures. Hands together."

Candy was a small terrier with a white body and brown cinnamon-colored spots on her rump and head. Mrs. Spence's upstairs neighbor was taking care of her while Mrs. Spence stayed at my house. When we went to pick her up, Candy jumped up and down and raced around the room, barking with joy.

Mrs. Spence's condo at Oak Village was on the bottom floor of a two-unit building. It was small and dark and looked out over a tiny backyard where she'd hung two mottled birdseed bells from some low tree branches.

"This is my home," she said, turning on the lights. "Nothing grand like yours, but there you go."

On the walls of her living room were dim watercolor paintings of seascapes and flowerbeds, and all her furniture looked worn but unused. On a dark-stained wooden table were some old black and white photos: men in uniform standing in a line, a few women in old-fashioned bathing suits lounging on a wooden raft, a man balancing a hatbox on his head, laughing.

Mrs. Spence came out of her room. "That's my family," she said. "Only pictures now."

Mrs. Spence gave me some ginger ale in a heavy tumbler, and she had tomato juice in a mug. We sat out on the back porch as she went through her mail, and I threw a ball for Candy, who would catch it in her mouth and bring it back.

"You two are friends," Mrs. Spence said when she saw me holding Candy in my lap.

"She doesn't have to stay with your neighbor while you're staying at my house," I said to her. "You can bring her over."

"Your parents told me no pets," she said.

"Who cares?" I said. "They won't know."

"I shouldn't," she said.

"But I want you to," I said. "I like her."

When we brought Candy back to the house, I told Mrs. Spence that I would be willing to play the piano with her in the house on the condition that she stay out of the room and that she not disturb me while I was practicing.

"Of course I won't!" she insisted. "I just want to hear you play, I don't necessarily have to *watch* you play, if it makes you nervous."

"It doesn't make me nervous," I said. "It's just that I have to play alone. Or I have to feel like I'm alone."

"Hopefully you won't always feel that way — in your life, I mean," she said. "But we'll do what you want. We'll be in here making dinner, and you can be in the other room playing your music."

The concrete church steps were cold, and my legs felt numb. I sat and listened to the woman play at her lesson. I had practiced every day that week. It took me awhile, but I had memorized the first four measures of the piece, and a bit beyond.

The church door opened and the woman came out, looking tired. I wanted to ask her about Mr. Nichols and whether he sat with her on the bench and did what he did to me, but before I could say anything, she was gone, striding down the sidewalk toward the bus stop.

In the auditorium, Mr. Nichols was wearing a puffy red down coat and a long scarf. He was pouring steaming liquid from a thermos into a large mug.

"It's freezing in here," he said, and ushered me to the radiator, where he put my coat and gloves over the pipes and warmed my hands the way he did before.

"You're frozen," he said. "Were you waiting outside?"

"All the doors were locked."

"Sorry about that. I sometimes forget to leave it unlocked when I come in — it locks behind me. I'll remember next time." He gestured to my piano. "You've practiced?" he asked.

"Yes," I said. "All week."

I sat at the bench and he took his seat by his piano, which was a relief. I played the first four measures through. And he told me to play them again, and I did.

"Did you go any further?" he asked.

"A little bit," I said.

"Brave boy," he said. "Go on."

I played the next few measures, which were rough but coherent. He got up and stood behind me. I felt my shoulders hunch, but I tried to ignore him.

"Play that section again."

I played it again, fumbling, worried that he might sit down.

"Nice," he said, moving back from me, toward the radiator. "Play all eight. See if you can do it. For me. All eight measures."

I played all eight, slowly — even at half-tempo the piece was beginning to come together! — and I felt suddenly hopeful.

He sat down on the bench beside me, this time facing away from the keyboard, toward the tall windows. He took his forearm and slipped it over my lap, grazing the tops of my thighs, and lifted my elbows.

"Let your arms rest on my arm, so that your hands are level with the keyboard," he said. "Your elbows should be parallel with your legs."

I adjusted, trying to avoid touching him any more than necessary.

"Now," he said, quietly. "Again."

I played. I felt the hard bone of his forearm against the underside of my arms. I finished the eight measures and waited for him to pull his arm away, but he just let it fall to rest over the tops of my thighs.

"It's snowing out," he said, distantly. "Look at the street lights, it's coming down hard."

He slowly withdrew his arm, and, relieved, I turned around. The snow was falling against the black sky.

Mrs. Spence and Candy would come to pick me up every day after school, and we'd go to the bakery and get doughnuts. Then we'd come home, and I'd go into the living room and practice. Gradually, Mrs. Spence moved from listening in the kitchen to listening at the dining room table with Candy on her lap, eating the doughnuts from the bakery. When I realized she'd moved a room closer to me, I decided not to make a big deal of it — as long as she stayed out of the living room itself.

At times I worried what it would be like when my parents got back. In some ways, I knew it would be easier because I would have the house back to myself — and no worries of Mrs. Spence in another room, gradually creeping closer. One time, I'd gotten up to get a glass of water and caught her off guard, sitting in the hallway in a dining room chair, with her ear pressed up against the living room door.

But a part of me worried, too, that when she left, the music I played would just drift idly through the hollow rooms of the house and fade, expire, without any other audience than the open mouth of the fireplace, the broad windows with their swirled antique panes.

The day before my parents came home, I had another lesson. Before I left for school, Mrs. Spence told me that she'd pick me up at the church because it was supposed to snow later that day, and she didn't want me walking home alone in the storm.

"And when you get home, you can play what you've learned," she said. "I don't mean to be pushy, but I can't wait to hear what happens next."

"It just gets better," I said.

"It's really so moving," she said. "I sing it in my head all day long."

The church was unlocked. Inside I could hear the distant whine of a vacuum, somewhere in the basement.

"You've practiced?" said Mr. Nichols.

"Uh-huh," I said, putting the music up on the piano tray. I had already taken off my coat before I came in, so there would be no reason for him to think that I was cold from being outside.

I sat down and played as carefully as I could. I concentrated on every note and every rest and tried to be smooth and flowing and to avoid my usual errors.

When I was through, he sat down next to me on the bench. I started to get up.

"Stay here," he said. "I'm going to play the piece for you. And I want you to listen closely to it."

He played the entire piece. Moving, rocking slightly back and forth so at times his shoulder brushed up against mine, his leg, pressing and raising the pedals, grazed against my leg.

When he finished, he sat back.

"We're going to play the first two pages," he said.

"I can't," I said. "I've only learned to the bottom of the first."

"We'll play it through, and you'll play the right hand and I'll play the left."

"Why?"

"Because you have to learn each separately. Each hand speaks alone, in its own voice, and then it speaks with the other. Before you can fully learn their dialogue, you must master each singular voice."

"Why now, though?" I asked. "I've been learning both hands together for weeks."

"Because you haven't learned them well enough," he said. "I didn't think we'd have to backtrack like this," he sighed. "But I see that we must."

"I've been practicing," I said.

"Begin," he said.

I sat bolt upright, trying to avoid his swaying body. I didn't want him to sit next to me. It didn't make any sense that he was there. Eventually, we got through to the end of the second page.

"Now close your eyes," he said. "This time, we'll try with our eyes closed."

"I can't," I said, shifting away from him. "There's no way."

"You can," he said, his hand firmly on my arm. "Watch, I won't even have to look." He turned toward me and rested his wide forehead against my shoulder.

"You begin," he said softly into my sweater. "You start."

We played. But I did not close my eyes. I kept them wide open, looking at the music and beyond it, at the construction paper drawings on the walls and an orange extension cord snaking across the room. I looked out the glass-paneled doors, down the long hallway where the large white doors to the church had been left open. I could see inside — the shining gold candlesticks on the altar, the deep polished wood of the benches, the silk banners hanging from the balcony.

When we got to the end of the piece, I sat still. I had played horribly, but he didn't seem to notice. His head remained where it was, and I could hear him breathing steadily through his nose.

"I have to go," I said, jumping up and grabbing my bag. "Someone's coming to pick me up. There's supposed to be another storm."

"You did it," he said, looking at me, blinking, as if he'd just woken up. "You didn't think you could do it, but I knew you could. And you did."

I grabbed my jacket and hurried across the auditorium. I pushed open the door, slamming hard into Mrs. Spence, who was hiding behind it.

"Mrs. Spence told us something very disturbing," said my father, a week or so after they'd returned. We were sitting at the dining room table, eating a reheated dinner Mrs. Spence had left in the freezer.

"About your teacher, Mr. Nichols," said my mother.

"Your piano teacher," said my father.

They explained to me what Mrs. Spence had seen him do.

"Thank God she was there," said my father.

"Why?" I said.

"Because she was able to tell us what happened," said my mother.

"Nothing happened," I said.

In the dim candlelight, their faces looked flushed, puzzled.

"He's just a weird guy, and a weird teacher," I said. "He's just intense."

"Being intense doesn't account for him touching you," said my mother.

"Nothing accounts for that," said my father.

No one said anything. Our utensils lay half-buried in the cold food.

"This could be a serious problem," said my mother. "She said that —"

"And you actually believe her?" I asked. "You don't even know her. She's a stranger!"

"She was here for a month," said my father. "How can you say she's a stranger?"

"It's an issue of perspective," I said. "And scale."

They looked at me quizzically and then turned toward each other.

"She *is* an old woman," said my father, quietly. "She was very emotional."

"And barely coherent," said my mother.

"She's not crazy," I said, interrupting them. "But she might be a liar."

"What?" they said in unison.

"I'm just saying that she might not be such a reliable source of information. But she's nice and everything."

"Do *you* think she's . . . reliable?" asked my mother. "Like I said, this is a very serious claim."

"Also like you said, she's a very emotional woman," I said. "She's all alone in the world. She has no one, really. I'd say I'm her only friend."

"So your teacher didn't do what she suggested?" asked my father.

"You two are friends?" said my mother. "You just said she was a stranger."

"It doesn't matter," I said. "I'm done with these lessons anyway."

"Why?" said my mother. "It sounds like you were very good. That's what Mrs. Spence said."

"She was emphatic about that," said my father.

"Well, then," I said. "I don't know. Maybe not. We'll see."

They looked confused, disoriented, which was thrilling to witness — their otherwise stringent selves, suddenly inverted.

"Just let me ask, off the subject, for one second," said my father, seeking stability in the shift in topic. "Did she have some kind of animal in the house? There are traces of white furlike hair on the rug in the kitchen." He paused. "And an odd smell — maybe dander."

"The house does smell a bit strange," my mother said.

"I don't think so," I said.

"Are you sure?" asked my father. "Maybe a cat?"

"No cat," I said.

"But there's fur," said my father again.

My mother put her hand on my father's arm. "Should we have trusted this woman?"

"Good question," I said.

*

When I got home from school the next day, Mrs. Spence was standing against her car in the driveway. I could see Candy thrashing a red blanket around in the back seat of the car — flashes of red and white through the steamed-up window.

"How was school?" she asked.

"Wonderful," I said, and walked inside.

She followed me in, her hands in the pockets of her quilted coat, a plastic bag slapping against her leg.

"You can't bring Candy in the house," I said. "My parents found out she'd been inside."

"They did?" she said, looking shocked. "But I cleaned."

"They suspected that something — some animal — had been in the house," I said. "But I told them that there wasn't one."

"You did?" she said.

"And they believed me," I said.

Mrs. Spence followed me into the kitchen.

"I brought doughnuts," she said, smiling weakly.

She put the doughnuts on a plate, and we sat down at the kitchen table.

After a while I said, "I'm not going to play the piano today. If that's why you're here."

"No. Of course not," she said. "That's fine."

"Then why are you here?"

"I'm here to say to you," she began, nervously. "I have to say, I don't know what I saw that night, looking through the windows at your lesson. It was all so strange — the music was so beautiful — and I love to hear you play — because you're so talented — but then, the way that man was leaning against you . . ."

Instantly, I felt the pressure of Mr. Nichols's head against my shoulder, and I could smell the musky, tart odor of his scalp near my face.

"I know it was wrong to tell your parents what I saw — without saying anything to you," she continued, staring into her clasped hands. "And I know you're probably angry at me and won't forgive me." She looked to be on the verge of crying.

"But I want you to know that I did it because I care for you," she said. "And I want you to know, if you don't know, that it's not right. No teacher should act that way with a pupil."

"I know," I said.

"You do?" she said, looking up at me.

"It's fucked up" — a violent sob buckled in my chest.

"It is," she said.

"And it's not worth it," I said, my eyes stinging. "I'm not going back."

"Don't go back!" she said.

"But, I don't know how —"

"I'll do it!" she said. "Let me!"

She got up and grabbed the phone. "Give me his number."

I found the number in the address book in a drawer by the stove. While I called out the numbers, she punched them carefully into the keypad. When she was done and was waiting, with the receiver poised at her ear, I held out my hand.

"Okay," I said. "Give it to me."

"No," she said, turning into the wall. "Let me do this."

"Give it to me now!" I said, and wrenched the phone from her hands.

"You have to let me do something!" she said, swatting at the receiver. "Please!"

I turned away from her, and she stood leaning into me. "Please," she said, as the line clicked and buzzed.

"I'll do this by myself," I told her.

Slowly, she moved away from me. She picked up her coat she'd slung over the chair. I thought she was going to leave, and I had an uncontrollable urge to hang up the phone and tell her no.

"Hello?" Mr. Nichols's voice said over the line.

Mrs. Spence hung up her coat on the rack. She picked up the plate of doughnuts and disappeared into the dining room. The house was quiet, and I could hear her sitting down at the table to listen, one room away.

CHARLES D'AMBROSIO

The Scheme of Things

FROM THE NEW YORKER

LANCE VANISHED BEHIND THE WHITE DOOR of the men's room, and when he came out a few minutes later he was utterly changed. Gone was the tangled nest of thinning black hair, gone was the shadow of beard, gone, too, was the grime on his hands, the crescents of black beneath his blunt, chewed nails. Shaving had sharpened the lines of his jaw and revealed the face of a younger man. His shirt was tucked neatly into his trousers and buttoned up to his throat. He looked as clean and bland as an evangelist. He bowed to Kirsten with a stagy sweep of his hand and entered the gas station. All business, he returned immediately with the attendant in tow, a kid of sixteen, seventeen.

"This here's my wife, Kirsten," Lance said.

Kirsten smiled.

"Pleased," the kid said. He crawled under the chassis of the car and inspected the tailpipe.

"Your whole underside's rusted to hell," he said, standing up, wiping his hands clean of red dust. "I'm surprised you haven't fallen through."

"I don't know much about cars," Lance said.

"Well," the kid said, his face bright with expertise, "you should replace everything, right up to the manifold. It's a big job. It'll take a day, and it'll cost you."

"You can do it?" Kirsten asked.

"Sure," the kid said. "No problem."

Lance squinted at the oval patch above the boy's shirt pocket. "Randy," he said, "what's the least we can do?"

"My name's Bill," the kid said. "Randy's a guy used to work here."

"So, Bill, what's the least we can get away with?"

"Strap it up, I suppose. It'll probably hold until you get where you're going. Loud as hell, though."

The kid looked at Kirsten. His clear blue eyes lingered on her chest.

"We represent a charity." Lance handed the kid one of the printed pamphlets, watching his eyes skim back and forth as he took in the information. "Outside of immediate and necessary expenses, we don't have much money."

"Things are sure going to hell," the kid said. He shook his head, returning the pamphlet to Lance.

"Seems that way," Lance said.

The kid hurried into the station and brought back a coil of pipe strap. While he was under the car, Lance sat on the warm hood, listening to the wind rustle in the corn. Brown clouds of soil rose from the fields and gave the air a sepia tint. Harvest dust settled over the leaves of a few dying elms, over the windows of a cinderblock building, over the trailers in the courtyard across the street. One of the trailer doors swung open. Two Indians and a cowgirl climbed down the wooden steps. It was Halloween.

"You got a phone?" Lance asked.

"Inside," the kid said.

Lance looked down and saw the soles of the kid's work boots beneath the car, a patch of dirty sock visible through the hole widening in one of them. He walked away, into the station.

The kid hadn't charged them a cent, and they now sat at an intersection, trying to decide on a direction. The idle was rough. The car detonated like a bomb.

"Here's your gum," Lance said.

He emptied his front and back pockets and pulled the cuff of his pants up his leg and reached under the elastic band of his gym socks. Pink and green and blue and red packages of gum piled up in Kirsten's lap. He pulled a candy bar from his shirt pocket and began sucking away at the chocolate coating.

"One pack would've been fine," Kirsten said. "A gumball would have been fine."

"Land of plenty, sweetheart," he said.

Kirsten softened up a piece of pink gum and blew a large round bubble until it burst and the gum hung like flesh from her nose.

"Without money, we're just trying to open a can of beans with a cucumber," Lance said. "It doesn't matter how hungry we are, how desirous of those beans we are — without the right tools, those beans might as well be on the moon." Lance laughed to himself. "Moon beans," he said.

Kirsten got out of the car. The day was turning cold, turning to night. She leaned through the open window, smelling the warm air that was wafting unpleasantly with the mixed scent of chocolate and diesel.

"What's your gut feel?" Lance asked.

"I don't know, Lance."

She walked toward the intersection. Ghosts and witches crossed from house to house, holding paper sacks and pillowcases. The streetlights sputtered nervously in the fading twilight. With the cold wind cutting through her T-shirt, Kirsten felt her nipples harden. She was small-breasted and sensitive and the clasp on her only bra had broken. She untucked the shirt and hunched her shoulders forward so that the nipples wouldn't show, but still the dark circles pressed against the white cotton. The casual clothes that Lance had bought her in Key Biscayne, Florida, had come to seem like a costume and were now especially flimsy and ridiculous here in Tiffin, Iowa.

A young girl crossed the road, and Kirsten followed her. She thought she might befriend the girl and take her home, a gambit, playing on the gratitude of the worried parents that Kirsten always imagined when she saw a child alone. The pavement gave way to gravel and the gravel to dirt, and finally a narrow path in the weeds dipped through a dragline ditch and vanished into a cornfield. The girl was gone. Kirsten waited at the edge of the field, listening to the wind, until she caught a glimpse of the little girl again, far down one of the rows, sitting and secretly eating candy from her sack.

"You'll spoil your dinner," Kirsten said.

The girl clutched the neck of her sack and shook her head. Entering the field felt to Kirsten like wading from shore and finding herself, with one fatal step, out to sea. She sat in the dirt, facing the girl. The corn rose over their heads and blew in waves, bending with the wind.

"Aren't you cold?" Kirsten said. "I'm cold."

"Are you a stranger?" the girl asked.

"What's a stranger?"

"Somebody that kills you."

"No, then, I'm not a stranger."

Kirsten picked a strand of silk that hung in the little girl's hair.

"I'm your friend," she said. "Why are you hiding?"

"I'm not hiding. I'm going home."

"Through this field?" Kirsten said.

"I know my way," the little girl said.

The girl was dressed in a calico frock and dirty pink pumps, but Kirsten wasn't quite sure it was a costume. A rim of red lipstick distorted the girl's mouth grotesquely, and blue moons of eyeshadow gave her face an unseeing vagueness.

"What are you supposed to be?" Kirsten asked.

The girl squeezed a caramel from its cellophane wrapper and said, "A grownup."

"It's getting dark," Kirsten said. "You aren't scared?"

The little girl shrugged and chewed the caramel slowly. Juice dribbled down her chin.

"Let me take you back home."

"No," the girl said.

"You can't stay out here all by yourself."

The girl recoiled when Kirsten grabbed her hand. "Let me go," she screamed, her thin body jolting away. "Let me go!" The fury in her voice shocked Kirsten, and she felt the small fingers slip like feathers from her hand. When the girl ran off through the rows of corn, it was as if the wind had taken her away. Instantly, she was nowhere and everywhere. In every direction, the stalks swayed and the dry leaves turned as if the little girl, passing by, had just brushed against them.

When Kirsten finally found her way out of the field, she was in another part of town. She walked the length of the street, looking for signs, deciding at last on a two-story house in the middle of the block. A trike lay tipped over in the rutted grass, and a plastic pool of water held a scum of leaves. Clay pots with dead marigolds — woolly brown swabs on bent, withered stalks — lined the steps. A family of carved pumpkins sat on the porch rail, smiling toothy candle-lit grins that flickered to black, guttering in laughter with every gust of wind. On the porch, newspapers curled beside a milk crate. Warm yellow light lit the downstairs, and a woman's shadow flitted across a steam-clouded kitchen window.

Kirsten heard a radio playing. She knocked on the door.

The woman answered. Her hair was knotted up on her head with a blue rubber band, a few fugitive strands dangling down over her ears, one graying wisp curling around her eye. A smudge of flour dusted her cheek.

"Yes?" the woman said.

"Evening, ma'am." Kirsten handed the woman a flyer. "I'm with B.A.D.," she said. "Babies Addicted to Drugs. Are you busy?"

The woman switched on the porch light and held the printed flyer close to her face. Closing one eye, she studied the bold-red statistics on the front of the page and then flipped it over and looked into the face of the dark, shriveled baby on the back.

"Doesn't hardly look human, does it?" Kirsten said.

"No, I can't say it does," the woman said.

"That's what's happening out there, ma'am. That, and worse." Kirsten looked off down the road, east to where the town ended and the world opened up to cornfields and darkening sky. She thought of the little girl.

"Smells nice inside," Kirsten said.

"Cookies," the woman said.

"You mind if I come in?"

The woman looked quickly down the road and, seeing nothing there, said, "Sure. For a minute."

Kirsten sat in a Naugahyde recliner that had been angled to face the television. Across from her was a couch covered with a clear plastic sheet. The woman returned with a plate of cookies. She set them in front of Kirsten and slipped a coaster under a coffee cup full of milk.

"My partner and me have been assigned to the Midwest territory," Kirsten said. "I got into this when I was living in New Jersey and saw it all with my own eyes and couldn't stand by and do nothing. Those babies were just calling out to me for help."

"I've got three children myself," the woman said.

"That's what the cookies are for," Kirsten said. She bit into one and tasted the warm chocolate.

"Homemade," the woman said. "But the kids like store-bought. All they want is Wing Dings or what have you."

"They'll appreciate it later, ma'am. I know they will. They'll remember it and love you."

In the low light, Kirsten again noticed the spectral smudge of flour on the woman's cheek — she had reached to touch herself in a still, private moment as she thought of something she couldn't quite recall, a doubt too weak to claim a place in the clamor of her day.

"That baby on the flyer isn't getting any homemade cookies. That baby was born addicted to drugs. There's women I've personally met who would do anything to get their drugs and don't care what all happens to their kids. There's babies getting pitched out windows and dumped in trash cans and born in public lavatories."

"Things are terrible, I'm sure, but I can't give you any money. I worked all day making the kids Halloween costumes — they want store-bought, of course, but they can't have them, not this year."

"What're they going to be?"

"Janie's a farmer, Randall's a ghost. Kenny's costume was the hardest. He's a devil with a cape and hood and a tail."

If she could coax five dollars out of this woman, Kirsten thought, she could buy a cheap bra out of a bin at the dime store. Her breasts ached. When she'd seen the trike on the lawn out front, she'd assumed that this woman would reach immediately for her pocketbook.

"With a ten-dollar donation, you get your choice of two magazine subscriptions, free of charge for a year." Kirsten showed the woman the list of magazines. "*Cosmo,*" she said. "*Vogue, Redbook,* all them."

"I'm sorry," the woman said.

The front window washed with white light.

"You had better go." The woman stood up. "I don't have any use for your magazines."

On the porch, they met a man, his face darkened with the same brown dirt and dust that had rolled through and clouded the sky that day. Spikes of straw stabbed his hair and the pale-gray molt of a barn swallow clung to his plaid shirt. A silent look passed between the man and the woman, and Kirsten hurried away, down the steps.

"I thought she was trick-or-treating," the woman said as she shut the door.

*

"Nothing?" Lance said. "Nothing?"

Kirsten tore the wrapping from another piece of gum. They had driven to the outskirts of town, where the light ended and the pavement gave way to gravel and the road, rutted like a washboard, snaked off toward a defile choked with cottonwoods. Every street out of town seemed to dead-end in farmland, and here a lighted combine swept back and forth over the field, rising and falling like a ship over high seas. The combine's engine roared as it moved past them, crushing a path through the dry corn.

"A man came home," Kirsten said.

"So?"

"So the lady got all nervous and said I had to go."

"Should've worked the man," Lance said. He ran his finger along the outline of her breasts, as if he were drawing a cartoon bust. "We've talked about that. A man'll give money just to be a man about things."

"I'm too skinny," Kirsten said.

"You're filling out, I've noticed. You're getting some shape to you."

Lance smiled his smile, a wide, white grin with a hole in the middle of it. Two of his teeth had fallen out, owing to a weakness for sweets. He worried his tongue in the empty space, slithering it in and out along the bare gum.

"I wish I had a fix right now," Kirsten said. She hugged herself to stop a chill radiating from her spine. The ghost of her habit trailed after her.

Again the voracious growling of the combine came near. Kirsten watched the golden kernels spray into the holding bin. A man sat up front in a glass booth, smoking a pipe, a yellow cap tilted back on his head.

"My cowboy brain's about dead," Lance said. "What do you think?"

Kirsten had died once and had made the mistake, before she understood how superstitious he was, of telling Lance about it. Her heart had stopped and she had drifted toward a white light that rose away from her like a wind-blown sheet, hovering over what she recognized as her cluttered living room. She was placid and smiling into the faces of people she had never seen before, people she realized instantly were relatives, aunts and uncles, cousins, the mother she had never known. Kirsten had grown up in foster care, but now this true mother reached toward her from within the source of light, her pale-pink hands fluttering like the wings of a bird. A sense of calm told Kirsten that this was the afterlife, where brand-new rules obtained. She woke in a Key Biscayne hospital, her foster mother in a metal chair beside the bed, two uniformed cops standing at the door, ready to read Kirsten her rights.

"Don't always ask me," Kirsten said.

"Just close your eyes, honey. Close 'em and tell me the first thing you see."

With her eyes closed, she saw the little girl, alone, running, lost in the corn.

"Let's get out of here," she said.

"That's what you saw?"

"Start the car, okay? I can't explain everything I see."

She had met him in Florida, in her second year of detention. Her special problem was heroin, his was methamphetamine. They lived in a compound of low pink cinder-block buildings situated maddeningly close to a thoroughfare with a strip of shops, out beyond a chain-link fence and a greenbelt. At night, neon lights lit up the swaying palm fronds and banana plants, fringing the tangled jungle with exotic highlights of pink and blue. They'd climbed the fence together, running through the greenbelt, disappearing into the fantastic jungle. A year passed in a blur of stupid jobs — for Lance, stints driving a cab, delivering flowers, and, for Kirsten, tearing movie tickets in half as a stream of happy dreamers clicked through the turnstiles, then sweeping debris from the floors in the dead-still hours when the decent world slept. Lance worked a second job deep-frying doughnuts in blackened vats of oil, dressed in a white suit.

But *this,* Lance had said, *this* would allow them to turn their backs on that year, on everything they'd done for survival. A regular at the doughnut shop had set them up with their kit — the picture ID, the magazine subscriptions, the pamphlets. Although the deal worked like a pyramid scheme, it wasn't entirely a scam; a thin layer of legality existed, and 10 percent of the money collected actually went to the babies. Another 10 percent was skimmed by collectors in the field, and the remainder was mailed to a P.O. box in Key Biscayne. Of that, the recruiters took a percentage, and the recruiters of the recruiters took an even bigger cut. That's the way it was supposed to work, but when Lance and Kirsten left Florida, the tenuous sense of obligation weakened and finally vanished, and Lance was no longer sending any money to the P.O. box. They were renegade now; they kept everything.

Lance got out of the car. He tried to break the dragging tailpipe free, but it wouldn't budge. He wiped his hands. Down the road the yellow lights of a farmhouse glowed like portals. A dog barked and the wind soughing through the corn called hoarsely.

"The worst they can do is say no," Lance said.

"They won't," Kirsten said.

Lance grabbed his ledger and a sheaf of pamphlets and his ID. They left the car and walked down the road in the milky light of a gibbous moon that lit the feathery edges of a high, isolated cloud. The house was white and seemed illuminated, as did the ghostly white fence and the silver silo. When they opened the gate, the dog barked wildly and charged them, quickly using up its length of chain; its neck snapped and the barking stopped, and when the dog regained its feet it followed them in a semicircle, as if tracing a path drawn by a compass.

Before they could knock, an old woman answered with a bowl of candy. Her hair was thin and white, more the memory or suggestion of hair than the thing itself. Her eyes were blue and the lines of her creased face held the image of the land around her, worn and furrowed. Her housedress drifted vaguely around her body like a fog.

"Evening, ma'am," Lance said.

When he was done delivering his introduction on the evils of drugs, he turned to Kirsten for her part, but she said nothing, letting the silence become a burden. The whole of the night — the last crickets chirring in the cold, the brown moths beating against the yellow light, the moon shadows and the quiet that came, faintly humming, from the land itself — pressed in close, weighing on the woman.

Finally, Kirsten said, "If you could give us a place to stay for the night, we'd be grateful."

Lance said, "Now, honey, we can't impose."

"I'm tired and I'm cold," Kirsten said.

Again the silence accumulated around them like a world filling with water.

"My husband's gone up to bed," the woman said at last. "I hate to wake Effie."

"No need," Kirsten said. "If we could just sleep tonight in your girl's room, we'll be gone in the morning."

"My girl?"

"That's a lovely picture she drew," Kirsten said, "and it's wonderful that you hang it in the living room. You must have loved her very much."

A quelling hand went to the woman's lips. She backed away from the door — not so much a welcome as a surrender, a ceding of the space — and Kirsten and Lance entered. Years of sunlight had slowly paled the wallpaper in the living room and drained the red from the plastic roses on the sill. A familiar path was padded into the carpet and a pair of suede slippers waited at their place by the sofa. The air in the house was warm and still and faintly stale like a held breath.

In the morning, Kirsten woke feeling queasy and sat up on the cramped child's mattress. She pulled aside the curtain. The old couple were in the backyard. The wife was hanging a load of wash on a line, socks, a bra, underwear, linens that unfurled like flags in the wind. The husband hoed weeds from a thinning garden of gaunt cornstalks, black-stemmed tomato plants, and a few last, lopsided pumpkins that sat sad-faced on the ground, saved from rot by a bedding of straw. A cane swung from a belt loop in his dungarees.

"Any dreams?" Lance said. He reached for Kirsten, squeezing her thigh.

"Who needs dreams?" Kirsten said, letting the curtain fall back.

"Bitter, bitter," Lance said. "Don't be bitter."

He picked his slacks off the floor and shook out the pockets, unfolding the crumpled bills and arranging the coins in separate stacks on his stomach.

"Let's see where we're at," he said.

Lance grabbed his notebook from the floor and thumbed the foxed, dirty pages in which he kept a meticulous tally of their finances.

"You don't need a pencil and paper," Kirsten said.

"Discipline is important," he said. "When we strike it rich, we don't want to be all stupid and clueless. Can you see them old folks out there?"

"They're out there."

"It must be something to live in a place like this," Lance said. He put down the notebook and peered out the window. "Just go out and get yourself some corn when you're hungry." He pressed his hand flat against the glass. In the field to the east, the corn had been gathered, the ground laid bare. "It looks weird out there."

Kirsten had noticed it also. "It looks like we're too late," she said.

"That's the whole problem with the seventies."

"It's 1989, Lance."

"Well, then, high time we do something about it." He pulled the curtain closed. "I'm sick and tired of washing my crotch in sinks."

"I'll go out and talk to them," Kirsten said.

"Where'd you go last night?" Lance said. "After the gas station."

She didn't want to say, and said, "Nowhere."

"Get a look at yourself in that mirror there," he said.

Kirsten sat in a child's chair, looking at herself in the mirror of a vanity that had also doubled as a desk at one time — beside the perfume bottles and a hairbrush and a box of costume jewelry were cups of crayons and pens and pencils and a yellowed writing tablet. Kirsten leaned her head to the side and began to brush her hair, combing the leaves and dirt out of it.

"Lance," she said.

"Yeah?"

"Don't take anything from these people."

"You can't hide anything from me," he said, with an assured, tolerant smile.

Kirsten set down the brush and walked out into the yard, where the old woman was stretched on her toes, struggling to hang a last billowing sheet.

"Lend me a hand here," she said. "The wind's blowing so —"

Kirsten held an end and helped fasten the sheet. Blowing dust clung to the wet cotton.

"I probably shouldn't even bother hanging out the wash, this time of year," the old woman said. She pronounced it "warsh."

The combine's swallowing mouth opened a path along the fence. The old woman shuddered and turned away.

"You have a beautiful place," Kirsten said. "All this land yours?"

"We got two sections. Daddy's too old to work it now, so we lease everything to a commercial outfit in Kalona."

"You must eat a lot of corn."

"Oh, hon, that's not sweet corn. That corn's for hogs. It's feed."

"Oh," she said.

"That blue Rabbit up the road yours?" The old man walked with an injured stoop, punting himself forward with the cane. He introduced himself — Effie Bowen, Effie and his wife, Gen. He was short of breath and gritted his teeth as if biting the difficult air. A rime of salt stained the brim of his red cap.

"That's us, I'm sorry to say."

He tipped the hat back, bringing his eyes out of the shade.

"Momma thinks I can tow you with the tractor," he said. "I say she's right. I went and looked at it this morning."

"I'm not sure we can afford any major repairs," Kirsten said.

"You work for a children's charity," the old woman said.

"That's right."

"We'll get you going," the man said. "Up to the Mennonites, right, Momma?"

The old woman nodded. "I put towels out. You kids help yourselves to a hot shower, and meanwhile Daddy and me'll tow your car up to the plain people and then we'll just see."

"We'd like to go into town," Kirsten said. "If that's okay."

"Sure," the old woman said. She looked at her husband. "Yeah?"

"Of course, yes. Yes."

Main Street was wide and empty, the storefronts colorless in the flat light. A traffic signal swaying over the only intersection ticked like a clock in the quiet. Feeling faint, her stomach cramping, Kirsten sat on the curb. A hand-lettered sign on a sheet of unpainted plywood leaned against a low stucco building, advertising FRESH EGGS, MILK, BROCCOLI, CHERRIES, BREAD, POTATOES, WATERMELON, STRAWBERRIES, ROOT BEER, ANTIQUES.

"No corn," Lance observed, pitching a rock at the sign. "So, you gonna tell me?"

She shook her head. "I just went for a walk, Lance. Nowhere," she said, pressing a print of her hand in the dust. She was wary of Lance, knowing that if she let him, he would tap her every mood. He believed that a rich and deserved life ran parallel to theirs, a life that she alone could see, and he would probe her dreams for directions and tease her premonitions for meanings, as if her nightmares and moods gave her access to a world of utter certainty, when in fact Kirsten knew the truth — that every dream was a reservoir of doubt. A life spent revolving through institutions had taught her that. Foster care, detox, detention — even the woman she called mother was an institution, a fumbling scheme. Her improvised family of shifting faces sat together in common rooms furnished with donated sofas and burned lampshades and ashtrays of cut green glass, in lounges that were more home to her than home ever was, the inmates more family than she'd ever known.

It was in those lounges, on mornings that never began, through nights that wouldn't end, that Kirsten had elaborated her sense of the other world. She had stripped her diet of the staples of institutional life — the starches, the endless urns of coffee and the sugar cubes and creamers, the cigarettes. She'd cropped her hair short and stopped wearing jewelry, and one afternoon, while the janitor mopped the hallway, she'd slipped the watch from her wrist and dumped it into his dingy bucket of water. She'd cleaned her room and kept it spare and was considered a model inmate, neat and quiet and nearly invisible. By experimenting, she discovered that the only deeply quiet time on the ward was in the dark hour before dawn, and so she'd begun to wake at 4:00 A.M., first with an alarm clock, then automatically, easing from sleep into a stillness that was as spacious and as close to freedom as anything inside detention could be. Then she would pull a candle from her dresser drawer, melt it to her bedpost, sit in her chair, and stare at the mirror bolted to her wall. For weeks, she waited for something to appear in the clear depth, looking into the glass as if into a great distance. An instinct told her she was trying too hard, but one morning her arms lost life and went leaden, her hands curled, and the mirror turned cloudy, her face fading as if it had sunk below the surface of the glass, and her true mother's fingers reached toward hers. The next morning, she learned that guiding the images made them go away, and she spent another disconsolate hour staring at herself. Eventually, she was able to sit without panic as her image sank and vanished, and often she emerged from her trances with her own hand stretched to meet the hand in the mirror.

Early in her detention, a social worker had advised Kirsten that the only thing better than heroin was a future, and that had been Lance's gift, a restlessness that seemed focused on tomorrow, a desire that made the days seem available. But he was impatient, and his sense of her gift was profane and depleting, with every half thought and reverie expected to strike pay dirt.

"Okay, fine," Lance said. "Let's hit the trailer court."

"I'm tired of those smelly trailers."

"We've talked about this I don't know how many times."

"I want the nice houses. Those people have the money."

"They have the money," he said, "because they don't fall for bullshit like ours."

They started up the steps of the biggest and nicest house on the street. With its wide and deep veranda, it seemed to have been built with a different prospect in mind, a more expansive view. Kirsten knocked and wiped her feet on the welcome mat and shuffled through her pamphlets and forms. Dressed in overalls, stuffed with straw, a scarecrow slumped on a porch swing, its head a forlorn sack knotted at the neck with a red kerchief. Kirsten knocked again, and then once more, but no one answered.

"See?" Lance said.

"See nothing," Kirsten said. She marched across the lawn to the neighbor's door. Lance sat on the curb, picking apart a leaf. No one answered her knock. She shuffled through her materials, stalling.

"Time to hit the trailer trash," Lance said.

Kirsten ran to the next house. A ghost hung from the awning, and the family name, Strand, was engraved on a wooden plaque above the door. She drew a deep breath and knocked. For some time now, she'd done things Lance's way. She'd solicited only the homes where she found signs of a shoddy slide — a car on blocks, a windowpane repaired with tape, some loss of contour in the slouching house itself — fissures in somebody else's hope that she and Lance could crawl through. But what had happened? They'd become sad little children, petty thieves and liars, swiping things that no one would miss — five dollars here, ten dollars there — and laying siege to it with large plans, intricate calculations. Lance had his theories, but lately it had occurred to Kirsten that he was conducting his life with folklore. He had a knack for discovering the reverse of everything — the good were bad, the rich were poor, the great were low and mean — and it was no surprise that they were now living lives that were upside down.

A little girl pulled the door open a crack, peering shyly up at Kirsten.

"Is your momma home?"

"Momma!"

The woman who came to the door, wiping her hands on a dish towel, was a fuller version of the little girl, with the same blond hair and blue eyes. Kirsten offered her one of the brochures.

The little girl clung to her mother's leg. She wore one yellow sock and one green, orange dance tights, a purple skirt, a red turtleneck.

Kirsten said, "Did you get dressed all by yourself this morning?"

The little girl nodded and buried her face in the folds of her mother's skirt.

The mother smiled. "Cuts down on the fighting, right, April? We have a deal. She dresses herself, then she has to eat all her breakfast." She handed Kirsten the pamphlet. "I just made some coffee," she said.

Kirsten leaned forward in a faded green chair by the window and watched Lance aimlessly tossing rocks and sticks in the street.

The woman brought two cups of coffee and a plate with Pop-Tarts, toasted and cut in thirds, fanned around the edges.

"You'd be surprised how many around here get into drugs," she said.

"I'm not sure it would surprise me, ma'am," Kirsten said. "Everywhere I go I hear stories from people who have been touched by this thing." She sipped her coffee. "This tragedy."

"I worry about this little one," the woman said.

Kirsten bit a corner of a Pop-Tart, feeling the hot cinnamon glaze on the roof of her mouth. On the mantel above the fireplace was a collection of ceramic owls. They stared steadily into the room with eyes so wide open and unblinking, they looked blind.

"My owls," the woman said. "I don't know how it is you start collecting. It just happens innocently, you think one is cute, then all of a sudden" — she waved her hand in the air — "you've got dumb owls all over the place."

"Keep them busy," Kirsten said.

"What's that?"

"April here — and all kids — if they have something to do they won't have time for drugs."

"That makes sense."

"People think of addicts as these lazy, do-nothing sort of people, but really it's a full-time job. Most of them work at it harder than these farmers I seen in these cornfields. It takes their entire life."

The woman cupped her hands over her knees, then clasped

them together. Either her wedding band was on the sill above the kitchen sink, left there after some chore, or she was divorced. Kirsten felt a rush of new words rise in her throat.

"You know what it's like to be pregnant, so I don't have to tell you what it means to have that life in you — and then just imagine feeding your baby poison all day. A baby like that one on the pamphlet, if they're born at all, they just cry all the time. You can't get them quiet."

It was a chaotic purse, and the woman had to burrow down through wadded Kleenex, key rings, and doll clothes before she pulled out a checkbook.

"I never knew my own mother," Kirsten said.

The woman's pen was poised above the check, but she set it down to look at Kirsten. It was a look Kirsten had lived with all her life and felt ashamed of, seeing something so small and frail and helpless at the heart of other people's sympathy. They meant well and it meant nothing.

"And I never really get away from this feeling," she went on. "Sadness, you could call it. My mother — my true mother, I mean — is out there, but I'll never know her. I sometimes get a feeling like she's watching me in the dark, but that's about it. You know that sense you get, where you think something's there and you turn around and, you know, there's nothing there?"

The woman did, she did, with nods of encouragement.

"When I think about it, though, I'm better off than these babies. Just look at that little one's dark face, his shriveled head. He looks drowned."

Then the woman filled in an amount and signed her name.

"I wish I was invisible," Lance said. "I'd just walk into these houses and they wouldn't even know."

"And do what?"

"Right now I'd make some toast."

"Hungry?"

"A little."

"Wouldn't they see the bread floating around?"

"Invisible bread."

"You get that idea from your cowboy brain?"

"Don't make fun of the cowboy brain," Lance said. "It got us out of that goddamn detention. It got us over that fence."

"We're ghosts to these people, Lance. They already don't see us."

"I'd like to kill someone. That'd make them see. They'd believe then."

"You're just talking," Kirsten said. "I think I'm getting my period."

"Great," Lance said. "All we need."

"Fuck you," Kirsten said. "I haven't had a period in two years."

She turned over one of the pamphlets. Seeing the baby's inconsolable face reminded Kirsten of a song her foster mother used to sing, but while the melody remained the lyrics were dead to her, because merely thinking of this mother meant collaborating in a lie, and everything in it was somehow corrupted. Words to songs never returned to Kirsten readily — she had to think hard just to recall a Christmas carol.

"Little babies like that one," she said, "they'll scream all the time. Their little hands are jittery. They have terrible fits where they keep squeezing their hands real tight and grabbing the air. They can't stop shaking, but when you try to hold them they turn stiff as a board."

"To be perfectly honest," Lance said, "I don't really give a fuck about those babies."

"I know."

"We just need money for gas."

"I know."

At the next house, a man answered, and immediately Kirsten smelled the sour odor of settledness through the screen door. A television played in the cramped front room. A spider plant sat on a stereo speaker, still in its plastic pot, the soil dry and hard yet with a pale shoot thriving, growing down to the shag carpet, as if it might find a way to root in the fibers. Pans in the sink he scrubbed as needed, coffee grounds and macaroni on the floor, pennies and dimes caught in clots of dog hair. A somber, unmoving light in rooms where the windows were never opened, the curtains always closed.

"Some got to be addicted," the man said, after Kirsten explained herself. "They never go away."

"That may be so," Kirsten admitted. "I've thought the same myself."

He went to the kitchen and opened the fridge.

"You want a beer?"

"No, thanks."

The blue air around the television was its own atmosphere, and when the man sank back in his chair, it was as if he'd gone there to breathe. He looked at Kirsten's breasts, then down at her feet, and finally at his own hands, which were clumsy and large, curling tightly around the bottle.

"Where you staying?"

"About a mile out of town," she said. She handed the man a pamphlet. "I've had that same despair you're talking about. When you feel nothing's going to change enough to wipe out all the problem."

"Bunch of niggers, mostly."

"Did you look at the one there?"

"Tar baby."

"That kid's white," Kirsten said. She had no idea if this was true.

He didn't say anything.

Kirsten nodded at the television. "Who's winning?"

"Who's playing?" the man said. He was using a coat hanger for an aerial. "The blue ones, I guess."

"But isn't it enough? If you can save one baby from this life of hell, isn't that okay?"

"Doesn't matter much," he said. "In the scheme of things."

"It would mean everything," Kirsten said, "if it was you."

"But," he said, "it's not me." The blur of the television interested him more. "Where?"

"Where what?"

"Where'd you say you were staying?"

"With these old people, Effie, Effie and his wife, Gen."

He dropped the pamphlet on the floor and pushed himself out of the chair. He swayed and stared dumbly into a wallet full of receipts.

"Well, tonight you say hi to them for me. You tell Effie and Gen Johnny says hi." When he looked at Kirsten, his eyes had gone neutral. "You tell them I'm sorry, and you give them this," he said, leaning toward Kirsten. Then his lips were gone from her mouth, and he was handing her the last five from his billfold.

When they returned to the farmhouse, their car was sitting in the drive and dinner was cooking. The kitchen windows were steamed, and the moist air, warm and fragrant, settled like a perfume on Kirsten's skin. She ran hot water and lathered her hands. The ball of soap was as smooth and worn as an old bone, a mosaic assembled from remnants, small pieces thriftily saved and then softened and clumped together. Everything in the house seemed to have that same quality, softened by the touch of hands — hands that had rubbed the brass plating from the doorknobs, hands that had worn the painted handles of spoons and ladles down to bare wood. Kirsten rinsed the soap away, and Gen offered her a towel.

"You don't have any other clothes, do you?" the old woman asked.

"No, ma'am," she said.

"Let's go pull some stuff out of the attic," Gen said. She drew a level line from the top of her head to the top of Kirsten's. "We're about the same size, I figure. You won't win any fashion awards — it's just old funny things, some wool pants, a jacket, a couple cardigan sweaters. But you aren't dressed for Iowa." She pronounced it "Ioway."

"I'd appreciate that, ma'am."

"Doing the kind of work you do, I don't imagine you can afford the extras," she said, as they climbed a set of steps off the upstairs hallway. "But in this country we don't consider a coat extra."

The old woman tugged a string and a bare bulb lit the attic. In the sudden glare, the room seemed at first to house nothing but a jumble of shadows. "I've held on to everything," she said.

"I met a man in town today," Kirsten said. "He said he knew you and Effie."

The old woman slit the tape on a box with her thumbnail and handed Kirsten a sweater that smelled faintly of dust and camphor.

Kirsten held the woman still and kissed her on the lips. "He said to give you that."

"Johnny?" Gen said. "He won't come out here."

Kirsten slipped into the sweater, a cardigan with black leather buttons like a baby's withered navel, a hardened ball of Kleenex in the pocket. She had never known a world of such economy, where things were saved and a room in a house could be set aside for storage. This woman had lived to pass her things on, but now there was no one to take them.

"It was a combine," Kirsten said. "It was this time of year."

The old woman nodded.

"Your little girl doesn't know she's dead. She's still out there."

"How do I know you know all this?"

"I saw her," Kirsten said. "And when me and Lance come to the door last night we never knocked."

From a rack against the wall, the old woman took down a wool overcoat.

"You were waiting up for her. You wait every year."

Gen stepped in front of a cheval mirror and held the coat against her body, modeling it for a moment.

"It wasn't Effie's fault."

"He feels the guilt all the same," the old woman said.

"He had to," Kirsten said.

"Had to what?"

"Live," she said. "He had to live his life, just the same as me and you."

They set four places with the good plates and silver and flowery napkins in the dining room. There was a ham pricked with cloves and ringed around with pineapple and black olives and green beans and salad and bread. Effie fussed over his wife as if he'd never had dinner with her, passing dishes and offering extra helpings, which she refused each time, saying, "Help yourself." Kirsten eventually caught on, seeing that this solicitude was the old man's sly way of offering a compliment and serving himself a little more at the same time. The food was good; it all glistened, the juices from the ham, the butter running off the beans, the oil on the salad. Gen spent most of the meal up on her feet, offering, spooning, heating, filling.

Effie's conversation made a wide, wandering tour of the land. Jesse James used to hide out in this country, he said. Then he was talking about no-till planting, soil that wasn't disked or plowed.

"You got corn in just about everything," he said. "In gasoline, spark plugs, crayons, toothpaste, disposable diapers —"

"No, really?" Lance said.

"You bet," the old man went on, "and paint, beer, whiskey. You name it."

He said one out of four hogs produced in this country came from Iowa — which he, too, pronounced "Ioway." Hogs till Hell wouldn't have it, he said, thundering the words. The topic of hogs led to a story he'd read about Fidel Castro roasting a pig in a hotel room in New York, and then he told about their travels, a trip to Ireland and another to Hawaii, which he pronounced "Hoy."

After dinner, there was pumpkin pie — prize-winning, Effie announced, as the pie tin took center stage on the cleared table.

It was delicious, the filling warm with a buttery vanishing feel on Kirsten's tongue. "What's in it?" she asked.

"Oh," Gen said, "cinnamon, ginger, nutmeg, allspice, vanilla — but real pumpkin's the key." Gen, satisfied with the satisfaction at her table, smiled at her husband, who gravely put down his fork.

"When you come," Effie said, "Momma said you mentioned our little girl."

The old man looked across the table at his wife, checking her eyes, or the turn of her mouth, for subtle signs, searching for agreement. It was as if he found what he needed in the space between them and spoke aloud only to verify that it was there, that someone else had seen it.

"Our little girl," Gen said.

"Your daughter," Kirsten said.

"I wondered if you were an old friend. Maybe from school. Most of them have grown and gone away. I used to see — it would have been so long ago but . . ." He trailed off, his pale-blue eyes wetly sparking in the weak, splintered light of the chandelier.

Lance said, "Kirsten's been to the other side. She's seen it."

"I would believe you," Effie said. "Some around here don't credit dowsers, but we always have. We never had reason not to. We always had plenty of water." He cleared his throat. "I'd pay anything if you could tell us — anything."

"There's the babies," Lance said.

"I'll help with those babies of yours. I'll donate to your cause. Where you going after this?"

"We're aiming west," Lance said.

Effie squared his fork with the edge of the table. "Well?"

Kirsten was about to speak when she felt a hand slide over her knee, the fingers feeling their way until they rested warmly in her hand, holding it tight. She glanced at the old woman.

"It was only that picture on your wall," she said to Effie.

The picture was the one every child drew a hundred times — the house, the leafy tree, the sun in one corner, the birds overhead, the walkway widening like a river as it flows out from the front door, the family standing on the green grass, a brother, a sister, a mother with her triangle dress, the father twice as big as everybody, the stick fingers overlapping — and that no one ever saved.

"It was just that picture," Kirsten said. "I wish I could say it was more, but it wasn't."

Effie picked up his fork and pressed it against the crumbs of pie-crust still on his plate, gathering them. He looked as though he had another question in mind.

"That was the last picture," the old woman said.

"She just drawn it at school," he said. "She put me and Gen in, her and her brother."

"Stephanie," Kirsten said, "and Johnny."

The old man glanced at his wife.

"She spelled all the names on the picture," Kirsten said.

Gen whispered yes, but it was Effie who had to speak up. "I never breathed right or walked right after," he said. "Never farmed, neither, except for my little garden out back."

"That was the best pie I ever had," Kirsten said.

"Show your ribbons, Momma," Effie said.

"Oh, no," Gen said, waving her hand, shooing away the approach, the temptation of something immodest.

"Well, that's right," Effie said. "The pie's right here, huh?" He looked around the table. "The pie's right here."

Kirsten hovered above the field and could hear the rumble of an engine and the crushed stalks snapping, a crackling noise that spread and came from everywhere at once, like fire. The stalks flailed and broke and dust and chaff flew up, and then, ahead, she saw the little girl running down the rows, lost in the maze, unable to search out a safe direction. Suddenly, the girl sat on the ground, her stillness an instinct, looking up through the leaves, waiting for the noise to pass. Kirsten saw her there — a little girl being good, quiet, obedient — but when the sound came closer she flattened herself against the dirt, as if the moment might pass her by. When it was too late, she kicked her feet, trying to escape, and was swallowed up. The noise faded, and a scroll of dirt and stover curved over the fields like handwriting. Then it was gone, and Kirsten saw her own reflection floating in the gray haze of the vanity.

"Lance," she said.

"What?"

"We're leaving," she said.

"Why, what?"

Kirsten gathered the old woman's clothes in a garbage sack and had Lance carry them to the car. She made the bed and fluffed the thin pillows. The house was quiet.

She sat at the small painted vanity, taking a blue crayon from the cup, and wrote a thank-you note. She wrote to the old woman that one second of love is all the love in the world, that one moment is all of them; she wrote that she'd really liked the pumpkin pie and meant it when she'd said it was the best she'd ever had, adding that she never expected to taste better; she thanked her for the hospitality and for fixing the car; and then she copied down the words to the song the woman she called Mother had sung:

> Where are you going, my little one, little one?
> Where are you going, my baby, my own?
> Turn around and you're two, turn around and you're four.
> Turn around and you're a young girl going out of the door.

Lance was gone for a long time, and Kirsten, looking over the note, considered tearing it up each time she read it. As she sat and waited, she felt a sudden warmth and reached under the elastic of her underpants. When Lance finally returned, he was covered in dry leaves and strings of tassel, as if he'd been out working in the fields. They went outside and pushed the car down the gravel drive, out to the road. It started up, beautifully quiet.

"Wait here," Kirsten said.

She walked back to the yard. It was cool, and the damp night air released a rich smell of dung and soil and straw, a smell Kirsten was sure belonged only to Iowa, and only at certain hours. She pulled her T-shirt over her head. She was reaching for the clothespin that held the old woman's bra when something made her look up. The old woman was standing at the upstairs window, her hand pressed flat against the glass. Kirsten took the bra from the line and slipped the straps over her shoulders. She fastened the clasp and leaned forward, settling her breasts in the small white cups. The women looked at each other for what seemed like an eternity, and then Kirsten pulled on her shirt and ran back to Lance.

Under the moonlight, they drove down mazy roads cut through the fields.

"Goddamn, the Lord sure hath provideth the corn around

here," Lance said. He imitated the old man compulsively. "I'll be plenty glad to get out of this Ioway. Ioway! Christ Almighty. I'm sorry, but those people were corny. And that old guy, jawing on about Castro's fucking pigs in the bathtub. What'd he say, they cooked a hog in that hotel room? What the hell." Lance was taking charge, his mind hard, forging connections. He was feeling good, he was feeling certain. "And goddamn I hate ham! Smells like piss!" He rolled down the window and yelled, "Goodbye, fucking Ioway!" He brushed corn silk from his sleeve and shook bits of leaves from his hair.

"Here's something for you." He reached in his pocket and handed her a long heavy chain.

"Looks to me like gold with emeralds and rubies mixed in," he said.

"That's costume jewelry, Lance."

"We'll get it appraised, and you'll see. It's real," he said, bullying the truth, hating its disadvantages. "They won't miss it, Kirsten. They're old, honey. They're gonna die and they got no heirs so don't you worry." He grinned widely and said, "I got something out of the deal, too." He waited. Kirsten just stared at the cheap gaudy chain, pouring it like water from one hand to the other.

Lance said, "Look in back."

When she turned around, all she saw through the rear window was a trail of dust turning red in the taillights.

"Under the blanket," Lance said.

Kirsten reached behind her and pulled away the blanket. The rear seat was overflowing with ears of corn. Lance had turned the whole back of the car into a crib.

"Ioway corn," he said. "Makes me hungry just thinking about it."

ALICE MUNRO

Silence

FROM THE NEW YORKER

ON THE SHORT FERRY RIDE from Buckley Bay to Denman Island, Juliet gets out of her car and stands at the front of the boat, in the late-spring breeze. A woman standing there recognizes her, and they begin to talk. It is not unusual for people to take a second look at Juliet and wonder where they've seen her before. She appears regularly on the provincial television channel, interviewing people who lead notable lives and deftly directing panel discussions for a program called *Issues of the Day.* Her hair is cut short now, as short as possible, and has taken on a very dark auburn color, which matches the frames of her glasses. She often wears black pants, as she does today, and an ivory silk shirt, and sometimes a black jacket. She is what her mother would have called a striking woman.

"Forgive me. People must always be bothering you," the woman says. She is about Juliet's age. Long black hair streaked with gray, no makeup, denim skirt. She lives on Denman, so Juliet asks her what she knows about the Spiritual Balance Centre.

"Because my daughter is there," Juliet says. "She's been on a retreat there, or a course — I don't know what they call it. For six months."

"There are a couple of places like that," the woman says. "They sort of come and go. I don't mean there's anything suspect about them. Just that they're generally off in the woods, you know, and don't have much to do with the community. Well, what would be the point of a retreat if they did?"

She says that Juliet must be looking forward to seeing her daughter again and Juliet says, yes, very much.

"I'm spoiled," she says. "She's twenty years old, my daughter —

she'll be twenty-one this month, actually — and we haven't been apart much."

The woman says that she has a son who is twenty and fifteen- and eighteen-year-old daughters, and there are days when she'd *pay* them all to go on a retreat.

Juliet laughs. "Well. I've only got the one. Of course, I can't guarantee that I won't be all for shipping her back, given a few weeks."

She finds this kind of fond but exasperated mother talk easy to slip into (Juliet is an expert at reassuring responses), but the truth is that Penelope has scarcely ever given her cause for complaint, and if she wanted to be totally honest at this point she would say that one day without some contact with her daughter is hard to bear, let alone six months. Penelope spent a summer working as a hotel chambermaid at Banff, and she has gone on bus trips to Mexico. A hitchhiking trip to Newfoundland. But, in order to save money, she has always lived with Juliet, and there has never before been a six-month break.

She gives me delight, Juliet could have said. *Not that she is one of those song-and-dance purveyors of sunshine and cheer and looking-on-the-bright-side. But she has grace and compassion and she is as wise as if she'd been on this earth for eighty years. Her nature is reflective — not all over the map, like mine. Somewhat reticent, like her father's. She is also angelically pretty — blond like my mother but not so frail. Strong and noble. Molded, I should say, like a caryatid. And, contrary to popular notions, I am not even faintly jealous. All this time without her — and no word from her, because Spiritual Balance does not allow letters or phone calls — all this time I've been in a sort of desert, and when her message came I was like an old patch of cracked earth getting a full drink of rain.*

"Hope to see you Sunday afternoon. It's time," Penelope's card had said.

Time to come home was what Juliet hoped this meant. But of course she would leave that up to Penelope.

Penelope had drawn a rudimentary map, and Juliet shortly found herself parked in front of an old church — that is, a church building that was seventy-five or eighty years old, covered with stucco, not as old or nearly as impressive as churches often were in the part of Canada where Juliet had grown up. Behind it was a more recent building, with a slanting roof and windows all across its front, as well as a simple outdoor stage and some benches and what looked like a volleyball court, with a sagging net. Everything was shabby, and the once cleared patch of land was being reclaimed by juniper and poplars.

A couple of people — she couldn't tell whether they were men or women — were doing some carpentry work on the stage, and others sat on the benches in separate small groups. All wore ordinary clothes, not yellow robes or anything of that sort. For a few minutes, no notice was taken of Juliet's car. Then one of the people on the benches rose and walked unhurriedly toward her. A short middle-aged man wearing glasses.

Juliet greeted him and asked for Penelope. He did not speak — perhaps there was a rule of silence — but nodded and turned away and went into the church. From which there shortly appeared not Penelope but a heavy, slow-moving woman with white hair, wearing jeans and a baggy sweater.

"What an honor to meet you," she said. "Do come inside. I've asked Donny to make us some tea."

She had a broad fresh face, a smile that was both roguish and tender, and what Juliet supposed one would call twinkling eyes. "My name is Joan," she said. Juliet had been expecting an assumed name like Serenity, or something with an Eastern flavor, nothing so plain and familiar as Joan.

"I've got the right place, have I? I'm a stranger on Denman," she said in a way that she hoped was disarming. "You know I've come to see Penelope?"

"Of course. Penelope." Joan prolonged the name, with a certain tone of celebration.

The inside of the church was darkened, with purple cloth hung over the high windows. The pews and other church furnishings had been removed, and plain white curtains had been strung up to form private cubicles, as in a hospital ward. The cubicle into which Juliet was directed had, however, no bed, just a small table and a couple of plastic chairs and some open shelves piled untidily with loose papers.

"I'm afraid we're still in the process of getting things fixed up in here," Joan said. "Juliet. May I call you Juliet?"

"Yes, of course."

"I'm not used to talking to a celebrity." Joan held her hands together in a prayer pose beneath her chin. "I don't know whether to be informal or not."

"I'm not much of a celebrity."

"Oh, you are. Now, don't say that. And I'll just get it off my chest right away, how I admire you for the work you do. It's a beam in the darkness. The only television worth watching."

"Thank you," Juliet said. "I had a note from Penelope."

"I know. But I'm sorry to have to tell you, Juliet, I'm very sorry and I don't want you to be too disappointed — Penelope is not here."

The woman says those words — *Penelope is not here* — as lightly as possible, as if Penelope's absence could be turned into a matter for amused contemplation, even for their mutual delight.

Juliet has to take a deep breath. For a moment she cannot speak. Dread pours through her. Foreknowledge. Then she pulls herself back to reasonable consideration of this fact. She fishes around in her bag.

"She said she hoped —"

"I know. I know," Joan says. "She did intend to be here, but the fact was she could not —"

"Where is she? Where did she go?"

"I cannot tell you that."

"You mean you can't or you won't?"

"I can't. I don't know. But I can tell you one thing that may put your mind at rest. Wherever she has gone, whatever she has decided, it is the right thing for her. It is the *right* thing for her spirituality and her growth."

Juliet decides to let this pass. She gags on the word *spirituality,* which seems to encompass — as she often says — everything from prayer wheels to High Mass. She had never expected that Penelope, with her intelligence, would get mixed up in anything like this.

"I just thought I should know," she says. "In case she wanted me to send on any of her things."

"Her possessions?" Joan seems unable to suppress a smile, though she modifies it at once with an expression of tenderness. "Penelope is not very concerned right now about *her possessions.*"

Sometimes Juliet realizes, in the middle of an interview, that the person across from her has reserves of hostility that were not apparent before the cameras started rolling. A person whom Juliet has underestimated, whom she has thought rather stupid, may turn out to have strength of this sort. Playful but deadly hostility. Her rule then is never to show that she is taken aback, never to display any hint of hostility in return.

"What I mean by growth is our inward growth, of course," Joan says.

"I understand," Juliet says, looking her in the eye.

"Penelope has had such a wonderful opportunity in her life to meet interesting people — goodness, she hasn't needed to meet interesting people, she's grown *up* with an interesting person, you're her *mother* — but, you know, sometimes there's a dimension that is missing. Grownup children feel that they've missed *out* on something —"

"Oh, yes," Juliet says. "I know that grownup children can have all sorts of complaints."

Joan has decided to come down hard.

"The spiritual dimension — I have to say this — was it not altogether lacking in Penelope's life? I take it she did not grow up in a faith-based home."

"Religion was not a banned subject. We could talk about it."

"But perhaps it was the *way* you talked about it. Your intellectual way. If you know what I mean. You are so clever," she adds kindly.

"So you say." Juliet is aware that any control she had over the interview, and over herself, is faltering, and may be lost.

"Not so I say, Juliet. So *Penelope* says. Penelope is a dear fine girl, but she came to us here in great hunger. Hunger for the things that were not available to her in her home. There you were, with your wonderful, busy, successful life. But, Juliet, do you not know that your daughter has known loneliness? That she has known unhappiness?"

"Don't most people feel that, at one time or another? Loneliness and unhappiness?"

"It's not for me to say. Oh, Juliet. You are a woman of marvelous insights. I've often watched you on television and I've thought, How does she get right to the heart of things like that, and all the time stay so nice and polite to people? I never thought I'd be sitting talking to you face to face. And, what's more, that I'd be in a position to *help* you —"

"I think that maybe you're mistaken about that."

"You feel hurt. It's natural that you should feel hurt."

"It's also my own business."

"Ah, well. Perhaps she'll get in touch with you. After all."

Penelope did get in touch with Juliet, a couple of weeks later. A birthday card arrived on her — Penelope's — birthday, the nineteenth of June. Her twenty-first birthday. It was the sort of card you send to an acquaintance whose taste you cannot guess. Not crude or jokey or truly witty. Just a drawing of a small bouquet of pansies tied by a thin purple ribbon whose tail spelled out the words "Happy Birthday."

There was no inscription and no signature. At first, Juliet thought that someone had sent this card to Penelope and forgotten to sign it, and that she, Juliet, had opened it by mistake. Someone who had Penelope's name and birth date on file. Her dentist, maybe, or her driving teacher. But when she checked the writing on the envelope, she saw that there had been no mistake: there was her own name, indeed, in Penelope's handwriting.

Postmarks gave you no clue anymore. They all said "Canada Post."

Juliet went to see Christa, who was in Vancouver now, too, in an assisted-living facility in Kitsilano. She had multiple sclerosis. Her room was on the ground floor, with a small private patio, and Juliet sat with her there, looking out at a sunny bit of lawn and the wisteria in bloom along a fence that concealed the garbage bins.

She told Christa the whole story of the trip to Denman Island. She had told nobody else and had hoped not to have to tell anybody. Every day, on her way home from work, she had wondered if perhaps Penelope would be waiting for her in the apartment. Or at least if there would be a letter, and then there had been — that unkind card — and she had torn it open with her hands shaking.

"It means something," Christa said. "It lets you know that she's okay. Something will follow. It will. Be patient."

Juliet talked bitterly for a while about Mother Shipton. That was what she had finally decided to call her, having toyed, and become dissatisfied, with Pope Joan. What bloody chicanery, she said. What creepiness, nastiness, behind her second-rate, sweetly religious façade. It was impossible to imagine Penelope's having been taken in by her.

Christa suggested that perhaps Penelope had visited the place because she had considered writing something about it. Some sort of investigative journalism. Field work. The personal angle — the long-winded personal angle — that was so popular nowadays.

"Investigating for six months?" Juliet said. "Penelope could have figured Mother Shipton out in ten minutes."

"It's weird," Christa admitted.

"You don't know more than you're letting on, do you?" Juliet said. "I hate to even ask that. I feel so at sea. I feel stupid. That woman intended me to feel stupid, of course. Like the character who blurts out something in a play and everybody turns away because they all know something she doesn't know —"

"No one writes that kind of play anymore," Christa said. "Now nobody knows anything. No — Penelope didn't take me into her confidence. Why should she? She knows I'd end up telling you. Just hold on. It's one of the trials of parenthood. She hasn't given you many, after all. In a year this will all be ancient history."

Juliet didn't tell Christa that in the end she had not been able to walk away from the Spiritual Balance Centre with dignity. She had turned and cried out beseechingly, furiously, "What did she *tell* you?"

Mother Shipton had stood there watching her, as if she had expected this. A fat pitying smile had stretched her closed lips as she shook her head.

During the next year, Juliet got phone calls, now and then, from people who had been friendly with Penelope. Her reply to their inquiries was always the same. Penelope had decided to take a year off from university. She was traveling. Her agenda was by no means fixed, and Juliet had no way of contacting her, nor any address she could supply.

She did not hear from anybody who had been a close friend. This might mean that people who had been close to Penelope knew quite well where she was. Or it might mean that they, too, were off on trips to foreign countries, had found jobs in other provinces, or had embarked on new lives, too crowded or chancy still to allow them to wonder about old friends. (Old friends, at that stage in life, meaning somebody they had not seen for half a year.)

Whenever Juliet came home, the first thing she did was look for the flashing light on her answering machine. Each time, she tried some silly trick — to do with how many steps she took to the phone, how she picked it up, how she breathed. *Let it be her.*

Nothing worked.

After a while, the world seemed emptied of the people that Penelope had known — the boyfriends she had dropped and the ones who had dropped her, the girls she had gossiped with and probably confided in. Because she had gone to Torrance House rather than to a public high school, most of her longtime friends had come from out of town. Alaska or Prince George or Peru.

There was no message at Christmas. But in June another card, very much in the style of the first. Not a word written inside. Juliet had a drink of wine before she opened it, then threw it away at once.

She had spurts of weeping, once in a while of uncontrollable shaking, but she emerged from these in quick fits of fury, walking around the house and slapping her fist into her palm. The fury was directed at Mother Shipton, but the image of that woman had faded, and finally Juliet had to recognize that she was really only a convenient target.

All pictures of Penelope were banished to her old bedroom, with the sheaves of drawings she had done before they left Whale Bay, her books, and the European one-cup coffeemaker with the plunger that she'd bought as a present for Juliet with the first money she'd made in her summer job at McDonald's. The door of her bedroom was shut and in time could be passed without disturbance.

Juliet gave a great deal of thought to leaving this apartment, giving herself the benefit of new surroundings. But, as she told Christa, she could not do it, because this was the only address that Penelope had, and mail would not be forwarded for more than three months. After that, there would be no place where her daughter could find her.

"She could always get you at work," Christa said.

"Who knows how long I'll be there?" Juliet said. "She's probably in some commune where they're not allowed to communicate. Run by a guru who sleeps with all the women and sends them out to beg on the streets. If I'd sent her to Sunday school and taught her to say her prayers this probably never would have happened. I should have done it. I should have. It would have been like an inoculation. I neglected her *spirituality*. As Mother Shipton said."

When Penelope was barely thirteen years old, she had gone away on a camping trip to the Kootenay Mountains of British Columbia, with a friend from Torrance House and the friend's family. Juliet was in favor of this trip. Penelope had been at Torrance House for only one year, and it pleased Juliet that she had already made so firm a friend and been readily accepted by her family. Also that she was going camping — something that regular children did and that Juliet, as a child, had never had the chance to do. Not that she would have wanted to — at Penelope's age, she had already been buried in books — but she welcomed signs that Penelope was turning out to be a more normal sort of girl than she herself had been.

Eric was apprehensive about the whole idea. He thought that Penelope was too young. He didn't like her going on a holiday with people he knew almost nothing about. And now that she went to boarding school, they saw too little of her as it was — so why should that time be shortened?

Juliet had another reason: she wanted Penelope out of the way for a couple of weeks, so that she could clear the air between herself and Eric. She wanted things resolved, and they were not resolved. She did not want to have to pretend that all was well, for the sake of the child.

Eric, on the other hand, would have liked nothing better than to see their trouble smoothed over, tucked out of the way. As he saw it, civility would restore good feeling, and the semblance of love would be enough to get by on until love itself could be rediscovered. And if there was never anything more than semblance — well, that would have to do. He could manage with that.

Having Penelope at home, forcing them to behave well — forcing Juliet to behave well, since she was the one, in his opinion, who had stirred up all the rancor — that would suit Eric very well.

Or so Juliet claimed, and created a new source of bitterness and blame, because he missed Penelope badly.

The reason for their quarrel was an old and ordinary one. In the spring, through some trivial disclosure — and the frankness or possibly the malice of their longtime neighbor Ailo, who had always had some reservations about Juliet — Juliet had discovered that Eric had slept with Christa again. She could not reasonably object to what had happened in the time before she and Eric were together. She did not. What she did object to — what she said had broken her heart — had happened after that. (Though still a long time ago, Eric pointed out.)

It had happened when Penelope was a year old and Juliet had taken her back to Ontario to visit her parents. To visit — as she emphasized now — her dying mother. While she was away, and loving and missing Eric with every shred of her being (she now believed this), Eric had simply returned to his old habits.

At first he confessed to once (drunk), but with further prodding, and some drinking in the here and now, he said that possibly it had been more than that.

Possibly? He could not remember? So many times he could not remember?

He could remember.

Christa came to see Juliet, to assure her that it had been nothing serious. (This was Eric's refrain as well.) Juliet told her to go away and never come back. Christa decided that now would be a good time to visit her sister in California.

Juliet's outrage at Christa was actually something of a formality. She did understand that a few rolls in the hay with an old girlfriend (Eric's disastrous description, in an ill-judged attempt to minimize things) were nowhere near as threatening as a hot embrace with some woman newly met. And her outrage at Eric was so fierce and irrepressible as to leave little room for blame of anybody else.

Her contentions were that he did not love her, had never loved her, had mocked her, with Christa, behind her back. He had made her a laughingstock in front of people like Ailo (who, Juliet said, had always hated her). He had treated her — and the love she felt (or had felt) for him — with contempt. He had lived a lie with her. Sex meant nothing to him, or, at any rate, it did not mean what it meant (had meant) to her — he would have it off with whoever was handy.

Only the last of these contentions had the smallest germ of truth in it, and in her quieter states she knew that. But even that little truth was enough to pull everything down around her. It shouldn't have done so, but it did. And Eric was not able — in all honesty he was not able — to see why. He was not surprised that she should object, make a fuss, even weep (though a woman like Christa wouldn't have), but that she should really be damaged, that she should consider herself bereft of all that had sustained her — and over something that had happened *twelve years ago* — this he could not understand.

Sometimes he believed that she was shamming, making too much of it, and at other times he was full of real grief that he had made her suffer. Their grief aroused them, and they made love magnificently. And each time he thought that that would be the end of it, that their miseries were over. Each time he was mistaken.

In bed, Juliet told him lightheartedly about Samuel and Mrs. Pepys, inflamed with passion under similar circumstances. (Since she had more or less given up on her classical studies, she was reading widely, and nowadays everything she read seemed to have to do with adultery.) Never so often and never so hot, Pepys had said, though he also recorded that his wife thought of murdering him in his sleep. Juliet laughed about this, but half an hour later, when Eric came to say goodbye before going out in the boat to check his prawn traps, she showed him a stony face and gave him a kiss of resignation, as if he'd been going to meet a woman out in the middle of the bay under a rainy sky.

There was more than rain. The water was hardly choppy when Eric went out, but later in the afternoon a wind came up suddenly, from the southeast, and tore up the waters of Desolation Sound and Malaspina Strait. It continued almost until dark — which did not really fall until around eleven o'clock in this last week of June. By then, a sailboat from Campbell River was missing, with three adults and two children aboard. Also two fish boats, one with two men aboard and the other with only one man — Eric.

The next morning was calm and sunny — the mountains, the waters, the shores, all sleek and sparkling.

It was possible, of course, that none of these people were lost, that they had found shelter and spent the night in any of the multitude of little bays along the coast. That was more likely to be true of the fishermen than of the family in the sailboat, who were not locals but vacationers from Seattle. Boats went out at once, that morning, to search the mainland and island shores and the water.

The drowned children were found first, in their life jackets, and by the end of the day the bodies of their parents were located as well. A grandfather who had accompanied them was not found until the following day. The bodies of the men who had been fishing together were lost, though the remnants of their boat washed up near Refuge Cove.

Eric's body was recovered on the third day. Juliet was not allowed to see it. Something had got at him, she was told (meaning some animal), after the body was washed ashore.

It was perhaps because of this — because there was no question of viewing the body and no need for an undertaker — that the idea caught hold among his old friends and fellow-fishermen of burning Eric on the beach. Juliet did not object to this. A death certificate had to be made out, so the doctor who came to Whale Bay once a week was telephoned at his office in Powell River, and he gave Ailo, who was a registered nurse and his weekly assistant, the authority to do it.

There was plenty of driftwood around, plenty of the sea-salted bark that makes a superior fire. In a couple of hours, all was ready. News had spread — somehow, even at such short notice, women began arriving with food. It was Ailo who took charge of this half-pagan ceremony — her Scandinavian blood, her upright carriage and flowing white hair made her a natural for the role of Widow of the Sea. Children ran about on the logs and were shooed away from the growing pyre, the shrouded, surprisingly meager bundle that was Eric. A coffee urn was supplied by one of the churches, and cartons of beer, bottles of alcohol of all sorts were left discreetly, for the time being, in the trunks of cars and the cabs of trucks.

The question arose of who would speak and who would light the pyre. The men who headed the preparations asked Juliet if she would do it. And Juliet, brittle and busy, handing out mugs of coffee, told them that they had it wrong — as the widow, she was supposed to throw herself into the flames. She actually laughed as she said this, and those who had asked her backed off, afraid that she was getting hysterical. The man who had often been Eric's partner in the boat agreed to do the lighting, but said that he was no speaker. It occurred to some that he would not have been a good choice anyway, since his wife was an evangelical Anglican, and he might have felt obliged to say things that would have distressed Eric, if he had been able to hear them. Then Ailo's husband offered. He was a little man who had been disfigured by a fire on a boat, years ago, a bitter socialist and atheist, and in his talk he rather lost track of Eric, except to claim him as a Brother in the Battle. He went on at surprising length, and this was ascribed, afterward, to the life that he led under the rule of Ailo. There was some restlessness in the crowd before he finally stopped speaking, some feeling that the event was not as splendid, or solemn, or heart-rending, as had been expected. But when the fire began to burn this feeling vanished, and there was great concentration, even, or especially, among the children, until the moment when one of the men cried, "Get the kids out of here." This was when the flames had reached the body, and there was a realization, rather late, that consumption of fat, of heart and kidneys and liver, might produce explosive or sizzling noises that would be disconcerting to hear. A good many of the children were hauled away by their mothers — some willingly, some to their dismay. And the final act of the fire became a mostly male ceremony. Slightly scandalous, though not in any way illegal.

Juliet stayed, wide-eyed, rocking on her haunches, face pressed against the heat. She was not quite there. She thought of whoever it was — Trelawny? — snatching Shelley's heart out of the flames. The heart, with its long history of significance. Strange to think how even at that time, not so long ago, one fleshly organ had been thought so precious, the site of courage and love. It was just flesh burning. Not Eric.

Penelope knew nothing of what was going on. There was a short item in the Vancouver paper — not about the burning on the beach, of course, just about the drowning — but no newspapers or radio reports reached her, deep in the Kootenay Mountains. When she got back to Vancouver, she phoned home from her friend Heather's house. Christa answered — she had got back from California too late for the ceremony, but was staying with Juliet, and helping as much as she could. She told Penelope that Juliet was not there — it was a lie — and asked to speak to Heather's mother. She explained what had happened and said that she would be driving Juliet to Vancouver — they would leave at once — and Juliet would tell Penelope herself when they got there.

Christa dropped Juliet at the house where Penelope was, and Juliet went inside alone. Penelope was waiting in the sunroom. She received the news with an expression of fright, then — when Juliet put her arms around her — of something like embarrassment. Perhaps in Heather's house, in the white-and-green-and-orange sunroom, with Heather's brothers shooting baskets in the backyard, news so dire could hardly penetrate. The burning was not mentioned — in this house and neighborhood it would have seemed uncivilized, grotesque. In this house, also, Juliet's manner was more sprightly than she intended.

Heather's mother entered after a tiny knock, with glasses of iced tea. Penelope gulped hers down and went to join Heather, who had been lurking in the hall. Heather's mother then had a talk with Juliet. She apologized for intruding with practical matters but said that time was short. She and Heather's father were driving east in a few days' time to see relatives. They would be gone for a month, and had planned to take Heather with them. But now Heather had decided that she did not want to go; she had begged to stay here in the house, with Penelope. A fourteen-year-old and a thirteen-year-old could not be left alone in the house, and it had occurred to her that Juliet might like some time away from Whale Bay, a respite, after what she had been through. After her tragic loss.

So Juliet found herself living in a different world, in a large spotless house, brightly and thoughtfully decorated, with what are called conveniences — but to her were luxuries — on every hand. This on a curving street lined with similar houses, behind trimmed bushes and extravagant flower beds. Even the weather, for that month, was flawless — warm, breezy, dazzling. Heather and Penelope went swimming, played badminton in the backyard, went to the movies, baked cookies, gorged, dieted, worked on their tans, filled the house with music whose lyrics seemed to Juliet sappy and irritating, sometimes invited girlfriends over, did not exactly invite boys but held long, taunting, aimless conversations with those who passed the house or gathered next door. By chance, Juliet heard Penelope say to one of the visiting girls, "Well, I hardly knew him really."

She was speaking about her father.

How strange.

She had never been afraid to go out in the boat, as Juliet was, when there was a chop on the water. She had pestered Eric to take her and was often successful. Following after him, in her businesslike orange life jacket, carrying what gear she could manage, Penelope always wore an expression of particular seriousness and dedication. She took note of the setting of the traps and became skillful, quick, and ruthless at the deheading and bagging of the catch. At a certain stage of her childhood — say, from eight to eleven — she had always said that she was going to have her own boat when she grew up. And Juliet had thought it was possible that Penelope would choose that life, since she was bright but not bookish, and exuberantly physical and brave. But Eric, out of Penelope's hearing, said that he hoped the idea would wear off; he wouldn't wish the life on anybody. He spoke about the hardship and uncertainty that he had chosen, although, at the same time, he took pride, Juliet thought, in those very things.

And now he had been dismissed. By Penelope, who had recently painted her toenails purple and was sporting a temporary tattoo on her midriff. He who had filled her life. She had dismissed him.

But Juliet was doing the same thing, in a way. Of course, she was busy looking for a job and a place to live. She had already put the house in Whale Bay up for sale — she could not imagine staying there now. She had sold the truck and given away Eric's tools, and the traps that had been recovered, and the dinghy. Ailo had come and taken the dog.

Juliet had applied for a job in the reference department of the university library and a job at the public library, and she had a feeling that she would get one or the other. She began to look for an apartment. The cleanness, tidiness, and manageability of city life kept surprising her. This was how people lived where men's work did not take place out-of-doors, and where the various operations connected with it did not end up indoors. Where the weather might be a factor in your mood but never in your life, where such dire matters as the changing habits and availability of prawns or salmon were merely interesting, or not remarked upon at all. The life she had been leading at Whale Bay, such a short time ago, seemed haphazard, cluttered, exhausting, by comparison. And she herself was cleansed of the moods of the last months — she was lively and capable, and better-looking.

Eric should see her now.

She thought about Eric in this way all the time. It was not that she failed to remember that he was dead — that did not happen for a moment. But nevertheless she kept referring to him, in her mind, as if he were still the person to whom her existence mattered more than it could to anyone else. As if he were still the person in whose eyes she hoped to shine. Also the person to whom she presented arguments, information, surprises. This was such a habit with her, and took place so automatically, that the fact of his death did not seem to interfere with it.

Nor was their last quarrel entirely resolved. She held him to account, still, for his betrayal. When she flaunted herself a little now, it was in response to that.

The storm, the recovery of the body, the burning on the beach — that was all like a pageant that she had been compelled to watch and to believe in. It still had nothing to do with Eric and herself.

She got the job at the university reference library; she found a two-bedroom apartment that she could just afford; Penelope went back to Torrance House as a day student. Their affairs at Whale Bay were wound up, their life there finished. Even Christa was moving out, coming to Vancouver in the spring.

On a day before Christa or spring had arrived, a day in February, Juliet stood in the shelter at the campus bus stop after work. The day's rain had stopped, there was a band of clear sky in the west, red where the sun had gone down, out over the Strait of Georgia. This sign of lengthening days, the promise of a change of season, had an effect on her that was unexpected and crushing.

She realized that Eric was dead.

It was as if all this time, while she was in Vancouver, he had been waiting for her somewhere else, waiting to see if she would resume her life with him. As if being with him were an option that had stayed open. Her life since she came to Vancouver had been lived against a backdrop of Eric, without her having quite understood that Eric did not exist. That nothing of him existed. That even the memory of him, in the daily and ordinary world, was in retreat.

So this was grief. She felt as if a sack of cement had been poured into her and quickly hardened. She could barely move. Getting onto the bus, getting off the bus, walking half a block to her building was like climbing a cliff. And now she had to hide this from Penelope.

At the supper table she began to shake. She could not loosen her fingers to drop her knife and fork. Penelope came around the table and pried her hands open. She said, "It's Dad, isn't it?"

Juliet afterward told a few people — Christa was one — that these seemed the most utterly absolving, the most tender words that anybody had ever said to her.

Penelope ran her cool hands up and down the insides of Juliet's arms. She phoned the library the next day to say that her mother was sick, and she took care of her for a couple of days, staying home from school until Juliet had recovered. Or at least until the worst was over.

During those days, Juliet told Penelope everything. About Christa, the fight, the burning on the beach (which she had so far managed, almost miraculously, to conceal from her). Everything.

"I shouldn't burden you with all this."

Penelope said, "Yeah, well, maybe not." But added staunchly, "I forgive you. I guess I'm not a baby."

Juliet went back into the world. The sort of fit she had had at the bus stop recurred, but never so powerfully.

Through her work at the library, she met some people from the provincial television channel and took a job they offered. She had worked there for about a year when she began to do interviews. All the indiscriminate reading she'd done for years (and that Ailo had so disapproved of, in her days at Whale Bay), all the bits and pieces of information she'd picked up, her random appetite and quick assimilation, now came in handy. She cultivated a self-deprecating, faintly teasing manner that seemed to go over well. On camera, few things fazed her. But at home she would march back and forth, letting out whimpers or curses as she recalled some perceived glitch or fluster or, worse still, a mispronunciation.

After five years, the birthday cards stopped coming.

"It doesn't mean anything," Christa said. "They were just to tell you that she's alive somewhere. Now she figures you've got the message. She trusts you not to send some tracker after her. That's all."

"Did I put too much on her?"

"Oh, Jule."

"I don't mean just with Eric dying. Other men, later. I let her see too much misery. My stupid misery."

For Juliet had had two affairs during the years that Penelope was between fourteen and twenty-one, and during both of these she had managed to fall hectically in love, in a way that left her ashamed afterward. One of the men was much older than she, and solidly married. The other was a good deal younger, and alarmed by her ready emotions. Later she wondered at these herself. She really had cared nothing for him, she said.

"I didn't think you did," said Christa, who was tired. "I don't know."

"Oh, Christ. I was such a fool. I don't get like that about men anymore. Do I?"

"No, Jule. No." Christa did not mention that this might be due to a lack of candidates.

"Actually, I didn't do anything so terrible," Juliet said then, brightening up. "Why do I keep lamenting that it's my fault? She's a conundrum, that's all. I need to face that. A conundrum and a cold fish," she added, in a parody of resolution.

"No," Christa said.

"No," Juliet said. "I know that's not true."

After the second June had passed without any word, Juliet decided to move. She found an apartment in a high-rise building in the West End. She meant to throw away the contents of Penelope's room, but in the end she stuffed it all into garbage bags and carried it with her. She had only one bedroom here, but there was storage space in the basement.

She took up jogging, in Stanley Park. She seldom mentioned Penelope, even to Christa. She had a boyfriend now, who had never heard anything about her daughter.

Christa grew thinner and moodier. Quite suddenly, one January, she died.

You don't go on forever appearing on television. However agreeable the viewers have found your face, there comes a time when they'd prefer somebody new. Juliet was offered other jobs — researching, writing voice-overs for nature shows — but she refused them cheerfully, describing herself as in need of a total change. Her boyfriend got a teaching job in China. She went back to classical studies — an even smaller department than it used to be. She intended to resume writing her thesis, to get her Ph.D. She moved out of the high-rise apartment and into a bachelor flat to save money.

The flat was in the basement of a house, but the sliding doors at the back opened out at ground level. And there she had a little brick-paved patio, a trellis with sweet peas and clematis, herbs and flowers in pots. For the first time in her life and in a very small way, she was a gardener.

Sometimes people said to her — in stores or on the campus bus — "Excuse me, but your face is so familiar," or "Aren't you the lady that used to be on television?" But after a year or so this passed. She spent a lot of time sitting and reading, drinking coffee at a sidewalk café, and nobody noticed her. She let her hair grow out. It was a silvery brown now, fine and wavy.

She did not have room to have people to dinner anymore, and she had lost interest in recipes. She ate meals that were nourishing enough, but monotonous. Without exactly meaning to, she lost contact with most of her friends.

It was no wonder. She lived a life now that was as different as possible from the life of the public, vivacious, concerned, endlessly well-informed woman she had been. She lived among books, reading through most of her waking hours, often being compelled to deepen, to alter, whatever premise she had started with. She sometimes missed the world news for a week at a time.

She had given up on her old thesis and become interested in some writers referred to as the Greek novelists, whose work came rather late in the history of Greek literature (starting in the first century B.C.E., as she had now learned to call it, and continuing into the early Middle Ages). Aristides, Longus, Heliodorus, Achilles Tatius. Much of their work was lost or fragmentary and was also reported to be indecent. But there was a romance written by Heliodorus, called the *Aethiopica* (originally stored in a private library and retrieved during the siege of Buda), which had been known in Europe since it was printed, in Basel, in 1534.

In this story, the queen of Ethiopia gives birth to a white baby and is afraid that she will be accused of adultery. So she puts the child, a daughter, in the care of the gymnosophists — that is, the naked philosophers, who are hermits and mystics. The girl, who is called Charicleia, is eventually taken to Delphi, where she becomes one of the priestesses of Artemis. There she meets a noble Thessalian named Theagenes, who falls in love with her and, with the help of a clever Egyptian, carries her off. The Ethiopian queen, as it turns out, has never ceased to long for her daughter and has hired this very Egyptian to search for her. Mischance and adventures continue until all the main characters meet at Meroë and Charicleia is rescued — rescued once more — just as she is about to be sacrificed by her own father.

Interesting themes were as thick as flies here, and the tale had a natural continuing fascination for Juliet. Particularly the part about the gymnosophists. She tried to find out as much as she could about these people — who were usually referred to as Hindu philosophers. Was India, in this case, presumed to be adjacent to Ethiopia? No — Heliodorus came late enough to know his geography better than that. The gymnosophists were wanderers, far spread, attracting and repelling those they lived among, with their ironclad devotion to purity of life and thought, their contempt for possessions, even for clothing and food. Whatever happened to her later, a girl who had spent time among them might well be left with some perverse hankering for a bare, ecstatic life.

Juliet had made a new friend, named Larry. He taught Greek, and he let Juliet store the garbage bags full of Penelope's belongings in the basement of his house. He liked to imagine how they might make the *Aethiopica* into a musical. Juliet collaborated in this fantasy, even to the point of making up some marvelously silly songs and preposterous stage effects. But she was secretly drawn to devising a different ending to the story, one that would involve renunciation, and a backward search, in which the girl would be sure to meet fakes and charlatans, impostors, shabby imitations of what she was really looking for. Which was reconciliation, at last, with the erring, repentant, essentially greathearted queen of Ethiopia.

Juliet was almost certain that she had seen Mother Shipton here in Vancouver. She had taken some clothes that she would never wear again (her wardrobe had grown increasingly utilitarian) to a Salvation Army thrift store, and as she set the bag down in the receiving room she saw a fat old woman in a muumuu, fixing tags onto trousers. The woman was chatting with the other workers — she had the air of a supervisor, a cheerful but vigilant overseer, or perhaps the air of a woman who would assume that role, whether she had any official superiority or not.

If she was in fact Mother Shipton, she had come down in the world. But not by very much. For if she was Mother Shipton, would she not have such reserves of buoyancy and self-approbation as to make real downfall impossible?

Reserves of advice, pernicious advice, as well.

She came to us here in great hunger.

Juliet had told Larry about Penelope. She had to have one person who knew.

"Should I have talked to her about a noble life?" she said. "Sacrifice? Opening your heart to the needs of strangers? I never thought of it. I must have acted as if it would be good enough if she turned out like me."

Larry wanted nothing from Juliet but her friendship and good humor. He was what used to be called an old-fashioned bachelor, asexual as far as she could tell (but probably she could not tell far enough), squeamish about any personal revelations, endlessly entertaining.

Two other men had appeared who wanted more from her. One of them she had met when he sat down at her sidewalk table. He was a recent widower. She liked him, but his loneliness was so raw and his pursuit of her so desperate that she became alarmed.

The other man was Christa's brother Gary, whom Juliet had met several times while Christa was alive. His company suited her — in many ways he was like Christa. His marriage had ended long ago, and he was not desperate — in fact, she knew from Christa that there had been women ready to marry him, whom he had avoided. But he was too rational — his choice of her verged on being cold-blooded. There was something humiliating about it. But why humiliating? It was not as if she loved him.

It was while she was still seeing Gary that she ran into Heather, on a downtown street. Juliet and Gary had just come out of a cinema where they had seen an early-evening movie, and they were talking about where to go for dinner. It was a warm night in summer, the light not yet gone from the sky.

A woman detached herself from a group on the sidewalk and came straight at Juliet. A thin woman, perhaps in her late thirties. Fashionable, with taffy streaks in her dark hair.

"Mrs. Porteous. Mrs. Porteous."

Juliet knew the voice, though she did not quite know the face. Heather.

"This is incredible," Heather said. "I'm here for three days and I'm leaving tomorrow. My husband's at a conference. I was just thinking that I hardly know anybody here anymore and then I turn around and see you."

Juliet asked her where she was living now and she said, "Connecticut. And just about three weeks ago I was visiting Josh — you remember my brother Josh? — I was visiting Josh and his family in

Edmonton, and I ran into Penelope. Just like this, on the street. No — actually, it was in the mall, that humongous mall they have. She had a couple of her kids with her — she'd brought them down to get uniforms for that school they go to. The boys. We were both flabbergasted. I didn't know her right away, but she recognized me. She'd flown down, of course. From that place way up north. But she says it's quite civilized, really. And she said that you were still living here. But I'm with these friends — they're my husband's friends — and I really haven't had time to ring you up."

Juliet made some gesture to say that of course there had not been time and she had not expected to be rung up.

She asked how many children Heather had.

"Three. They're all monsters. I hope they grow up in a hurry. But my life's a picnic compared with Penelope's. *Five.*"

"Yes."

"I have to run now — we're going to see a movie. But it was great meeting you like this. My mom and dad moved to White Rock. They used to see you all the time on TV. They used to brag to their friends that you'd lived in our house. They say you're not on anymore. Did you get sick of it?"

"Something like that."

"I'm coming, I'm coming." She hugged and kissed Juliet, the way everybody did now, and ran to join her companions.

So. Penelope did not live in Edmonton — she had *come down* to Edmonton. Flown down. That meant she must live in Whitehorse or Yellowknife. Where else was there that she could describe as "quite civilized"? Maybe she was being ironical, mocking Heather a bit, when she said that.

She had five children, and two, at least, were boys. They were being outfitted with school uniforms. That meant a private school. That meant money.

Heather had not known Penelope at first. Did that mean that she had aged? That she was out of shape after five pregnancies, that she had not *taken care of herself*? As Heather had. As Juliet had, to a certain extent. That Penelope was one of those women to whom the whole idea of such a struggle seemed ridiculous, a confession of insecurity? Or just something that she had no time for — far outside of her consideration?

Juliet had thought of Penelope as being involved with transcendentalists, as having become a mystic and spending her life in contemplation. Or else — rather the opposite, but still radically simple and pure — earning her living in a rough and risky way, fishing, perhaps with a husband, perhaps with some husky little children, in the cold waters of the Inside Passage off the British Columbia coast.

Not at all. She was living the life of a prosperous practical matron. Married to a doctor, maybe, or to one of those civil servants who were managing the northern parts of the country just as their control was being gradually, but with some fanfare, relinquished to the native people. If she ever met Penelope again they would laugh about how wrong she had been. When they talked about their weird separate meetings with Heather, they would laugh.

No. No. The fact was that she had already laughed too much around Penelope. Too many things had been jokes. Just as too many things — personal things, loves that were maybe just self-gratification — had been tragedies. She had been lacking in motherly inhibitions and propriety and self-control.

Penelope had told Heather that she, Juliet, was still living in Vancouver. She had not said anything about the breach. Surely not. If she had, Heather would not have spoken so easily.

How did Penelope know that she was still here, unless she had checked in the phone directory? And, if she had, what did that mean?

Nothing. Don't make it mean anything.

She walked to the curb to join Gary, who had tactfully moved away from the scene of the reunion.

Whitehorse, Yellowknife. It was painful indeed to know the names of these places — places she could fly to. Places where she could loiter in the streets, devise plans for catching glimpses.

But she was not so mad. She must not be so mad.

At dinner, she realized that the news she had just absorbed had put her into a better situation for marrying Gary, or living with him — whatever it was that he wanted. There was nothing to worry about, or wait for, concerning Penelope. Penelope was not a phantom. She was safe, as far as anybody is safe, and she was probably as happy as anybody is happy. She had detached herself from Juliet and very likely from the memory of Juliet, and Juliet could not do anything but detach herself in turn.

But she had told Heather that Juliet was living in Vancouver. Had she said "Juliet"? Or "Mother"? "My mother"?

Juliet told Gary that Heather was the child of old friends. She had never spoken to him about Penelope, and he had never given any sign of knowing about Penelope's existence. It was possible that Christa had told him, and he had remained silent out of the feeling that it was none of his business. Or that he had forgotten. Or that Christa had never mentioned anything about Penelope, not even her name.

If Juliet were to live with him, the fact of Penelope would never surface — Penelope would not exist.

Nor did Penelope exist. The Penelope that Juliet sought was gone. The woman Heather had spotted in Edmonton, the mother who had flown down with her sons to get school uniforms, who had changed in face and body so that Heather did not recognize her, was nobody Juliet knew.

Did Juliet believe this?

If Gary saw that she was agitated, he pretended not to notice. But it was probably on this evening that they both understood that they would not be together. If it had been possible for them to be together, she might have said to him that night:

My daughter went away without telling me goodbye, and in fact she probably did not know then that she was going. She did not know that it was for good. Then gradually I believe it dawned on her how much she wanted to stay away. It was just the way that she found to manage her life.

It's maybe the explaining to me she can't face. Or has no time for, really. You know, we always have the idea that there is this reason or that reason. And I could tell you plenty about what I did wrong. But I think the reason may not be something so easily dug out. More like some kind of purity in her nature. Yes. Some fineness and strictness and purity, some rock-hard honesty in her.

My father used to say of someone he disliked that he had no use for that person. Couldn't those words mean simply what they say? Penelope does not have a use for me.

Or can't stand me.

Juliet has friends — not so many now, but friends. Larry continues to visit and to make jokes. She keeps on with her studies. The word *studies* does not seem to describe very well what she does — *investigations* would be better.

And, being short of money, she works some hours a week at the café where she used to spend so much time at the sidewalk table.

She finds this job a good balance for her involvement with the old Greeks — so much so that she believes she wouldn't quit even if she could afford to.

She keeps on hoping for a word from Penelope, but not in any strenuous way. She hopes, as people who know better hope for undeserved blessings, spontaneous remissions, or things of that sort.

TOM BISSELL

Death Defier

FROM VIRGINIA QUARTERLY REVIEW

GRAVES HAD BEEN SICK FOR THREE DAYS when, on the long, straight highway between Mazar and Kunduz, a dark blue truck coming toward them shed its rear wheel in a spray of orange-yellow sparks. The wheel, as though excited by its sudden liberty, bounced twice not very high and once very high and hit their windshield with a damp crack. "Christ!" Donk called out from the back seat. The driver, much too late, wrenched on the steering wheel, and they fishtailed and then spun out into the dunes alongside the road. Against one of the higher sandbanks the Corolla slammed to a dusty halt. Sand as soft and pale as flour poured into the partially open windows. The shattered but still intact windshield sagged like netting. After a moment Donk touched his forehead, his eyebrow bristles as tender as split stitches. Thin, watery blood streaked down his fingers.

From the front passenger seat Graves asked if everyone — Donk, Hassan, the driver — was all right. No one spoke. Graves sighed. "Glad to hear it." He gave his dune-pinned door two small, impotent outward pushes, then spent the next few moments staring out the splintery windshield. The air-freshener canister that had been suckered to the windshield lay quietly frothing lilac-scented foam in Graves's lap. The spun-around Corolla now faced Kunduz, the city they had been trying to escape. "I'm glad I'm not a superstitious man," Graves said at last. The driver's hands were still gripped around the steering wheel.

Donk climbed out on the Corolla's open side, cupping his throbbing eye socket and leaning forward, watching his blood patter onto the sand in perfect red globules. He did not have the faintest idea what he had struck his head against until Hassan, wincing and rubbing his shoulder, muscled his way out of the car behind him. Hassan looked at Donk and shrug-smiled, his eyes rimmed with such a fine black line they looked as if they had been Maybellined. His solid belly filled the stretched sack of his maroon cardigan sweater, and his powder-blue *shalwar khameez* — the billowy national pants of Afghanistan, draped front and back with a flap of cloth that resembled an untied apron — were splattered with Donk's blood. The whole effect gave Hassan an emergency-room air. Donk did not return Hassan's smile. The night before, in Kunduz, after having a bite of Spam and stale brie in the rented compound of an Agence France Presse correspondent, Donk and Graves found their hotel room had been robbed. Graves had lost many personal items, a few hundred dollars, and his laptop, while Donk had parted with virtually all of his photographic equipment, including an irreplaceably good wide lens he had purchased in London on the way over. Hassan, charged with watching the room while they were out, claimed to have abandoned his sentry duties only once, for five minutes, to go to the bathroom. He had been greatly depressed since the robbery. Donk was fairly certain Hassan had robbed them.

Donk fastened around his head the white scarf he had picked up in Kunduz's bazaar. Afghan men tended to wear their scarves atop their heads in vaguely muffin-shaped bundles or around their necks with aviator flair. Afghanistan's troublous Arab guests, on the other hand, were said to tie the scarves around their skulls with baldness-mimicking tightness, the hem just millimeters above their eyes while the scarf's tasseled remainder trailed down their spines. This was called "terrorist style," and Donk adopted it now. It was the only way he could think to keep the blood out of his eyes. He also sort of liked how it looked.

"Hassan," Graves snapped as he climbed out of the Corolla. It was an order, and Graves — a tall, thin Brit with an illusionless, razor-burned face — had a voice seemingly engineered to give orders. He had thick brown hair and the ruined teeth of a man who had spent a large amount of time in the unfluoridated parts of the world. His hands were as filthy as the long sleeves of his white thermal underwear top, though his big fingernails seemed as bright and smooth as shells. Graves made his way to the truck, twenty yards down the road and askew on its three remaining wheels. He glanced down at the tire, innocently at rest in the middle of the highway, that had shattered the Corolla's windshield. Donk noted that Graves looked as stately as was imaginable for a sick man wearing one of those silly war-reporter khaki vests and red Chuck Taylor All Stars. Hassan rushed to catch up to him, as Graves had not waited.

This left Donk and the driver, a kind of bear-man miracle with moist brown eyes and a beard it was hard to imagine he had not been born with, to have a look under the Corolla and assess the damage. Monoglots both, they could do little better than exchange artfully inflected grunts. Nothing seemed visibly wrong. The axle, for instance, was not bent, which had been Donk's greatest fear. But the steering wheel refused to budge, and the ignition responded to the driver's twist with a click.

"Hmn," Donk consoled him.

"Mmn," the driver agreed.

Donk looked over at Graves, who was speaking through Hassan to the truck's stranded driver. Graves was nodding with exquisitely false patience as the curly-haired boy, who looked no older than twenty, grasped his head with both hands and then waved his arms around at the desert in huge gestures of innocence. Bursts of dune-skimmed sand whistled across the three of them. The bed of the boy's truck was piled ten-deep with white bags of internationally donated wheat. His truck, Donk noticed, was not marked with any aid group's peaceable ideogram.

It had been a strange morning, even by Donk's standards. A few hours ago some "nasties," as Graves called them, had appeared on the outskirts of Kunduz, though they were supposed to have been driven out of the area a week ago. In fact, they were supposed to have been surrendering. Graves and Donk had jumped out of bed and rushed downstairs into the still-dark autumn morning air to see what they could see, hopping around barefoot on the frigid concrete. The battle was still far away, the small, faint pops of gunfire sounding as dry as firecrackers. It appeared that, after some desultory return fire, Kunduz's commander called in an American air strike. The great birds appeared with vengeful instantaneousness and screamed across the city sky. The sound was terrific, atmosphere-shredding, and then they were gone. The horizon, a few moments later, burped up great dust bulbs. But within the hour the gunfire had moved closer. The well-armed defenders of Kunduz had been scrambling everywhere as Donk and Graves packed up what little remained of their gear into this hastily arranged taxi and sped out of town to the more securely liberated city of Mazar.

"Bloody fool," Graves said now, when he walked back over to Donk. He was speaking of the curly-haired boy.

"Call him a wog if it makes you feel better," Donk said. "I don't mind."

Graves cast a quick look back at the boy, now squatting beside his hobbled truck and chatting with Hassan. "He's stolen that wheat, you know."

"Where was he going?"

"He won't say."

"What's he doing now?"

"He's going to wait here, he says. I told him there were nasties about. Bloody fool." He looked at Donk, his face softened by sudden concern. "How's that eye, then?"

"Bleeding."

Graves leaned into him optometristically, trying to inspect the messy wound through the do-rag. "Nasty," he said finally, pulling away. "How many wars did you say you've covered?"

"Like war wars? Shooting wars? Or just wars?"

Graves nodded. "Shooting wars."

"Not counting this one, three. But I've never been shot at until today." While they were leaving Kunduz their Corolla had been hit with a short burst of Kalashnikov fire, though it was unclear whether the bullets were intended for them. The driver had used the strafe — it sounded and felt like a flurry of ball-peen hammer strikes — to establish a median traveling speed of 125 miles per hour. They had very nearly plowed over a little boy and his pony just before the city's strangely empty westernmost checkpoint.

"And how did you find it?" Graves asked, as though genuinely curious.

"I found it like getting shot at."

"That was rather how I found it." Graves's face pinched with fresh discomfort. He sighed, then seemed to go paler. His eyelids were sweaty. Graves stepped toward the Corolla searchingly, arms out, and lowered himself onto the bumper. "Think I need a rest." The driver fetched a straw-covered red blanket from the Corolla and wrapped it around Graves's shoulders.

They had been in Kunduz for two days when Donk noticed Graves tenderly hugging himself, no matter the heat thrown off by their hotel room's oil-burning stove. His pallor grayed by the day, and soon he was having trouble seeing. Initially Graves had not been concerned. They went about their business of covering the war, Donk snapping Kunduz's ragtag liberators and the dead-eyed prisoners locked up in one of the city's old granaries, Graves reading ten hours' worth of CNN updates a day on his laptop and worrying over his past, present, and future need to "file." But his fever worsened, and he took a day's bed rest while Donk toured Kunduz on foot with the city's local commander, a happily brutal man who twice tried selling Donk a horse. When Donk returned to the hotel a few minutes before curfew that evening, he found Graves twisted up in his vomit-stained sheets, his pillow lying in a sad crumple across the room. "Deborah," Graves had mumbled when Donk stirred him. "Listen. Turn the toaster? Please turn the toaster?"

Donk did not know Graves well. He had met him only ten days ago in Pyanj, Tajikistan, where many of the journalists were dovetailing stories by day and playing poker with worthless Tajik rubles by night. All were waiting for official clearance before venturing into Afghanistan. Graves — with an impatience typical of print journalists, their eyewitness being more perishable — elected to cast a few pearly incentives at the feet of the swinish border guards and asked Donk if he wanted to tag along. Donk, dispatched here by a British newsweekly, was under no real pressure to get in. His mandate was not one of breaking news but of chronicling the country's demotic wartime realities. He did not even have a return flight booked. But he agreed.

Donk did not regret following Graves, even as he forced mefloquine hydrochloride tablets into his mouth, crusty with stomach ejecta, splashing in some canteen water to chase them. Graves, Donk was certain, had malaria, even though it was late November, a season at the outer edge of probability for contracting the disease, and even though he knew Graves had been taking mefloquine since October. The next day Donk convinced one of Kunduz's aid workers — a grim, black Belgian — to give him a small cache of chloroquine phosphate pills, as mefloquine was mostly useful as a malaria preventative. The chloroquine seemed to help, and Graves, still as shivery as a foundling, had recommenced with his worries about filing a story. Graves was rather picky with his stories, seeking only narratives that presented this war in its least inspiring light. Unfortunately, Kunduz seemed fairly secure and the people weirdly grateful. Indeed, despite predictions of a long, bloody, province-by-province conflict, 60 percent of the country had fallen to American-led forces in this, the war's fourth week.

After they were robbed Graves noted that his chloroquine pills were among the missing items. As the regrouped nasties waged this morning's hopeless surprise counterattack, neither Donk nor Graves had the presence of mind to beg more pills before they left, though Donk was fairly certain the aid workers would have pulled out of Kunduz too. That one could simply leave a firefight and come back a bit later was one of the odder things about this shadowy war. Roads were safe one day, suicide the next. Warlords thought to be relatively trustworthy one week were reported to have personally overseen the meticulous looting of an aid-group warehouse the next. All of this seemed designed to prevent anyone from actually fighting. From the little Donk had seen and heard, gun battles here seemed founded upon one's ability to spray bullets blindly around rocks and walls and then beat a quick, spectacular retreat.

"How do you feel?" Donk asked Graves now.

Graves, still sitting on the bumper, flashed his ruined teeth. The dirty wind had given his eyes a teary under-rim. "How do I look?"

"Fading. We need to get you somewhere."

Graves looked down, angrily blinking away his eyes' moisture. "Where are we, anyway?"

"About an hour outside Kunduz."

"That's another hour from Mazar?"

"Roughly."

Graves glanced around, but the dunes were too high to see anything but the road, and the road was too straight to reveal anything but the dunes. "Not far enough, I imagine."

"Probably not."

"We could hitch. Someone is bound to be along."

"Someone is. *Who* is the problem."

"You don't think the poor devils would use *roads,* for God's sake, do you? This far north? They'd be bombed within minutes."

"I have no idea."

With shiatsu delicacy Graves massaged his face with his fingertips. A bright bracelet of untanned flesh encircled his wrist.

Graves's watch, too, had been stolen. His hands fell into his lap then, and he sighed. "I hope you're not worried, Duncan."

Donk decided not to remind Graves, for what would have been the fortieth time, that he preferred to be called Donk. The nickname — a diminutive form of *donkey* — dated to one of the boyhood camping trips he and his father and older brother, Jason, used to take every year in the Porcupine Mountains of Michigan's Upper Peninsula. If he had never especially liked the name, he had come to understand himself through its drab prism. DONK ST. PIERRE was stamped in raised black type upon his ivory business card; it was the name above which his photographs were today published. People often mistook his work for that of some Flemish eccentric. When colleagues first met him, something Donk called The Moment inescapably came to pass. Faced not with a tall, spectral, chain-smoking European but a short, overweight midwesterner with frizzy black hair and childishly small hands, their smiles faded, their eyes crumpled, and a discreet little sound died just past their glottis. "I'm not worried," Donk said. "I'll be even less worried when we figure out where we're going."

Graves stared at Donk as though weighing him in some crucial balance. "You seemed rather jittery in Pyanj. Wasn't sure you'd be up to this."

When Donk said nothing, Graves stood, listing momentarily before he steadied himself against the Corolla with one hand. Hassan loped back over to them, grinning beneath the pressure of one of his patented "discoveries," always uncanny in their relative uselessness. "My friends, I have discovered that nearby there is village. Good village, the driver says. Safe, friendly village. We will be welcome there. He told for me the way. Seven, eight kilometers."

Although this was much better information than Hassan was usually able to manage, Graves's expression was sour. Sweat dripped off his nose, and he was breathing hard. Merely standing had wiped him out. "Did he tell you that, or did you ask him?"

Hassan seemed puzzled. "I ask-ed him. Why?"

"Because, Hassan, information is only as reliable as the question that creates it."

"Mister Graves, I am not understanding you."

"He's saying," Donk said, "that our wheat-stealing friend may be telling us to go somewhere we shouldn't."

Hassan looked at them both in horror. "My friends, *no*. This is not possible. He is good man. And we are gracious, hospitable people here. We would never —"

Graves, cruelly, was ignoring this. "How's the car?"

Donk shook his head. "Wheel won't turn, engine won't start. Back wheels are buried in sand. And there's the windshield issue. Other than that, it's ready to go."

Graves walked out into the middle of the highway, drawing the blanket up over his head. Each end of the road streaked off into a troubling desert nothingness and appeared to tunnel into the horizon itself. It was before noon in northern Afghanistan, and the country felt as empty and skull-white as a moon. Not our familiar moon but another, harder, stranger moon. Above, the clouds were like little white bubbles of soap that had been incompletely sponged off the hard slate of the blue morning sky. Donk was compelled to wonder if nothingness and trouble were not, in fact, indistinguishable. Graves marched back over to the Corolla and savagely yanked his duffle from the front seat. "We walk to this village, then."

When it became apparent to the driver that they were leaving, he spoke up, clearly agitated. Hassan translated. "He says he won't leave his car."

"I don't blame him," Graves said, and peeled off three twenties to pay the man.

After leaving the main highway they walked along a scarred, inattentively paved road toward the village Hassan had promised was only six or seven, or was it eleven, kilometers away. Human Conflict, Donk thought, rather abstractly. It was one of his lively but undisciplined mind's fascinations. It differed from land to land, as faces differed. But the basic elements (ears, nose, mouth; aid workers, chaos, exhilaration) were always the same. It was the one thing that survived every era, every philosophy, the one legacy each civilization surrendered to the next. For Donk, Human Conflict was curiously life-affirming, based as it was on avoiding death — indeed, on inflicting death preemptively on others. He loved Human Conflict not as an ideal but as a milieu, a state of mind one absorbed but was not absorbed by, the crucial difference between combatants and non-. His love of Human Conflict was as unapologetic as it was without nuance. He simply *enjoyed* it. "Duncan," a therapist had once asked him, "have you ever heard of the term *chronic habitual suicide?*" Donk never saw that therapist, or any other, again.

He kicked from his path a billiard-ball-sized chunk of concrete. How was it that these people, the Afghans, could, for two hundred years, hold off or successfully evade several of the world's most go-getting empires and not find it within themselves to pave a fucking road? And yet somehow Afghanistan was, at least for the time being, the world's most significant place. Human Conflict had a way of doing that too. He remembered back two weeks ago to a press conference in the Presidential Palace in Tashkent, the capital of neighboring Uzbekistan, where the fragrant, rested-looking journalists who had arrived with the American secretary of state had surrounded him. Donk had taken his establishing shots of the secretary — looking determined and unusually Vulcan behind his press-conference podium — and quickly withdrawn. In one of the palace's uninhabited corners he found a splendid globe as large as an underwater mine, all of its countries' names in Cyrillic. Central Asia was turned out toward the room; North America faced the wall. Seeing the planet displayed from that strange side had seemed to Donk as mistaken as an upside-down letter. But it was not wrong. That globe was in fact perfectly accurate.

Up ahead, Graves was walking more slowly now, almost shuffling. Donk was allowing Graves the lead largely because Graves needed the lead. He was one of those rare people one did not actually mind seeing take charge. But Graves, wrapped in his red blanket, looked little better than a confused pensioner. The sun momentarily withdrew behind one of the bigger bubbly cloud formations. The temperature dropped with shocking immediacy, the air suddenly as sharp as angel hair and the morning light going blotted and cottony. Donk watched Graves's shoelaces come slowly and then floppily untied. For some reason Donk was too embarrassed for Graves to say anything.

"Mister Donk," Hassan said quietly, drawing beside him. "Is Mister Graves all right?"

Donk managed a weak, testy smile. "Mister Graves is fine."

Hassan nodded. "May I, Mister Donk, ask you questions?"

"You may."

"Where were you born in America?"

"Near the Sea of Tranquility."

"I ask, what is your favorite food?"

"Blueberry filling."

"American women are very beautiful, they say. They say too they have much love."

"That's mostly true. One should only sleep with beautiful women, even though they have the least love. Write that down. With women it's all confidence, Hassan. Write that down, too. You might look at me and think, But this is a fat man! And it's true. But I grow on people. You're not writing."

"I hear that American women make many demands. Not like Afghan women."

"Did you steal my cameras?"

"Mister Donk! No!"

"That's not nice, you know," Graves said suddenly, glancing back. "Teasing the boy like that."

"I was wondering when I'd get your attention."

"Leave the boy alone, Duncan. He's dealt with enough bad information to last his entire lifetime."

"I am not a boy," Hassan said suddenly.

"Don't listen to him," Graves said to Hassan. "War's made Mister Duncan barmy."

"How are you feeling?" Donk asked Graves. "Any better?"

Graves dropped his eyes to his open palm. "I was just checking my cell phone again. Nothing." Some enigma of telecommunications had prevented his Nokia from functioning the moment they crossed into Afghanistan. He absently tried to put away the phone but missed his pocket. Graves stopped and stared at the Nokia, a plastic purple amethyst half buried in the sand. Donk scooped it up and handed it back to Graves, who nodded distantly. Suddenly the sky filled with a deep, nearly divine roar. Their three heads simultaneously tipped back. Nothing. American F/A-18s and F-14s were somewhere cutting through that high blue, releasing satellite- and laser-guided bombs or returning from dropping bombs or looking for new places to drop bombs. Graves shook his head, quick and hard, as though struggling to believe that these jets really existed. Only after the roar faded did they push on, all of them now walking Wizard-of-Oz abreast. Graves still seemed angry. "Sometimes," he said, "I wonder if all the oil companies and the American military purposefully create these fucking crises to justify launching all those pretty missiles and dropping all these dreadful expensive bombs. Air Force. Error Farce is more like it."

"Coalition troops," Donk reminded him. "Those could be British jets."

"Somehow, Duncan, I doubt that."

Donk swigged from his canteen and wiped his mouth with his forearm. Talking politics with Graves was like being handed an armful of eels and then being asked to pretend that they were bunnies. He did not typically mind arguing, certainly not with a European, especially about the relative merits of the Land of the Red, White, and Blue. But Graves did not seem up to it. Donk settled on what he hoped was a slightly less divisive topic. "I wonder if they caught him yet."

"They're not going to catch him. The first private from Iowa to find him is going to push him up against a cave wall and blow a hole in his skull." Graves seemed unable to take his eyes off his feet.

"Well," Donk said, "let's hope so."

Graves looked over at him with lucid, gaunt-faced disappointment. He snorted and returned his gaze to his Converse All Stars, their red fabric so dusty they now appeared pink. "I can't believe someone as educated as you would think that's appropriate."

"I'm not that educated." Donk noted that Graves was practically panting, his mouth open and his tongue peeking over the fenceposts of his lower front teeth. Donk touched him on the shoulder. "Graves, hey. You really look like you need to rest again."

Graves's reaction was to nod, stop, and collapse into a rough squat, his legs folding beneath him at an ugly, painful-looking angle. Donk handed Graves his canteen while Hassan, standing nearby, mashed some raisins into his mouth. Graves watched a chewing Hassan watch him for a while, then closed his eyes. "My head," he said. "Suddenly it's splitting."

"Malaria," Donk said, kneeling next to him. "The symptoms are cyclical. Headaches. Fever. Chills. The sweats."

"Yes," Graves said heavily. "I know. Until the little buggers have clogged my blood vessels. Goodbye, vital organs."

"Malaria isn't fatal," Donk said.

Graves shook his head. It occurred to Donk that Graves's face, which tapered slightly at his temples and swelled again at his jawline, was shaped rather like a foot. "Untreated malaria is often fatal."

Donk looked at him evenly. Graves's thermal underwear top had soaked through. The sharp curlicues of grayish hair that swirled in the hollow of Graves's throat sparkled with sweat. His skin was shinier than his eyes by quite a lot.

"Tell me something," Graves said suddenly. "Why were you so nervous-seeming in Pyanj?"

Donk sighed. "Because nothing was happening. When nothing is happening I get jumpy."

Graves nodded quickly. "I heard that about you."

"You did?"

"That was a splendid shot, you know. The dead Tajik woman in Dushanbe. Brains still leaking from her head. You were there — what? — three minutes after she was shot? I wonder, though. You see her when you sleep, Duncan?"

It was probably Donk's most famous photo, and his first real photo. The woman had been gunned down by Russian soldiers in the Tajik capital during one of the ugly, early paroxysms of street fighting. The Russians were in Tajikistan as peacekeepers after the Soviet collapse. Her death had been an accident, crossfire. She had known people were fighting on that street, but she walked down it anyway. You saw a lot of that in urban warfare. Chronic habitual suicide. In the photo her groceries were scattered beside her. One of her shoes was missing. A bit of her brain in the snow — just a bit, as though it were some glistening red fruit that had been spooned onto a bed of sugar — the rest shining wetly in a dark gash just above her ear. Her mouth was open. The photo had run on the wires all over the world and, from what he had heard, infuriated the Russian authorities, which explained the difficulty he always had getting into Russia. "I guess I'm not a very haunted person," Donk said finally.

Graves was still smiling in a manner Donk recognized for its casual hopelessness. It was a war zone look. He had seen it on aid workers' faces and correspondents' faces but most often on soldiers' faces. He had witnessed it, too, on the bearded faces of the POWs in Kunduz's granary. Hassan had stopped eating his raisins and now watched the two men. He saw it too — perhaps because, Donk thought, it was his own default expression.

"But you love death, though, Duncan, yes?" Graves asked. "You have to. We all do. That's why we do this, isn't it?"

Donk began to pat himself down in search of something. He did not know what. He disliked such emotional nudism. He stopped pawing himself then and, feeling not a little caught out, traced his finger around in the sand. He made a peace sign, an easy shape to make. "Graves, I have learned not to generalize much about people in our line of work. The best combat photographer I ever saw was the mother of two children."

"Russian?"

"Israeli."

Graves leaned forward slightly. "Do you know what Montaigne says?"

Donk neither moved nor breathed nor blinked. He heard *Montaigne* as *Montane.* "Can we walk again now?"

"Montaigne believed that death was easiest for those who thought about it the most. That way it was possible for a man to die resigned. 'The utility of living consists not in the length of days' — Montaigne said this — 'but in the use of time.'" Graves smiled again.

Donk decided to switch tacks. "Your Royal Illness," he said cheerfully, getting to his feet, "I bid you, rise and walk."

Graves merely sat there, shivering. His khaki vest looked two sizes too large for him, his hair no longer so thick-looking now that it was soaked to his skull, his snowy scalp showing through. Graves seemed reduced, as unsightly as a wet rodent. "Isn't it strange," he asked, "that in the midst of all this a man can die from a mosquito bite?"

Donk's voice hardened: "(A) Graves, give me a break. (B) You're not going to die."

He laughed, lightly. "Today, no. Probably not."

Donk had a thought. *Deborah. Turn the toaster.* This Deborah had to be Graves's girlfriend or common-law wife. The man did not seem traditional husband material, somehow. "Graves, you need to walk. For Deborah."

Graves's puzzled face lifted up, and for a moment he looked his imperious self again. "Who the devil is Deborah?"

"Mister Donk —" Hassan said urgently, all but pulling on Donk's sleeve.

"Graves," Donk said, "I *need* you to get *up.*"

Graves lay back, alone in his pain, his skull finding the pillow of his duffle bag. "It's my head, Duncan. I can't bloody *think.*"

"Mister Donk!" Hassan said, but it was too late. The Jeep was approaching in a cloud of dust.

*

The owner of the Jeep was a thirtyish man named Ahktar. He wore blue jeans and a thin gray windbreaker and, as it happened, was only lightly armed, outwardly friendly, and claimed to live in the village they were headed toward. It was his "delight," he said, to give them a ride. He spoke a little English. "My father," he explained once they were moving along, "is chief of my village. I go to school in Mazar city, where I learn English at the English Club."

"You're a student now?" Donk asked, surprised. He found he could not stop looking at Ahktar's thick mustache and toupee-shaped hair, both as impossibly black as photocopier ink.

He laughed. "No. Many years ago."

Hassan and Donk bounced around on the Jeep's stiff back seat as Ahktar took them momentarily off road, avoiding a dune that had drifted out into the highway. Jumper cables and needle-nose pliers jangled around at Donk's feet. Graves was seat-belted in the shotgun position next to Ahktar, jostling in the inert manner of a crash-test dummy. Donk had yet to find the proper moment to ask why in Afghanistan the steering wheels were found on the right side of the car when everyone drove on the right side of the road. He thought he had found that moment now, but before he could ask, Ahktar hit a bump and Donk bashed his head against the vehicle's metal roof. "Your Jeep," Donk said, rubbing his head through his terrorist-style do-rag.

"Good Jeep!" Ahktar said.

"It's a little . . . military-seeming."

Ahktar looked at him in the rearview and shook his head. He had not heard him.

Donk leaned forward. "Military!" he shouted over the Jeep's gruff, lawnmowerish engine. "It looks like you got it from the military!"

"Yes, yes," Ahktar said, clearly humoring Donk. "I do!"

Donk leaned back. "This is a military Jeep, isn't it?" he asked Hassan.

"His father maybe is warlord," Hassan offered. "A good warlord!"

"Where are you from?" Ahktar asked Donk. "America?"

"That's right," Donk said.

"You know Lieutenant Marty?" Ahktar asked.

"Lieutenant Marty? No, I'm sorry. I don't."

Ahktar seemed disappointed. "Captain Herb?"

"No. Why do you ask?"

Ahktar reached into the side pocket of his gray coat and handed back to Donk a slip of paper with the names "Captain Herb" and "Lieutenant Marty" written on it, above what looked to be a pi-length satellite phone number. "Who are they?" Donk asked, handing the paper back.

"American soldiers," he said happily. "We are friends now because I help them with some problems."

"Is there a phone in your village? We could call them."

"Sorry, no," Ahktar apologized. "We have radios in my village, but nearest phone is Kunduz. I think today I will not go to Kunduz. They are having problems there." He motioned toward Graves, who seemed to be napping. "From where in America is your friend?"

"I'm not an American," Graves muttered with as much force as Donk had heard him manage all day. "I'm *English.*"

"What?" Ahktar asked, leaning toward him.

Graves's eyes cracked open, dim and sticky like a newborn's. "I'm *English.* From England. The people your countrymen butchered by the thousand a hundred and fifty years ago."

"Yes," Ahktar said soberly, downshifting as they came to a hill. Something in the Jeep's heater was rattling like a playing card in bicycle spokes. The waves of air surging from its vents went from warm, to hot, to freezing, to hot again. Ahktar drew up in his seat. "Here is village."

As they plunged down the highway, hazy purple mountains materialized along the horizon. From the road's rise Ahktar's village appeared as an oblong smear of homes and buildings located just before a flattened area where the mountain range's foothills began. Now came a new, low-ground terrain covered with scrabbly, drought-ruined grass. Along the road were dozens of wireless and long-knocked-over telephone poles. The Jeep rolled through the village's outer checkpoint. Set back off the highway, every fifty yards, were some small stone bubble-domed homes, their chimneys smoking. They looked to Donk like prehistoric arboretums. None of it was like anything Donk had ever before seen in Central Asia. The virus of Soviet architecture — with its practically right angles, frail plaster, and monstrous frescoes — had not spread here. In the remoter villages of Tajikistan he had seen poverty to rival northern Afghanistan's, but there the Soviet center had always held. In these never-mastered lands south of the former Soviet border, everything appeared old and shot up and grievously unattended. These discrepancies reminded Donk of what borders really meant, and what, for better or worse, they protected.

The road narrowed. The houses grew tighter, bigger, and slightly taller. The smoky air thickened, and soon they were rolling through Ahktar's village proper. He saw a few shops crammed with junk — ammunition and foodstuffs and Aladdin's lamp for all he knew — their window displays tiered backward like auditorium seating. Black, curly-haired goats hoofed at the dirt. Dogs slinked from doorway to doorway. Dark, hawk-nosed men wearing shirts with huge floppy sleeves waved at Ahktar. Most looked Tajik, and Donk cursed his laziness for not learning at least how to count in Tajik during all the months he had spent in Tajikistan. Walking roadside were beehive-shaped figures whose bedspread-white and sky-blue garments managed to hide even the basest suggestion of human form. These were women. Around their facial areas Donk noted narrow, tightly latticed eye slots. Children ran happily beside the Jeep, many holding pieces of taut string. "Kites," Graves observed weakly. "They're flying kites."

Ahktar's face turned prideful. "Now we are free, you see." He pointed at the sky. Donk turned his head sideways and peered up out the window. Floating above the low buildings of Ahktar's village were, indeed, scores of kites. Some were boxes, others quadrangular; some swooped and weaved like osprey; others hung eerily suspended.

Hassan looked up also. "We could not fly kites before," he said quietly.

"Yes," Donk said. "I know. Let freedom ring."

"When they leave our village," Ahktar — a bit of a present-tense addict, it seemed — went on, "we see many changes, such as shaving of the beards. The men used to grow big beards, of course very long, and they checked!"

Donk smiled, in spite of himself. "So you had a long beard?"

"Of course I have. I show you my pictures. It was a very long beard! Now everybody is free to shave or grow as their own choice."

It seemed impious to point out that virtually every man momentarily centered within the frame of Donk's murky plastic window had a griffin's nest growing off his chin.

"When did they leave?" Donk asked. "Was it recently?"

"Oh, yes," Ahktar said. "Very recently!" He cut the engine and rolled them down a rough dirt path through a part of the village that seemed a stone labyrinth. Sack-burdened peasants struggled past plain mud homes. Kunduz suddenly seemed a thriving desert metropolis in comparison. A high-walled compound guarded by two robed young men cradling Kalashnikovs stood where the path dwindled into a driveway. Inches before the compound's metal gate the Jeep rolled to a soft stop. Ahktar climbed out of the vehicle, and Donk followed.

"What's this?" Donk asked.

"My father's house. I think you are in trouble. If so, he is the man you are wanting to talk to now."

"We're not in trouble," Donk said. "My friend is sick. We just need to get him some medicine. We're not in any trouble. Our car broke down."

Ahktar lifted his hands, as though to ease Donk. "Yes, yes." He moved toward the compound's gate. "Come. Follow."

"What about my friend?" But Donk turned to see that the guards were helping Graves from the Jeep and leading him toward Ahktar's father's compound. Surprisingly, Graves did not spurn their assistance or call them bloody Hindoos, but simply nodded and allowed his arms to find their way around each guard's neck. They dragged him along, Graves's legs serving as occasional, steadying kickstands. Hassan followed behind them, again nervously eating the raisins he kept in his pocket.

The large courtyard, its trees stripped naked by autumn, was patrolled by a dozen more men holding Kalashnikovs. They were decked out in the same crossbred battle dress as the soldiers Donk had seen loitering around Kunduz: camouflage pants so recently issued by the American military they still held their crease, shiny black boots, *pakuls* (the floppy national hat of Afghanistan), rather grandmotherly shawls, and shiny leather bandoliers. While most of the bandoliers were empty, a few of these irregulars had hung upon them three or four small bulb-like grenades. They looked a little like explosive human Christmas trees.

"Wait one moment, please," Ahktar said, strolling across the courtyard and ducking into one of the many dark, doorless portals at its northern edge. The guards deposited Graves at a wooden table, and a minute later he was brought a pot of tea. Donk and Hassan, exchanging glances, walked over to Graves's table and sat down in the cold, dim light. The soldiers on the compound's periphery had yet to acknowledge them. They simply walked back and forth, back and forth, along the walls. Something about their manner, simultaneously alert and robotic, led Donk to guess that their weapons' safeties were off. If Kalashnikovs even had safeties, which, come to think of it, Donk was fairly sure they did not.

"Nothing quite like a safe, friendly village," Graves said in a thin voice. He sipped his tea, holding the round, handleless cup with both hands.

"How do you feel, Mister Graves?" Hassan asked eagerly.

"Hassan, I feel dreadful."

"I'm sorry to hear this, Mister Graves."

Graves set down the teacup and frowned. He looked at Hassan. "Be a lad and see if you can't scare up some sugar for me, would you?"

Hassan stared at him, empty-faced.

Graves chuckled at the moment he seemed to recognize that the joke had not been funny. "I'm joking, Hassan." He poured them both a cup of tea, and with a dramatic shiver quickly returned his arm to the warm, protective folds of his blanket. "Bloody freezing, isn't it?"

"It's actually a little warmer," Donk said, turning from his untouched tea to see Ahktar and an older gentleman walking over to join them. Ahktar's father was a towering man with a great, napkin-shaped cinnamon beard. He wore long, clean, white-yellow robes, his leather belt as broad as a cummerbund. Stuffed into this belt was what looked to be a .45. He was almost certainly Tajik and had large, crazed eyes and a nose that looked as hard as a sharp growth of bark. But he was smiling — something he did not do well, possibly for lack of practice. When he was close he threw open his arms and proclaimed something with an air of highly impersonal sympathy.

"My father says you are welcome," Ahktar said. He did not much resemble his father; he was smaller, darker skinned. Doubtless Ahktar had a Pashtun mother around here somewhere. Donk could almost assemble her features. His father said something else, then nudged Ahktar to translate. "He says too that you are his great and protected guests." His father spoke again, still with his effortful smile. "He says he is grateful for American soldiers and grateful for you American journalists, who care only of the truth."

"English," Graves said quietly.

"Whatever trouble you are in, my father will help you. It is his delight."

"Ahktar," Donk stepped in gently, "I told you. We're not in any trouble. My friend here is very sick. Our car broke down. We were trying to go to Mazar. It's very simple." Ahktar said nothing. "Well," Donk asked, "are you going to tell your father that?"

"I tell him that already."

"Then can we go to Mazar from here?"

The muscles of Ahktar's face tightened with regret. "Unfortunately, that is problem. No one is going to Mazar today." He seemed suddenly to wish that he were not standing beside his father, who of course asked what had just been said. Ahktar quietly back-translated for him, obviously hoping that his pea of an answer would be smothered beneath the mattress of translation.

"Why can't we go to Mazar?" Donk pressed.

At this mention of Mazar his father spoke again, angrily now. Ahktar nodded obediently. "My father wishes you to know you are safe here. Mazar is maybe not so safe."

"But Mazar's perfectly safe. It's been safe for days. I have friends there."

"My father is friendly with American soldiers in Mazar. Very friendly. And now we are helping them with some problems they are having in this region. We have authority for this. Unfortunately, Mazar's Uzbek commander and my father are not very friendly, and there my father has no authority. Therefore it would be good for you to stay."

After a pause, Donk spoke: "Who, may I ask, is your father?"

"My father is General Ismail Mohammed. He was very important part of United National Islamic Front for the Salvation of Afghanistan, which fought against —"

"But Mazar's commander was part of that same front."

"Yes," Ahktar said sadly. "Here is problem."

Donk had met a suspiciously large number of generals during his time in Afghanistan and was not sure how to judge General Mohammed's significance. Warlord? Ally? Both? He let it drop. "Do you have medicine here?"

Again Ahktar shrugged. "Some. But unfortunately it is with my father's soldiers now. They are out taking care of some problems for Lieutenant Marty."

"Is Lieutenant Marty with them?"

"Oh, no. Lieutenant Marty is in Mazar."

"Where we can't go."

"Yes."

There really were, Donk had often thought, and thought again now, two kinds of people in the world: Chaos People and Order People. For Donk this was not a bit of cynical, Kipling-ish wisdom to be doled out among fellow journalists in barren intercontinental barrooms. It was not meant in a condescending way. No judgment; it was a purely empirical matter. Chaos People, Order People. Anyone who doubted this had never tried to wait in line, board a plane, or get off a bus among Chaos People. The next necessary division of the world's people took place along the lines of whether they actually knew what they were. The Japanese were Order People and knew it. Americans and English were Chaos People who thought they were Order People. The French were the worst thing to be: Order People who thought they were Chaos People. But Afghans, like Africans and Russians and the Irish, were Chaos People who knew they were Chaos People, and while this lent the people themselves a good amount of charm, it made their countries berserk, insane. Countries did indeed go insane. Sometimes they went insane and stayed insane. Chaos People's countries particularly tended to stay insane. Donk miserably pulled off his do-rag, the bloody glue that held the fabric to his skin tearing from his ruined eyebrow so painfully that he had to work to keep the tears from his eyes. "So tell me, Ahktar. What are we supposed to do here?"

Before anyone could answer, Graves had a seizure.

A few hours later Donk was sitting outside the room in which Graves had been all but quarantined. He was petting a stray, wolfish mongrel with filaments of silver hair threaded through its black coat, waiting for the village medicine man to emerge from Graves's room. This man had claimed he was a doctor and offered up to Donk a large pouch of herbs as evidence. Donk did not have the heart to argue. The compound was quiet but for some small animals fighting or playing along the eaves just above Donk's head and the occasional overhead roar of a jet. Hassan, sitting a few feet away, watched Donk stroke the dog's head in revulsion.

"Why," he asked finally, "do you do that?"

Donk had always taken pity on Central Asian dogs, especially after learning that one could fend off a possible attack by miming the act of picking up a stone, at which the dogs usually turned and ran away. He lowered his lips to the creature's head and planted upon it a chaste kiss. The dog smelled of oily musk. "Because it's lonely," Donk said.

"That is a filthy animal," Hassan told him. "You should not touch such a filthy animal, Mister Donk."

Donk chose not to point out that Hassan was, if anything, far dirtier. The boy had spent a night with Donk and Graves in Kunduz. His body odor had been so potent, so overwhelmingly cheesy, that Donk was not able to sleep. Misplaced Muslim piety, he thought with uncharacteristic bitterness.

"You're right," Donk said at last. "The dog's filthy. But so am I. So there we are."

Hassan humphed.

During the seizure Donk had stuffed his bloody do-rag in Graves's mouth to keep him from biting off his tongue, even though he knew convulsive people rarely, if ever, bit off their own tongues. It was one of those largely ceremonial things people did in emergencies. Donk had pushed Graves up on the table and held him down. Graves shuddered for a few moments, his eyes filled with awful awareness, his chest heaving like the gills of a suffocating fish. Then, mercifully, he went unconscious. Donk used the rest of his iodined water to try to rehydrate Graves, but he quickly vomited it up. At this General Mohammed had sent for his medicine man.

Donk knew there were at least two kinds of malaria. The less serious strain was stubborn and hard to kill — flu-like symptoms could recur as long as five decades after the initial infection — but it was rarely lethal. The more serious strain quickly turned life-threatening if untreated. He was no longer wondering which strain Graves had contracted. Graves was conscious now — Donk could hear him attempting to reason with the village doctor — but his voice was haggard and dazed.

Donk looked around. Thirty or forty yards away a small group of General Mohammed's soldiers watched him, their Kalashnikovs slung over their shoulders. They looked beaten, bullied, violent. Hair-trigger men. Their faces were like shadows. And these were the *winners.* Donk found himself, suddenly, missing women. Seeing them, staring at them, smelling them. Afghanistan had mailed into Donk's brain a series of crushingly similar mental post cards: men, men, desert, men, men, men, guns, men, guns, guns, desert, guns, men. One might think that life without women would lead to a simpler, less fraught existence. No worries about hair or odor. Saying whatever you wanted. But one's eyes tired of men, as one's nerves certainly tired of guns.

It was not just women, however. Donk missed sex even more. He needed, he admitted, an inordinate amount of sex. Heavy people needed things — hence their heaviness. Sex was a large part of the reason he had been reluctant to leave Chicago to come to Afghanistan. He was having a *Guinness Book* amount of it with Tina, who was maybe his girlfriend, his first in a long time. As luck would have it, Tina was menstruating the night before he left. They had had sex anyway, in her bathroom, and left bloody foot- and handprints all over the white tile. They Windexed away the blood together. It had not been freaky. It had almost been beautiful, and he loved her. But for him distance was permission, and newness arousal itself. Plane tickets and hotel rooms were like lingerie. He had already slept with an AP reporter in Tashkent. He did not regret it, exactly, because he had every intention of lying about it later. It occurred to him that he had also lied to Graves. About not being haunted. Strangely, he felt bad about that lie. It seemed like something Graves should have known. But Donk had not known where to begin.

A decade ago Donk worked as a staff photographer for a dozen family newspapers peppered throughout central Wisconsin, all somehow owned by the same unmarried man. His life then had been sitting through school-board meetings and upping the wattage of the smiles of local luminaries, drinking three-dollar pitchers of Bud after work and suffering polite rejection from strangers he misjudged as unattractive enough to want to speak to him. That life began to end when the last of five sudden strokes stripped Donk's father of his mind and sent him off into dementia. Donk was the only one of his siblings who lived within 1,000 miles of Milwaukee, where his father was hospitalized; his mother had long refused to speak to the man. So, alone, Donk set up camp beside his father's deathbed.

Death was a peculiar thing. Some endured unenviable amounts of firsthand death without its one clearest implication ever occurring to them. Donk had never much thought about his own death before. The prospect had always felt to him like a television show he knew was on channel eleven and started at eight but had never watched and never planned to. Donk stared at the monitors, listened to the hiss of his father's bed's mattress as the nurses pistoned it up and down, timed the steady beep whose provenance he did not care to isolate. It was all he could do to keep from thinking that all of it was assembled to provide the man a few last deprived moments of life. Donk realized that even if he were beside his father at the moment his final journey began, the man would still die alone, as Donk would die alone, as we all died alone. Horribly, doubly alone, for just as no one went with us, no one greeted us when it was over.

Nurses found him weeping in the hospital's cafeteria. When his father's doctor brought some final forms for Donk to fill out, she slipped into his catatonic hand a small packet of diazepam. The nervous breakdown Donk expected. The estrangement from his surviving family — who could not understand his "sudden obsession" with dying — he expected. Quitting his job and investing his small inheritance he expected. Becoming a freelance combat photographer he did not. People who were not correspondents laughed when Donk told the story, which he often did. It sounded so unbelievable. But people were not born combat photographers any more than they were born lawyers. One day you were waiting tables, the next you were in law school. One day you were heartbroken and megalomaniacal, the next you were faxing visa requests to embassies using stolen letterhead. Only Tajikistan's had answered him. If Tajikistan's embassy wondered why the *Waukesha Freeman* felt it needed a photographer in Dushanbe, it did not share that curiosity with Donk. He was awarded his first visa to his first war, a genuine hot war, a civil war. He told everyone he met in Dushanbe that he was "stringing," even though he was not sure what that word really entailed. In Tajikistan he saw his first gunshot wound, his first dead baby. He learned that combat photographers either "spooked" or did not. To his surprise, Donk did not. At least, he spooked no more than he had the afternoon he watched his father burp, sigh, and stop breathing. The photo of the gunned-down old woman, taken after five months and $3,000 of squandered savings, led to Donk's covering the reconciliation trials in Rwanda for one of India's biggest dailies. There he learned that he no longer had much patience for American minorities' claims of oppression. Rwanda led to Jerusalem, shortly after the intifada. There he learned of the subterranean connections world media outlets had expertly tunneled beneath continents of human misery, and how often you passed the same faces when traveling through them. Jerusalem led to Dagestan, where he spent a day with a Tatar Muslim warlord whose nom de guerre was Hitler and who made an awkward pass at Donk when they were alone. He learned that of all the countries in the world America was most hesitant to publish graphic "bang-bang" photos. He learned that arms and cocaine were the world's second and third most profitable exports, after human sex slaves. He learned how to shop for a Kevlar vest. He learned how to take a good picture while running. He learned, when all else failed, to follow refugees. And he learned that the worse and more ugly the reality around him, the more impervious to it and better he felt, the more he forgot his father. He learned that the only thing that frightened him, truly frightened him, was quiet, because he knew death was quiet, the longest quiet. He learned that the persona that came with this strange fearlessness was able to win, if only for a night, a certain kind of troubled heart belonging to a certain kind of woman more worldly than Donk had any previous right to expect, and he learned that he was the type of man to abuse this ability.

His brother and sister called him a fear addict, a desperate idiot on a danger bender. He had never "dealt" with their father's death, they claimed. Donk's brother, Jason, was a first-team whiskey addict (three interventions and counting: "What, this again?" he had asked, after the most recent). His sister, Marie, lived in Anchorage, too far away to provide Donk with any idea of what, exactly, she was into. Judging from her insensate 3:00 A.M. phone calls, it was high-impact. Who were they to speak of fear, of "dealing with the natural process" of death? Death was actually the least natural thing Donk could imagine, involving, as it did, not living. Death's stature as a physiological event did not mean it was natural. The trapped mink does not accept its own death; it chews off its leg. No, death was something else, categoryless and dreadful, something to be fought off, defied, spat upon. Human Conflict, he thought. Death was the unappeasable aggressor. And he stroked the dog's small head.

The medicine man stepped from Graves's room. Without consulting him Donk rushed inside. It was a little past eleven in the morning now, the light in Graves's room brighter than he expected. Graves was supine on a thick mass of blankets with another, thinner blanket mostly covering him. He seemed very still. His eyes were dry. Though he did not look at Donk, he raised his hand in brief acknowledgment. Donk crouched next to Graves's makeshift bed and said nothing. Then, on an impulse, he took Graves's hand and held it crossways in his own, as though hoping to offer him some mysterious transfer of strength.

"Did you once think," Graves asked, "about how dirty dying is? I'm lying here in my own shit. You can smell it, can't you? I should really do something about this." He shifted positions, and then Donk could smell Graves's shit, thin and sour and soupy. In response Donk squeezed Graves's hand. "In England," Graves went on, wincing briefly, "I think something like eighty percent of all deaths now take place in hospitals. I watched my mother and my father die in hospitals. They went quietly. It was lovely, in its way. But fifty years ago only forty percent of the English population died in hospitals. We sequester the dying, you see. Because it *is* ugly, it *is* dirty. I think we don't want to know that. We want to keep that little truth hidden away. But think a moment about how most people have died, Duncan. They've died in places just like this. So if I'm going to die here, I'm joining legions. For some reason this makes me happy." Graves's head rolled an inch on its pillow and, for the first time, he looked at Donk.

Donk stared back at Graves, the connection allowing him to locate the voice, as faraway as a quasar, in his mind. "You're not going to die."

Graves smiled. "Old men have to die. The world grows moldy, otherwise."

Graves, Donk knew, was forty. His sympathy left him in one brash gust. "What did the doctor say?"

"Oh, you mean St. John's Wort, M.D.? Hell if I know. He all but sprinkled me with voodoo dust. Duncan, calm down. I'm either going to make it through this or I won't. I'm not upset. I just have to wait." He closed his eyes. "'Of all the wonders that I yet have heard, / It seems to me most strange that men should fear; / Seeing that death, a necessary end, / Will come when it will come.' That Shakespeare. Preternatural, isn't it? Any occasion one can think of, and there he is."

Donk knew he could barely quote Shakespeare if he were spotted "To be" and "not to be." In a low voice he said, "You *are* going to die, Graves, if you've already convinced yourself you're going to die."

"A puzzle."

Donk let go of his hand. "It's not a fucking puzzle."

"Getting upset, Duncan, isn't going to help me."

"Then what is going to help you?"

"Medicine. Medicine they don't have here."

"Where?" Donk asked. "Where do I go?"

Graves looked at him again. Suddenly Donk saw the fear just below the flat blue composure of Graves's eyes, a stern, dignified terror barricaded so completely inside of him it barely recognized itself. Graves's lips were shaking. "Jesus, Duncan. I — you — you could rent that chap Ahktar's Jeep. You could —"

With that Donk rushed out, collared Hassan, and went to find General Mohammed and Ahktar. Seven hundred dollars was hidden beneath the insole of Donk's boot. This would be enough, he hoped, for a safety deposit on the Jeep. He would drive to Mazar with Hassan. He would walk into UNICEF's office or Doctors Without Borders or find Lieutenant Marty and he would come back here. Graves was too sick to travel, and if they broke down again or were stopped — it was too complicated. That was the one truly upsetting thing about Human Conflict. It made everything far too complicated. Donk found General Mohammed alone in his quarters. He was wearing glasses, surprisingly enough, sitting at a plain wooden desk, reading a book in Persian. His .45 was flat on the tabletop. Behind the general, on the wall, hung a green and black flag last used in Afghanistan during the reign of its deposed king, thirty years ago. Without knocking, Donk announced he was renting Ahktar's Jeep and going to Mazar. Without looking up, General Mohammed informed him that Ahktar had, only an hour before, left in his Jeep to take care of a few more problems. He would be back sometime tomorrow perhaps maybe. Donk stood silently in the general's doorway, feeling himself growing smaller. Perhaps maybe. The national motto of Afghanistan.

"He says," Hassan translated for General Mohammed, "that Mister Graves is very sick. He says he has spoken to his doctor."

"Yes," Donk said, looking at the general. "He's going to die."

General Mohammed frowned and spoke again. The man's face, Donk thought, was 70 percent nose. Hassan: "His doctor says there is one thing that can help him."

"What's that?" Donk asked, the second word cracking as it left his mouth. He was still looking at the general.

"There is a grass that grows in a valley in the mountains. A special grass. Medicine grass?"

"Medicinal grass."

"Yes. This grass his doctor can boil for Mister Graves, he says. Then Mister Graves can drink the broth." General Mohammed spoke again, nodded, and returned to his book. "He says Mister Graves will get better." Hassan shrugged.

"He has malaria," Donk told Hassan numbly. "Grass won't help malaria. He needs antibiotics."

Donk had not meant for Hassan to translate this, but he did. "Yes," General Mohammed said through Hassan. As the general went on, Hassan began to shift and nod. "Okay, now he says that once he suffered this himself. Six years ago, in the summer?" General Mohammed kept talking. "And many of his men as well. They were all very ill, he says, just like Mister Graves. He says they have seen much of Mister Graves's sickness here. But they drank the boiled grass, and a day later they were well."

"Do they have any of the grass here?"

"No. He says it is in a valley in the mountains beyond the village." Hassan listened. "He is saying now he can tell for you how to find the grass and give you two of his men. Together, he says, you can go get the grass. Then, Mister Graves will be well." Hassan smiled.

"I need a vehicle," Donk said. He did not intend to find the grass. He would simply drive to Mazar. If General Mohammed's shadow-faced men did not care for this, they could shoot him. They could give Donk his own shadow face.

The general was reading again. When Hassan translated Donk's request, he breathed in deeply and turned a page. He spoke. Hassan: "It is not a far walk, he says. His men will show you."

"Tell him I need a vehicle."

General Mohammed peered at Donk over the top edge of his glasses and spoke, it was clear, for the last time. Hassan shook his head: "He says he is sorry, Mister Donk, but they have too many problems today to spare any vehicles to go to Mazar."

When Donk returned to Graves's room, he found him asleep, his white face and reddish purple cheeks agleam with perspiration, his forehead creased and dented. He was holding his purple Nokia. NO SIGNAL, its LCD read. Again Donk sat next to Graves's bed. Getting close to Graves was now like entering a force field of heat. He could smell Graves's bad breath, which smelled like shit, and his shit, which smelled like bad breath. Donk did not now believe and never had much believed in God, or in human goodness. He did not think that each of us had a "time" we "had to go," or even that this special mountain grass would do fuck-all for Graves. He believed in and tried to think about very little. He believed in photography, which he loved, and death, which he hated. He thought about how he had been using one to deny the other. He thought about how clearly he felt death in Graves's bright room, the same greedy, cool-edged core of heat that a decade ago he had felt zeroing in on his father. He refused to abandon Graves to it. Of course this was just more ceremony. Graves was dying as he looked at him. But death, too, was ceremony, the one sacrament that, in time, singed every tongue.

Donk touched his own lips, absently. They were cold.

Hassan disagreed that helping Donk find medicinal grass was an implied part of his duties. He had no wish to leave the relative safety of this village. He seemed surprised, in fact, that Donk even wanted him along. Donk began to wonder if robbing them was not Hassan's polite if highly indirect way of attempting to end their association. The two soldiers General Mohammed lent Donk most clearly did not want to go find the grass either. The only person who wished less than they to go out and find this grass was Donk. General Mohammed assured them that leaving by 1:00 P.M. would afford them plenty of time to find the valley, fill a satchel with grass, and return by the evening. Before they left, one of General Mohammed's wives fed them all a pile of meatless *pilau* that they chased down with gallons of cherry compote.

Just outside the village Donk watched as the two loaner soldiers loaded a small donkey with canvas pouches and plastic bags emblazoned with the Marlboro logo.

"Why," Donk asked Hassan, "are they bringing a goddamned donkey? We're only going to be gone for a few hours."

Hassan asked them, but the soldiers did not respond and kept loading the donkey with plastic bags. "I am thinking," Hassan hazarded, "that this donkey belongs to one of them. Like pet? Maybe they want it to receive its exercise today."

That these were not General Mohammed's ablest men was evident in several ways. They had been lucky enough to receive the American camouflage uniforms, but in place of the boots Donk saw on proud display among the general's other soldiers, these men were wearing what he realized only incrementally were tire treads held to their feet by twine.

"I have a rule," Donk told Hassan to tell the soldiers, neither of whose names he had any interest in learning. "I'm going to call it Rule One. Rule One is: No talking. Unless it's an emergency, or unless they see the grass. Otherwise I don't want to hear any talking. Okay?"

Hassan looked troubled. "Mister Donk, why this rule?"

"Because I'm sick of talking, I'm sick of languages I don't understand, and I'm sick of words in general. I just want to walk."

"Can I talk if I talk English?"

Donk looked at him. "Did you steal my cameras?"

"Mister Donk! Why would I steal your cameras? Where would I put them?"

"You can talk in English. A little. But ask me first."

Hassan shook his head, lamely mouthed Donk's edict to the soldiers, then walked away a few feet and moped defeatedly. The soldiers had scarcely listened, their limited attention still fully commandeered by the donkey. The donkey was a youngish creature with a rust-and-toffee coat and teeth the size of shot glasses. Once it was loaded up, one of the soldiers smacked the donkey with proprietary cruelty on its bulbous, muscular hindquarters. The donkey trundled forward a few steps, then stopped and shook its head, its long ears flapping. The first soldier, whose angular and almost handsome face was nearly hidden behind a bushy black beard that began growing just below his eyes, laughed and shook his head. The second soldier, a smaller man whose beard was redder and less ambitious, walked over to the donkey and whipped it with a switch. This time the donkey walked and did not stop. Donk stared at the animal with dejected, secret confederacy, then followed after it.

They hiked for an hour without talking, saw no one, and reached the range's first serious hill just after two. They cleared it easily, and though another, steeper hill lay just ahead, Donk was pleased. These foothills were not very challenging. Even this range's highest faraway peaks were snowless. In Tajikistan he had trekked over far more punishing country. The trails were well worn and dusty, and the wind was low. The sun was bright, and beneath it Afghanistan looked like a blizzard of gray and brown. A nature hike, minus all the nature. Donk thought back to the Porcupines in Upper Michigan, trips his brother, Jason, now referred to as "hurt-feelings competitions." But Donk did not remember them this way. Donk was always deputized to carry the party's RV-sized tent, as well as anything that related to the inevitable screaming match that doubled as the tent's assembly. Donk had been a shortish, overweight boy, a puffing congenital sweater. Jason had likened his younger brother's hunched, miserable appearance under thirty pounds of fatly wrapped weatherproofed nylon to that of a donkey. The word's phonic closeness to *Duncan* or, worse, *Dunc,* his family nickname, did not immediately occur to Jason, and for the remainder of the trip Duncan inured himself to being known as "Donkey Boy." On their last night in the Porcupines — traditionally the one time their father let the boys drink beer before they headed back to Milwaukee — Duncan plunged his hand into their cooler's watery, lukewarm dregs in search of a can of Miller Lite. "Hey, Donk," Jason called over, distracted with the fire, "grab me one too?" Donk knew, even before Jason and his father had exchanged looks of revelation, that he had just been rechristened. The nickname spread as though it were a plot. His mother was the longest holdout, but after six months he was Donk even to her. He thought that nothing could have ever happened to him out there. That was what the trips now meant to him. They were pre-danger. Pre-death. Once, after he had had too much to drink during one of his infrequent visits back to the Midwest, Jason had unkindly disclosed that the trips' whole purpose had been their father's attempt to rid Donk of what the man always called "that goddamn baby fat." This had hurt Donk, a little.

"Mister Donk," Hassan said, apprehensive to be violating Rule One, "you are well?"

"Fine," Donk said. "Some dirt in my eye."

Hassan almost smiled. "Both eyes?"

Hassan was smarter than Donk realized. Everyone, Donk thought, was smarter than you realized. "Yes, Hassan. Both eyes."

Hassan fretted with the front flap of his *shalwar khameez.* "Mister Donk, I have maybe an emergency."

"Oh?"

"I think perhaps General Mohammed's soldiers are not pleased."

"What makes you say that?"

Hassan was quiet a moment, listening to the soldiers. They were ten feet back, softly chatting, their rifles' thin black straps cutting across their chests and their tire-tread sandals slapping against the hard soil. Their language sounded to Donk, strangely, like yodeling. Hassan edged closer to Donk and whispered, "They are talking about leaving us."

"Fuck them, then. I have a compass. I can find our way back. We don't need them."

"But what of the grass?"

Donk had completely forgotten about the grass.

"I am thinking," Hassan said, looking straight ahead, "that these are bad men."

The second hill took longer to climb. It was steeper, the path more friable. The sun's warmth had opened Donk's eyebrow, and sweat soaked into the wound lividly. The donkey, especially, was having trouble, its hard little hooves slipping in the thick gray gravel. Red Beard decided the best way to hasten the donkey's ascent was to whip it across the face with his switch. The donkey hissed at him, its huge, rotten teeth bared, its gelatinous eyes rolling wildly in their sockets. Red Beard whipped it again, this time across the nose. Black Beard observed all this with nodding satisfaction. Hassan shook his head wretchedly and turned away and kept walking. As the beating went on, it gathered a terrible energy, as crying does, as pain does, and Donk took a seat on a pathside stone and watched. As bad as he felt for the animal, he was not about to step between it and Red Beard, whose streak of ferruginous cruelty was certain to run deeper than Donk could even begin to imagine. Thus he was cheered when the donkey, bouncing bronco-style on its hind legs, its huge testicles jouncing, cunningly maneuvered its position in such a way as to deliver into Red Beard's chest a quick and astonishingly forceful double-barreled kick. Red Beard managed, somehow, to stay on his feet. After a few moments of absorption, however, his expression loosened, opened to a hundred new possibilities of pain. He dropped his stick and, gently, sat down. He rolled onto his side and rocked back and forth in the dirt. Donk noticed, remotely, that Red Beard was barefoot. The donkey had kicked him right out of his tire-tread sandals. With equal remoteness Donk watched Black Beard calmly level his Kalashnikov at the donkey and squeeze off three quick rounds into its hindquarters. The donkey kicked blindly a few more times and then galumphed down the path, back toward the village, screaming. That was, Donk thought, really the only word for the sound he was now hearing. Screaming, screaming. It did not get far. With the Kalashnikov's stock tucked snugly into his shoulder, Black Beard tracked the donkey and fired twice. The donkey's head kicked up, the reports' echoes saturating the afternoon air. The donkey staggered ahead for a few steps more, tried to turn around, then dropped onto its side. Its legs were still moving at different speeds and in different directions. In the meantime Red Beard had struggled to his feet. With one arm wrapped around his cracked ribcage he limped over to Donk and spoke.

Hassan was shaking with terror; his voice broke register as he translated. "Mister Donk, he says he is injured and requests that we go back."

Donk nodded at Red Beard thoughtfully, his hands tucked away in his hooded sweatshirt's front pockets to hide the fact that they were trembling. "Tell him, Hassan, that when we have the grass we can go back."

"He says he is injured very badly."

"Tell him this is his own stupid fucking fault."

"You tell him this!" Hassan cried.

Black Beard, his Kalashnikov now slung over his shoulder, was pulling off the donkey the pouches and Marlboro bags. Donk was about to speak when he noticed Black Beard quickly stand and look off warily to the east, instinctively reaching around for his rifle but not unshouldering it. Before Donk had even turned his head he heard the hollow patter of an approaching horse, then a low snorty sound. Upon the horse was a soldier. He rode in slowly, stopping at the midpoint between Donk and Black Beard, whose hand was still frozen in mid-reach for his rifle. The soldier looked to Donk, then to the dead donkey. Finally he rode over and circled the donkey's corpse, looking over at Black Beard only after he had made a complete orbit. "Salaam," the soldier said, his horse's ears smoothed back, clear evidence of its distress at the sight of its murdered cousin. "Salaam," Black Beard returned, his hand lowering. The soldier was an American. His fatigues were lightly camouflaged, a few blobby splashes of faint green and wavy brown upon a dirty tan background. His backpack's two olive-green straps ran vertically down his chest. Another, thicker strap corseted his waist, and two more cinched around his thigh, where a 9 mm pistol was sheathed in a camouflaged holster. Affixed upon his shoulder was the bulky black control pad for his air-to-ground radio, its CB hooked to his waist. Somewhat ostentatiously, Donk felt, he was wearing a floppy Afghan *pakul,* and around his neck was the same make of white scarf Donk had bought in Kunduz. He galloped over to Donk, young and triumphantly blue-eyed, his nose snoutlike and his chin weak. A southerner, Donk guessed. Obviously he was one of the commandos Donk had only heard about, Special Forces boys leading on horseback whole garrisons of guerillas, shining lasers into the nasties' mountain hidey-holes for the F/A-18s' laser-guided bombs, and vacuuming up customs and language as they went. Some of these guys, it was rumored, had been here as early as September 14. It was against SF doctrine to travel alone, and Donk imagined that right about now he was zooming up in the digital viewfinder of the binoculars that belonged to this commando's partner, who was no doubt watching from a hill or was perhaps even hidden in some impossibly nearby rocks.

"Sir," the commando said to Donk. "You're an American?"

Donk pulled his hands from his sweatshirt's pockets and stood. "I am."

The commando, squinting, gazed down at Donk from his mount. He threw off the hard, unapproachable aura of sunlight on sheet metal. "Are you wounded?"

"What?"

The soldier tapped himself above the eye.

"No," Donk said, touching himself there and, with a flinch, regretting it. "It's nothing. A car accident."

"Sir, I've been following you. And I have to ask what you're doing out here, for one, and for two, why are your men discharging their weapons in a hostile area?"

"They executed our donkey," Donk said. "I'm not sure why. And they're not my men. They're General Ismail Mohammed's."

The horse footed back a few steps, its huge, stone-smooth muscles sliding around one another beneath a dark brown coat as shiny as chocolate pudding. The commando, with the steadiness of a centaur, had not taken his eyes off Donk. "That leaves what you're doing out here."

"I'm a journalist. My friend is back in General Mohammed's village, like I said. He's very sick. I'm out here looking for grass."

The commando stared at him. "Pardon me, sir, but the stuff

practically falls out of the trees here. There's no need to be out this —"

"Not marijuana. Grass. A special kind of grass."

"Ho-kay," he said.

"Look, forget that. Can you help me?"

"Sir, I don't really have any guidance."

"Any what?"

"Guidance, sir. I can't talk to the media."

Donk always admired military men, young military men in particular, for their peculiarly unsullied minds. "I'm not looking for an interview. My friend has malaria. He's back in General Mohammed's village. He's dying."

"Sir, be advised that these mountains are not safe for civilians. They're crawling with hostiles. And I don't mean to sound like a hard-ass, but I'm not really authorized to use this radio for anything other than ordering air strikes. We're doing pest control, sir, and I strongly recommend you get back to that village."

"Where's your commanding officer?"

"He's in Mazar-i-Sharif, sir."

"Lieutenant Marty, right?"

The commando paused. "I'm not at liberty to say, sir."

"Look, do you have any malaria medicine? Antibiotics? Anything you have. Believe me when I say it's an emergency."

The commando pulled back on the reins. The horse turned with the finicky heaviness particular to its species, and the commando started off.

Donk was not surprised. "This is all about reporters fucking you guys over in Vietnam, isn't it?" he called after him. "Well, you should know I was about six when Saigon fell. Were you even born?"

The commando stopped and turned back to him. "Leave this area, sir. Now."

Donk saluted the commando, who politely returned the salute and *ya*'d his horse to a full gallop. The cool, thin dust swallowed them both just before they would have vanished over the nearest hill's lip. Donk asked Hassan to inform Black Beard and Red Beard that his mission was now under the protection of the American military, owners of fearsome fighter planes, magical horseback summoners of aerial bombs, benevolent providers of PX-surplus camouflage. Neither Red Beard nor Black Beard had much of anything to say after that.

Shortly after 4:00 P.M. they found the valley where the grass was supposed to grow, a large scooped-out gouge of grayish sand and brown, rocky soil amid a ragged perimeter of half a dozen steep hills. A long, twisty road wended through the valley and disappeared into an identically shady pass at each end. The hill they were now atop had provided them the least hospitable, most distinctly mountainous trek yet. Its top ridge was cold, windy, and dustless. As they stood in the sunlight looking down into the valley, Donk saw why the commando had wanted him to return to General Mohammed's village. Along the valley's road was a smudged line of charcoal-colored transport trucks and pickups. Black Beard withdrew from one of his satchels a pair of binoculars. After having a look, he handed the binoculars without comment to Donk. They were, Donk saw, cheap enough to have been pulled from a cereal box. Nonetheless, they helped him discern that the smudges were blast marks; the dark charcoal color could be credited to the fact that each vehicle had been incinerated from the outside in. It took them another twenty minutes to climb down into the valley, and they walked along the road's wreckage as warily and silently as animals. The bombing had not happened terribly recently. Not a single piece of hardware was smoking, and the truck husks had the brittle, crumbly look of a scorched old log one cleared from a well-trafficked campsite's pit before building a new fire. The wreckage looked picked over, and the shrapnel was in careful little piles. Black Beard and Red Beard muttered to themselves.

"What are they saying?" Donk asked Hassan.

Hassan shook his head. "Their prayers for the dead."

"But these men were their enemies."

"Of course," Hassan said, looking at Donk hatefully.

Donk approached the bombed convoy's lead vehicle. Its tires had melted and its doors were gone. The empty cab and bed were both largely intact, though they had been severed from each other after sustaining what looked like a direct hit. There were no craters, Donk knew, because this campaign's bombs were designed to explode a few feet above their targets. Donk walked farther down the blasted line. He did not see any bodies at all until the penultimate vehicle, a nearly vaporized Datsun pickup so skeletal it looked like a blackened blueprint of a Datsun pickup. The charred driver was barely distinguishable from the wreckage around him. He was just a crispy torso of shrunken unrealness. His face and hair had been burned off, his head a featureless black oval. Donk reached for the camera he did not have and stepped closer, discovering that the reason no one had moved his body was that it was melted to its seat. His stomach gurgled and turned. Something in him clenched. He did not have his camera. The image would never swim up at him from the bottom of a plastic platter filled with developing fluid. It would stay exactly this way . . . Donk strangled the thought off.

"Mister Donk!" Hassan called over to him.

He turned, rubbing his beating heart through his chest. "Yes, Hassan. What is it?"

He pointed at the Beards. "They say the grass is nearby."

Donk took in this information. He felt the same mild surprise he remembered experiencing when he learned, thanks to a concert Tina had taken him to, that people were still writing symphonic music. Surprise that he would be so surprised. The grass actually existed. How unaccountable. "Where?"

Hassan pointed across the valley. "They say over there."

Donk looked. At the far side of the valley stood a sparse stand of trees, the first trees he had seen all day. They made him feel better, somehow. Around the trees was a long, squarish field of desiccated grass the color of wheat. The road this annihilated convoy had been traveling along would have taken them right past that field. They walked, Black Beard and Red Beard having now unshouldered their weapons. To walk across this valley felt to Donk like standing in the middle of an abandoned coliseum. Above, the sky was getting darker. The day was silent. Donk noticed, as they grew closer to the trees, that they had not yet completely shed their leaves, little pom-poms of bright orange and yellow still tipping their branches. The setting sun was pulling a long, curtained shadow across this valley. He realized, then, that even if they pushed themselves, they were not going to make it back to the village before nightfall. He hurried himself ahead, and Hassan and the Beards jogged to keep pace with him. He did not care to learn who or what ruled these hills at night.

"Mister Donk," Hassan said, "please slow!"

"Fuck off," he called back. Donk's thoughts suddenly felt to him alien and disfigured, exalted by fear, disconnected from the internal key that transformed them into language. He veered off the road and sprinted toward the trees through the grass abruptly growing all around him. His boots were scything up great cheerful swaths of the stuff. He did not know why he was not gathering up any of it. He was not certain what might make one kind of grass more restorative than another. He had a quiet, appalled thought at all the things he did not know. He then remembered to believe that the grass was not going to help Graves. Not at all.

"Mister Donk!" Hassan called again. Donk turned to see Hassan following him across the field of grass in an unsteady, not-quite-running way. "They say we must be careful here! Mister *Donk!*" Black Beard, now shouting something himself, endured a moment of visible decision-making, then left the road and followed after Hassan.

Donk's head swiveled forward. He was almost to the trees. The grass just under the trees looked especially boilable, thick and tussocky. Then, oddly, Donk seemed to be looking at the trees and the grass from much higher up. His horizon lifted, then turned over. Donk had heard nothing, but when he landed he smelled something like cooked meat, cordite, loam. He lay there in the grass, blinking. With his fingers he pulled up a thick handful of grass, then let it go. He looked over. Hassan was beside him, ten feet away, screaming, though still Donk could hear nothing. Hassan's mouth was bloody, and his cardigan sweater was gone but for some shreds, and what Donk initially believed to be large, fat, red leeches were crawling all over his stomach and chest. On the other side of him Black Beard was creeping away on all fours, shaking his head in a dazed way. After a few feet he stopped and lay down. Donk thought that he, Donk, was okay. But for some reason he could not sit up. His legs felt funny, as did his back. He did not panic and lifted his left leg to watch the tendons and veins and muscles fall away from it as though it were a piece of chicken that had been boiled too long. Then he was bleeding. The blood did not come out of him in a glug but in a steady, silent gush. There was so much of it. He lowered his leg and from his supine position saw broken-ribbed Red Beard struggling down the road. Yes, he thought, that's right. Go get help. Donk thought he was going to be all right. It did not hurt yet. Oh wait yes it did. Suddenly it hurt very, very much. Donk always believed that you learned a lot about a place from the first thing you heard said there. In Chechnya it was: "It doesn't work." In Rwanda: "I don't know." In Afghanistan: "Why are you here?" He had not stepped on a mine. Slowly, he knew that. No reason to waste an expensive mine in such a remote place. He had stepped instead on a bomblet, a small and festively yellow cluster of ordnance that had not detonated above the eradicated convoy but rather bounced away, free and clear, and landed here in the grass. Hassan was no longer screaming but simply lying there and looking up at the sky. He, too, was mechanically blinking. Hassan needed help. Donk did not care if he stole his cameras. Donk could help him. Donk, suddenly, loved him. But first he had to rest. He could not think about all this until he had some fucking rest. Could he get some rest? He had to help Graves, because if he did not, Graves would die. He thought of his father, how he had looked in the end. God, Donk thought, I do not want to die. But he did not much care for old age either. A problem there. "Dad!" Donk yelled out suddenly. He did not know why; something in him unclenched. Or maybe he had not said anything at all. It was hard to tell, and it was getting dark. So: rest. Rest here one minute and off we go. Red Beard could use the company. Use the help. Ho-kay. He was all right. He just needed to figure this out.

JOY WILLIAMS

The Girls

FROM IDAHO REVIEW

THE GIRLS WERE SEARCHING ARLEEN'S ROOM and had just come upon her journal. The girls were thirty-one and thirty-three. Arleen was of a dowdy unspecific age, their parents' houseguest. She had arrived with the family's city pastor, an Episcopal priest, who had been in a depression for a number of months because his lover had died. The priest spent most of his time in the garden wearing only a bright red banana sling, his flabby body turning a magnificent somber brown. The girls were certain their parents regretted inviting him for he was not at all amusing, the way he could be frequently, in the pulpit.

Arleen was presently occupied with washing her long hair in the shower down the hall. It had taken the girls many clandestine visits to her room to find anything of interest. The journal was in the zippered pocket of her open suitcase.

"I know I looked here before."

"She must move it around."

"Should we start at the beginning or should we start with the last entry, that would be last night I suppose."

"That was the Owl Walk. She went on the Owl Walk with Mommy and came back and said so seriously, 'No Owls.'"

The girls found that hysterical.

The sound of water on the curtain ceased and the girls hurried downstairs. They made tea and curled up on the sofa with their cats. There were two cats living and two cats dead. The dead cats were Roland and Georgia O'Keeffe, their cremains in elaborate colorful urns on the mantelpiece. The ceramic feet on Roland's urn were rabbits. The ones on Georgia O'Keeffe, mice. The urns had been conceived and created by the girls.

"Good morning, Arleen," they said together when Arleen appeared, her hair wadded wetly on her back. She peered at them and smiled shyly. The back of her blouse was soaked because of the sack of hair. She wore khaki shorts. They were the weird kind to which leggings could be buttoned to create a pair of trousers.

"I was hoping," Arleen said, "that the kitty litter box could be taken out of the bathroom?"

The girls and the cats stared at her.

"It smells," Arleen said.

"It *smells?"* the girls said.

There was silence. "I took a lovely long walk early this morning," Arleen said. "I bicycled out to the moors and then I walked. It began to rain, quite hard, and then it suddenly stopped and was beautiful."

The girls mimed extreme wonder at this remarkable experience.

"It reminded me of something I read once about the English moors and the month of April," Arleen said. *"'April, who laughs her girlish laughter and a moment after weeps her girlish tears is apt to be a mature hysteric on the moors.'"* She looked at them, smiling quickly, then dipped her head. She had a big ragged part in her hair that made the girls almost dizzy.

"April is far behind us, Arleen," the girls said. "It is June. You've been here almost two weeks."

Arleen nodded. "It's been very good for Father Snow."

"What is *your* home like?" the girls inquired. They'd found one couldn't be too obvious with Arleen.

"It has stairs," Arleen mused. "Very steep stairs. Sometimes I don't go out, because coming back there would be the stairs, and often when I am out, I don't return because of the stairs. Otherwise it's quite adequate."

"Are you fearful of crime?" the girls said. They widened their eyes.

"No," Arleen said. She had very much the manner of someone waiting to be dismissed. The girls loved it. They spooned honey into their tea.

"Did you have a nice birthday, Arleen?" they asked. It had been announced several evenings before by Father Snow that it was Arleen's birthday. The girls had remarked that The Birthday was more or less an idiotic American institution regarded with some wonder by the rest of the world. Arleen had blushed. The girls had said that they did not sanction birthdays but that they adored Christmas. Last year they had given Mommy and Daddy adagio dance lessons and a needlepoint book, the pages depicting scenes from their life together — Mommy and Daddy and the girls.

No one had given Arleen anything on her birthday, but she and Father Snow had taken the opportunity to present their house present — a silver-plated cocktail shaker with Mommy and Daddy's initials engraved upon it.

"We were looking for something suitable but not insufferably dull," Father Snow said.

"No, no, you shouldn't have," Mommy said.

"We have ten of those!" the girls said, and rushed to show, hauling them out of the pantry, even the dented and tarnished ones. The cocktail shaker had proved to be a most popular house present over the years.

"I had a lovely birthday," Arleen said. She looked at her wrist and scratched it. "Is Father Snow outside?"

The girls pointed toward the garden. They had long pale shapely arms.

Arleen nodded vaguely and turned to leave, stumbling a bit on the sill.

Between themselves, the girls referred to Father Snow as Father Ice, an irony that gave them satisfaction for his fat sorrow elicited considerable indignation in them. Where was his faith? He didn't have the faith to fill a banana sling. Where was his calm demeanor? It had fled from him. He was the furthest thing from ice they could imagine, the furthest from their admiration of ice, the lacy sheaths, the glare, the brilliance and hardness of ice. There had never been enough of it in their lives. A little, but not much.

Cuddling and kissing the living cats, the girls walked to the kitchen window and looked out into the garden. Arleen was on the ground at Father Ice's feet, her head flung back, drying her hair. Father Ice was talking with his eyes shut, tears streaming down his cheeks.

What a pair! the girls thought. They kissed the cats' stomachs. Father Ice's mouth was flapping away. His lover, a gaunt young man named Donny, had cooked for Father Ice and pressed his vestments. Father Ice had broken down at dinner the previous night over a plate of barbecued butterflied lamb, recalling, it could only be assumed, the manner in which Donny had once prepared this dish. He had just recovered from having broken down an hour earlier at cocktails.

The girls, through the glass, watched Arleen closely.

"She's in love with him, can you believe it. That is not just friendship."

"That kind of love is so safe."

The girls had never been in love. They did not plan on marrying. They would go to the dance clubs and perch on stools, in their little red dresses, their little black ones and white ones, darling provocative tight little dresses, and they would toss their hair and laugh as they gazed into each other's eyes. There were always men around. Men were drawn to them, but one would not be courted without the other, even for amusement — they would not be separated. They were like Siamese twins. They were not Siamese twins, of course, they weren't twins at all, nor were they even born on the same day a year apart, which was why they didn't care for birthdays. Men did not mind the fact that they would not be separated. It excited them agreeably in fact. They didn't believe they didn't stand a chance in the long run.

The girls dropped the cats and moved away from the window, retiring to the large glassed-in porch on the south side of the house to work on their constructions. These were attractive assemblages, neither morbid nor violent nor sexually repressed as was so common with these objects, but tasteful, cold, and peculiar. One of the several young men who were fascinated with the girls made the beautiful partitioned boxes in which selections were placed. One of them contained a snip of lace from Mommy's wedding dress. They hadn't asked her for it, but she hadn't recognized it when she saw it either. There were many things of that nature in the boxes.

They heard Mommy's voice. She was saying, "Now how would you describe the sound it made? An asthmatic squeal is what the bird book said though I wouldn't describe it that way. It certainly did not sound like an asthmatic squeal to me."

Arleen muttered something in reply. She had apparently come back into the house. It was a three-storied nineteenth-century house with fish-scale shingles and wide golden floorboards. It was a wonderful house. Mommy and Daddy almost always had houseguests in the summer. The girls didn't like it; it was as though

Mommy and Daddy didn't want to be alone with them in the loveliest of months. The houseguests didn't stay long, usually no more than a week, but no sooner did they depart than others would arrive. The girls found few of them remarkable. There had been one young woman who held their interest for a weekend by drawing in pencil dozens of semi-Gothic, semi-Saracenic buildings, clearly intended to be visions of the starved or the drugged. They watched her closely, thinking her tremendously chic and fraudulent, and were disappointed when she left abruptly, taking, for it was never seen again, one of Mommy's Hermès beach towels, the one with the Lorraine cross. Most of the guests never returned, but Father Snow had been invited several times. Priests were freeloaders in the girls' opinion, party-crashers, and although Father Snow could give a good performance in the right surroundings — they had observed this at high holidays — he was no exception. They had not encountered Arleen before. At first, certainly, she had not appeared to be a problem. She was shy, deferential, and plain. Her skin ran to bumps around the mouth and she wore red sneakers, the left one slit, she admitted, to accommodate a bunion. She did have lovely auburn hair. The one story she told concerned her hair. She had lovely hair as a child as well and had worn it in a long braid. She had cut it off one morning and given it to a man she had a crush on, a married man, a post office employee or some such thing. It had not been returned and the man had moved away. The girls loved that story. It was so droll, so retarded practically.

The girls heard Mommy's voice again and cocked their heads. She was planning the marketing. If Arleen would like to go into town, they could get flowers as well, and Arleen could give her opinion about a sweater Mommy was considering buying. Daddy said that when you look death in the eye, you want to do it as calmly as a stroller looks into a shop window. But Mommy never looked into a shop window that way. She looked into shop windows with excitement and distress. Sometimes what Daddy said didn't take Mommy into account.

"Girls!" Mommy called.

The girls put aside their constructions and glided into the kitchen where Mommy was putting away the tea things.

"Arleen said she saw the cats playing with a mockingbird earlier. She said they had snapped its legs clean off."

"Clean off?" the girls repeated, marveling at the infelicitous phrasing.

Mommy nodded. She was wearing a lovely floral dressing gown and silk slippers, just like the girls.

"Those weren't our cats," the girls said, "our cats are sweet cats, old stay-at-home cats, they play with store-bought toys only," knowing full well that even this early in the summer the cats had slaughtered no less than a dozen songbirds by visible count, that they were efficient and ruthless and that the way in which they so naturally expressed their essential nature was something the girls admired very much.

"Are you aware," Arleen said, "that domestic cats kill 4.4 million birds every year in this country alone?"

"Awful," Mommy said faintly.

"Mommy, Mommy, Mommy, don't you listen to such dreadful things. Such dreadful things don't happen in our garden," the girls said, hugging her, pretending to hang off her, touching her soft waist with their narrow hands, prattling on until Mommy made a smile.

"On a lighter note," the girls then announced, glaring at Arleen, "we are going to the beach."

There they spent the remainder of the day, nude and much admired, glistening with frequently applied oil. They talked about Mommy and Daddy. This they did not usually do, preferring to keep them inside themselves in quite a definite and distinct way, not touching them with words not even inside words, but just holding them inside, trapped as it were, aware of them quite clearly but not thinking about them, fooling around with them that way.

But Mommy and Daddy were changing. They seemed to be actually crumbling in the girls' eyes. This was of concern. Daddy was smoking and drinking more and surrendering himself to bleak pronouncements. He was sometimes gruff with them as though they were not everything to him! And Mommy's enchantment with life seemed to be waning. They were behaving uncertainly; it was harder for them to be discriminating. Daddy had wanted to burn like a hot fire, and he had not. Clearly, he had not. Something was hastening toward him, and Mommy too, hastening but slowly at once, cloaked in the minutes and months.

The girls returned home, subdued, coming through the garden, passing beneath the rose arbor where the birds' nest was concealed prettily among the climbing canes. The girls grimaced at it, knowing it contained two rotting eggs, having investigated it some days before. They had not informed Mommy of the nest's pulpy contents and they never would, of course.

In the kitchen there was a message for them, written on Mommy's heavy stationery, in Mommy's rounded hand.

Father Snow and Arleen have gone downtown for ice cream cones. Daddy and I are taking our naps.

The girls skipped upstairs and into Father Snow's room. There was nothing there but two black round stones on the table by the single bed.

"He doesn't think that's him and Donny, does he?"

"How ghastly."

In Arleen's room, they immediately went to the suitcase but couldn't find the journal. The journal was missing again, it was nowhere. Then they found it. Triumphant, they scarcely acknowledged Arleen standing in the doorway. She was a smudgy thing, round-shouldered, carrying a whale-shaped purse, a wretched souvenir of this perfect island.

Then she was gone.

"Well, that was considerate of her."

"It *is* our house."

But just as they opened the book, which was covered with a disgusting pink and rawly fibrous cover, Arleen appeared again and spoke the words as they appeared on the first page.

"'Headaches . . . Palpitations . . . Isolated . . . Guilt . . .' And that's a sketch of a photograph your mother showed me. It's you and your parents when you were little girls."

The girls peered at it, at a loss. The woman had no talent whatsoever. On impulse, they bent forward and sniffed it.

"Your mother thinks of her heart as a speeding car," Arleen said. "Too big, too fast, out of control, no one at the wheel. And in her head too, a speeding . . . Further on, there are accounts of some of her dreams."

"She didn't tell you her dreams!" The girls didn't believe it for a moment, that Mommy would tell this *troll* her dreams.

Arleen gently tugged her journal from their hands and smiling thinly at them, left.

The girls sat for several moments in a perturbed silence. Later, in their own room, which comprised the entire third floor and was exotic and theatrical, they bathed and dressed and put up their hair. It was now dusk; the downstairs parlor where they were all to gather for cocktails was filled with a soft and moteless light.

The girls tiptoed down the stairs. Daddy was telling Father Snow about a former houseguest who claimed he could get out of his body anytime he wanted to and turn around and look at it. The girls remembered *that* weekend. They rolled their eyes.

"I never believed him," Mommy said. "But then it's a very subjective matter, I would think."

"Must have gotten a taste for it," Father Snow said.

"I would never, I don't think," Mommy said.

This was regarded as amusing by all. The girls were scandalized by the friendship between Mommy and Daddy and this weird duo. They couldn't bear it for another night.

"Oh, girls, you look lovely!" Mommy exclaimed.

Father Snow was stirring martinis. He wore a jacket and tie. Arleen was wearing . . . something dreadful. The drinks in their crystal glasses were passed around. Father Snow liked to offer a small prayer before the cocktail hour began. To the girls it was merely one of his excruciatingly annoying habits. Prayer is a means of getting rid of some of our own ignorance about ourselves, Father Snow had always said. Mommy and Daddy and Arleen bowed their heads. The girls, as they always did, looked around the room. The mirrors, the embroidered footstool, the good Chinese rug, the little brass clocks, the wallpaper of madder rose. They adored it, this was theirs.

"A toast," Father Snow said, "a toast to those not with us tonight." He looked at them unhappily. "We all have to do this at once," he said. They all took a sip of their drinks.

"Was Donny your first best boy?" the girls asked brightly.

"I wish I could snap out of this," Father Snow said. "I do apologize."

"Maybe you're in the wrong line of work," the girls said with concern.

"I am thinking of resigning my parish," Father Snow said, chewing on an olive, "and dealing with people on a one-to-one basis. Seeing them through. One by one."

Daddy remarked that he and Mommy were with him 100 percent on that.

"Poor Donny," Father Snow said. "He led a fairly incoherent existence and then he died."

"But that's because he was so typical," the girls said. "And there is nothing, absolutely nothing, wrong with that. But what was the matter with his teeth? He had that high-water mark like on his teeth." The girls found the ensuing awkward moment quite satisfying.

Father Snow blinked. "I loved him very much."

The girls sighed. He seemed to them like a mollusk at that moment. He was hardly worth the effort.

"Mommy," they said, "tell the story about the night Daddy proposed."

"Oh," Mommy said, "yes. He knelt before me and said, 'Let's merely see each other every day for the rest of our lives.'" She passed Arleen a cracker with a bit of foul and expensive cheese daubed upon it. This was declined. "Almost thirty-five years ago now."

"Tell the whole story," the girls squealed. "We love the story. Tell how Daddy ran over that man that winter night, the man who was standing beside his disabled car on the highway, but Daddy didn't stop even though he knew he'd very likely killed him because you were going to a concert, it was the night Daddy was going to propose to you, and Daddy didn't want your life together compromised or delayed. You had your life before you!"

Father Snow visibly paled.

"It was Janáček's 'Fairy Tale' that evening," Mommy said. "Debussy and Beethoven were also on the program."

Father Snow looked very ill at ease. Mommy reached out and squeezed his hand. "If this happened," Mommy said, "you'd be able to accept it, wouldn't you? If it had happened, you'd understand."

Father Snow squeezed back. "Only if it had," he said.

"That story has not been previously aired in public," Daddy said.

The girls closed their eyes and hummed a little. They loved the story — the night, the waves of snow descending, the elegant evening clothes, the nonexistent girls, some stranger sacrificed.

Father Snow drained his drink. "I'm going to make another batch of these if I may," he said. He extricated his hand from Mommy's and dumped more gin in the shaker, swirled it once and poured, without ceremony. There simply were some situations that did not allow for the sacralization of the ordinary, which he otherwise made every effort to observe.

He swallowed and groped for Mommy's hand again, recoiling slightly when he found it.

"Do you think we could do something about it?" Mommy said tentatively. "Is it possible after all these years?"

"Repent?" he said, his voice cracking. "Repent," he said.

Mommy looked at him with some annoyance. "I've always thought that was a rather commonly easy thing to do." She wanted to offer more cheese to all, but her hand was trapped. "I do feel sorry," she said. "We do."

"But the word is misunderstood!" Father Snow said. "The word translated throughout the New Testament as *repentance* is, in the Greek, *meta-noia,* which means change of mind. *Meta* means transference, as in *metaphor*— transference of meaning. Transformation."

"Repent," Mommy said. "So unhelpful. So common, really."

"The English word *repentance* is derived from the Latin *poenitare,* which merely means to feel sorry, suggesting a change in the heart rather than in the mind. *Poenitare* is a most inadequate word, which doesn't reflect the challenge involved," Father Snow said excitedly.

"We've had a good life," Daddy said, smoking. "Full. Can't take that away from us."

Father Snow looked at his drink. The moment of exhilaration had passed. He was now merely drunk and missing Donny in the same sad keen way. "Very difficult. Another way of thinking, a different approach to everything in life . . ." he said uncertainly.

The cats came into the room and leapt up onto Arleen's lap. The cats would do this to people they sensed hated them, and this amused the girls. But Arleen stroked them, first the one, then the other. From one's side she plucked a bloodsucker the size of a swollen dime. She held it between her fingers, a fat full thing with tiny waving legs, and dropped it in the dish Daddy was using as an ashtray. From behind the ear of the other cat, Arleen snapped off another. Its removal occasioned a slight clicking sound. She dropped it beside the other one. The things stumbled around in the ashes in the little china dish. The attractive floral pattern that was so Mommy, that Mommy admired on all her china, was totally obscured. In this pretty room, this formal room with the silk shades, the portraits of ancestors, and the lark beneath the bell jar.

"That's disgusting, Arleen," the girls said. They had no doubt that she had produced them fraudulently. Their pets, their darlings, could not possibly be harboring such things. "Are you a magician? Isn't that unchristian?"

"No, no," Arleen said, ducking her head shyly. "I'm hardly a magician. I'm an adviser, a companion."

"Arleen's no amateur," Father Snow said.

"A companion?" the girls said.

"The woman can listen to anything and come to a swift decision," Father Snow said. "I rely more on the ritual stuff. Words. Blah blah blah."

Arleen turned to Mommy. "You should get rid of them."

"The cats?" Mommy said. "Oh, I know, sometimes they *spray* . . ."

"The girls," Arleen said. "High time for them to be gone."

The girls gaped at her.

"Your mother's not well, you're killing her," Arleen said simply.

Mommy looked at them. She looked as though she didn't know what to think. Daddy lay his burning cigarette in the dish, then ground it out and lit another. The ashes moved with continuing, even renewed, effort.

Mommy spread more cheese on the crackers, quickly, quickly. Wads of it, a bit more than was nice actually. She stood up to pass the plate, tottering a bit.

"Oh, do sit down," the girls said, exasperated.

She did, abruptly, looking stunned as though she had seen something quite unusual, though more puzzling than extraordinary.

Father Snow said, "Clarissa, are you all right?" for Clarissa was Mommy's name.

"Dear?" Daddy said.

She smiled slyly and gave a little grunt. It was all so not like Mommy. She swayed and slid to the floor not at all gracefully, entangling herself in the cord of a lamp and striking her head on the lintel of the fireplace.

The girls clutched each other and cried out.

Arleen moved to cradle Clarissa's head, and Father Snow, with surprising sureness, crouched beside them both. He had quite regained his composure, as though for the moment he had put the old dead behind him and was moving on to the requirements of the quickening new.

CORY DOCTOROW

Anda's Game

FROM SALON.COM

ANDA DIDN'T REALLY START TO PLAY the game until she got herself a girl-shaped avatar. She was twelve, and up until then, she'd played a boy-elf because her parents had sternly warned her that if you played a girl you were an instant perv-magnet. None of the girls at Ada Lovelace Comprehensive would have been caught dead playing a girl character. In fact, the only girls she'd ever seen in-game were being played by boys. You could tell, cos they were shaped like a boy's idea of what a girl looked like: hooge buzwabs and long legs all barely contained in tiny, pointless leather bikini-armor. Bintware, she called it.

But when Anda was twelve, she met Liza the Organiza, whose avatar was female but had sensible tits and sensible armor and a bloody great sword that she was clearly very good with. Liza came to school after PE, when Anda was sitting and massaging her abused podge and hating her entire life from stupid sunrise to rotten sunset. Her PE kit was at the bottom of her school bag, and her face was that stupid red color that she *hated* and now it was stinking maths, which was hardly better than PE but at least she didn't have to sweat.

But instead of maths, all the girls were called to assembly, and Liza the Organiza stood on the stage in front of Miss Cruickshanks, the principal, and Mrs. Danzig, the useless counselor.

"Hullo, chickens," Liza said. She had an Australian accent. "Well, aren't you lot just precious and bright and expectant with your pink upturned faces like a load of flowers staring up at the sky? Warms me fecking heart it does."

That made her laugh, and she wasn't the only one. Miss Cruickshanks and Mrs. Danzig didn't look amused, but they tried to hide it.

"I am Liza the Organiza, and I kick arse. Seriously." She tapped a key on her laptop and the screen behind her lit up. It was a game — not the one that Anda played, but something space-themed, a space station with a rocket ship in the background. "This is my avatar." Sensible boobs, sensible armor, and a sword the size of the world. "In-game, they call me the Lizanator, Queen of the Spacelanes, El Presidente of the Clan Fahrenheit." The Fahrenheits had chapters in every game. They were amazing and deadly and cool, and to her knowledge, Anda had never met one in the flesh. They had their own *island* in her game. Crikey.

On screen, the Lizanator was fighting an army of wookie-men, sword in one hand, laser-blaster in the other, rocket-jumping, spinning, strafing, making impossible kills and long shots, diving for power-ups and ruthlessly running her enemies to ground.

"The *whole* Clan Fahrenheit. I won that title through popular election, but they voted me in cos of my prowess in *combat.* I'm a world-champion in six different games, from first-person shooters to strategy games. I've commanded armies and I've sent armies to their respawn gates by the thousands. Thousands, chickens: my battle record is 3,522 kills in a single battle. I have taken home cash prizes from competitions totaling more than 400,000 pounds. I game for four to six hours nearly every day, and the rest of the time, I do what I like.

"One of the things I like to do is come to girls' schools like yours and let you in on a secret: girls kick arse. We're faster, smarter, and better than boys. We play harder. We spend too much time thinking that we're freaks for gaming and when we do game, we never play as girls because we catch so much shite for it. Time to turn that around. I am the best gamer in the world and I'm a girl. I started playing at ten, and there were no women in games — you couldn't even buy a game in any of the shops I went to. It's different now, but it's still not perfect. We're going to change that, chickens, you lot and me.

"How many of you game?"

Anda put her hand up. So did about half the girls in the room.

"And how many of you play girls?"

All the hands went down.

"See, that's a tragedy. Practically makes me weep. Gamespace smells like a boy's *armpit.* It's time we girled it up a little. So here's my offer to you: if you will play as a girl, you will be given probationary memberships in the Clan Fahrenheit, and if you measure up, in six months, you'll be full-fledged members."

In real life, Liza the Organiza was a little podgy, like Anda herself, but she wore it with confidence. She was solid, like a brick wall, her hair bobbed bluntly at her shoulders. She dressed in a black jumper over loose dungarees with giant, goth boots with steel toes that looked like something you'd see in an in-game shop, though Anda was pretty sure they'd come from a real-world goth shop in Camden Town.

She stomped her boots, one-two, thump-thump, like thunder on the stage. "Who's in, chickens? Who wants to be a girl out-game and in?"

Anda jumped to her feet. A Fahrenheit, with her own island! Her head was so full of it that she didn't notice that she was the only one standing. The other girls stared at her, a few giggling and whispering.

"That's all right, love," Liza called, "I like enthusiasm. Don't let those staring faces rattle yer: they're just flowers turning to look at the sky. Pink scrubbed shining expectant faces. They're looking at you because *you* had the sense to get to your feet when opportunity came — and that means that someday, girl, you are going to be a leader of women, and men, and you will kick arse. Welcome to the Clan Fahrenheit."

She began to clap, and the other girls clapped too, and even though Anda's face was the color of a lollipop-lady's sign, she felt like she might burst with pride and good feeling, and she smiled until her face hurt.

> Anda,

her sergeant said to her,

> how would you like to make some money?

> Money, Sarge?

Ever since she'd risen to platoon leader, she'd been getting more missions, but they paid *gold* — money wasn't really something you talked about in-game.

The Sarge — sensible boobs, gigantic sword, longbow, gloriously orcish ugly phiz — moved her avatar impatiently.

> Something wrong with my typing, Anda?

> No, Sarge,
she typed.

> You mean gold?

> If I meant gold, I would have said gold. Can you go voice?

Anda looked around. Her door was shut and she could hear her parents in the sitting room, watching something loud on telly. She turned up her music just to be safe and then slipped on her headset. They said it could noise-cancel a Blackhawk helicopter — it had better be able to overcome the little inductive speakers suction-cupped to the underside of her desk. She switched to voice.

"Hey, Lucy," she said.

"Call me Sarge!" Lucy's accent was American, like an old TV show, and she lived somewhere in the middle of the country where it was all vowels, Iowa or Ohio. She was Anda's best friend in-game, but she was so hard-core it was boring sometimes.

"Hi, Sarge," she said, trying to keep the irritation out of her voice. She'd never smart off to a superior in-game, but v2v it was harder to remember to keep to the game norms.

"I have a mission that pays real cash. Whichever paypal you're using, they'll deposit money into it. Looks fun, too."

"That's a bit weird, Sarge. Is that against Clan rules?" There were a lot of Clan rules about what kind of mission you could accept and they were always changing. There were curb-crawlers in gamespace, and the way that the Clan leadership kept all the mummies and daddies from going ape-poo about it was by enforcing a long, boring code of conduct that was meant to ensure that none of the Fahrenheit girlies ended up being virtual prozzies for hairy old men in raincoats on the other side of the world.

"What?" Anda loved how Lucy quacked *What?* It sounded especially American. She had to force herself from parroting it back. "No, jeez. All the executives in the Clan pay the rent doing missions for money. Some of them are even rich from it, I hear! You can make a lot of money gaming, you know."

"Is it really true?" She'd heard about this but she'd assumed it was just stories, like the kids who gamed so much that they couldn't tell reality from fantasy. Or the ones who gamed so much that they stopped eating and got all anorexic. She wouldn't mind getting a little anorexic, to be honest. Bloody podge.

"Yup! And this is our chance to get in on the ground floor. Are you in?"

"It's not — you know, *pervy,* is it?"

"Gag me. No. Jeez, Anda! Are you nuts? No — they want us to go kill some guys."

"Oh, we're good at that!"

The mission took them far from Fahrenheit Island to a cottage on the far side of the largest continent on the gameworld, which was called Dandelionwine. The travel was tedious, and twice they were ambushed on the trail, something that had hardly happened to Anda since she joined the Fahrenheits: attacking a Fahrenheit was bad for your health, because even if you won the battle, they'd bring a war to you.

But now they were far from the Fahrenheits' power base, and two different packs of brigands waylaid them on the road. Lucy spotted the first group before they got into sword range and killed four of the six with her bow before they closed for hand-to-hand. Anda's sword — gigantic and fast — was out then, and her fingers danced over the keyboard as she fought off the player who was attacking her, her body jerking from side to side as she hammered on the multibutton controller beside her. She won — of course! She was a Fahrenheit! Lucy had already slaughtered her attacker. They desultorily searched the bodies and came up with some gold and a couple of scrolls, but nothing to write home about. Even the gold didn't seem like much, given the cash waiting at the end of the mission.

The second group of brigands was even less daunting, though there were twenty of them. They were total noobs and fought like statues. They'd clearly clubbed together to protect themselves from harder players, but they were no match for Anda and Lucy. One of them even begged for his life before she ran him through,

> please sorry u cn have my gold sorry!!!!!!

Anda laughed and sent him to the respawn gate.

> You're a nasty person, Anda,

Lucy typed.

> I'm a Fahrenheit!!!!!!!!!!

she typed back.

The brigands on the road were punters, but the cottage that was their target was guarded by an altogether more sophisticated sort. They were spotted by sentries long before they got within sight of the cottage, and they saw the warning spell travel up from the sentries' hilltop like a puff of smoke, speeding away toward the cottage. Anda raced up the hill while Lucy covered her with her bow, but that didn't stop the sentries from subjecting Anda to a hail of flaming spears from their fortified position. Anda set up her standard dodge-and-weave pattern, assuming that the sentries were nonplayer characters — who wanted to *pay* to sit around in gamespace watching a boring road all day? — and to her surprise, the spears followed her. She took one in the chest, and only some fast work with her shield and all her healing scrolls saved her. As it was, her constitution was knocked down by half and she had to retreat back down the hillside.

"Get down," Lucy said in her headset. "I'm gonna use the BFG."

Every game had one — the Big Friendly Gun, the generic term for the baddest-arse weapon in the world. Lucy had rented this one from the Clan armory for a small fortune in gold and Anda had laughed and called her paranoid, but now Anda helped Lucy set it up and thanked the gamegods for her foresight. It was a huge, demented flaming crossbow that fired five-meter bolts that exploded on impact. It was a beast to arm and a beast to aim, but they had a nice, dug-in position of their own at the bottom of the hill and it was there that they got the BFG set up, deployed, armed, and ranged.

"Fire!" Lucy called, and the game did this amazing and cool animation that it rewarded you with whenever you loosed a bolt from the BFG, making the gamelight dim toward the sizzling bolt as though it were sucking the illumination out of the world as it arced up the hillside, trailing a comet-tail of sparks. The game played them a groan of dismay from their enemies, and then the bolt hit home with a crash that made her point-of-view vibrate like an earthquake. The roar in her headphones was deafening, and behind it she could hear Lucy on the voice-chat, cheering it on.

"Nuke 'em till they glow and shoot 'em in the dark! Yee-haw!" Lucy called, and Anda laughed and pounded her fist on the desk. Gobbets of former enemy sailed over the treeline dramatically, dripping hyper-red blood and ichor.

In her bedroom, Anda caressed the controller-pad, and her avatar punched the air and did a little rugby victory dance that the All-Blacks had released as a limited edition promo after they won the World Cup.

Now they had to move fast, for their enemies at the cottage would be alerted to their presence and waiting for them. They spread out into a wide flanking maneuver around the cottage's sides, staying just outside of bow range, using scrying scrolls to magnify the cottage and make the foliage around them fade to translucency.

There were four guards around the cottage, two with nocked arrows and two with whirling slings. One had a scroll out and was surrounded by the concentration marks that indicated spellcasting.

"GO GO GO!" Lucy called.

Anda went! She had two scrolls left in her inventory, and one was a shield spell. They cost a fortune and burned out fast, but whatever that guard was cooking up, it had to be bad news. She cast the spell as she charged for the cottage, and lucky thing, because there was a fifth guard up a tree who dumped a pot of boiling oil on her that would have cooked her down to her bones in ten seconds if not for the spell.

She power-climbed the tree and nearly lost her grip when whatever the nasty spell was bounced off her shield. She reached the fifth man as he was trying to draw his dirk and dagger and lopped his bloody head off in one motion, then backflipped off the high branch, trusting to her shield to stay intact for her impact on the cottage roof.

The strategy worked — now she had the drop (literally!) on the remaining guards, having successfully taken the high ground. In her headphones, the sound of Lucy making mayhem, the grunts as she pounded her keyboard mingling with the in-game shrieks as her arrows found homes in the chests of two more of the guards.

Shrieking a berserker wail, Anda jumped down off the roof and landed on one of the two remaining guards, plunging her sword into his chest and pinning him in the dirt. Her sword stuck in the ground, and she hammered on her keys, trying to free it, while the remaining guard ran for her on screen. Anda pounded her keyboard, but it was useless: the sword was good and stuck. Poo. She'd blown a small fortune on spells and rations for this project with the expectation of getting some real cash out of it, and now it was all lost.

She moved her hands to the part of the keypad that controlled motion and began to run, waiting for the guard's sword to find her avatar's back and knock her into the dirt.

"Got 'im!" It was Lucy, in her headphones. She wheeled her avatar about so quickly it was nauseating, and she saw that Lucy was on her erstwhile attacker, grunting as she engaged him close in. Something was wrong, though: despite Lucy's avatar's awesome stats and despite Lucy's own skill at the keyboard, she was being taken to the cleaners. The guard was kicking her ass. Anda went back to her stuck sword and recommenced whanging on it, watching helplessly as Lucy lost her left arm, then took a cut on her belly, then another to her knee.

"Shit!" Lucy said in her headphones as her avatar began to keel over. Anda yanked her sword free — finally — and charged at the guard, screaming a ululating war cry. He managed to get his avatar swung around and his sword up before she reached him, but it didn't matter: she got in a lucky swing that took off one leg, then danced back before he could counterstrike. Now she closed carefully, nicking at his sword hand until he dropped his weapon, then moving in for a fast kill.

"Lucy?"

"Call me Sarge!"

"Sorry, Sarge. Where'd you respawn?"

"I'm all the way over at Body Electric — it'll take me hours to get there. Do you think you can complete the mission on your own?"

"Uh, sure." Thinking, *Crikey,* if that's what the guards *outside* were like, how'm I gonna get past the *inside* guards?

"You're the best, girl. Okay, enter the cottage and kill everyone there."

"Uh, sure."

She wished she had another scrying scroll in inventory so she could get a look inside the cottage before she beat its door in, but she was fresh out of scrolls and just about everything else.

She kicked the door in and her fingers danced. She'd killed four of her adversaries before she even noticed that they weren't fighting back.

In fact, they were generic avatars, maybe even nonplayer characters. They moved like total noobs, milling around in the little cottage. Around them were heaps of shirts, thousands and thousands of them. A couple of the noobs were sitting in the back, incredibly, still crafting more shirts, ignoring the swordswoman who'd just butchered four of their companions.

She took a careful look at all the avatars in the room. None of them were armed. Tentatively, she walked up to one of the players and cut his head off. The player next to him moved clumsily to one side and she followed him.

"Are you a player or a bot?" she typed.

The avatar did nothing. She killed it.

"Lucy, they're not fighting back."

"Good, kill them all."

"Really?"

"Yeah — that's the orders. Kill them all and then I'll make a phone call and some guys will come by and verify it and then you haul ass back to the island. I'm coming out there to meet you, but it's a long haul from the respawn gate. Keep an eye on my stuff, okay?"

"Sure," Anda said, and killed two more. That left ten. *One two one two and through and through,* she thought, lopping their heads off. Her vorpal blade went snicker-snack. One left. He stood off in the back.

> *no porfa necesito mi plata*

Italian? No, Spanish. She'd had a term of it in Third Form, though she couldn't understand what this twit was saying. She could always paste the text into a translation bot on one of the chat channels, but who cared? She cut his head off.

"They're all dead," she said into her headset.

"Good job!" Lucy said. "Okay, I'm gonna make a call. Sit tight."

Bo-ring. The cottage was filled with corpses and shirts. She picked some of them up. They were totally generic: the shirts you crafted when you were down at Level 0 and trying to get enough skillz to actually make something of yourself. Each one would fetch just a few coppers. Add it all together and you barely had two thousand gold.

Just to pass the time, she pasted the Spanish into the chatbot.

> no [colloquial] please, I need my [colloquial] [money|silver]

Pathetic. A few thousand golds — he could make that much by playing a couple of the beginner missions. More fun. More rewarding. Crafting shirts!

She left the cottage and patrolled around it. Twenty minutes later, two more avatars showed up. More generics.

> are you players or bots?

she typed, though she had an idea they were players. Bots moved better.

> any trouble?

Well all right then.

> no trouble

> good

One player entered the cottage and came back out again. The other player spoke.

> you can go now

"Lucy?"

"What's up?"

"Two blokes just showed up and told me to piss off. They're noobs, though. Should I kill them?"

"No! Jeez, Anda, those are the contacts. They're just making sure the job was done. Get my stuff and meet me at Marionettes Tavern, okay?"

Anda went over to Lucy's corpse and looted it, then set out down the road, dragging the BFG behind her. She stopped at the bend in the road and sneaked a peek back at the cottage. It was in flames, the two noobs standing amid them, burning slowly along with the cottage and a few thousand golds' worth of badly crafted shirts.

That was the first of Anda and Lucy's missions, but it wasn't the last. That month, she fought her way through six more, and the paypal she used filled with real, honest-to-goodness cash, pounds sterling that she could withdraw from the cashpoint situated exactly 501 meters away from the school gate, next to the candy shop that was likewise 501 meters away.

"Anda, I don't think it's healthy for you to spend so much time with your game," her da said, prodding her bulging podge with a finger. "It's not healthy."

"Daaaa!" she said, pushing his finger aside. "I go to PE every stinking day. It's good enough for the Ministry of Education."

"I don't like it," he said. He was no movie star himself, with a little pot belly that he wore his belted trousers high upon, a wobbly extra chin, and two bat wings of flab hanging off his upper arms. She pinched his chin and wiggled it.

"I get loads more exercise than you, Mr. Kettle."

"But I pay the bills around here, little Miss Pot."

"You're not seriously complaining about the cost of the game?" she said, infusing her voice with as much incredulity and disgust as she could muster. "Ten quid a week and I get unlimited calls, texts, and messages! Plus play, of course, and the in-game encyclopedia and spellchecker and translator bots!" (This was all from rote — every member of the Fahrenheits memorized this or something very like it for dealing with recalcitrant, ignorant parental units.) "Fine then. If the game is too dear for you, Da, let's set it aside and I'll just start using a normal phone, is that what you want?"

Her da held up his hands. "I surrender, Miss Pot. But *do* try to get a little more exercise, please? Fresh air? Sport? Games?"

"Getting my head trodden on in the hockey pitch, more like," she said, darkly.

"Zackly!" he said, prodding her podge anew. "That's the stuff! Getting my head trodden on was what made me the man I are today!"

Her da could bluster all he liked about paying the bills, but she had pocket money for the first time in her life: not book tokens and fruit tokens and milk tokens that could be exchanged for "healthy" snacks and literature. She had real money, cash money that she could spend outside of the 500-meter sugar-free zone that surrounded her school.

She wasn't just kicking arse in the game, now — she was the richest kid she knew, and suddenly she was everybody's best pal, with handfuls of Curly Wurlies and Dairy Milks and Mars Bars that she could selectively distribute to her schoolmates.

"Go get a BFG," Lucy said. "We're going on a mission."

Lucy's voice in her ear was a constant companion in her life now. When she wasn't on Fahrenheit Island, she and Lucy were running missions into the wee hours of the night. The Fahrenheit armorers, nonplayer characters, had learned to recognize her and they had the Clan's BFGs oiled and ready for her when she showed up.

Today's mission was close to home, which was good: the road trips were getting tedious. Sometimes, nonplayer characters or Game Masters would try to get them involved in an official in-game mission, impressed by their stats and weapons, and it sometimes broke her heart to pass them up, but cash always beat gold and experience beat experience points: *Money talks and bullshit walks,* as Lucy liked to say.

They caught the first round of sniper/lookouts before they had a chance to attack or send off a message. Anda used the scrying spell to spot them. Lucy had kept both BFGs armed, and she loosed rounds at the hilltops flanking the roadway as soon as Anda gave her the signal, long before they got into bow range.

As they picked their way through the ruined chunks of the dead player-character snipers, Anda still on the lookout, she broke the silence over their voicelink.

"Hey, Lucy?"

"Anda, if you're not going to call me Sarge, at least don't call me 'Hey, Lucy!' My dad loved that old TV show and he makes that joke every visitation day."

"Sorry, Sarge. Sarge?"

"Yes, Anda?"

"I just can't understand why anyone would pay us cash for these missions."

"You complaining?"

"No, but —"

"Anyone asking you to cyber some old pervert?"

"No!"

"Okay then. I don't know either. But the money's good. I don't care. Hell, probably it's two rich gamers who pay their butlers to craft for them all day. One's fucking with the other one and paying us."

"You really think that?"

Lucy sighed a put-upon, sophisticated, American sigh. "Look at it this way. Most of the world is living on like a dollar a day. I spend five dollars every day on a frappuccino. Some days, I get two! Dad sends Mom three thousand a month in child support — that's a hundred bucks a day. So if a day's money here is a hundred dollars, then to an African or whatever my frappuccino is worth like *five hundred dollars*. And I buy two or three every day.

"And we're not rich! There's craploads of rich people who wouldn't think twice about spending five hundred bucks on a coffee — how much do you think a hot dog and a Coke go for on the space station? A thousand bucks!

"So that's what I think is going on. There's someone out there, some Saudi or Japanese guy or Russian mafia kid who's so rich that this is just chump change for him, and he's paying us to mess around with some other rich person. To them, we're like the Africans making a dollar a day to craft — I mean, sew — T-shirts. What's a couple hundred bucks to them? A cup of coffee."

Anda thought about it. It made a kind of sense. She'd been on hols in Bratislava where they got a posh hotel room for ten quid — less than she was spending every day on sweeties and fizzy drinks.

"Three o'clock," she said, and aimed the BFG again. More snipers pat-patted in bits around the forest floor.

"Nice one, Anda."

"Thanks, Sarge."

They smashed half a dozen more sniper outposts and fought their way through a couple packs of suspiciously bad-ass brigands before coming upon the cottage.

"Bloody hell," Anda breathed. The cottage was ringed with guards, forty or fifty of them, with bows and spells and spears, in entrenched positions.

"This is nuts," Lucy agreed. "I'm calling them. This is nuts."

There was a muting click as Lucy rang off and Anda used up a scrying scroll to examine the inventories of the guards around the corner. The more she looked, the more scared she got. They were loaded down with spells, a couple of them were guarding BFGs and what looked like an even *bigger* BFG, maybe the fabled BFG10K, something that was removed from the game economy not long after gameday one as too disruptive to the balance of power. Supposedly, one or two existed, but that was just a rumor. Wasn't it?

"Okay," Lucy said. "Okay, this is how this goes. We've got to do this. I just called in three squads of Fahrenheit veterans and their noob prentices for backup." Anda summed that up in her head to a hundred player characters and maybe three hundred nonplayer characters: familiars, servants, demons . . .

"That's a lot of shares to split the pay into," Anda said.

"Oh ye of little tits," Lucy said. "I've negotiated a bonus for us if we make it — a million gold and three missions' worth of cash. The Fahrenheits are taking payment in gold — they'll be here in an hour."

This wasn't a mission anymore, Anda realized. It was war. Gamewar. Hundreds of players converging on this shard, squaring off against the ranked mercenaries guarding the huge cottage over the hill.

Lucy wasn't the ranking Fahrenheit on the scene, but she was the designated general. One of the gamers up from Fahrenheit Island brought a team flag for her to carry, a long spear with the magical standard snapping proudly from it as the troops formed up behind her.

"On my signal," Lucy said. The voice chat was like a wind tunnel from all the unmuted breathing voices, hundreds of girls in hundreds of bedrooms like Anda's, all over the world, some sitting down before breakfast, some just coming home from school, some roused from sleep by their ringing game-sponsored mobiles. "GO GO GO!"

They went, roaring, and Anda roared too, heedless of her parents downstairs in front of the blaring telly, heedless of her throat lining, a Fahrenheit in berserker rage, sword swinging. She made straight for the BFG10K — a siege engine that could level a town wall, and it would be hers, captured by her for the Fahrenheits if she could do it. She spelled into insensibility the merc who was cranking it, rolled and rolled again to dodge arrows and spells, healed herself when an arrow found her leg and sent her tumbling, springing to her feet before another arrow could strike home, watching her hit points and experience points move in opposite directions.

HERS! She vaulted the BFG10K and snicker-snacked her sword through two mercs' heads. Two more appeared — they had the thing primed and aimed at the main body of Fahrenheit fighters, and they could turn the battle's tide just by firing it — and she killed them, slamming her keypad, howling, barely conscious of the answering howls in her headset.

Now *she* had the BFG10K, though more mercs were closing on her. She disarmed it quickly and spelled at the nearest bunch of mercs, then had to take evasive action against the hail of incoming arrows and spells. It was all she could do to cast healing spells fast enough to avoid losing consciousness.

"LUCY!" she called into her headset. "LUCY, OVER BY THE BFG10K!"

Lucy snapped out orders, and the opposition before Anda began to thin as Fahrenheits fell on them from behind. The flood was stemmed, and now the Fahrenheits' greater numbers and discipline showed. In short order, every merc was butchered or run off.

Anda waited by the BFG10K while Lucy paid off the Fahrenheits and saw them on their way. "Now we take the cottage," Lucy said.

"Right," Anda said. She set her character off for the doorway. Lucy brushed past her.

"I'll be glad when we're done with this — that was bugfuck nutso." She opened the door and her character disappeared in a fireball that erupted from directly overhead. A door-curse, a serious one, one that cooked her in her armor in seconds.

"SHIT!" Lucy said in her headset.

Anda giggled. "Teach *you* to go rushing into things," she said. She used up a couple scrying scrolls making sure that there was nothing else in the cottage save for millions of shirts and thousands of unarmed noob avatars that she'd have to mow down like grass to finish out the mission.

She descended upon them like a reaper, swinging her sword heedlessly, taking five or six out with each swing. When she'd been a noob in the game, she'd had to endure endless fighting practice, "grappling" with piles of leaves and other nonlethal targets, just to get enough experience points to have a chance of hitting anything. This was every bit as dull.

Her wrists were getting tired, and her chest heaved and her hated podge wobbled as she worked the keypad.

> Wait, please, don't — I'd like to speak with you

It was a noob avatar, just like the others, but not just like it after all, for it moved with purpose, backing away from her sword. And it spoke English.

> nothing personal,

she typed.

> just a job

> There are many here to kill — take me last at least. I need to talk to you.

> talk, then,

she typed. Meeting players who moved well and spoke English was hardly unusual in gamespace, but here in the cleanup phase, it felt out of place. It felt *wrong.*

> My name is Raymond, and I live in Tijuana. I am a labor organizer in the factories here. What is your name?

> i don't give out my name in-game

> What can I call you?

> kali

It was a name she liked to use in-game: Kali, Destroyer of Worlds, like the Hindu goddess.

> Are you in India?

> london

> You are Indian?

> naw im a whitey

She was halfway through the room, mowing down the noobs in twos and threes. She was hungry and bored and this Raymond was weirding her out.

> Do you know who these people are that you're killing?

She didn't answer, but she had an idea. She killed four more and shook out her wrists.

> They're working for less than a dollar a day. The shirts they make are traded for gold and the gold is sold on eBay. Once their avatars have leveled up, they too are sold off on eBay. They're mostly young girls supporting their families. They're the lucky ones: the unlucky ones work as prostitutes.

Her wrists *really* ached. She slaughtered half a dozen more.

> The bosses used to use bots, but the game has countermeasures against them. Hiring children to click the mouse is cheaper than hiring programmers to circumvent the rules. I've been trying to unionize them because they've got a very high rate of injury. They have to play for eighteen-hour shifts with only one short toilet break. Some of them can't hold it in and they soil themselves where they sit.

> look,

she typed, exasperated.

> it's none of my lookout, is it. the world's like that. lots of people with no money. im just a kid, theres nothing i can do about it.

> When you kill them, they don't get paid.

no porfa necesito mi plata

> When you kill them, they lose their day's wages. Do you know who is paying you to do these killings?

She thought of Saudis, rich Japanese, Russian mobsters.

> not a clue

> I've been trying to find that out myself, Kali.

They were all dead now. Raymond stood alone amongst the piled corpses.

> Go ahead,

he typed

> I will see you again, I'm sure.

She cut his head off. Her wrists hurt. She was hungry. She was alone there in the enormous woodland cottage, and she still had to haul the BFG10K back to Fahrenheit Island.

"Lucy?"

"Yeah, yeah, I'm almost back there, hang on. I respawned in the ass end of nowhere."

"Lucy, do you know who's in the cottage? Those noobs that we kill?"

"What? Hell no. Noobs. Someone's butler. I dunno. Jesus, that spawn gate —"

"Girls. Little girls in Mexico. Getting paid a dollar a day to craft shirts. Except they don't get their dollar when we kill them. They don't get anything."

"Oh, for Chrissakes, is that what one of them told you? Do you believe everything someone tells you in-game? Christ. English girls are so naive."

"You don't think it's true?"

"Naw, I don't."

"Why not?"

"I just don't, okay? I'm almost there, keep your panties on."

"I've got to go, Lucy," she said. Her wrists hurt, and her podge overlapped the waistband of her trousers, making her feel a bit like she was drowning.

"What, now? Shit, just hang on."

"My mom's calling me to supper. You're almost here, right?"

"Yeah, but —"

She reached down and shut off her PC.

Anda's da and mum were watching the telly again with a bowl of crisps between them. She walked past them like she was dreaming and stepped out the door onto the terrace. It was nighttime, eleven o'clock, and the chavs in front of the council flats across the square were kicking a football around and swilling lager and making rude noises. They were skinny and rawboned, wearing shorts and string vests with strong, muscular limbs flashing in the streetlights.

"Anda?"

"Yes, Mum?"

"Are you all right?" Her mum's fat fingers caressed the back of her neck.

"Yes, Mum. Just needed some air is all."

"You're very clammy," her mum said. She licked a finger and scrubbed it across Anda's neck. "Gosh, you're dirty — how did you get to be such a mucky puppy?"

"Owww!" she said. Her mum was scrubbing so hard it felt like she'd take her skin off.

"No whingeing," her mum said sternly. "Behind your ears, too! You are *filthy.*"

"Mum, *owwww!*"

Her mum dragged her up to the bathroom and went at her with a flannel and a bar of soap and hot water until she felt boiled and raw.

"What *is* this mess?" her mum said.

"Lilian, leave off," her da said, quietly. "Come out into the hall for a moment, please."

The conversation was too quiet to hear and Anda didn't want to, anyway: she was concentrating too hard on not crying — her ears *hurt.*

Her mum enfolded her shoulders in her soft hands again. "Oh, darling, I'm sorry. It's a skin condition, your father tells me, Acanthosis Nigricans — he saw it in a TV special. We'll see the doctor about it tomorrow after school. Are you all right?"

"I'm fine," she said, twisting to see if she could see the "dirt" on the back of her neck in the mirror. It was hard because it was an awkward placement — but also because she didn't like to look at her face and her soft extra chin, and she kept catching sight of it.

She went back to her room to Google "Acanthosis Nigricans."

A condition involving darkened, thickened skin. Found in the folds of skin at the base of the back of the neck, under the arms, inside the elbow, and at the waistline. Often precedes a diagnosis of type-2 diabetes, especially in children. If found in children, immediate steps must be taken to prevent diabetes, including exercise and nutrition as a means of lowering insulin levels and increasing insulin sensitivity.

Obesity-related diabetes. They had lectures on this every term in health class — the fastest-growing ailment among British teens, accompanied by photos of orca-fat sacks of lard sat up in bed surrounded by an ocean of rubbery, flowing podge. Anda prodded her belly and watched it jiggle.

It jiggled. Her thighs jiggled. Her chins wobbled. Her arms sagged.

She grabbed a handful of her belly and *squeezed it,* pinched it hard as she could, until she had to let go or cry out. She'd left livid red fingerprints in the rolls of fat and she was crying now, from the pain and the shame and oh, God, she was a fat girl with diabetes —

"Jesus, Anda, where the hell have you been?"

"Sorry, Sarge," she said. "My PC's been broken —" Well, out of service, anyway. Under lock and key in her da's study. Almost a month now of medications and no telly and no gaming and double PE periods at school with the other whales. She was miserable all day, every day now, with nothing to look forward to except the trips after school to the news agents at the 501-meter mark and the fistfuls of sweeties and bottles of fizzy drink she ate in the park while she watched the chavs play footy.

"Well, you should have found a way to let me know. I was getting worried about you, girl."

"Sorry, Sarge," she said again. The PC Baang was filled with stinky spotty boys — literally stinky, it smelled like goats, like a train-station toilet — being loud and obnoxious. The dinky headphones provided were greasy as a slice of pizza, and the mouthpiece was sticky with excited-boy saliva from games gone past.

But it didn't matter. Anda was back in the game, and just in time, too: her money was running short.

"Well, I've got a backlog of missions here. I tried going out with a couple other of the girls" — a pang of regret shot through Anda at the thought that her position might have been usurped while she was locked off the game — "but you're too good to replace, okay? I've got four missions we can do today if you're game."

"Four missions! How on earth will we do four missions? That'll take days!"

"We'll take the BFG10K." Anda could hear the savage grin in her voice.

The BFG10K simplified things quite a lot. Find the cottage, aim the BFG10K, fire it, whim-wham, no more cottage. They started with five bolts for it — one BFG10K bolt was made up of twenty regular BFG bolts, each costing a small fortune in gold — and used them all up on the first three targets. After returning it to the armory and grabbing a couple of BFGs (amazing how puny the BFG seemed after just a couple hours' campaigning with a really *big* gun!) they set out for number four.

"I met a guy after the last campaign," Anda said. "One of the noobs in the cottage. He said he was a union organizer."

"Oh, you met Raymond, huh?"

"You knew about him?"

"I met him too. He's been turning up everywhere. What a creep."

"So you knew about the noobs in the cottages?"

"Um. Well, yeah, I figured it out mostly on my own and then Raymond told me a little more."

"And you're fine with depriving little kids of their wages?"

"Anda," Lucy said, her voice brittle. "You like gaming, right, it's important to you?"

"Yeah, 'course it is."

"How important? Is it something you do for fun, just a hobby you waste a little time on? Are you just into it casually, or are you *committed* to it?"

"I'm committed to it, Lucy, you know that." God, without the game, what was there? PE class? Stupid Acanthosis Nigricans and, someday, insulin jabs every morning? "I love the game, Lucy. It's where my friends are."

"I know that. That's why you're my right-hand woman, why I want you at my side when I go on a mission. We're bad-ass, you and me, as bad-ass as they come, and we got that way through discipline and hard work and really *caring* about the game, right?"

"Yes, right, but —"

"You've met Liza the Organiza, right?"

"Yes, she came by my school."

"Mine too. She asked me to look out for you because of what she saw in you that day."

"Liza the Organiza goes to Ohio?"

"Idaho. Yes — all across the U.S. They put her on the tube and everything. She's amazing, and she cares about the game, too — that's what makes us all Fahrenheits: we're committed to each other, to teamwork, and to fair play."

Anda had heard these words — lifted from the Fahrenheit mission statement — many times, but now they made her swell a little with pride.

"So these people in Mexico or wherever, what are they doing?

They're earning their living by exploiting the game. You and me, we would never trade cash for gold or buy a character or a weapon on eBay — it's cheating. You get gold and weapons through hard work and hard play. But those Mexicans spend all day, every day, crafting stuff to turn into gold to sell off on the exchange. *That's where it comes from* — that's where the crappy players get their gold from! That's how rich noobs can buy their way into the game that we had to play hard to get into.

"So we burn them out. If we keep burning the factories down, they'll shut them down and those kids'll find something else to do for a living and the game will be better. If no one does that, our work will just get cheaper and cheaper: the game will get less and less fun, too.

"These people *don't* care about the game. To them, it's just a place to suck a buck out of. They're not players, they're leeches, here to suck all the fun out."

They had come upon the cottage now, the fourth one, having exterminated four different sniper nests on the way.

"Are you in, Anda? Are you here to play, or are you so worried about these leeches on the other side of the world that you want out?"

"I'm in, Sarge," Anda said. She armed the BFGs and pointed them at the cottage.

"Boo-yah!" Lucy said. Her character notched an arrow.

> Hello, Kali

"Oh, Christ, he's back," Lucy said. Raymond's avatar had sneaked up behind them.

> Look at these,

he said, and his character set something down on the ground and backed away. Anda edged up on them.

"Come on, it's probably a booby trap, we've got work to do," Lucy said.

They were photo objects. She picked them up and then examined them. The first showed ranked little girls, fifty or more, in clean and simple T-shirts, skinny as anything, sitting at generic white-box PCs, hands on the keyboards. They were hollow-eyed and grim, and none of them older than she.

The next showed a shantytown, shacks made of corrugated aluminum and trash, muddy trails between them, spray-painted graffiti, rude boys loitering, rubbish and carrier bags blowing.

The next showed the inside of a shanty, three little girls and a little boy sitting together on a battered sofa, their mother serving them something white and indistinct on plastic plates. Their smiles were heartbreaking and brave.

> That's who you're about to deprive of a day's wages

"Oh, hell, *no,*" Lucy said. "Not again. I killed him last time and I said I'd do it again if he ever tried to show me photos. That's it, he's dead." Her character turned toward him, putting away her bow and drawing a short sword. Raymond's character backed away quickly.

"Lucy, don't," Anda said. She interposed her avatar between Lucy's and Raymond. "Don't do it. He deserves to have a say." She thought of old American TV shows, the kinds you saw between the Bollywood movies on telly. "It's a free country, right?"

"God*damn* it, Anda, what is *wrong* with you? Did you come here to play the game or to screw around with this pervert dork?"

> what do you want from me raymond?

> Don't kill them — let them have their wages. Go play somewhere else

> They're leeches,

Lucy typed,

> they're wrecking the game economy and they're providing a gold-for-cash supply that lets rich assholes buy their way in. They don't care about the game and neither do you

> If they don't play the game, they don't eat. I think that means that they care about the game as much as you do. You're being paid cash to kill them, yes? So you need to play for your money, too. I think that makes you and them the same, a little the same.

> go screw yourself,

Lucy typed. Anda edged her character away from Lucy's. Raymond's character was so far away now that his texting came out in tiny type, almost too small to read. Lucy drew her bow again and nocked an arrow.

"Lucy, DON'T!" Anda cried. Her hands moved of their own volition and her character followed, clobbering Lucy barehanded so that her avatar reeled and dropped its bow.

"You BITCH!" Lucy said. She drew her sword.

"I'm sorry, Lucy," Anda said, stepping back out of range. "But I don't want you to hurt him. I want to hear him out."

Lucy's avatar came on fast, and there was a click as the voicelink dropped. Anda typed one-handed while she drew her own sword.

> dont lucy come on talk2me

Lucy slashed at her twice, and she needed both hands to defend herself or she would have been beheaded. Anda blew out through her nose and counterattacked, fingers pounding the keyboard. Lucy had more experience points than she did, but she was a better player, and she knew it. She hacked away at Lucy, driving her back and back, back down the road they'd marched together.

Abruptly, Lucy broke and ran, and Anda thought she was going away and decided to let her go, no harm no foul, but then she saw that Lucy wasn't running away, she was running *toward* the BFGs, armed and primed.

"Bloody hell," she breathed, as a BFG swung around to point at her. Her fingers flew. She cast the fireball at Lucy in the same instant that she cast her shield spell. Lucy loosed the bolt at her a moment before the fireball engulfed her, cooking her down to ash, and the bolt collided with the shield and drove Anda back, high into the air, and the shield spell wore off before she hit ground, costing her half her health and inventory, which scattered around her. She tested her voicelink.

"Lucy?"

There was no reply.

> I'm very sorry you and your friend quarreled.

She felt numb and unreal. There were rules for Fahrenheits, lots of rules, and the penalties for breaking them varied, but the penalty for attacking a fellow Fahrenheit was — she couldn't think the word, she closed her eyes, but there it was in big glowing letters: EXPULSION.

But Lucy had started it, right? It wasn't her fault.

But who would believe her?

She opened her eyes. Her vision swam through incipient tears. Her heart was thudding in her ears.

> The enemy isn't your fellow player. It's not the players guarding the fabrica, it's not the girls working there. The people who are working to destroy the game are the people who pay you and the people who pay the girls in the fabrica, who are the same people. You're being paid by rival factory owners, you know that? THEY are

the ones who care nothing for the game. My girls care about the game. You care about the game. Your common enemy is the people who want to destroy the game and who destroy the lives of these girls.

"Whassamatter, you fat little cow? Is your game making you cwy?" She jerked as if slapped. The chav who was speaking to her hadn't been in the Baang when she arrived, and he had mean, close-set eyes and a football jersey, and though he wasn't any older than she, he looked mean, and angry, and his smile was sadistic and crazy.

"Piss off," she said, mustering her braveness.

"You wobbling tub of guts, don't you DARE speak to me that way," he said, shouting right in her ear. The Baang fell silent and everyone looked at her. The Pakistani who ran the Baang was on his phone, no doubt calling the coppers, and that meant that her parents would discover where she'd been and then —

"I'm talking to you, girl," he said. "You disgusting lump of suet — Christ, it makes me wanta puke to look at you. You ever had a boyfriend? How'd he shag you — did he roll yer in flour and look for the wet spot?"

She reeled back, then stood. She drew her arm back and slapped him, as hard as she could. The boys in the Baang laughed and went *whoooooo!* He purpled and balled his fists and she backed away from him. The imprint of her fingers stood out on his cheek.

He bridged the distance between them with a quick step and *punched her,* in the belly, and the air whooshed out of her and she fell into another player, who pushed her away, so she ended up slumped against the wall, crying.

The mean boy was there, right in front of her, and she could smell the chili crisps on his breath. "You disgusting whore —" he began and she kneed him square in the nadgers, hard as she could, and he screamed like a little girl and fell backward. She picked up her schoolbag and ran for the door, her chest heaving, her face streaked with tears.

"Anda, dear, there's a phone call for you."

Her eyes stung. She'd been lying in her darkened bedroom for hours now, snuffling and trying not to cry, trying not to look at the empty desk where her PC used to live.

Her da's voice was soft and caring, but after the silence of her room, it sounded like a rusting hinge.

"Anda?"

She opened her eyes. He was holding a cordless phone, silhouetted against the open doorway.

"Who is it?"

"Someone from your game, I think," he said. He handed her the phone.

"Hullo?"

"Hullo, chicken." It had been a year since she'd heard that voice, but she recognized it instantly.

"Liza?"

"Yes."

Anda's skin seemed to shrink over her bones. This was it: expelled. Her heart felt like it was beating once per second; time slowed to a crawl.

"Hullo, Liza."

"Can you tell me what happened today?"

She did, stumbling over the details, backtracking and stuttering. She couldn't remember, exactly — did Lucy move on Raymond and Anda asked her to stop and then Lucy attacked her? Had Anda attacked Lucy first? It was all a jumble. She should have saved a screenmovie and taken it with her, but she couldn't have taken anything with her, she'd run out —

"I see. Well, it sounds like you've gotten yourself into quite a pile of poo, haven't you, my girl?"

"I guess so," Anda said. Then, because she knew that she was as good as expelled, she said, "I don't think it's right to kill them, those girls. All right?"

"Ah," Liza said. "Well, funny you should mention that. I happen to agree. Those girls need our help more than any of the girls anywhere in the game. The Fahrenheits' strength is that we are cooperative — it's another way that we're better than the boys. We care. I'm proud that you took a stand when you did — glad I found out about this business."

"You're not going to expel me?"

"No, chicken, I'm not going to expel you. I think you did the right thing —"

That meant that Lucy would be expelled. Fahrenheit had killed

Fahrenheit — something had to be done. The rules had to be enforced. Anda swallowed hard.

"If you expel Lucy, I'll quit," she said, quickly, before she lost her nerve.

Liza laughed. "Oh, chicken, you're a brave thing, aren't you? No one's being expelled, fear not. But I wanta talk to this Raymond of yours."

Anda came home from remedial hockey sweaty and exhausted, but not as exhausted as the last time, nor the time before that. She could run the whole length of the pitch twice now without collapsing — when she'd started out, she could barely make it halfway without having to stop and hold her side, kneading her loathsome podge to make it stop aching. Now there was noticeably less podge, and she found that with the ability to run the pitch came the freedom to actually pay attention to the game, to aim her shots, to build up a degree of accuracy that was nearly as satisfying as being really good in-game.

Her da knocked at the door of her bedroom after she'd showered and changed. "How's my girl?"

"Revising," she said, and hefted her maths book at him.

"Did you have a fun afternoon on the pitch?"

"You mean 'did my head get trod on'?"

"Did it?"

"Yes," she said. "But I did more treading than getting trodden on." The other girls were *really* fat, and they didn't have a lot of team skills. Anda had been to war: she knew how to depend on someone and how to be depended upon.

"That's my girl." He pretended to inspect the paint work around the light switch. "Been on the scales this week?"

She had, of course: the school nutritionist saw to that, a morning humiliation undertaken in full sight of all the other fatties.

"Yes, Da."

"And — ?"

"I've lost a stone," she said. A little more than a stone, actually. She had been able to fit into last year's jeans the other day.

She hadn't been in the sweets shop in a month. When she thought about sweets, it made her think of the little girls in the sweatshop. Sweatshop, sweetshop. The sweets shop man sold his wares close to the school because little girls who didn't know better would be tempted by them. No one forced them, but they were ***kids*** and grownups were supposed to look out for kids.

Her da beamed at her. "I've lost three pounds myself," he said, holding his tum. "I've been trying to follow your diet, you know."

"I know, Da," she said. It embarrassed her to discuss it with him.

The kids in the sweatshops were being exploited by grownups, too. It was why their situation was so impossible: the adults who were supposed to be taking care of them were exploiting them.

"Well, I just wanted to say that I'm proud of you. We both are, your mum and me. And I wanted to let you know that I'll be moving your PC back into your room tomorrow. You've earned it."

Anda blushed pink. She hadn't really expected this. Her fingers twitched over a phantom game-controller.

"Oh, Da," she said. He held up his hand.

"It's all right, girl. We're just proud of you."

She didn't touch the PC the first day, nor the second. The kids in the game — she didn't know what to do about them. On the third day, after hockey, she showered and changed and sat down and slipped the headset on.

"Hello, Anda."

"Hi, Sarge."

Lucy had known the minute she entered the game, which meant that she was still on Lucy's buddy list. Well, that was a hopeful sign.

"You don't have to call me that. We're the same rank now, after all."

Anda pulled down a menu and confirmed it: she'd been promoted to sergeant during her absence. She smiled.

"Gosh," she said.

"Yes, well, you earned it," Lucy said. "I've been talking to Raymond a lot about the working conditions in the factory, and, well —" She broke off. "I'm sorry, Anda."

"Me too, Lucy."

"You don't have anything to be sorry about," she said.

They went adventuring, running some of the game's standard missions together. It was fun, but after the kind of campaigning they'd done before, it was also kind of pale and flat.

"It's horrible, I know," Anda said. "But I miss it."

"Oh, thank God," Lucy said. "I thought I was the only one. It was fun, wasn't it? Big fights, big stakes."

"Well, poo," Anda said. "I don't wanna be bored for the rest of my life. What're we gonna do?"

"I was hoping you knew."

She thought about it. The part she'd loved had been going up against grownups who were not playing the game, but *gaming* it, breaking it for money. They'd been worthy adversaries, and there was no guilt in beating them, either.

"We'll ask Raymond how we can help," she said.

"I want them to walk out — to go on strike," he said. "It's the only way to get results: band together and withdraw your labor." Raymond's voice had a thick Mexican accent that took some getting used to, but his English was very good — better, in fact, than Lucy's.

"Walk out in-game?" Lucy said.

"No," Raymond said. "That wouldn't be very effective. I want them to walk out in Ciudad Juarez and Tijuana. I'll call the press in, we'll make a big deal out of it. We can win — I know we can."

"So what's the problem?" Anda said.

"The same problem as always. Getting them organized. I thought that the game would make it easier. We've been trying to get these girls organized for years: in the sewing shops, and the toy factories, but they lock the doors and keep us out and the girls go home and their parents won't let us talk to them. But in the game, I thought I'd be able to reach them —"

"But the bosses keep you away?"

"I keep getting killed. I've been practicing my sword fighting, but it's so hard —"

"This will be fun," Anda said. "Let's go."

"Where?" Lucy said.

"To an in-game factory. We're your new bodyguards." The bosses hired some pretty mean mercs, Anda knew. She'd been one. They'd be *fun* to wipe out.

Raymond's character spun around on the screen, then planted a kiss on Anda's cheek. Anda made her character give him a playful shove that sent him sprawling.

"Hey, Lucy, go get us a couple BFGs, okay?"

ALIX OHLIN

Simple Exercises for the Beginning Student

FROM SWINK

HE DID NOT HAVE FRIENDS. He was silent much of the time. He picked his nose, and when told to stop he would remove his finger slowly and stare at the snot, as if hypnotized, then put his hand in his pocket without wiping it. He had bad dreams: for one whole year, he woke, white and crying, from nightmares about snakes. The next year it was clouds. He could not explain why the clouds frightened him and shook his head, trembling and sweaty under the covers. Although his mother, Rachel, made an effort to find the nicest clothes she could within the budget, the same clothes that other kids were wearing, as soon as he put them on the clothes drooped and sagged, changing from their store rack normalcy into something disheveled, misshapen, patchlike.

Sometimes his eyes looked blurry and unfocused, but when Rachel took him to the eye doctor, his vision tested fine.

For his eighth birthday, he asked for piano lessons. Rachel and Brian, the father, looked at each other, then back at him. The three of them lived in a two-bedroom apartment. They had one bedroom, and he had the other. In the kitchen there was only enough room to stand up, and so in the living room, cramped together, were the dining table and chairs, the couch, and the TV. Rachel and Brian both worked, but between their credit card debt and the car payments, they were barely making the rent. And there was something else. Rachel was pregnant; she was the only one who knew. She'd been pregnant once before, since Kevin, but she didn't keep it. This time would be different. At night, with her eyes closed, she breathed in deeply, and at the innermost point of her breath she felt the baby, tight and insistent and coiled. It wanted to be born.

"Kevin," she said, "since when do you want to play the piano?"

"Since now."

"Listen, buddy," Brian said. He motioned Kevin over the couch, and Kevin stood between his legs. "I don't know if you've noticed, but we don't have a piano."

"The teacher does."

"But you have to practice," Brian said. "That's part of taking lessons — you spend like an hour a week at the teacher's or whatever, and then you go home, and you have to practice. Like homework."

Kevin looked up at his father, his eyes both wary and blank. Rachel saw that he hadn't thought of this. Where did he get the idea for piano lessons in the first place? If he didn't even know that practicing was part of it? It was a mystery. Her son came to her and placed his hand on her knee, silently.

"It's okay," she said. "We just have to think about this." She felt Brian staring at her. She knew what he wanted: for Kevin to play hockey, stickball in the street, be more of a boy, be more like other boys. But this was impossible: somehow, she knew, it was already too late.

On the day of the first lesson Kevin wore a blue sweater and brown cords and smoothed his hair across his forehead with his fingers. He was excited. Bright images flickered through his mind, just out of visible reach: a grand piano, a stone castle, people dancing. Rachel called, "Are you ready?"

"Coming." He walked out of his room, hearing the beats of his own tread, his socks hitting the carpet, dum dum dum dum. His mother stood in the hallway with her boots on, holding his coat. When he put it on, she handed him his hat, then picked up her coat.

"I want to go alone," he said.

She put her hands on her hips, like she always did.

"Well, you can't."

"Why?"

She ticked off the reasons on her hand. "Because it's the first day. Because you don't know where it is. Because I need to meet the teacher." The teacher was a friend of a friend of a friend. She had just moved into the neighborhood and was charging low rates.

"Tell me where it is," Kevin said, "and I'll find it. You told Dad I could walk there."

"I meant later."

"Now," he said.

"Kevin, come on."

"I'll only go if I go alone," he said.

"You have to go. I made the appointment."

"I know," he said, and held up his hands for his mitts. Rachel gave them to him and they stared at each other for a long moment. Their eyes were the same color, very pale blue, although what was watery in Kevin's face looked tired and opaque in Rachel's. Then Rachel sighed and he knew that he had won. She bent down and told him carefully which way to go. She watched him walk down the street, his arms sticking stiffly out from the coat, his mitts drooping down from the wrists.

They lived in an apartment building next to a small park with brown grass splotched with snow. He was supposed to go halfway around the park to the exact other side from home. Then go left, then go right on Oakhill. The house where he was going was 1330 Oakhill. He had to look for the left part of it. It would say *A. A* was for *Anita.* The teacher's name was Anita Tanizaki. In his mind's eye his mother's handwriting rose up from a piece of paper: *Mrs. Anita Tanizaki.* A-ni-ta. I-need-a Tanizaki, he said to himself. Get me a Tanizaki this instant! I will now perform the famous Tanizaki maneuver. It has never been done in this country before.

He skirted the park, kicking the iced crusts of snow with his boots. From the big street a few blocks away he could hear a siren, like that of a fire engine, bubbling and boiling. It came closer. He closed his eyes and listened to it: a note falling through the air like skiing downhill. With his eyelids shut, the sound was the color red splashed over the sky. Then it faded to pink, and then it was gone.

He opened his eyes and started walking again. A car passed him; there was nobody else walking around. It was Saturday morning. He went left, then right. Inside his mitts his fingers closed against his palms, making warm sweat. He found the house without any problem. There was ice on the steps and he slipped a little going up them, and almost lost his balance. He stamped his feet on the ice to steady himself, then pressed his finger against the doorbell, ding-dong. No sound came from the house, no music, no movement, and for a moment the world wavered and threatened to collapse. Nothing was the way he planned it. Then he heard a rustle behind the door, and it opened.

"Come in," said Mrs. Anita Tanizaki. He stepped inside and took his boots off on the mat and hung up his coat. She waited for him at the end of the hallway, not smiling. She had short dark hair in waves all over her head like frosting on a cake. The house seemed very dark and smelled like a restaurant, like food cooked and eaten hours before.

"So, come in," she said again. He followed her into the living room, where she gestured to the piano. He had never seen one up close before. It was smaller than he had thought it would be, and blacker. All of a sudden he was frightened: it just stood there, its wood body staunch and foreign. It looked back at him like an animal. Mrs. Tanizaki sat down on the bench and patted the spot next to her, and he joined her. They both looked down at the piano's keys as if the thing might start playing itself. Then Mrs. Tanizaki reached down and stroked a white key with her finger, from the top to the bottom, holding it down. The note resounded, pure and direct, resembling nothing except itself.

She hit another key, then a black one, then another white.

"I'm going to be honest with you, Kevin," Mrs. Tanizaki said. "This is my first lesson. Your first lesson, and my first lesson. We're going to be learning together. Here's what I can tell you right away. I love the piano. I love the touch of it" — here she made more strokes with the one finger, from the top to the bottom, the pad of her fingertip sliding — "and the sound" — here she added another note, with the left hand, and her elbow touched Kevin, and he flinched. She either didn't notice or pretended not to — "and the way it looks. I can't teach you to love the piano, but I can teach you some basic things about it. So, now we will start." She took his finger and pressed it down on a key.

"C," she said.

"Okay."

"Not 'do you see.' Middle *C*. This note is the middle of everything. It's the center of the piano. Look down, don't look at me, it doesn't matter what I look like. Press it again."

"C," he said.

*

When Kevin got home he was in a daze. He waited at the table without speaking while Rachel heated up some vegetable soup and cheese toast. His eyes had a misted quality, as if he were staring into the distance, even though he wasn't. Actually, he looked stoned. That's what my son looks like when he's happy, she thought, with a glow like pride.

To pay for the lessons, they gave up cable TV. But then Brian started watching hockey and basketball games in bars, drinking with his friend Steve, so it was not clear how well this worked out, budgetwise.

Mrs. Tanizaki had a son named Lawrence. He was fifteen. The next time Kevin had a piano lesson Lawrence crept into the room behind Kevin's and Mrs. Tanizaki's backs. Kevin could feel him there. Mrs. Tanizaki, who was guiding the fingers of Kevin's right hand up a scale from middle C, stopped at the top.

"This is Lawrence," she said. "Lawrence, this is Kevin."

Lawrence didn't nod or anything. His black hair flopped over his glasses. He was both gangly in the arms and legs area and fat in the middle.

"I'm hungry, Mom," he said to Mrs. Tanizaki.

She sighed. "Excuse me, Kevin. Lawrence, make yourself a sandwich."

"Don't want a sandwich."

"Then you can wait until we're done here, and I'll make lunch. There will be no lunch until I'm done teaching. Do you understand?"

Lawrence left the room. Kevin and Mrs. Tanizaki returned intently to the scale, and the song they were singing with it: do re mi fa sol la ti do. C D E F G A B C. After E you tucked your thumb under the rest of your hand and started over. Kevin didn't understand why the notes of the song had different names from the notes, but maybe one was for singing and one was for playing. When Mrs. Tanizaki sang, her voice was hollow and slightly rough. It was not at all clear like the piano. She made him sing too, and his voice was ugly and unrecognizable to him. He tried to sing as softly as possible, hearing one set of notes but not the other, while his fingers moved thickly up the keys.

"Now you do it by yourself," she told him. Kevin swallowed.

"Do re mi fa," he sang, trailing off. Behind him he could hear a wet chewing sound. Lawrence was back in the room eating a sandwich.

"Excuse me, Kevin," Mrs. Tanizaki said in her grave way. "Lawrence, either close your mouth when you chew, or leave the room. Or, maybe you could do both."

Kevin looked down at the keyboard while Lawrence shuffled out of the room. He was learning to memorize the shape of the keys, their color and configuration, the scuff marks on some of them, the way they added up to a whole entity like the face of a person. In his bedroom now, or at school, his fingers skimmed along surfaces, over the blanket or the desk, as if divining for sound. Inseparable from the keys was the smell of Mrs. Tanizaki's house, a spicy sour smell of leftover dinner, and her smell too, different from his mother's but distantly related to it, an older woman smell, and the darkness of the room, and the one lamp that pooled light over the piano. He was drawn inside all of this. Still, at times, he woke up at night and remembered the visions he'd had about the dancing and the castle, a piece of color at the edge of his sight like a scarf fluttering in the wind, and he knew that as piercing as the notes were, as clearly as they answered to his fingers on the white and black keys, still they were only notes, they weren't the music.

Rachel told Brian about the baby.

"I think it's a girl," she said. "I just have a feeling." They lay side by side in bed.

"I want to keep it, Bri," she said. She waited a moment, then went on.

"I know it's going to be hard, but we won't regret it. I promise. It'll be worth it."

He said, "If that's what you want."

He put his arm around her and went to sleep and Rachel stayed awake for hours, watching shadows and streetlights weave through the window. She waited for something else to happen, but nothing did.

She went to the doctor. Everything looked fine. She heard the baby's heart beating along with the pulse of her own blood. Brian acted kind yet impartial; when she talked about the baby, he listened. He said nothing against the baby, said nothing about the money, about the apartment, about how or whether they could live on just his paycheck. Rachel avoided these subjects also, knowing they were knotty, invited danger. She kept her worries to herself. She tried to maintain the certainty she'd held in the pit of her stomach, the push of the extra life inside her, but somehow the energy of these feelings seeped away from her, more and more quickly, each day. In the mornings she felt nauseated; in the afternoons she felt great. At night she was exhausted and went to sleep right after dinner.

One Saturday, at lunch, she asked Kevin if he understood what the word *pregnant* meant, and he said yes. She told him that he was going to have a little brother or sister. He put down his forkful of macaroni and cheese and appraised her.

"You don't look pregnant," he said, and gestured a bulge over his stomach.

"It doesn't show yet. But it will soon."

"Okay," he said.

He started eating again and Rachel felt herself plummet down into empty space. But then he said, with his mouth full, "Mrs. Tanizaki has a son."

"She does?"

"He's fifteen," Kevin said, and swallowed.

"Is he your friend?" Rachel said, not understanding.

He shook his head. "No. He sits in the room and eats sandwiches during my lessons."

"Oh."

"Lawrence is fifteen and I'm eight," Kevin said. "When the baby's eight, I'll be sixteen."

"Yes, that's right."

"Sixteen," he repeated. "I'll really play piano by then. I'll play for the baby."

Rachel smiled. "That's right," she said.

Mrs. Tanizaki loaned Kevin a book called *Simple Exercises for the Beginning Student.* When she presented it to him, the moment took on the aspect of a ceremony. Lawrence was not in the room, and it was very quiet. Mrs. Tanizaki stood up, took the book off the top of the piano, and put it in Kevin's hands.

"I'm going to lend this book to you, Kevin," she said. "It's my book, and I want it back eventually. But you can use it for now. I'm going to assign you exercises from it each week, and you'll practice them. Every day."

Kevin nodded and held the book loosely, afraid to damage or mark it in any way. It was a short, wide book with yellow pages. The cover was dog-eared and bent. He opened the cover and saw penciled handwriting on the inside that said, *Anita Osaka.* I-need-a, I-need-a, he said to himself. He looked at her and she said, "That was my name before I married Mr. Tanizaki. I've had this book for a long time. That's why you have to be careful with it and give it back."

"Okay."

"I trust you, Kevin. I know you'll take good care of the book and practice every day."

"Okay."

"Do you understand? Say yes, Kevin, not this 'Okay' all the time."

"Yes," he whispered. He was close to desperation. He had not told Mrs. Tanizaki that he had no piano to practice on. He was afraid to tell her because he thought she might say that he couldn't take lessons anymore. Every two weeks his mother gave him an envelope with a check in it for Mrs. Tanizaki, and he brought it and laid it on the piano. It stayed there, undiscussed, until he left. They never talked about his family, or where he lived, or anything. The piano was their only shared element. Now he didn't know what to do. The book was ancient and valuable; he shouldn't have it. In his hands, as if by itself, the pages flipped open and he saw the long black lines stretch across the pages, notes rising and falling in small streams. As he looked, the notes wrapped themselves around him like ribbons of seaweed. He could not tell her.

He took the book home and laid it on his bed. Then he took his school notebook and ripped out three pages and fastened them side-to-side with Scotch tape. He took a pencil and drew middle C in the center of one page. It looked lopsided and thick and the bottom right side of it spread downward as if the key had been left out in the sun and begun to melt. He thought of Mrs. Tanizaki's face and of the sound of Lawrence's chewing and the smell of food that laid itself over all his lessons and he was angry then, and he ripped up the pages and threw them in the garbage can.

But the next day he started over, and he drew eight white notes and five black ones, enough for a scale and for the simple exercises for the right hand, and in the bedroom he practiced from the book, his fingers going rustle-tap-rustle against the paper. Before he figured out that he needed to put the paper over a book from school, he broke through the paper twice and ruined it. Eventually he drew the best and longest-lasting one.

Rachel, cleaning out the garbage can a week afterward, found all the draft and messed-up piano pages. By this time, she was showing, and although she was not yet too ungainly, the consciousness of weight invaded all her actions, including the way she bent to pick up the garbage can or lowered herself onto the couch to examine the papers. When Brian came home from work and turned on the news, she brought him a beer.

"Brian," she said, "we need to get Kevin a piano, so he can practice. Maybe we can find him one of those, what are they, like a synthesizer? The little flat thing that wouldn't be too expensive?"

He looked at her, but not in the face. Lately she'd noticed that he didn't meet her eyes; he looked at her stomach or his gaze seemed to fasten on her neck, not quite making it any higher than that, as if gripped by that weight she carried, her additional gravity.

"You want to buy a goddamn piano?" he said.

"Not a real piano," she said. "Just something for him to practice on. He loves it, Brian, it's really amazing. He could turn out to be a genius, I mean who knows?"

"Yeah," he said.

"Or, maybe, if we gave Mrs. Tanizaki a little extra money she'd let him go over there and play her piano. She can't use it all the time, can she? I bet she'd do that. I bet she would." Brian put down his beer and held her hand and looked at her lap. His voice when he spoke was tender and soft.

"Rachel," he said. "I don't know how to tell you this, but I want you to listen to me. I think you're losing it. I think you really are."

The next morning, she got a call from Brian's boss asking if he was sick, which he wasn't. He didn't come home after work. She didn't call Steve, or his parents. She wasn't going to ask anybody else where her own husband was. She wasn't about to do that, not in this lifetime.

A month passed and Brian did not come back. Kevin practiced daily on the paper piano. He could play "Twinkle, Twinkle, Little

Star" and "Au clair de la lune." On paper the melodies whispered and tapped but on the piano, in three dimensions, the sound burst out, strong and plain, in a way that shocked him. A lot of times when he touched the wrong notes it wasn't because he didn't practice but because the keys were higher and farther apart than in his drawing of them. If Mrs. Tanizaki noticed his surprise or his fumbling readjustments, she didn't say anything. She spoke to him quietly as he played.

"Good, Kevin. Wrists up. Fingers bent. Don't look at me, it doesn't matter what I look like. Keep going. That's good."

Sometimes she rapped against the piano with a little stick, to help him keep time. It made him feel sick to his stomach. Other times, while he was playing, she disappeared behind him, even leaving the room. He hadn't seen Lawrence for a while, and he wondered if Mrs. Tanizaki had to go make Lawrence his sandwiches in the kitchen. These days Rachel was not making lunch for Kevin anymore. When he got home he would make his lunch in the microwave and eat it by himself at the table with the taps of Mrs. Tanizaki's stick still beating inside his ears. His mother would be sitting on the couch, looking out the window at the park. She was there and not there at the same time. He thought that the baby in her stomach was dragging her down; it was round like a bowling ball and maybe that heavy.

Rachel had decisions to make, she had to figure out what to do — about her job, the rent, the future. The words *what to do* ran together in her mind until they lost meaning and became a chant instead, *what to do what to do what to do.* At times she felt she was drowning in air — it was too thick and it bore down and she could not move or breathe. The baby was due in two months. This much she knew: she was going to name the baby Jennifer, she was going to put little barrettes in her hair, she could practically feel the silky skin of the baby's cheek against hers. A fifty-dollar bill came in the mail, in an envelope with no return address. She was waiting to find the strength inside of her, waiting for it and building it up. In the meantime she rested and Kevin played piano in his room.

It was summer and Kevin did not have school. He stayed in his room playing the piano. The apartment was hot and dense. He played "Pop! Goes the Weasel." Rachel was lying down in the bedroom. The doorbell rang and he answered it. It was his father.

Kevin looked at him. Rachel had told him that Brian was away on a trip but he hadn't believed her. But maybe it was true.

"Hey, buddy," Brian said. "How's it going?"

"Okay."

"Just okay? Not good, not great?"

"Good."

"Good," Brian said. "Here, I brought you something." He held out a plastic bag. Kevin took it and looked inside. It was a toy truck.

"Can I come in?"

Kevin stepped aside and Brian walked in. Rachel was standing in the living room rubbing the sleep from her eyes. Each time she went to sleep she seemed to fall deeper and deeper, and it took her forever to wake. Even the sight of her husband couldn't shake her into action; she stood there blinking.

"Hey," Brian said. "I came to see how you guys are doing."

Rachel rubbed her stomach.

"It's a girl," she said. "Jennifer."

Kevin closed the door and the sound of it made Brian turn around. He smiled at Kevin. Rachel and Brian sat on the couch and Brian talked. It was like he had been storing up words for all the time he'd been away, shut them up like in a closet, and when he got home and opened his mouth they tumbled out on top of one another, falling and falling. But the things he was talking about had nothing to do with his trip: he was talking about baseball scores and his job and jokes he'd heard. Kevin sat down next to him, on the other side of Rachel. He put his hand next to Brian's knee. He could feel the weight of the leg under his jeans. A while later Rachel went into the kitchen to make dinner and Brian stood in the doorway, still talking. After dinner, Kevin went to his room, and he could hear his parents' voices rumbling in a steady rhythm through the walls. With a book and the paper piano on his lap he used their rhythm in a song; he made it the bass clef to a melody he made up as he went, a tap-tap beat up and down and around the scale.

In the middle of the night he thought he heard a scream, and he jumped up out of bed. He stood outside their door, listening. He thought he heard his mother sob. Was it the baby? So heavy that it dropped out of her, ripped her open?

"Mom?" he said.

"Go to sleep, Kev," Brian said. "Everything's fine."

Kevin looked at the closed door.

"Mom?" he said.

Finally she called, "It's okay."

He was still standing there and Brian said, "Did you hear her, bud? Go back to bed."

In the morning when he left for his piano lesson they were still asleep. He drank a glass of juice and ate some toast and walked around the park, green and weedy now. He rang the doorbell at Mrs. Tanizaki's.

"Come in, Kevin," she said. "Today I've got a surprise for you."

He followed her into the house. Lawrence stood in the doorway of the kitchen, chewing. When Kevin passed him Lawrence opened his mouth wide and showed Kevin the pile of chewed-up food on his tongue. Kevin stared.

"When you're finished eating," Mrs. Tanizaki called, "we'll be waiting for you, Lawrence." Lawrence smiled at Kevin with his mouth still open and his tongue still covered with food. His eyes were barely visible behind his glasses and his hair. Kevin sped past him.

"Sit over here, Kevin," Mrs. Tanizaki said. She pointed to the chair at the back of his room, the one where Lawrence used to sit chewing his sandwiches. "Where is your book?" she said. He opened his backpack and took it out.

"Open to the last page," she said. "I want you to learn this piece. This section in your book is just a small part of the piece. But Lawrence knows the whole piece and he plays it very well. So, I asked him to play it for you. And I want you to listen to it very carefully."

"Okay."

"Lawrence, are you ready?"

Lawrence came into the room with his mouth closed and sat down on the piano bench. Kevin looked at his slouching back. All he could think about was Lawrence chewing, with bits of food falling out of his mouth and landing on the white and black keys. When Lawrence started playing, he could hardly hear the music. He was thinking about the food and the notes were wooden and dull. He wanted Lawrence to stop but he would not. He closed his eyes. Lawrence's fingers moved over the piano without ceasing, and he pictured them and made them into his own fingers, and he was playing and finally he heard the piano. He heard it without

Lawrence in it. And there it was. The notes lined up, they partnered and separated and circled; they moved swiftly through a clear, empty hall; there were no smells in this place, just a pale and pure background, like water. Then he thought, this is the castle. These are the dancers.

A cascade, a chord, a castle.

The music stopped and he opened his eyes. Mrs. Tanizaki smiled down at him, not at his face but at his hands, and he looked and saw that they were balled into fists. Lawrence made a snorting sound.

"Thank you, Lawrence," Mrs. Tanizaki said. "Kevin, would you like to thank Lawrence for his performance?"

"Okay."

"Kevin," she said.

"I mean thank you," he said.

"No big deal. Can I go now, Mom?"

"Yes, Lawrence."

Lawrence slipped heavily off the bench and disappeared into the kitchen, where Kevin could hear him opening and closing the refrigerator door. He took his place at the piano. "Now, you try," Mrs. Tanizaki said, opening the book. Kevin's fingers moved thick and sluggish through the first bars. It sounded nothing like what he had just heard. He thought about his paper piano and his mother and his father there or not there and his fingers making empty sounds on a flat surface and he bit down, hard, on the inside of his cheek. His fingers stopped. "It's all right, Kevin," Mrs. Tanizaki said. "It takes practice. If you go home and you practice you'll be able to play the piece. I guarantee it."

He looked at her dark eyes. She was the teacher. He bent his head over the keys.

When he got home his father was not there. His mother looked dazed: she kept moving her hands over her swollen stomach, from top to bottom, over and over.

"I don't think he's coming back this time," she said. "He packed a bag." Kevin set his own backpack down, as if it incriminated him, and put his hands in his pockets.

"The duffel bag," Rachel said. "He took the duffel bag this time." She looked at Kevin, his thin arms poking out of his T-shirt, and remembered lunch.

"Sit down at the table," she said. "He's not coming back, okay? But we're going to be fine. I'm going to make lunch."

She heated up some soup in the microwave and brought it to the table and poured him a glass of milk. She sat down opposite him and crossed her arms.

"How was your lesson?"

"I'm not going back," Kevin said.

"What do you mean? You love the piano."

He shook his head. He picked up his spoon and slurped soup. Although he'd had his eyes closed during Lawrence's performance, nonetheless he couldn't stop picturing Lawrence's hands moving quickly, unhesitatingly, over the keys, gathering the notes into perfect strands, as Mrs. Tanizaki watched. The two of them sat together at the piano under the pool of light. It was their world and he did not belong there. He saw himself walking slowly toward them, a sheet of paper in his hand, and Mrs. Tanizaki did not hear him, but Lawrence did; he turned and saw Kevin and he was laughing, his head flung back.

"I hate her," he said. He couldn't say her name. "I'm not going back."

"You really don't want to? You don't like the piano anymore?"

"I'm not going anymore."

"Come here," she said. "Stop eating and come here."

He obeyed her. He walked around the table and stood next to her. They looked into each other's pale blue eyes. Then his lower lip, still orange with soup, trembled; tears slipped down his cheeks. Rachel felt her blood pump in her veins — moving through her, waking her up — and she put her hands on the small, slack muscles of his upper arms.

"I won't let you stop," she said, and her fingers sent strength into his skin. Her voice was the world's warmest sound. It pulled and pulled him until he found himself leaning close against her, and he pressed his forehead to her neck.

EDWARD P. JONES

Old Boys, Old Girls

FROM THE NEW YORKER

THEY CAUGHT HIM AFTER HE HAD KILLED THE SECOND MAN. The law would never connect him to the first murder. So the victim — a stocky fellow Caesar Matthews shot in a Northeast alley only two blocks from the home of the guy's parents, a man who died over a woman who was actually in love with a third man — was destined to lie in his grave without anyone officially paying for what had happened to him. It was almost as if, at least on the books the law kept, Caesar had got away with a free killing.

Seven months after he stabbed the second man — a twenty-two-year-old with prematurely gray hair who had ventured out of Southeast for only the sixth time in his life — Caesar was tried for murder in the second degree. During much of the trial, he remembered the name only of the first dead man — Percy, or "Golden Boy," Weymouth — and not the second, Antwoine Stoddard, to whom everyone kept referring during the proceedings. The world had done things to Caesar since he'd left his father's house for good at sixteen, nearly fourteen years ago, but he had done far more to himself.

So at trial, with the weight of all the harm done to him and because he had hidden for months in one shit hole after another, he was not always himself and thought many times that he was actually there for killing Golden Boy, the first dead man. He was not insane, but he was three doors from it, which was how an old girlfriend, Yvonne Miller, would now and again playfully refer to his behavior. Who the fuck is this Antwoine bitch? Caesar sometimes thought during the trial. And where is Percy? It was only when the judge sentenced him to seven years in Lorton, D.C.'s prison in Virginia, that matters became somewhat clear again, and in those last moments before they took him away he saw Antwoine spread out on the ground outside the Prime Property nightclub, blood spurting out of his chest like oil from a bountiful well. Caesar remembered it all: sitting on the sidewalk, the liquor spinning his brain, his friends begging him to run, the club's music flooding out of the open door and going *thumpety-thump-thump* against his head. He sat a few feet from Antwoine and would have killed again for a cigarette. "That's you, baby, so very near insanity it can touch you," said Yvonne, who believed in unhappiness and who thought happiness was the greatest trick God had invented. Yvonne Miller would be waiting for Caesar at the end of the line.

He came to Lorton with a ready-made reputation, since Multrey Wilson and Tony Cathedral — first-degree murderers both, and destined to die there — knew him from his Northwest and Northeast days. They were about as big as you could get in Lorton at that time (the guards called Lorton the House of Multrey and Cathedral), and they let everyone know that Caesar was good people, "a protected body," with no danger of having his biscuits or his butt taken.

A little less than a week after Caesar arrived, Cathedral asked him how he liked his cellmate. Caesar had never been to prison but had spent five days in the D.C. jail, not counting the time there before and during the trial. They were side by side at dinner, and neither man looked at the other. Multrey sat across from them. Cathedral was done eating in three minutes, but Caesar always took a long time to eat. His mother had raised him to chew his food thoroughly. "You wanna be a old man livin on oatmeal?" "I love oatmeal, Mama." "Tell me that when you have to eat it every day till you die."

"He all right, I guess," Caesar said of his cellmate, with whom he had shared fewer than a thousand words. Caesar's mother had died before she saw what her son became.

"You got the bunk you want, the right bed?" Multrey said. He was sitting beside one of his two "women," the one he had turned out most recently. "She" was picking at her food, something Multrey had already warned her about. The woman had a family — a wife and three children — but they would not visit. Caesar would never have visitors, either.

"It's all right." Caesar had taken the top bunk, as the cellmate had already made the bottom his home. A miniature plastic panda from his youngest child dangled on a string hung from one of the metal bedposts. "Bottom, top, it's all the same ship."

Cathedral leaned into him, picking chicken out of his teeth with an inch-long fingernail sharpened to a point. "Listen, man, even if you like the top bunk, you fuck him up for the bottom just cause you gotta let him know who rules. You let him know that you will stab him through his motherfuckin heart and then turn around and eat your supper, cludin the dessert." Cathedral straightened up. "Caes, you gon be here a few days, so you can't let nobody fuck with your humanity."

He went back to the cell and told Pancho Morrison that he wanted the bottom bunk, couldn't sleep well at the top.

"Too bad," Pancho said. He was lying down, reading a book published by the Jehovah's Witnesses. He wasn't a Witness, but he was curious.

Caesar grabbed the book and flung it at the bars, and the bulk of it slid through an inch or so and dropped to the floor. He kicked Pancho in the side, and before he could pull his leg back for a second kick Pancho took the foot in both hands, twisted it, and threw him against the wall. Then Pancho was up, and they fought for nearly an hour before two guards, who had been watching the whole time, came in and beat them about the head. "Show's over! Show's over!" one kept saying.

They attended to themselves in silence in the cell, and with the same silence they flung themselves at each other the next day after dinner. They were virtually the same size, and though Caesar came to battle with more muscle, Pancho had more heart. Cathedral had told Caesar that morning that Pancho had lived on practically nothing but heroin for the three years before Lorton, so whatever fighting dog was in him could be pounded out in little or no time. It took three days. Pancho was the father of five children, and each time he swung he did so with the memory of all five and what he had done to them over those three addicted years. He wanted to return to them and try to make amends, and he realized on the morning of the third day that he would not be able to do that if Caesar killed him. So fourteen minutes into the fight he sank to the floor after Caesar hammered him in the gut. And though he could have got up he stayed there, silent and still. The two guards laughed. The daughter who had given Pancho the panda was nine years old and had been raised by her mother as a Catholic.

That night, before the place went dark, Caesar lay on the bottom bunk and looked over at pictures of Pancho's children, which Pancho had taped on the opposite wall. He knew he would have to decide if he wanted Pancho just to move the photographs or to put them away altogether. All the children had toothy smiles. The two youngest stood, in separate pictures, outdoors in their First Communion clothes. Caesar himself had been a father for two years. A girl he had met at an F Street club in Northwest had told him he was the father of her son, and for a time he had believed her. Then the boy started growing big ears that Caesar thought didn't belong to anyone in his family, and so after he had slapped the girl a few times a week before the child's second birthday she confessed that the child belonged to "my first love." "Your first love is always with you," she said, sounding forever like a television addict who had never read a book. As Caesar prepared to leave, she asked him, "You want back all the toys and things you gave him?" The child, as if used to their fighting, had slept through this last encounter on the couch, part of a living-room suite that they were paying for on time. Caesar said nothing more and didn't think about his 18k.-gold cigarette lighter until he was eight blocks away. The girl pawned the thing and got enough to pay off the furniture bill.

Caesar and Pancho worked in the laundry, and Caesar could look across the noisy room with all the lint swirling about and see Pancho sorting dirty pieces into bins. Then he would push uniform bins to the left and everything else to the right. Pancho had been doing that for three years. The job he got after he left Lorton was as a gofer at construction sites. No laundry in the outside world wanted him. Over the next two weeks, as Caesar watched Pancho at his job, his back always to him, he considered what he should do next. He wasn't into fucking men, so that was out. He still had not decided what he wanted done about the photographs on the cell wall. One day at the end of those two weeks, Caesar saw the light above Pancho's head flickering and Pancho raised his head and looked for a long time at it, as if thinking that the answer to all his problems lay in fixing that one light. Caesar decided then to let the pictures remain on the wall.

Three years later, they let Pancho go. The two men had mostly stayed at a distance from each other, but toward the end they had been talking, sharing plans about a life beyond Lorton. The relationship had reached the point where Caesar was saddened to see the children's photographs come off the wall. Pancho pulled off the last taped picture and the wall was suddenly empty in a most forlorn way. Caesar knew the names of all the children.

Pancho gave him a rabbit's foot that one of his children had given him. It was the way among all those men that when a good-luck piece had run out of juice it was given away with the hope that new ownership would renew its strength. The rabbit's foot had lost its electricity months before Pancho's release. Caesar's only good-fortune piece was a key chain made in Peru; it had been sweet for a bank robber in the next cell for nearly two years until that man's daughter, walking home from third grade, was abducted and killed.

One day after Pancho left, they brought in a thief and three-time rapist of elderly women. He nodded to Caesar and told him that he was Watson Rainey and went about making a home for himself in the cell, finally plugging in a tiny lamp with a green shade, which he placed on the metal shelf jutting from the wall. Then he climbed onto the top bunk he had made up and lay down. His name was all the wordplay he had given Caesar, who had been smoking on the bottom bunk throughout Rainey's efforts to make a nest. Caesar waited ten minutes and then stood and pulled the lamp's cord out of the wall socket and grabbed Rainey with one hand and threw him to the floor. He crushed the lamp into Rainey's face. He choked him with the cord. "You come into my house and show me no respect!" Caesar shouted. The only sound Rainey could manage was a gurgling that bubbled up from his mangled mouth. There were no witnesses except for an old man across the way, who would occasionally glance over at the two when he wasn't reading his Bible. It was over and done with in four minutes. When Rainey came to, he found everything he owned piled in the corner, soggy with piss. And Caesar was again on the top bunk.

They would live in that cell together until Caesar was released, four years later. Rainey tried never to be in the house during waking hours; if he was there when Caesar came in, he would leave. Rainey's names spoken by him that first day were all the words that would ever pass between the two men.

A week or so after Rainey got there, Caesar bought from Multrey a calendar that was three years old. It was large and had no markings of any sort, as pristine as the day it was made. "You know this one ain't the year we in right now," Multrey said as one of his women took a quarter from Caesar and dropped it in her purse. Caesar said, "It'll do." Multrey prized the calendar for one thing: its top half had a photograph of a naked woman of indeterminate race sitting on a stool, her legs wide open, her pussy aimed dead at whoever was standing right in front of her. It had been Multrey's good-luck piece, but the luck was dead. Multrey remembered what the calendar had done for him, and he told his woman to give Caesar his money back, lest any new good-fortune piece turn sour on him.

The calendar's bottom half had the days of the year. That day, the first Monday in June, Caesar drew in the box that was January 1st a line that went from the upper left-hand corner down to the bottom right-hand corner. The next day, a June Tuesday, he made a line in the January 2nd box that also ran in the same direction. And so it went. When the calendar had all such lines in all the boxes, it was the next June. Then Caesar, in that January 1st box, made a line that formed an X with the first line. And so it was for another year. The third year saw horizontal marks that sliced the boxes in half. The fourth year had vertical lines down the centers of the boxes.

This was the only calendar Caesar had in Lorton. That very first Monday, he taped the calendar over the area where the pictures of Pancho's children had been. There was still a good deal of empty space left, but he didn't do anything about it, and Rainey knew he couldn't do anything, either.

The calendar did right by Caesar until near the end of his fifth year in Lorton, when he began to feel that its juice was drying up. But he kept it there to mark off the days and, too, the naked woman never closed her legs to him.

In that fifth year, someone murdered Multrey as he showered. The killers — it had to be more than one for a man like Multrey — were never found. The Multrey woman who picked at her food had felt herself caring for a recent arrival who was five years younger than her, a part-time deacon who had killed a Southwest bartender for calling the deacon's wife "a woman without one fuckin brain cell." The story of that killing — the bartender was dropped head first from the roof of a ten-story building — became legend, and in Lorton men referred to the dead bartender as "the Flat-Head Insulter" and the killer became known as "the Righteous Desulter." The Desulter, wanting Multrey's lady, had hired people to butcher him. It had always been the duty of the lady who hated food to watch out for Multrey as he showered, but she had stepped away that day, just as she had been instructed to by the Desulter.

In another time, Cathedral and Caesar would have had enough of everything — from muscle to influence — to demand that someone give up the killers, but the prison was filling up with younger men who did not care what those two had been once upon a time. Also, Cathedral had already had two visits from the man he had killed in Northwest. Each time, the man had first stood before the bars of Cathedral's cell. Then he held one of the bars and opened the door inward, like some wooden door on a person's house. The dead man standing there would have been sufficient to unwrap anyone, but matters were compounded when Cathedral saw a door that for years had slid sideways now open in an impossible fashion. The man stood silent before Cathedral, and when he left he shut the door gently, as if there were sleeping children in the cell. So Cathedral didn't have a full mind, and Multrey was never avenged.

There was an armed-robbery man in the place, a tattooer with homemade inks and needles. He made a good living painting on both muscled and frail bodies the names of children; the Devil in full regalia with a pitchfork dripping with blood; the words "Mother" or "Mother Forever" surrounded by red roses and angels who looked sad, because when it came to drawing happy angels the tattoo man had no skills. One pickpocket had had a picture of his father tattooed in the middle of his chest; above the father's head, in medieval lettering, were the words "Rotting in Hell," with the letter "H" done in fiery yellow and red. The tattoo guy had told Caesar that he had skin worthy of "a painter's best canvas," that he could give Caesar a tattoo "God would envy." Caesar had always told him no, but then he awoke one snowy night in March of his sixth year and realized that it was his mother's birthday. He did not know what day of the week it was, but the voice that talked to him had the authority of a million loving mothers. He had long ago forgotten his own birthday, had not even bothered to ask someone in prison records to look it up.

There had never been anyone or anything he wanted commemorated on his body. Maybe it would have been Carol, his first girlfriend twenty years ago, before the retarded girl entered their lives. He had played with the notion of having the name of the boy he thought was his put over his heart, but the lie had come to light before that could happen. And before the boy there had been Yvonne, with whom he had lived for an extraordinary time in Northeast. He would have put Yvonne's name over his heart, but she went off to work one day and never came back. He looked for her for three months, and then just assumed that she had been killed somewhere and dumped in a place only animals knew about. Yvonne was indeed dead, and she would be waiting for him at the end of the line, though she did not know that was what she was doing. "You can always trust unhappiness," Yvonne had once said, sitting in the dark on the couch, her cigarette burned down to the filter. "His face never changes. But happiness is slick, can't be trusted. It has a thousand faces, Caes, all of them just ready to re-form into unhappiness once it has you in its clutches."

So Caesar had the words "Mother Forever" tattooed on his left biceps. Knowing that more letters meant a higher payment of cigarettes or money or candy, the tattoo fellow had dissuaded him from having just plain "Mother." "How many hours you think she spent in labor?" he asked Caesar. "Just to give you life." The job took five hours over two days, during a snowstorm. Caesar said no to angels, knowing the man's ability with happy ones, and had the words done in blue letters encased in red roses. The man worked from the words printed on a piece of paper that Caesar had given him, because he was also a bad speller.

The snow stopped on the third day and, strangely, it took only another three days for the two feet of mess to melt, for with the end of the storm came a heat wave. The tattoo man, a good friend of the Righteous Desulter, would tell Caesar in late April that what happened to him was his own fault, that he had not taken care of himself as he had been instructed to do. "And the heat ain't helped you neither." On the night of March 31st, five days after the tattoo had been put on, Caesar woke in the night with a pounding in his left arm. He couldn't return to sleep so he sat on the edge of his bunk until morning, when he saw that the "e"s in "Mother Forever" had blistered, as if someone had taken a match to them.

He went to the tattoo man, who first told him not to worry, then patted the "e"s with peroxide that he warmed in a spoon with a match. Within two days, the "e"s seemed to just melt away, each dissolving into an ugly pile at the base of the tattoo. After a week, the diseased "e"s began spreading their work to the other letters, and Caesar couldn't move his arm without pain. He went to the infirmary. They gave him aspirin and Band-Aided the tattoo. He was back the next day, the day the doctor was there.

He spent four days in D.C. General Hospital, his first trip back to Washington since a court appearance more than three years before. His entire body was paralyzed for two days, and one nurse confided to him the day he left that he had been near death. In the end, after the infection had done its work, there was not much left of the tattoo except an "o" and an "r," which were so deformed they could never pass for English, and a few roses that looked more like red mud. When he returned to prison, the tattoo man offered to give back the cigarettes and the money, but Caesar never gave him an answer, leading the man to think that he should watch his back. What happened to Caesar's tattoo and to Caesar was bad advertising, and soon the fellow had no customers at all.

Something had died in the arm and the shoulder, and Caesar was never again able to raise the arm more than thirty-five degrees. He had no enemies, but still he told no one about his debilitation. For the next few months he tried to stay out of everyone's way, knowing that he was far more vulnerable than he had been before the tattoo. Alone in the cell, with no one watching across the way, he exercised the arm, but by November he knew at last he would not be the same again. He tried to bully Rainey Watson as much as he could to continue the façade that he was still who he had been. And he tried to spend more time with Cathedral.

But the man Cathedral had killed had become a far more constant visitor. The dead man, a young bachelor who had been Cathedral's next-door neighbor, never spoke. He just opened Cathedral's cell door inward and went about doing things as if the cell were a family home — straightening wall pictures that only Cathedral could see, turning down the gas on the stove, testing the shower water to make sure that it was not too hot, tucking children into bed. Cathedral watched silently.

Caesar went to Cathedral's cell one day in mid-December, six months before they freed him. He found his friend sitting on the bottom bunk, his hands clamped over his knees. He was still outside the cell when Cathedral said, "Caes, you tell me why God would be so stupid to create mosquitoes. I mean, what good are the damn things? What's their function?" Caesar laughed, thinking it was a joke, and he had started to offer something when Cathedral looked over at him with a devastatingly serious gaze and said, "What we need is a new God. Somebody who knows what the fuck he's doing." Cathedral was not smiling. He returned to staring at the wall across from him. "What's with creatin bats? I mean, yes, they eat insects, but why create those insects to begin with? You see what I mean? Creatin a problem and then havin to create somethin to take care of the problem. And then comin up with somethin for that second problem. Man oh man!" Caesar slowly began moving away from Cathedral's cell. He had seen this many times before. It could not be cured even by great love. It sometimes pulled down a loved one. "And roaches. Every human bein in the world would have the sense not to create roaches. What's their function, Caes? I tell you, we need a new God, and I'm ready to cast my vote right now. Roaches and rats and chinches. God was out of his fuckin mind that week. Six wasted days, cept for the human part and some of the animals. And then partyin on the seventh day like he done us a big favor. The nerve of that motherfucker. And all your pigeons and squirrels. Don't forget them. I mean really."

In late January, they took Cathedral somewhere and then brought him back after a week. He returned to his campaign for a new God in February. A ritual began that would continue until Caesar left: determine that Cathedral was a menace to himself, take him away, bring him back, then take him away when he started campaigning again for another God.

There was now nothing for Caesar to do except try to coast to the end on a reputation that was far less than it had been in his first years at Lorton. He could only hope that he had built up enough good will among men who had better reputations and arms that worked 100 percent.

In early April, he received a large manila envelope from his attorney. The lawyer's letter was brief. "I did not tell them where you are," he wrote. "They may have learned from someone that I was your attorney. Take care." There were two separate letters in sealed envelopes from his brother and sister, each addressed to "My Brother Caesar." Dead people come back alive, Caesar thought many times before he finally read the letters, after almost a week. He expected an announcement about the death of his father, but he was hardly mentioned. Caesar's younger brother went on for five pages with a history of what had happened to the family since Caesar had left their lives. He ended by saying, "Maybe I should have been a better brother." There were three pictures as well, one of his brother and his bride on their wedding day, and one showing Caesar's sister, her husband, and their two children, a girl of four or so and a boy of about two. The third picture had the girl sitting on a couch beside the boy, who was in Caesar's father's lap, looking with interest off to the left, as if whatever was there were more important than having his picture taken. Caesar looked at the image of his father — a man on the verge of becoming old. His sister's letter had even less in it than the lawyer's: "Write to me, or call me collect, whatever is best for you, dear one. Call even if you are on the other side of the world. For every step you take to get to me, I will walk a mile toward you."

He had an enormous yearning at first, but after two weeks he tore everything up and threw it all away. He would be glad he had done this as he stumbled, hurt and confused, out of his sister's car less than half a year later. The girl and the boy would be in the back seat, the girl wearing a red dress and black shoes, and the boy in blue pants and a T-shirt with a cartoon figure on the front. The boy would have fallen asleep, but the girl would say, "Nighty-night, Uncle," which she had been calling him all that evening.

An ex-offenders' group, the Light at the End of the Tunnel, helped him to get a room and a job washing dishes and busing tables at a restaurant on F Street. The room was in a three-story building in the middle of the 900 block of N Street, Northwest, a building that, in the days when white people lived there, had had two apartments of eight rooms or so on each floor. Now the first-floor apartments were uninhabitable and had been padlocked for years. On the two other floors, each large apartment had been divided into five rented rooms, which went for twenty to thirty dollars a week, depending on the size and the view. Caesar's was small, twenty dollars, and had half the space of his cell at Lorton. The word that came to him for the butchered, once luxurious apartments was *warren.* The roomers in each of the cut-up apartments shared two bathrooms and one nice-sized kitchen, which was a pathetic place because of its dinginess and its fifty-watt bulb and because many of the appliances were old or undependable or both. Caesar's narrow room was at the front, facing N Street. On his side of the hall were two other rooms, the one next to his housing a mother and her two children. He would not know until his third week there that along the other hall was Yvonne Miller.

There was one main entry door for each of the complexes. In the big room to the left of the door into Caesar's complex lived a man of sixty or so, a pajama-clad man who was never out of bed in all the time Caesar lived there. He *could* walk, but Caesar never saw him do it. A woman, who told Caesar one day that she was "a home health-care aide," was always in the man's room, cooking, cleaning, or watching television with him. His was the only room with its own kitchen setup in a small alcove — a stove, icebox, and sink. His door was always open, and he never seemed to sleep. A green safe, three feet high, squatted beside the bed. "I am a moneylender," the man said the second day Caesar was there. He had come in and walked past the room, and the man had told the aide to have "that young lion" come back. "I am Simon and I lend money," the man said as Caesar stood in the doorway. "I will be your best friend, but not for free. Tell your friends."

He worked as many hours as they would allow him at the restaurant, Chowing Down. The remainder of the time, he went to movies until the shows closed and then sat in Franklin Park, at Fourteenth and K, in good weather and bad. He was there until sleep beckoned, sometimes as late as two in the morning. No one bothered him. He had killed two men, and the world, especially the bad part of it, sensed that and left him alone. He knew no one, and he wanted no one to know him. The friends he had had before Lorton seemed to have been swept off the face of the earth. On the penultimate day of his time at Lorton, he had awoken terrified and thought that if they gave him a choice he might well stay. He might find a life and a career at Lorton.

He had sex only with his right hand, and that was not very often. He began to believe, in his first days out of prison, that men and women were now speaking a new language and that he would never learn it. His lack of confidence extended even to whores, and this was a man who had been with more women than he had fingers and toes. He began to think that a whore had the power to crush a man's soul. "What kinda language you speakin, honey? Talk English if you want some." He was thirty-seven when he got free.

He came in from the park at two-forty-five one morning and went quickly by Simon's door, but the moneylender called him back. Caesar stood in the doorway. He had been in the warren for less than two months. The aide was cooking, standing with her back to Caesar in a crisp green uniform and sensible black shoes. She was stirring first one pot on the stove and then another. People on the color television were laughing.

"Been out on the town, I see," Simon began. "Hope you got enough poontang to last you till next time." "I gotta be goin," Caesar said. He had begun to think that he might be able to kill the man and find a way to get into the safe. The question was whether he should kill the aide as well. "Don't blow off your friends that way," Simon said. Then, for some reason, he started telling Caesar about their neighbors in that complex. That was how Caesar first learned about an "Yvonny," whom he had yet to see. He would not know that she was the Yvonne he had known long ago until the second time he passed her in the hall. "Now, our sweet Yvonny, she ain't nothin but an old girl." Old girls were whores, young or old, who had been battered so much by the world that they had only the faintest wisp of life left; not many of them had hearts of gold. "But you could probably have her for free," Simon said, and he pointed to Caesar's right, where Yvonne's room was. There was always a small lump under the covers beside Simon in the bed, and Caesar suspected that it was a gun. That was a problem, but he might be able to leap to the bed and kill the man with one blow of a club before he could pull it out. What would the aide do? "I've had her myself," Simon said, "so I can only recommend it in a pinch." "Later, man," Caesar said, and he stepped away. The usual way to his room was to the right as soon as he entered the main door, but that morning he walked straight ahead and within a few feet was passing Yvonne's door. It was slightly ajar, and he heard music from a radio. The aide might even be willing to help him rob the moneylender if he could talk to her alone beforehand. He might not know the language men and women were speaking now, but the language of money had not changed.

It was a cousin who told his brother where to find him. That cousin, Nora Maywell, was the manager of a nearby bank, at Twelfth and F

Streets, and she first saw Caesar as he bused tables at Chowing Down, where she had gone with colleagues for lunch. She came in day after day to make certain that he was indeed Caesar, for she had not seen him in more than twenty years. But there was no mistaking the man, who looked like her uncle. Caesar was five years older than Nora. She had gone through much of her childhood hoping that she would grow up to marry him. Had he paid much attention to her in all those years before he disappeared, he still would not have recognized her — she was older, to be sure, but life had been extraordinarily kind to Nora and she was now a queen compared with the dirt-poor peasant she had once been.

Caesar's brother came in three weeks after Nora first saw him. The brother, Alonzo, ate alone, paid his bill, then went over to Caesar and smiled. "It's good to see you," he said. Caesar simply nodded and walked away with the tub of dirty dishes. The brother stood shaking for a few moments, then turned and made his unsteady way out the door. He was a corporate attorney, making nine times what his father, at fifty-seven, was making, and he came back for many days. On the eighth day, he went to Caesar, who was busing in a far corner of the restaurant. It was now early September and Caesar had been out of prison for three months and five days. "I will keep coming until you speak to me," the brother said. Caesar looked at him for a long time. The lunch hours were ending, so the manager would have no reason to shout at him. Only two days before, he had seen Yvonne in the hall for the second time. It had been afternoon and the dead light bulb in the hall had been replaced since the first time he had passed her. He recognized her, but everything in her eyes and body told him that she did not know him. That would never change. And, because he knew who she was, he nodded to his brother and within minutes they were out the door and around the corner to the alley. Caesar lit a cigarette right away. The brother's gray suit had cost $1,865.98. Caesar's apron was filthy. It was his seventh cigarette of the afternoon. When it wasn't in his mouth, the cigarette was at his side, and as he raised it up and down to his mouth, inhaled, and flicked ashes, his hand never shook.

"Do you know how much I want to put my arms around you?" Alonzo said.

"I think we should put an end to all this shit right now so we can get on with our lives," Caesar said. "I don't wanna see you or anyone else in your family from now until the day I die. You should understand that, Mister, so you can do somethin else with your time. You a customer, so I won't do what I would do to somebody who ain't a customer."

The brother said, "I'll admit to whatever I may have done to you. I will, Caesar. I will." In fact, his brother had never done anything to him, and neither had his sister. The war had always been between Caesar and their father, but Caesar, over time, had come to see his siblings as the father's allies. "But come to see me and Joanie, one time only, and if you don't want to see us again then we'll accept that. I'll never come into your restaurant again."

There was still more of the cigarette, but Caesar looked at it and then dropped it to the ground and stepped on it. He looked at his cheap watch. Men in prison would have killed for what was left of that smoke. "I gotta be goin, Mister."

"We are family, Caesar. If you don't want to see Joanie and me for your sake, for our sakes, then do it for Mama."

"My mama's dead, and she been dead for a lotta years." He walked toward the street.

"I know she's dead! I know she's dead! I just put flowers on her grave on Sunday. And on three Sundays before that. And five weeks before that. I know my mother's dead."

Caesar stopped. It was one thing for him to throw out a quick statement about a dead mother, as he had done many times over the years. A man could say the words so often that they became just another meaningless part of his makeup. The pain was no longer there as it had been those first times he had spoken them, when his mother was still new to her grave. The words were one thing, but a grave was a different matter, a different fact. The grave was out there, to be seen and touched, and a man, a son, could go to that spot of earth and remember all over again how much she had loved him, how she had stood in her apron in the doorway of a clean and beautiful home and welcomed him back from school. He could go to the grave and read her name and die a bit, because it would feel as if she had left him only last week.

Caesar turned around. "You and your people must leave me alone, Mister."

"Then we will," the brother said. "We will leave you alone. Come to one dinner. A Sunday dinner. Fried chicken. The works. Then we'll never bother you again. No one but Joanie and our families.

No one else." Those last words were to assure Caesar that he would not have to see their father.

Caesar wanted another cigarette, but the meeting had already gone on long enough.

Yvonne had not said anything that second time, when he said, "Hello." She had simply nodded and walked around him in the hall. The third time they were also passing in the hall, and he spoke again, and she stepped to the side to pass and then turned and asked if he had any smokes she could borrow.

He said he had some in his room, and she told him to go get them and pointed to her room.

Her room was a third larger than his. It had an icebox, a bed, a dresser with a mirror over it, a small table next to the bed, a chair just beside the door, and not much else. The bed made a T with the one window, which faced the windowless wall of the apartment building next door. The beautiful blue and yellow curtains at the window should have been somewhere else, in a place that could appreciate them.

He had no expectations. He wanted nothing. It was just good to see a person from a special time in his life, and it was even better that he had loved her once and she had loved him. He stood in the doorway with the cigarettes.

Dressed in a faded purple robe, she was looking in the icebox when he returned. She closed the icebox door and looked at him. He walked over, and she took the unopened pack of cigarettes from his outstretched hand. He stood there.

"Well, sit the fuck down before you make the place look poor." He sat in the chair by the door, and she sat on the bed and lit the first cigarette. She was sideways to him. It was only after the fifth drag on the cigarette that she spoke. "If you think you gonna get some pussy, you are sorely mistaken. I ain't givin out shit. Free can kill you."

"I don't want nothin."

"'I don't want nothin. I don't want nothin.'" She dropped ashes into an empty tomato-soup can on the table by the bed. "Mister, we all want somethin, and the sooner people like you stand up and stop the bullshit, then the world can start bein a better place. It's the bullshitters who keep the world from bein a better place." Together, they had rented a little house in Northeast and had been planning to have a child once they had been there two years. The night he came home and found her sitting in the dark and talking about never trusting happiness, they had been there a year and a half. Two months later, she was gone. For the next three months, as he looked for her, he stayed there and continued to make it the kind of place that a woman would want to come home to. "My own mother was the first bullshitter I knew," she continued. "That's how I know it don't work. People should stand up and say, 'I wish you were dead,' or 'I want your pussy,' or 'I want all the money in your pocket.' When we stop lyin, the world will start bein heaven." He had been a thief and a robber and a drug pusher before he met her, and he went back to all that after the three months, not because he was heartbroken, though he was, but because it was such an easy thing to do. He was smart enough to know that he could not blame Yvonne, and he never did. The murders of Percy "Golden Boy" Weymouth and Antwoine Stoddard were still years away.

He stayed that day for more than an hour, until she told him that she had now paid for the cigarettes. Over the next two weeks, as he got closer to the dinner with his brother and sister, he would take her cigarettes and food and tell her from the start that they were free. He was never to know how she paid the rent. By the fourth day of bringing her things, she began to believe that he wanted nothing. He always sat in the chair by the door. Her words never changed, and it never mattered to him. The only thanks he got was the advice that the world should stop being a bullshitter.

On the day of the dinner, he found that the days of sitting with Yvonne had given him a strength he had not had when he had said yes to his brother. He had Alonzo pick him up in front of Chowing Down because he felt that if they knew where he lived, they would find a way to stay in his life.

At his sister's house, just off Sixteenth Street, Northwest, in an area of well-to-do black people some called the Gold Coast, they welcomed him, Joanie keeping her arms around him for more than a minute, crying. Then they offered him a glass of wine. He had not touched alcohol since before prison. They sat him on a dark-green couch in the living room, which was the size of ten prison cells. Before he had taken three sips of the wine, he felt good enough not to care that the girl and the boy, his sister's children, wanted to be in his lap. They were the first children he had been around in more than ten years. The girl had been calling him Uncle since he entered the house.

Throughout dinner, which was served by his sister's maid, and during the rest of the evening, he said as little as possible to the adults — his sister and brother and their spouses — but concentrated on the kids, because he thought he knew their hearts. The grownups did not pepper him with questions and were just grateful that he was there. Toward the end of the meal, he had a fourth glass of wine, and that was when he told his niece that she looked like his mother and the girl blushed, because she knew how beautiful her grandmother had been.

At the end, as Caesar stood in the doorway preparing to leave, his brother said that he had made this a wonderful year. His brother's eyes teared up and he wanted to hug Caesar, but Caesar, without smiling, simply extended his hand. The last thing his brother said to him was "Even if you go away not wanting to see us again, know that Daddy loves you. It is the one giant truth in the world. He's a different man, Caesar. I think he loves you more than us because he never knew what happened to you. That may be why he never remarried." The issue of what Caesar had been doing for twenty-one years never came up.

His sister, with her children in the back seat, drove him home. In front of his building, he and Joanie said goodbye and she kissed his cheek and, as an afterthought, he, a new uncle and with the wine saying, *Now, that wasn't so bad,* reached back to give a playful tug on the children's feet, but the sleeping boy was too far away and the girl, laughing, wiggled out of his reach. He said to his niece, "Good night, young lady," and she said no, that she was not a lady but a little girl. Again, he reached unsuccessfully for her feet. When he turned back, his sister had a look of such horror and disgust that he felt he had been stabbed. He knew right away what she was thinking, that he was out to cop a feel on a child. He managed a goodbye and got out of the car. "Call me," she said before he closed the car door, but the words lacked the feeling of all the previous ones of the evening. He said nothing. Had he spoken the wrong language, as well as done the wrong thing? Did child molesters call little girls "ladies"? He knew he would never call his sister. Yes, he had been right to tear up the pictures and letters when he was in Lorton.

He shut his eyes until the car was no more. He felt a pained rumbling throughout his system and, without thinking, he staggered away from his building toward Tenth Street. He could hear music coming from an apartment on his side of N Street. He had taught his sister how to ride a bike, how to get over her fear of falling and hurting herself. Now, in her eyes, he was no more than an animal capable of hurting a child. They killed men in prison for being that kind of monster. Whatever avuncular love for the children had begun growing in just those few hours now seeped away. He leaned over into the grass at the side of the apartment building and vomited. He wiped his mouth with the back of his hand. "I'll fall, Caesar," his sister had said in her first weeks of learning how to ride a bicycle. "Why would I let that happen?"

He ignored the aide when she told him that the moneylender wanted to talk to him. He went straight ahead, toward Yvonne's room, though he had no intention of seeing her. Her door was open enough for him to see a good part of the room, but he simply turned toward his own room. His shadow, cast by her light behind him, was thin and went along the floor and up the wall, and it was seeing the shadow that made him turn around. After noting that the bathroom next to her room was empty, he called softly to her from the doorway and then called three times more before he gave the door a gentle push with his finger. The door had not opened all the way when he saw her half on the bed and half off. Drunk, he thought. He went to her, intending to put her full on the bed. But death can twist the body in a way life never does, and that was what it had done to hers. He knew death. Her face was pressed into the bed, at a crooked angle that would have been uncomfortable for any living person. One leg was bunched under her, and the other was extended behind her, but both seemed not part of her body, awkwardly on their own, as if someone could just pick them up and walk away.

He whispered her name. He sat down beside her, ignoring the vomit that spilled out of her mouth and over the side of the bed. He moved her head so that it rested on one side. He thought at first that someone had done this to her, but he saw money on the dresser and felt the quiet throughout the room that signaled the end of it all, and he knew that the victim and the perpetrator were one and the same. He screwed the top on the empty whiskey bottle near her extended leg.

He placed her body on the bed and covered her with a sheet and a blanket. Someone would find her in the morning. He stood at the door, preparing to turn out the light and leave, thinking this was how the world would find her. He had once known her as a clean woman who would not steal so much as a needle. A woman with a well-kept house. She had been loved. But that was not what they would see in the morning.

He set about putting a few things back in place, hanging up clothes that were lying over the chair and on the bed, straightening the lampshade, picking up newspapers and everything else on the floor. But, when he was done, it did not seem enough.

He went to his room and tore up two shirts to make dust rags. He started in a corner at the foot of her bed, at a table where she kept her brush and comb and makeup and other lady things. When he had dusted the table and everything on it, he put an order to what was there, just as if she would be using them in the morning.

Then he began dusting and cleaning clockwise around the room, and by midnight he was not even half done and the shirts were dirty with all the work, and he went back to his room for two more. By three, he was cutting up his pants for rags. After he had cleaned and dusted the room, he put an order to it all, as he had done with the things on the table — the dishes and food in mouse-proof cannisters on the table beside the icebox, the two framed posters of mountains on the wall that were tilting to the left, the five photographs of unknown children on the bureau. When that work was done, he took a pail and a mop from her closet. Mice had made a bed in the mop, and he had to brush them off and away. He filled the pail with water from the bathroom and soap powder from under the table beside the icebox. After the floor had been mopped, he stood in the doorway as it dried and listened to the mice in the walls, listened to them scurrying in the closet.

At about four, the room was done and Yvonne lay covered in her unmade bed. He went to the door, ready to leave, and was once more unable to move. The whole world was silent except the mice in the walls.

He knelt at the bed and touched Yvonne's shoulder. On a Tuesday morning, a school day, he had come upon his father kneeling at his bed, Caesar's mother growing cold in that bed. His father was crying, and when Caesar went to him his father crushed Caesar to him and took the boy's breath away. It was Caesar's brother who had said they should call someone, but their father said, "No, no, just one minute more, just one more minute," as if in that next minute God would reconsider and send his wife back. And Caesar had said, "Yes, just one minute more." *The one giant truth . . .* , his brother had said.

Caesar changed the bed clothing and undressed Yvonne. He got one of her large pots and filled it with warm water from the bathroom and poured into the water cologne of his own that he never used and bath-oil beads he found in a battered container in a corner beside her dresser. The beads refused to dissolve, and he had to crush them in his hands. He bathed her, cleaned out her mouth. He got a green dress from the closet, and underwear and stockings from the dresser, put them on her, and pinned a rusty cameo on the dress over her heart. He combed and brushed her hair, put barrettes in it after he sweetened it with the rest of the cologne, and laid her head in the center of the pillow now covered with one of his clean cases. He gave her no shoes and he did not cover her up, just left her on top of the made-up bed. The room with the dead woman was as clean and as beautiful as Caesar could manage at that time in his life. It was after six in the morning, and the world was lighting up and the birds had begun to chirp. Caesar shut off the ceiling light and turned out the lamp, held on to the chain switch as he listened to the beginnings of a new day.

He opened the window that he had cleaned hours before, and right away a breeze came through. He put a hand to the wind, enjoying the coolness, and one thing came to him: he was not a young man anymore.

He sat on his bed smoking one cigarette after another. Before finding Yvonne dead, he had thought he would go and live in Baltimore and hook up with a vicious crew he had known a long time ago. Wasn't that what child molesters did? Now, the only thing he knew about the rest of his life was that he did not want to wash dishes and bus tables anymore. At about nine-thirty, he put just about all he owned and the two bags of trash from Yvonne's room in the bin in the kitchen. He knocked at the door of the woman in the room next to his. Her son opened the door, and Caesar asked for his mother. He gave her the $147 he had found in Yvonne's room, along with his radio and tiny black-and-white television. He told her to look in on Yvonne before long and then said he would see her later, which was perhaps the softest lie of his adult life.

On his way out of the warren of rooms, Simon called to him. "You comin back soon, young lion?" he asked. Caesar nodded. "Well, why don't you bring me back a bottle of rum? Woke up with a taste for it this mornin." Caesar nodded. "Was that you in there with Yvonny last night?" Simon said as he got the money from atop the safe beside his bed. "Quite a party, huh?" Caesar said nothing. Simon gave the money to the aide, and she handed Caesar ten dollars and a quarter. "Right down to the penny," Simon said. "Give you a tip when you get back." "I won't be long," Caesar said. Simon must have realized that was a lie, because before Caesar went out the door he said, in as sweet a voice as he was capable of, "I'll be waitin."

He came out into the day. He did not know what he was going to do, aside from finding some legit way to pay for Yvonne's funeral. The D.C. government people would take her away, but he knew where he could find and claim her before they put her in potter's field. He put the bills in his pocket and looked down at the quarter in the palm of his hand. It was a rather old one, 1967, but shiny enough. Life had been kind to it. He went carefully down the steps in front of the building and stood on the sidewalk. The world was going about its business, and it came to him, as it might to a man who had been momentarily knocked senseless after a punch to the face, that he was of that world. To the left was Ninth Street and all the rest of N Street, Immaculate Conception Catholic Church at Eighth, the bank at the corner of Seventh. He flipped the coin. To his right was Tenth Street, and down Tenth were stores and the house where Abraham Lincoln had died and all the white people's precious monuments. Up Tenth and a block to Eleventh and Q Streets was once a High's store where, when Caesar was a boy, a pint of cherry-vanilla ice cream cost twenty-five cents, and farther down Tenth was French Street, with a two-story house with his mother's doilies and a foot-long porcelain black puppy just inside the front door. A puppy his mother had bought for his father in the third year of their marriage. A puppy that for thirty-five years had been patiently waiting each working day for Caesar's father to return from work. *The one giant truth . . . Just one minute more.* He caught the quarter and slapped it on the back of his hand. He had already decided that George Washington's profile would mean going toward Tenth Street, and that was what he did once he uncovered the coin.

At the corner of Tenth and N, he stopped and considered the quarter again. Down Tenth was Lincoln's death house. Up Tenth was the house where he had been a boy and where the puppy was waiting for his father. A girl at the corner was messing with her bicycle, putting playing cards in the spokes, checking the tires. She watched Caesar as he flipped the quarter. He missed it and the coin fell to the ground, and he decided that that one would not count. The girl had once seen her aunt juggle six coins, first warming up with the flip of a single one and advancing to the juggling of three before finishing with six. It had been quite a show. The aunt had shown the six pieces to the girl — they had all been old and heavy one-dollar silver coins, huge monster things, which nobody made anymore. The girl thought she might now see a reprise of that event. Caesar flipped the quarter. The girl's heart paused. The man's heart paused. The coin reached its apex and then it fell.

EANS

The Secret Goldfish

FROM THE NEW YORKER

HE HAD A WEIRD GROWTH ALONG HIS DORSAL FIN and that gape-mouth grimace you see in older fish. Way too big for his tank, too, having outgrown the standard goldfish age limit. Which is what? About one month? He was six years old — outlandishly old for a fish. One afternoon, Teddy, as he was called then, now just Ted, took notice of the condition of Fish's tank: a wedge of sunlight plunged through the window of his bedroom and struck the water's surface, disappearing. The water was so clotted it had become a solid mass, a putty within which Fish was presumably swimming, or dead. Most likely dead. Where's Fish? Where's Fish? Teddy yelled to his mom. She came into his room, caught sight of the tank, and gave a small yelp. Once again, a fish had been neglected.

Everyone knows the story. The kids beg and plead: Please, please get us a fish (or a dog), we'll feed it, we will, honest, we'll take care of it and you won't have to do a single thing. We'll clean the tank walls with the brush and make sure the filter charcoal is replaced regularly and refill the water when it evaporates. Please, please, we can handle it, we're old enough now, we are, it'll be so much fun, it will, so much fun. But in the end they don't. They dump too much food in no matter how often they're told to be careful, to use just a pinch, and even after they've read biblical-sounding fables about the fish who ate too much and grew too large for its bowl, shattering the sides, they watch gleefully while he consumes like mad, unable to stop. It's fun to watch him eat, to witness the physical manifestation of a fact: the level of Fish's hunger is permanently set too high. In the metaphysics of the fish universe, gluttony is not a sin.

The delicate wafers of food fall lightly onto the water, linger on the surface tension, and are broken apart on infinitely eager lips. She overfeeds, too (on the days when she's pretty sure the kids haven't fed him). Her shaking mechanics are sloppy. The light flakes become moist, collude, collect their inertia, and all too often fall out of the can in a large clump. Really, she hasn't neglected the poor fish. *Neglect* seems a word too heavy with submerged intent. Something was bound to slip to the side amid the chaos of the domestic arena. But Fish has sustained himself in terrible conditions. He is the king of all goldfish survivors.

Her own childhood goldfish — named Fred — ended his days in Grayling Pond, a hole near her house in northern Michigan, dug out by the state D.N.R. on a pond-production grant. (Why the Great Lakes state needed more ponds is anyone's guess.) Garnished with a wide band of lily pads, the water a pale yellow, speckled with skeeter-bug ripples, the pond was close to becoming a marsh. Hope you survive, Fred, her father had said as he slopped the fish out of the pail and into the pond. She did not forget the sight of her beloved fish as he slipped from the lip of the bucket and rode the glassine tube of water into the pond. The rest of the summer she imagined his orange form — brilliantly bright and fluorescent against the glimmer of water — in a kind of slow-motion replay. Dumbest animals on earth, she remembered her father adding. Nothing dumber than a carp. Except maybe a catfish, or your goddamn mother.

Not long after that afternoon at Grayling Pond, her father left the house in a fit of rage. Gone for good, her mother said. Thank Christ. Then, a few months later, he was killed in a freak accident, crushed between hunks of ice and the hull of a container ship in Duluth. Superior's slush ice was temperamental that winter, chewing up the coastline, damaging bulkheads. Her father had signed on as one of the men who went down with poles and gave furtive pokes and prods, in the tradition of those Michigan rivermen who had once dislodged logjams with their peaveys and pike poles, standing atop the timber in their spiked boots, sparring with magnificent forces. Accounts varied, but the basic story was that the ice shifted, some kind of crevasse formed, and he slipped in. Then the lake gave a heave and his legs were crushed, clamped in the jaw of God's stupid justice. As she liked to imagine it, he had just enough time to piece together a little prayer asking for forgiveness for being a failure of a father ("Dear Heavenly Father, forgive me for my huge failings as a father to my dear daughter and even more for my gaping failure as a husband to my wife") and for dumping Fred ("and for getting rid of that fish my daughter loved more than me"), and then to watch as the pale winter sun slipped quickly away while the other men urged him to remain calm and told him that he'd be fine and they'd have him out in a minute or so, while knowing for certain that they wouldn't.

Long after her father was gone, she imagined Fred lurking in the lower reaches of Grayling Pond, in the coolest pockets, trying to conserve his energy. Sometimes, when she was cleaning upstairs and dusting Teddy's room, she would pause in the deep, warm, silent heart of a suburban afternoon and watch Fish as he dangled asleep, wide-eyed, unmoving, just fluffing his fins softly on occasion. One time she even tried it herself, standing still, suspended in the dense fluid of an unending array of demanding tasks — cleaning, cooking, washing, grocery shopping, snack getting — while outside the birds chirped and the traffic hissed past on the parkway.

The marriage had fallen apart abruptly. Her husband — who worked in the city as a corporate banker and left the house each morning at dawn with the *Times,* still wrapped in its bright-blue delivery bag, tucked beneath his arm — had betrayed his vows. One evening, he'd arrived home from work with what seemed to be a new face: his teeth were abnormally white. He'd had them bleached in the city. (In retrospect, she saw that his bright teeth were the first hint of his infidelity.) He had found a dentist on Park Avenue. Soon he was coming home late on some nights and not at all on others, under the vague pretense of work obligations. In Japan, he explained, people sleep overnight in town as a sign of their dedication to business; they rent cubicles just wide enough for a body, like coffins, he said, and for days when he did not return she thought of those small compartments and she chose to believe him. (Of course I know about the Japanese, she had said, emphatically.) Then one night she found him in the bathroom with a bar of soap, rubbing it gently against his wedding ring. It's too tight, he said. I'm just trying to loosen it. When others were perplexed by the fact that she had not deduced his infidelity, picked up on the clues, during those fall months, she felt compelled (though she never did) to describe the marriage in all of its long complexity — fifteen years — starting with the honeymoon in Spain: the parador in Chinchón, outside Madrid, that had once been a monastery, standing naked with him at the balcony door in the dusky night air listening to the sounds of the village and the splash of the pool. She had given up her career for the relationship, for the family. She had given up plenty in order to stay home for Teddy's and Annie's formative years, to make sure those brain synapses formed correctly, to be assured that the right connections were fused. (Because studies had made it clear that a kid's success depends on the first few years. It was important to develop the fine motor skills, to have the appropriate hand play, not to mention critical reasoning skills, before the age of four!) So, yes, she guessed the whole decision to give herself over to the domestic job had been an act of free will, but now it felt as though the act itself had been carried out in the conditions of betrayal that would eventually unfold before her.

Fish had come into the family fold in a plastic Baggie of water, bulging dangerously, knotted at the top, with a mate, Sammy, who would end up a floater two days later. Pet Universe had given free goldfish to all the kids on a preschool field trip. In less than a year, Fish had grown too big for his starter bowl and begun to tighten his spiraled laps, restricted in his movements by his gathering bulk and the glass walls of the bowl. Then he graduated to a classic five-gallon bowl, where, in the course of the next few years, he grew, until one afternoon, still deep in what seemed to be a stable domestic situation, with the kids off at school, she went out to Pet Universe and found a large tank and some water-prep drops and a filter unit, one that sat on the rim and produced a sleek, fountainlike curl of water, and some turquoise gravel and a small figurine to keep the fish company: a cartoonish pirate galleon — a combination of Mark Twain riverboat and man-of-war — with an exaggerated bow and an orange plastic paddle wheel that spun around in the tank's currents until it gobbed up and stuck. The figurine, which was meant to please the eyes of children, had that confused mix of design that put commercial viability ahead of the truth. Teddy and Annie hated it. Ultimately, the figure served one purpose. It rearranged the conceptual space of the tank and gave the illusion that Fish now had something to do, something to work around, during his languorous afternoon laps, and she found herself going in to watch him, giving deep philosophical consideration to his actions: Did Fish remember that he had passed that way before? Was he aware of his eternal hell, caught in the tank's glass grip? Or did he feel wondrously free, swimming — for all he knew — in Lake Superior, an abundant, wide field of water, with some glass obstructions here and there? Was he basically free of wants, needs, and everything else? Did he wonder at the food miraculously appearing atop the surface tension, food to be approached with parted lips?

One evening, after observing Fish, when she was at the sink looking out the window at the yard, she saw her husband there, along the south side, holding his phone to his ear and lifting his free hand up and down from his waist in a slight flapping gesture that she knew indicated that he was emotionally agitated.

Shortly after that, the tank began to murk up. Through the dim months of January and February, the filter clotted, the flow stopped, and stringy green silk grew on the lip of the waterfall. The murk thickened. In the center of the darkness, Fish swam in random patterns and became a sad, hopeless entity curled into his plight. He was no longer fooled by his short-term memory into thinking that he was eternally free. Nor was he bored by the repetitive nature of his laps, going around the stupid ship figurine, sinking down into the gravel, picking — typical bottom-feeder — for scraps. Instead, he was lost in the eternal roar of an isotropic universe, flinging himself wildly within the expanding big bang of tank murk. On occasion, he found his way to the light and rubbed his eye against the glass, peering out in a judgmental way. But no one was there to see him. No one seemed available to witness these outward glances. Until the day when Teddy, now just Ted, noticed and said, Mom, Mom, the tank, and she went and cleaned it, but only after she had knocked her knuckle a few times on the glass and seen that he was alive, consumed in the dark but moving and seemingly healthy. Then she felt awe at the fact that life was sustainable even under the most abhorrent conditions. She felt a fleeting connection between this awe and the possibility that God exists. But then she reminded herself that it was only Fish. Just frickin' Fish, she thought. Here I am so weepy and sad, trying to make sense of my horrible situation, that something like this will give me hope. Of course, she was probably also thinking back to that afternoon, watching her father sluice Fred down into the warm waters of the shallow pond in Michigan. Her memory of it was profoundly clear. The vision of the fish itself — pristine and orange — traveling through the water as it spilled from the bucket was exact and perfect.

She set to work scooping out the water with an old Tupperware bowl, replacing it in increments so the chlorine would evaporate, driving to Pet Universe to get another cotton filter, some water-clarifying drops, and a pound sack of activated charcoal nuggets. She disassembled the pump mechanism — a small magnet attached to a ring of plastic that hovered, embraced by a larger magnet. Somehow the larger magnet cooperated with the magnet on the plastic device and used physical laws of some sort to suck the water up and through the filter, where it cascaded over the wide lip and twisted as it approached the surface. It seemed to her as her fingers cleaned the device that it was not only a thing of great simplicity and beauty but also something much deeper, a tool meant to sustain Fish's life and, in turn, his place in the family. The afternoon was clear, blue-skied, wintry bright — and out the kitchen window she saw the uncut lawn, dark straw brown, matted down in van Gogh swirls, frosted with cold. Past the lawn, the woods, through which she could see the cars moving on the parkway, stood stark and brittle in the direct implications of the winter light. It was a fine scene, embarrassingly suburban, but certainly fine. Back upstairs, she saw Fish swimming jauntily in his new conditions and she was pretty sure that he was delighted, moving with swift strokes from one end of the tank to the other, skirting the figurine professionally, wagging his back fin — what was that called? was it the caudal fin? — fashionably, like a cabaret dancer working her fan. A beautiful tail, unfurling in a windswept motion in the clearing water. When she leaned down for a closer look, it became apparent that the fin was much, much larger than it seemed when it was in action and twining in on itself. When Fish paused, it swayed open beautifully — a fine, healthy, wide carp tail. Along his sides, he had the usual scars of an abused fish, a wound or two, a missing scale, a new, smaller growth of some kind down near his anal fin. But otherwise he seemed big, brutally healthy, still blinking off the shock of the sudden glare.

Then the tank fell back into its murk, got worse, stank up, and became, well, completely, utterly, fantastically murky. Here one might note tangentially: if, as Aristotle claims, poetry is something of graver import than history — partly because of the naturalness of its statements — then Fish was more important than any domestic history, because Fish was poetic, in that he had succumbed to the darkness that had formed around him, and yet he was unwilling to die — or, rather, he *did not* die. He kept himself alive. He kept at it. Somehow he gathered enough oxygen from the water — perhaps by staying directly under the trickle that made its way over the lip of the filter. Of course, by nature he was a bottom-feeder, a mudfish, accustomed to slime and algae and to an environment that, for other fish, would be insufferable. No trout could sustain itself in these conditions. Not even close. A good brookie would've gone belly up long ago. A brookie would want cool pockets of a fast-moving stream, sweet riffles, bubbling swirls, to live a good life. But Fish stood in his cave of slime, graver than the history of the household into which his glass enclave had been placed: Dad packing his suitcases, folding and refolding his trousers and taking his ties off the electric tie rack and carefully folding them inside sheets of tissue, and then taking his shoes and putting each pair, highly glossed oxfords (he was one of the few to make regular use of the shoeshine stand at Grand Central), into cotton drawstring sacks, and then emptying his top dresser drawer, taking his cuff links, his old wallets, and a few other items. All of this stuff, the history of the house, the legal papers signed and sealed and the attendant separation agreement and, of course, the divorce that left her the house — all this historical material was transpiring outside the gist of Fish. He could chart his course and touch each corner of the tank and still not know shit. But he understood something. That much was clear. The world is a mucky mess. It gets clotted up, submerged in its own gunk. End of story.

He brushed softly against the beard of algae that hung from the filter device, worked his way over to the figurine, leaned his flank against her side, and felt the shift of temperature as night fell — Teddy liked to sleep with the window cracked a bit — and the oxygen content increased slightly as the water cooled. During the day, the sun cranked through the window, the tank grew warm, and he didn't move at all, unless someone came into the room and knocked on the tank or the floor, and then he jerked forward slightly before quickly settling down. A few times the downstairs door slammed hard enough to jolt him awake. Or there was a smashing sound from the kitchen. Or voices. "What in the world should we do?" "I would most certainly like this to be amicable, for the sake of the kids." Or a shoe striking the wall in the adjacent master bedroom. At times he felt a kinship with the figurine, as if another carp were there alongside him, waiting, hovering. Other times he felt a slight kinship with the sides of the tank, which touched his gill flaps when he went in search of light. God, if only he knew that he, Fish, was at the very center of the domestic arena, holding court with his own desire to live. He might have died happily right there! But he was not a symbolic fish. He seemed to have no desire to stand as the tragic hero in this drama.

Sent out, told to stay out, the kids were playing together down in the yard so that, inside, the two central figures, Dad and Mom, might have one final talk. The kids were standing by the playhouse — which itself was falling to decrepitude, dark-gray smears of mildew growing on its fake logs — pretending to be a mom and a dad themselves, although they were a bit too old and self-conscious for play-acting. Perhaps they were old enough to know that they were faking it on two levels, regressing to a secondary level of play-acting they'd pretty much rejected but playing Mom and Dad anyway, Teddy saying, I'm gonna call my lawyer if you don't settle with me, and Annie responding, in her high sweet voice, I knew you'd lawyer up on me, I just knew it, and then both kids giggling in that secretive, all-knowing way they have. Overhead, the tree branches were fuzzed with the first buds of spring, but it was still a bit cold, and words hovered in vapor from their mouths and darkness was falling fast over the trees, and beyond the trees the commuter traffic hissed unnoticed.

If you were heading south on the Merritt Parkway on the afternoon of April 3rd, and you happened to look to your right through the trees after Exit 35, you might've seen them, back beyond the old stone piles, the farm fences that no longer held significance except maybe as a reminder of the Robert Frost poem about good fences and good neighbors and all of that: two kids leaning against an old playhouse while the house behind them appeared cozy, warm, and, clearly, expensive. A fleeting tableau without much meaning to the commuting folk aside from the formulaic economics of the matter: near the parkway = reduced value, but an expensive area + buffer of stone walls + old trees + trendiness of area = more value.

There is something romantic and heartening about seeing those homes through the trees from the vantage of the parkway — those safe, confided Connecticut lives. Inside the house, the secret goldfish is going about his deeply moving predicament, holding his life close to the gills, subdued by the dark but unwilling to relinquish his cellular activities, the Krebs cycle still spinning its carbohydrate breakdown. The secret goldfish draws close to the center of the cosmos. In the black hole of familial carelessness, he awaits the graceful moment when the mother, spurred on by Teddy, will give yet another soft shriek. She'll lean close to the glass and put her eye there to search for Fish. Fish will be there, of course, hiding in the core of the murk near the figurine, playing possum, so that she will, when she sees him, feel the pitiful sinking in her gut — remembering the preschool field trip to Pet Universe — and a sorrow so deep it will send her to her knees to weep. She'll think of the sad little pet funeral she hoped to perform when Fish died (when Fish's sidekick died, Dad flushed him away): a small but deeply meaningful moment in the backyard, with the trowel, digging a shoebox-size hole, putting the fish in, performing a small rite ("Dear Lord, dear Heavenly Father, dear Fish God, God of Fish, in Fish's name we gather here to put our dear fish to rest"), and then placing atop the burial mound a big rock painted with the word FISH. It would be a moment designed to teach the children the ways of loss, and the soft intricacies of seeing something that was once alive now dead, and to clarify that sharp defining difference, to smooth it over a bit, so that they will remember the moment and know, later, recalling it, that she was a good mother, the kind who would hold pet funerals.

But Fish is alive. His big old carp gills clutch and lick every tiny trace of oxygen from the froth of depravity in the inexplicably determinate manner that only animals have. He will have nothing to do with this household. And later that evening, once Dad is gone, they'll hold a small party to celebrate his resurrection, because they had assumed — as was natural in these circumstances — that he was dead, or near enough death to be called dead, having near-death visions, as the dead are wont: that small pinpoint of light at the end of the tunnel and visions of an existence as a fish in some other ethery world, a better world for a fish, with fresh clear water bursting with oxygen and other carp large and small in communal bliss and just enough muck and mud for good pickings. After the celebration, before bedtime, they'll cover the top of the clean tank in plastic wrap and, working together, moving slowly with the unison of pallbearers, being careful not to slosh the water, carry it down the stairs to the family room, where with a soft patter of congratulatory applause they'll present Fish with a new home, right next to the television set.

JOYCE CAROL OATES

The Cousins

FROM HARPER'S MAGAZINE

Lake Worth, Florida
September 14, 1998

Dear Professor Morgenstern,

How badly I wish that I could address you as "Freyda"! But I don't have the right to such familiarity.

I have just read your memoir. I have reason to believe that we are cousins. My maiden name is "Schwart" (not my father's actual name, I think it was changed at Ellis Island in 1936), but my mother's maiden name was "Morgenstern" and all her family was from Kaufbeuren as yours were. We were to meet in 1941 when we were small children, you and your parents and sister and brother were coming to live with my parents, my two brothers, and me in Milburn, New York. But the boat that was carrying you and other refugees, the *Marea,* was turned back by U.S. Immigration at New York Harbor.

(In your memoir you speak so briefly of this. You seem to recall a name other than *Marea.* But I am sure that *Marea* was the name, for it seemed so beautiful to me like music. You were so young of course. So much would happen afterward, you would not remember this. By my calculation you were 6, and I was 5.)

All these years I had not known that you were living! I had not known that there were survivors in your family. It was told to us by my father that there were not. I am so happy for you and your success. To think that you were living in the U.S. since 1956 is a shock to me. That you were a college student in New York City while I was living (my first marriage, not a happy one) in upstate New York! Forgive me, I did not know of your previous books, though I would be intrigued by "biological anthropology," I think! (I have nothing of your academic education, I'm so ashamed. Not only not college but I did not graduate from high school.)

Well, I am writing in the hope that we might meet. Oh very soon, Freyda! Before it's too late.

I am no longer your 5-year-old cousin dreaming of a new "sister" (as my mother promised) who would sleep with me in my bed and be with me always.

Your "lost" cousin,
Rebecca

Lake Worth, Florida
September 15, 1998

Dear Professor Morgenstern,

I wrote to you just the other day. Now I see to my embarrassment that I may have sent the letter to a wrong address. If you are "on sabbatical leave" from the University of Chicago, as it says on the dust jacket of your memoir. I will try again with this, care of your publisher.

I will enclose the same letter. Though I feel it is not adequate, to express what is in my heart.

Your "lost" cousin,
Rebecca

P.S. Of course I will come to you, wherever & whenever you wish, Freyda!

Lake Worth, Florida
October 2, 1998

Dear Professor Morgenstern,

I wrote to you last month but I'm afraid that my letters were misaddressed. I will enclose these letters here, now that I know you are at the "Institute for Advanced Research" at Stanford University, Palo Alto, California.

It's possible that you have read my letters and were offended by them. I know, I am not a very good writer. I should not have said what I did about the Atlantic crossing in 1941, as if you would not know these facts for yourself. I did not mean to correct you, Professor Morgenstern, regarding the name of the very boat you and your family were on in that nightmare time!

In an interview with you reprinted in the Miami newspaper I was embarrassed to read that you have received so much mail from "relatives" since the memoir. I smiled to read where you said, "Where were all these relatives in America when they were needed?"

Truly we were here, Freyda! In Milburn, New York, on the Erie Canal.

Your cousin,
Rebecca

Palo Alto, CA
1 November 1998

Dear Rebecca Schward,

Thank you for your letter and for your response to my memoir. I have been deeply moved by the numerous letters I've received since the publication of *Back from the Dead: A Girlhood* both in the United States and abroad, and truly wish that I had time to reply to each of these individually and at length.

Sincerely,
FM
Freyda Morgenstern
Julius K. Tracey '48 Distinguished
Professor of Anthropology,
University of Chicago

Lake Worth, Florida
November 5, 1998

Dear Professor Morgenstern,

I'm very relieved now, I have the correct address! I hope that you will read this letter. I think you must have a secretary who opens your mail and sends back replies. I know, you are amused (annoyed?) by so many now claiming to be relatives of "Freyda Morgenstern." Especially since your television interviews. But I feel very strongly, I am your true cousin. For I was the (only) daughter of Anna Morgenstern. I believe that Anna Morgenstern was the (only) sister of your mother, Sara, a younger sister. For many weeks my mother spoke of her sister, Sara, coming to live with us, your father and your Elzbieta, who was older than you by 3 or 4 years, and your brother, Leon, who was also older than you, not by so much.

We had photographs of you. I remember so clearly how your hair was so neatly plaited and how pretty you were, a "frowning girl" my mother said of you, like me. We did look alike then, Freyda, though you were much prettier of course. Elzbieta was blonde with a plump face. Leon was looking happy in the photograph, a sweet-seeming boy of maybe 8. To read that your sister and brother died in such a terrible way in "Theresienstadt" was so sad. My mother never recovered from the shock of that time, I think. She was so hoping to see her sister again. When the *Marea* was turned back in the harbor, she gave up hope. My father did not allow her to speak German, only English, but she could not speak English well, if anyone came to the house she would hide. She did not speak much afterward to any of us and was often sick. She died in May 1949.

Reading this letter I see that I am giving a wrong emphasis, really! I never think of these long-ago things.

It was seeing your picture in the newspaper, Freyda! My husband was reading the *New York Times* & called me to him saying wasn't it strange, here was a woman looking enough like his wife to be a sister, though in fact you & I do not look so much alike, in my opinion, not any longer, but it was a shock to see your face, which is very like my mother's face as I remember it.

And then your name, *Freyda Morgenstern.*

At once I went out & purchased *Back from the Dead: A Girlhood.* I have not read any Holocaust memoirs out of a dread of what I would learn. Your memoir I read sitting in the car in the parking lot of the bookstore not knowing the time, how late it was, until my eyes could not see the pages. I thought, "It's Freyda! It's her! My sister I was promised." Now I am 62 years old, and so lonely in this place of retired wealthy people who look at me & think that I am one of them.

I am not one to cry. But I wept on many pages of your memoir though I know (from your interviews) you wish not to hear such reports from readers & have only contempt for "cheap American pity." I know, I would feel the same way. You are right to feel that way. In Milburn I resented the people who felt sorry for me as the "gravedigger's daughter" (my father's employment) more than the others who did not give a damn if the Schwarts lived or died.

I am enclosing my picture, taken when I was a girl of 16. It is all I have of those years. (I look very different now, I'm afraid!)

How badly I wish I could send you a picture of my mother, Anna Morgenstern, but all were destroyed in 1949.

Your cousin,
Rebecca

Palo Alto, CA
16 November 1998

Dear Rebecca Schwart,

Sorry not to have replied earlier. I think yes it is quite possible that we are "cousins" but at such a remove it's really an abstraction, isn't it?

I am not traveling much this year, trying to complete a new book before my sabbatical ends. I am giving fewer "talks" and my book tour is over, thank God. (The venture into memoir was my first and will be my last effort at non-academic writing. It was far too easy, like opening a vein.) So I don't quite see how it would be feasible for us to meet at the present time.

Thank you for sending your photograph. I am returning it.

Sincerely,
FM

Lake Worth, Florida
November 20, 1998

Dear Freyda,

Yes, I am sure we are "cousins"! Though like you I don't know what "cousins" can mean.

I have no living relatives, I believe. My parents have been dead since 1949 & I know nothing of my brothers, whom I have not glimpsed in many years.

I think you despise me as your "American cousin." I wish you could forgive me for that. I am not sure how "American" I am, though I was not born in Kaufbeuren as you were but in New York Harbor in May 1936. (The exact day is lost. There was no birth certificate or it was lost.) I mean, I was born on the refugee boat! In a place of terrible filth, I was told.

It was a different time then, 1936. The war had not begun & people of our kind were allowed to "emigrate" if they had money.

My brothers, Herschel & Augustus, were born in Kaufbeuren & of course both our parents. My father called himself "Jacob

Schwart" in this country. (This is a name I have never spoken to anyone who knows me now. Not to my husband of course.) I knew little of my father except he had been a printer in the old world (as he called it with scorn) and at one time a math teacher in a boys' school. Until the Nazis forbade such people to teach. My mother, Anna Morgenstern, was married very young. She played piano, as a girl. We would listen to music on the radio sometime if Pa was not home. (The radio was Pa's.)

Forgive me, I know you are not interested in any of this. In your memoir you spoke of your mother as a record keeper for the Nazis, one of those Jewish "administrators" helping in the transport of Jews. You are not sentimental about family. There is something so craven to it, isn't there. I respect the wishes of one who wrote *Back from the Dead,* which is so critical of your relatives & Jews & Jewish history & beliefs as of postwar "amnesia." I would not wish to dissuard you of such a true feeling, Freyda!

I have no true feelings myself, I mean that others can know.

Pa said you were all gone. Like cattle sent back to Hitler, Pa said. I remember his voice lifting, NINE HUNDRED SEVENTY-SIX REFUGEES, I am sick still hearing that voice.

Pa said for me to stop thinking about my cousins! They were not coming. They were *gone.*

Many pages of your memoir I have memorized, Freyda. And your letters to me. In your words, I can hear your voice. I love this voice so like my own. My secret voice I mean, that no one knows.

I will fly to California, Freyda. Will you give me permission? "Only say the word & my soul shall be healed."

Your cousin,
Rebecca

Lake Worth, Florida
November 21, 1998

Dear Freyda,

I am so ashamed, I mailed you a letter yesterday with a word misspelled: "dissuade." And I spoke of no living relatives, I meant no one remaining from the Schwart family. (I have a son from my first marriage, he is married with two children.)

I have bought other books of yours. *Biology: A History, Race and Racism: A History.* How impressed Jacob Schwart would be, the little girl in the photographs was never gone but has so very far surpassed him!

Will you let me come to see you in Palo Alto, Freyda? I could arrive for one day, we might have a meal together & I would depart the next morning. This is a promise.

Your (lonely) cousin,
Rebecca

Lake Worth, Florida
November 24, 1998

Dear Freyda,

An evening of your time is too much to ask, I think. An hour? An hour would not be too much, would it? Maybe you could talk to me of your work, anything in your voice would be precious to me. I would not wish to drag you into the cesspool of the past, as you speak of it so strongly. A woman like yourself capable of such intellectual work & so highly regarded in your field has no time for maudlin sentiment, I agree.

I have been reading your books. Underlining & looking up words in the dictionary. (I love the dictionary, it's my friend.) So exciting to consider *How does science demonstrate the genetic basis of behavior?*

I have enclosed a card here for your reply. Forgive me I did not think of this earlier.

Your cousin,
Rebecca

Palo Alto, CA
24 November 1998

Dear Rebecca Schwart,

Your letters of Nov. 20 & 21 are interesting. But the name "Jacob Schwart" means nothing to me, I'm afraid. There are numerous "Morgensterns" surviving. Perhaps some of these are your cousins, too. You might seek them out if you are lonely.

As I believe I have explained, this is a very busy time for me. I work much of the day and am not feeling very sociable in the evening. "Loneliness" is a problem engendered primarily by the too-close proximity of others. One excellent remedy is work.

Sincerely,
FM

P.S. I believe you have left phone messages for me at the Institute. As my assistant has explained to you, I have no time to answer such calls.

Lake Worth, Florida
November 27, 1998

Dear Freyda,

Our letters crossed! We both wrote on Nov. 24, maybe it's a sign.

It was on impulse I telephoned. "If I could hear her voice" — the thought came to me.

You have hardened your heart against your "American cousin." It was courageous in the memoir to state so clearly how you had to harden your heart against so much, to survive. Americans believe that suffering makes saints of us, which is a joke. Still I realize you have no time for me in your life now. There is no "purpose" to me.

Even if you won't meet me at this time, will you allow me to write to you? I will accept it if you do not reply. I would only wish that you might read what I write, it would make me so happy (yes, less lonely!), for then I could speak to you in my thoughts as I did when we were girls.

Your cousin,
Rebecca

P.S. In your academic writing you refer so often to "adaptation of species to environment." If you saw me, your cousin, in Lake Worth, Florida, on the ocean just south of Palm Beach, so very far from Milburn, N.Y., and from the "old world," you would laugh.

Palo Alto, CA
1 December 1998

Dear Rebecca Schwart,

My tenacious American cousin! I'm afraid it is no sign of anything, not even "coincidence," that our letters were written on the same day and that they "crossed."

This card. I admit I am curious at the choice. It happens this is a card on my study wall. (Did I speak of this in the memoir? I don't think so.) How do you happen to come into possession of this reproduction of Caspar David Friedrich's *Sturzacker* — you have not been to the museum in Hamburg, have you? It's rare that any

American even knows the name of this artist much esteemed in Germany.

Sincerely,
FM

Lake Worth, Florida
4 December 1998

Dear Freyda,

The post card of Caspar David Friedrich was given to me, with other cards from the Hamburg museum, by someone who traveled there. (In fact my son, who is a pianist. His name would be known to you, it's nothing like my own.)

I chose a card to reflect your soul. As I perceive it in your words. Maybe it reflects mine also. I wonder what you will think of this new card, which is German also but uglier.

Your cousin,
Rebecca

Palo Alto, CA
10 December 1998

Dear Rebecca,

Yes I like this ugly Nolde. Smoke black as pitch and the Elbe like molten lava. You see into my soul, don't you! Not that I have wished to disguise myself.

So I return *Towboat on the Elbe* to my tenacious American cousin. THANK YOU but please do not write again. And do not call. I have had enough of you.

FM

Palo Alto, CA
11 December 1998/2:00 A.M.

Dear "Cousin"!

Your 16-yr-old photo I made a copy of. I like that coarse mane of hair and the jaws so solid. Maybe the eyes were scared, but we know how to hide that, don't we cousin.

In the camp I learned to stand tall. I learned to be big. As animals make themselves bigger, it can be a trick to the eye that comes true. I guess you were a "big" girl, too.

I have always told the truth. I see no reason for subterfuge. I despise fantasizing. I have made enemies "among my kind" you can be sure. When you are "back from the dead" you do not give a damn for others' opinions & believe me, that has cost me in this so-called "profession" where advancement depends upon ass-kissing and its sexual variants not unlike the activities of our kindred primates.

Bad enough my failure to behave as a suppliant female through my career. In the memoir I take a laughing tone speaking of graduate studies at Columbia in the late 1950s. I did not laugh much then. Meeting my old enemies, who had wished to crush an impious female at the start of her career, not only female but a Jew & a refugee Jew from one of the camps, I looked them in the eye, I never flinched, but they flinched, the bastards. I took my revenge where & when I could. Now those generations are dying out, I am not pious about their memories. At conferences organized to revere them, Freyda Morgenstern is the "savagely witty" truth-teller.

In Germany, where history was so long denied, *Back from the Dead* has been a bestseller for five months. Already it has been nominated for two major awards. Here is a joke, and a good one, yes?

In this country, no such reception. Maybe you saw the "good" reviews. Maybe you saw the one full-page ad my cheapskate publisher finally ran in the *New York Review of Books.* There have been plenty of attacks. Worse even than the stupid attacks to which I have become accustomed in my "profession."

In the Jewish publications, & in Jewish-slanted publications, such shock/dismay/disgust. A Jewish woman who writes so without sentiment of mother & other relatives who "perished" in Theresienstadt. A Jewish woman who speaks so coldly & "scientifically" of her "heritage." As if the so-called Holocaust is a "heritage." As if I have not earned my right to speak the truth as I see it and will continue to speak the truth, for I have no plans to retire from research, writing, teaching, & directing doctoral students for a long time. (I will take early retirement at Chicago, these very nice benefits, & set up shop elsewhere.)

This piety of the Holocaust! I laughed, you used that word so reverentially in one of your letters. I never use this word that slides off American tongues now like grease. One of the hatchet-reviewers called Morgenstern a traitor giving solace to the enemy (which enemy? there are many) by simply stating & restating, as I will each time I am asked, that the "holocaust" was an accident in history as all events in history are accidents. There is no purpose to history as to evolution, there is no goal or progress. Evolution is the term given to what is. The pious fantasizers wish to claim that the Nazis' genocidal campaign was a singular event in history, that it has elevated us above history. This is bullshit, I have said so & will continue to say so. There are many genocides, as long as there has been mankind. History is an invention of books. In biological anthropology we note that the wish to perceive "meaning" is one trait of our species among many. But that does not posit "meaning" in the world. If history did exist it is a great river/cesspool into which countless small streams & tributaries flow. In one direction. Unlike sewage it cannot back up. It cannot be "tested" — "demonstrated." It simply is. If the individual streams dry up, the river disappears. There is no "river-destiny." There are merely accidents in time. The scientist notes that without sentiment or regret.

Maybe I will send you these ravings, my tenacious American cousin. I'm drunk enough, in a festive mood!

Your (traitor) cousin,
FM

Lake Worth, Florida
15 December 1998

Dear Freyda,

How I loved your letter, that made my hands shake. I have not laughed in so long. I mean, in our special way.

It's the way of hatred. I love it. Though it eats you from the inside out. (I guess.)

It's a cold night here, a wind off the Atlantic. Florida is often wet-cold. Lake Worth/Palm Beach are very beautiful & very boring. I wish you might come here & visit, you could spend the rest of the winter, for it's often sunny of course.

I take your precious letters with me in the early morning walking on the beach. Though I have memorized your words. Until a year ago I would run, run, run for miles! At the rain-whipped edge of a hurricane I ran. To see me, my hard-muscled legs & straight backbone, you would never guess I was not a young woman.

So strange that we are in our sixties, Freyda! Our baby-girl dolls have not aged a day.

(Do you hate it, growing old? Your photographs show such a vigorous woman. You tell yourself, "Every day I live was not meant to be" & there's happiness in this.)

Freyda, in our house of mostly glass facing the ocean you would have your own "wing." We have several cars, you would have your own car. No questions asked where you went. You would not have to meet my husband, you would be my precious secret.

Tell me you will come, Freyda! After the New Year would be a good time. When you finish your work each day we will go walking on the beach together. I promise we would not have to speak.

Your loving cousin,
Rebecca

Lake Worth, Florida
17 December 1998

Dear Freyda,

Forgive my letter of the other day, so pushy & familiar. Of course you would not wish to visit a stranger.

I must make myself remember: though we are cousins, we are strangers.

I was reading again *Back from the Dead.* The last section, in America. Your three marriages — "ill-advised experiments in intimacy/ lunacy." You are very harsh & very funny, Freyda! Unsparing to others as to yourself.

My first marriage too was blind in love & I suppose "lunacy." Yet without it, I would not have my son.

In the memoir you have no regret for your "misbegotten fetuses" though for the "pain and humiliation" of the abortions illegal at the time. Poor Freyda! In 1957 in a filthy room in Manhattan you nearly bled to death, at that time I was a young mother so in love with my life. Yet I would have come to you, if I had known.

Though I know that you will not come here, yet I hold out hope that, suddenly yes you might! To visit, to stay as long as you wish. Your privacy would be protected.

I remain the tenacious cousin,
Rebecca

Lake Worth, Florida
New Year's Day 1999

Dear Freyda,

I don't hear from you, I wonder if you have gone away? But maybe you will see this. "If Freyda sees this even to toss away . . ."

I am feeling happy & hopeful. You are a scientist & of course you are right to scorn such feelings as "magical" & "primitive," but I think there can be a newness in the New Year. I am hoping this is so.

My father, Jacob Schwart, believed that in animal life the weak are quickly disposed of, we must hide our weakness always. You & I knew that as children. But there is so much more to us than just the animal, we know that, too.

Your loving cousin,
Rebecca

Palo Alto, CA
19 January 1999

Rebecca:

Yes I have been away. And I am going away again. What business is it of yours?

I was coming to think you must be an invention of mine. My worst weakness. But here on my windowsill propped up to stare at me is "Rebecca, 1952." The horse-mane hair & hungry eyes.

Cousin, you are so faithful! It makes me tired. I know I should be flattered, few others would wish to pursue "difficult" Professor Morgenstern now I'm an old woman. I toss your letters into a drawer, then in my weakness I open them. Once, rummaging through Dumpster trash I retrieved a letter of yours. Then in my weakness I opened it. You know how I hate weakness!

Cousin, no more.
FM

Lake Worth, Florida
23 January 1999

Dear Freyda,

I know! I am sorry.

I shouldn't be so greedy. I have no right. When I first discovered that you were living, last September, my thought was only "My cousin Freyda Morgenstern, my lost sister, she is alive! She doesn't need to love me or even know me or give a thought to me. It's enough to know that she did not perish and has lived her life."

Your loving cousin,
Rebecca

Palo Alto, CA
30 January 1999

Dear Rebecca,

We make ourselves ridiculous with emotions at our age, like showing our breasts. Spare us, please!

No more would I wish to meet you than I would wish to meet myself. Why would you imagine I might want a "cousin" — "sister" — at my age? I would like it that I have no living relatives any longer, for there is no obligation to think *Is he/she still living?*

Anyway, I'm going away. I will be traveling all spring. I hate it here. California suburban boring & without a soul. My "colleagues/friends" are shallow opportunists to whom I appear to be an opportunity.

I hate such words as "perish." Does a fly "perish," do rotting things "perish," does your enemy "perish"? Such exalted speech makes me tired.

Nobody "perished" in the camps. Many "died" — "were killed." That's all.

I wish I could forbid you to revere me. For your own good, dear cousin. I see that I am your weakness, too. Maybe I want to spare you.

If you were a graduate student of mine, though! I would set you right with a swift kick in the rear.

Suddenly there are awards & honors for Freyda Morgenstern. Not only the memoirist but the "distinguished anthropologist" too. So I will travel to receive them. All this comes too late of course. Yet like you I am a greedy person, Rebecca. Sometimes I think my soul is in my gut! I am one who stuffs herself without pleasure, to take food from others.

Spare yourself. No more emotion. No more letters!
FM

Chicago, IL
29 March 1999

Dear Rebecca Schwart,

Have been thinking of you lately. It has been a while since I've heard from you. Unpacking things here & came across your letters & photograph. How stark-eyed we all looked in black-and-white! Like x-rays of the soul. My hair was never so thick & splendid as yours, my American cousin.

I think I must have discouraged you. Now, to be frank, I miss you. It has been two months nearly since you wrote. These honors & awards are not so precious if no one cares. If no one hugs you in congratulations. Modesty is beside the point & I have too much pride to boast to strangers.

Of course, I should be pleased with myself: I sent you away. I know, I am a "difficult" woman. I would not like myself for a moment. I would not tolerate myself. I seem to have lost one or two of your letters, I'm not sure how many, vaguely I remember you saying you & your family lived in upstate New York, my parents had arranged to come stay with you? This was in 1941? You provided facts not in my memoir. But I do remember my mother speaking with such love of her younger sister, Anna. Your father changed his name to "Schwart" from — what? He was a math teacher in Kaufbeuren? My father was an esteemed doctor. He had many non-Jewish patients who revered him. As a young man he had served in the German army in the first war, he'd been awarded a Gold Medal for Bravery & it was promised that such a distinction would protect him while other Jews were being transported. My father disappeared so abruptly from our lives, immediately we were transported to that place, for years I believed he must have escaped & was alive somewhere & would contact us. I thought my mother had information she kept from me. She was not quite the Amazon-mother of *Back from the Dead* . . . Well, enough of this! Though evolutionary anthropology must scour the past relentlessly, human beings are not obliged to do so.

It's a blinding-bright day here in Chicago, from my aerie on the 52nd floor of my grand new apartment building I look out upon the vast inland sea Lake Michigan. Royalties from the memoir have helped me pay for this, a less "controversial" book would not have earned. Nothing more is needed, yes?

Your cousin,
Freyda

Lake Worth, Florida
April 3, 1999

Dear Freyda,

Your letter meant much to me. I'm so sorry not to answer sooner. I make no excuses. Seeing this card I thought, "For Freyda!"

Next time I will write more. Soon I promise.

Your cousin,
Rebecca

Chicago, IL
22 April 1999

Dear Rebecca,

Rec'd your card. Am not sure what I think of it. Americans are ga-ga for Joseph Cornell as they are for Edward Hopper. What is *Lanner Waltzes*? Two little-girl doll figures riding the crest of a wave & in the background an old-fashioned sailing ship with sails billowing? "Collage"? I hate riddle-art. Art is to see, not to *think*.

Is something wrong, Rebecca? The tone of your writing is altered, I think. I hope you are not playing coy, to take revenge for my chiding letter of January. I have a doctoral student, a bright young woman not quite so bright as she fancies herself, who plays such games with me at the present time, at her own risk! I hate games, too.

(Unless they are my own.)

Your cousin,
Freyda

Chicago, IL
6 May 1999

Dear Cousin:

Yes, I think you must be angry with me! Or you are not well.

I prefer to think that you are angry. That I did insult you in your American soft heart. If so, I am sorry. I have no copies of my letters to you & don't recall what I said. Maybe I was wrong. When I am coldly sober, I am likely to be wrong. When drunk, I am likely to be less wrong.

Enclosed here is a stamped addressed card. You need only check one of the boxes: [ ] angry [ ] not well.

Your cousin,
Freyda

P.S. This Joseph Cornell *Pond* reminded me of you, Rebecca. A doll-girl playing her fiddle beside a murky inlet.

Lake Worth, Florida
September 19, 1999

Dear Freyda,

How strong & beautiful you were, at the awards ceremony in Washington! I was there, in the audience at the Folger Library. I made the trip just for you.

All of the writers honored spoke very well. But none so witty & unexpected as "Freyda Morgenstern," who caused quite a stir.

I'm ashamed to say, I could not bring myself to speak to you. I waited in line with so many others for you to sign *Back from the Dead* & when my turn came you were beginning to tire. You hardly glanced at me, you were vexed at the girl assistant fumbling the book. I did no more than mumble, "Thank you," & hurried away.

I stayed just one night in Washington, then flew home. I tire easily now, it was a mad thing to do. My husband would have prevented me if he'd known where I was headed.

During the speeches you were restless onstage, I saw your eyes wandering. I saw your eyes on me. I was sitting in the third row of the theater. Such an old, beautiful little theater in the Folger Library. I think there must be so much beauty in the world we haven't seen. Now it is almost too late we yearn for it.

I was the gaunt-skull woman with the buzz cut. The heavy dark glasses covering half my face. Others in my condition wear gaudy turbans or gleaming wigs. Their faces are bravely made up. In Lake Worth/Palm Beach there are many of us. I don't mind my baldie head in warm weather & among strangers, for their eyes look through me as if I am invisible. You stared at me at first & then looked quickly away & afterward I could not bring myself to address you. It wasn't the right time, I had not prepared you for the sight of me. I shrink from pity & even sympathy is a burden. I had not known that I would make the reckless trip until that morning, for so much depends upon how I feel each morning, it's not predictable.

I had a present to give to you, I changed my mind & took away again feeling like a fool. Yet the trip was wonderful for me, I saw my cousin so close! Of course I regret my cowardice now it's too late.

You asked about my father. I will tell you no more than that I do not know my father's true name. "Jacob Schwart" was what he called himself & so I was "Rebecca Schwart," but that name was lost long ago. I have another more fitting American name, & I have also my husband's last name, only to you, my cousin, am I identified as "Rebecca Schwart."

Well, I will tell you one more thing: in May 1949 my father who was the gravedigger murdered your aunt Anna and wished to murder me but failed, he turned the shotgun onto himself & killed himself when I was 13 struggling with him for the gun & my strongest memory of that time was his face in the last seconds & what remained of his face, his skull & brains & the warmth of his blood splattered onto me.

I have never told anyone this, Freyda. Please do not speak of it to me, if you write again.

Your cousin
Rebecca

(I did not intend to write such an ugly thing, when I began this letter.)

Chicago, IL
23 September 1999

Dear Rebecca,

I'm stunned. That you were so close to me — and didn't speak.

And what you tell me of —. What happened to you at age 13.

I don't know what to say. Except yes I am stunned. I am angry, & hurt. Not at you, I don't think I am angry at you but at myself.

I've tried to call you. There is no "Rebecca Schwart" in the Lake Worth phone directory. Of course, you've told me there is no "Rebecca Schwart." Why in hell have you never told me your married name? Why are you so coy? I hate games, I don't have time for games.

Yes I am angry with you. I am upset & angry you are not well. (You never returned my card. I waited & waited & you did not.)

Can I believe you about "Jacob Schwart"! We conclude that the ugliest things are likely to be true.

In my memoir that isn't so. When I wrote it, 54 yrs later it was a text I composed of words chosen for "effect." Yes there are true facts in *Back from the Dead*. But facts are not "true" unless explained. My memoir had to compete with other memoirs of its type & so had to be "original." I am accustomed to controversy, I know how to tweak noses. The memoir makes light of the narrator's pain & humiliation. It's true, I did not feel that I would be one of those to die; I was too young, & ignorant, & compared to others I was healthy. My big blonde sister Elzbieta the relatives so admired, looking like a German girl-doll, soon lost all that hair & her bowels turned to bloody suet. Leon died trampled to death, I would learn afterward. What I say of my mother, Sara Morgenstern, is truthful only at the start. She was not a kapo but one hoping to cooperate with the Nazis to help her family (of course) & other Jews. She was a good organizer & much trusted but never so strong as the memoir has her. She did not say those cruel things, I have no memory of anything anyone said to me except orders shouted by authorities. All the quiet spoken words, the very breath of our lives together, was lost. But a memoir must have spoken words, & a memoir must breathe life.

I am so famous now — infamous! In France this month I am a new bestseller. In the U.K. (where they are outspoken anti-Semites, which is refreshing!) my word is naturally doubted yet still the book sells.

Rebecca, I must speak with you. I will enclose my number here. I will wait for a call. Past 10:00 P.M. of any night is best, I am not so cold-sober & nasty.

Your cousin,
Freyda

P.S. Are you taking chemotherapy now? What is the status of your condition? *Please answer.*

Lake Worth, Florida
October 8

Dear Freyda,

Don't be angry with me, I have wanted to call you. There are reasons I could not but maybe I will be stronger soon & I promise, I will call.

It was important for me to see you, and hear you. I am so proud of you. It hurts me when you say harsh things about yourself, I wish you would not. "Spare us" — yes?

Half the time I am dreaming & very happy. Just now I was smelling snakeroot. Maybe you don't know what snakeroot is, you have lived always in cities. Behind the gravedigger's stone cottage in Milburn there was a marshy place where this tall plant grew. The wildflowers were as tall as five feet. They had many small white flowers that look like frost. Very powdery, with a strange strong smell. The flowers were alive with bees humming so loudly it seemed like a living thing. I was remembering how waiting for you to come from over the ocean I had two dolls — Maggie, who was the prettiest doll, for you, and my doll, Minnie, who was plain & battered but I loved her very much. (My brother Herschel found the dolls at the Milburn dump. We found many useful things at the dump!) For hours I played with Maggie & Minnie & you, Freyda. All of us chattering away. My brothers laughed at me. Last night I dreamt of the dolls that were so vivid to me I had not glimpsed in 57 yrs. But it was strange, Freyda, you were not in the dream. I was not, either.

I will write some other time. I love you.

Your cousin,
Rebecca

Chicago, IL
12 October

Dear Rebecca,

Now I am angry! You have not called me & you have not given me your telephone number & how can I reach you? I have your street address but only the name "Rebecca Schwart." I am so busy, this is a terrible time. I feel as if my head is being broken by a mallet. Oh I am very angry at you, cousin!

Yet I think I should come to Lake Worth, to see you.

Should I?

F

DAVID BEZMOZGIS

Natasha

FROM HARPER'S MAGAZINE

> It is the opposite which is good to us.
>
> — Heraclitus

WHEN I WAS SIXTEEN I WAS HIGH most of the time. That year, my parents bought a new house at the edge of Toronto's sprawl. A few miles north were cows; south, the city. I spent most of my time in basements. The suburbs offered nothing, and so I lived a predominantly subterranean life. At home, separated from my parents by door and stairs, I smoked hash, watched television, read, and masturbated. In other basements I smoked, watched television, and refined my style with girls.

In the spring my uncle Fima, my grandmother's youngest brother, met his second wife. She arrived from Moscow for two weeks to get acquainted. Dusa, our dentist, had known the woman in Russia and recommended her. She was almost forty, my uncle forty-four. The woman was another in a string of last chances. A previous last chance had led to his first marriage. That marriage, to a fellow Russian emigrant, had failed within six months. My uncle was a good man, a hard worker, and a polymath. He read books, newspapers, and travel brochures. He could speak with equal authority about the Crimean War and the Toronto Maple Leafs. Short months after arriving in Toronto he took a job giving tours of the city to visiting Russians. But he wasn't rich and never would be. He was also honest to a fault and nervous with people. My grandmother's greatest fear was that he would always be alone in the world. Zina, the woman, had greasy brown hair, cut in a mannish style. She was thin, her body almost without contour. The first time I saw her was when my uncle brought her to our house for dinner.

She wore tight blue pants, high heels, and a yellow silk blouse that accentuated her conspicuously long nipples. The top buttons of her blouse were undone, and a thin gold chain with a Star of David clung to her breastbone. When she kissed me in greeting, she smelled of sweat and lilac.

Zina strode into our house as if she were on familiar territory, and her confidence had the effect of making my uncle act as though he were the stranger. He stumbled through the introductions and almost knocked over his chair. He faltered as he tried to explain how they had spent the day, and Zina chided him and finished his sentences. When my mother served the raspberry torte, Zina fed my uncle from her fork. In Russia she was a "teacher of English," and she sprinkled her conversation with English words and phrases. The soup my mother served was "tasty," our dining room "divine," and my father "charming." After dinner, in the living room, she placed her hand on my uncle's knee. I was, as usual, high, and I became fixated on the hand. It rested on my uncle's knee like a small pale animal. Sometimes it would arch or rise completely to make a point, always to settle back on the knee. Under her hand, my uncle's knee barely moved.

After her two weeks in Canada, Zina returned to Moscow. Before she left, my mother and aunt took her shopping and bought her a new wardrobe. They believed that Zina would be good for my uncle. The last thing he needed was a timid wife. Maybe she was a little aggressive, but to make it in this country you couldn't apologize every step like him. My grandmother was anxious because Zina had a young daughter in Moscow, but she conceded that at this age to find a woman without a child probably meant there was something wrong with her. My uncle did not disagree. There were positives and negatives, he said.

The decision was made quickly, and days after Zina's departure, my uncle wrote her a letter inviting her to return and become his wife. One month later Zina was back in Toronto. This time my entire family went to the airport to greet her. We stood at the gate and waited as a stream of Russian faces filtered by. Near the end of the stream, Zina appeared. She was wearing an outfit my mother had purchased for her. She carried a heavy suitcase. When she saw my uncle, she dropped the suitcase and ran to him and kissed him on his cheeks and on his mouth. A thin blond girl, also carrying a suitcase, picked up Zina's abandoned bag and dragged both suitcases through the gate. The girl had large blue eyes, and her straight blond hair was cut into bangs. She strained toward us with the bags and stopped behind Zina, her face without expression, and waited for her mother to introduce her. Her name was Natasha. She was fourteen. My mother said, Meet your new cousin. Later, as we drove my grandparents home, my grandmother despaired that the girl's father was obviously a *shaygets.*

One week after their arrival, everyone went down to North York City Hall for the civil ceremony. A retired judge administered the vows, and we took photos in the atrium. There was no rabbi, no *chuppa,* no stomping of the glass. Afterward we all went to our house for a barbecue. One after another, people made toasts. My uncle and Zina sat at the head of the table like a real married couple. For a wedding gift they were given money to help them rent a larger apartment. My uncle's one bedroom would not do. This wasn't Russia, and the girl couldn't continue to sleep in the living room. The one time my grandparents had gone to visit, Natasha emerged from the shower naked and, without so much as acknowledging their presence, went into the kitchen. While my grandparents tried to listen to my uncle and Zina talk about Zina's plans to get her teaching certificate, Natasha stood in the kitchen and ate an apple.

At the barbecue, my mother seated Natasha between me and my cousin Jana. It was our duty to make her feel welcome. She was new to the country, she had no friends, she spoke no English, she was now family. Jana, two years my senior, had no interest in a fourteen-year-old girl. Especially one who dressed like a Polish hooker, didn't speak English, and wasn't saying anything in Russian either. Midway through the barbecue, a car full of girls came for Jana, and Natasha became my responsibility. My mother encouraged me to show her around the house.

Without enthusiasm I led Natasha around the house. Without enthusiasm she followed. For lack of anything else to say, I would enter a room and announce its name in Russian. We entered the kitchen and I said *kitchen,* my parents' bedroom and I said *bedroom,* the living room and I said *the room where we watch television,* since I had no idea what it was called in Russian. Then I walked her down into the basement. Through the blinds we could see the backyard and the legs of our newly incarnated family. I said, That's it, *the whole house.* Natasha looked around the room, then shut the blinds, rendering the already dim basement almost dark. She dropped down into one of the two velour beanbag chairs in front of the television. Chairs that I had been earnestly and consistently humping since the age of twelve.

— You have all of this to yourself?

— Yes.

— It must be nice.

— It is.

— What do you do here?

— Watch television, read.

— That's it?

— That's most of it.

— Do you bring girls here?

— Not really.

— Have you had sex down here?

— What?

— You don't have to say if you don't want to. I don't really care. It doesn't mean anything.

— You're fourteen.

— So what? That doesn't mean anything either. I've done it a hundred times. If you want, I'll do it with you.

— We're cousins.

— No, we're not.

— Your mother married my uncle.

— It's too bad. He's nice.

— He is.

— I feel sorry for him. She'll ruin his life.

— It's hard to imagine his life getting worse.

— She'll make it worse.

— She's your mother.

— She's a whore. Do you want to know how it sounds when they do it?

— Not particularly.

— They do it at least three times a day. He groans like he is being killed, and she screams like she is killing him.

A month after the wedding, my uncle, Zina, and Natasha found a new two-bedroom apartment ten minutes' walk from our house. Summer vacation had just begun, and instead of going off to camp

I had made an arrangement to work for Rufus, my dealer. Rufus was twenty and, while keeping up his business, was also studying philosophy at the University of Toronto. Aside from providing me with drugs, he also recommended books. Because of him I graduated from John Irving and Mordecai Richler to Camus, Heraclitus, Catullus, and Kafka. That summer, in exchange for doing the deliveries, I got free dope (notwithstanding whatever I shorted off potheads) and a little money. I also got to borrow the books Rufus had been reading over the course of the year. This, to me, was a perfectly legitimate way to spend two months, though my parents insisted that I find a job. Telling them about the job I already had was out of the question, and so the summer started off on a point of conflict.

A week into my summer vacation, my mother resolved our conflict. If I had no intention of finding a job, she would put me to good use. Since I was home by myself, I would be conscripted into performing an essential service. I was alone and Natasha was alone. She didn't know anyone in the city and was making a nuisance of herself. From what I could understand, she wasn't actually doing anything to be a nuisance, but her mere presence in the apartment was inconvenient. My family felt that my uncle needed time alone with his new wife, and having Natasha around made him uncomfortable. Besides, she was difficult. My uncle reported that she refused to speak to her mother and literally hadn't said a word in weeks.

The morning after my mother decided that I would keep Natasha company, I went to my uncle's new apartment. I hadn't seen him, Zina, or Natasha since the wedding and the barbecue. They hadn't been back to our house, and I had had no reason to go there. In fact, in all the years that my uncle lived in Toronto, I had never been to his apartment. Despite occasional invitations, I avoided the place because I preferred not to see how he lived.

By the time I arrived, my uncle had already left for work. Zina met me at the door wearing a blue Soviet housedress that could have passed for a hospital gown. Again, she wore no bra. I was greeted by nipples, then Zina. She put her hand on my arm and ushered me into the kitchen, where she was filling out forms to obtain credentials from the Board of Education. A stack of forms was laid out on the table along with black bread and cucumbers. She made me a sandwich I did not want and told me what a wonderful man my uncle was. How she was very fortunate to find such a man and how good things would be as soon as Natasha became accustomed to their new life. We were co-conspirators, she and I, both working for Natasha's well-being. She was convinced that I would be able to help her. She sensed that Natasha liked me. Natasha didn't like many people.

— I'm her mother, and no matter what she says I would cut off my right arm for her. But she has always been different. Even as a baby she hardly smiled.

Zina led me to Natasha's door, knocked, and announced that I was here. After a brief pause Natasha opened the door. She was wearing blue jeans and a souvenir T-shirt from Niagara Falls. I could see behind her into the room. There was a small bed and a table. On one wall was an old poster of Michael Jackson circa *Thriller.* In bold red letters a phonetic approximation of Michael Jackson's name was written in Cyrillic. I read the name slowly letter by letter, since I was effectively illiterate. It gave me something to do while Natasha and Zina glared at each other in acrimonious silence.

— I'm an enemy because I took her away from her criminal friends. I'm an enemy because I wanted to give her a better life. Now she won't say a word, but one day she'll thank me.

Without breaking her silence, Natasha grabbed my hand and led me out of the apartment. As we went past the door, Zina called after us, telling me to watch out for Natasha. I was to make sure that she didn't do anything stupid. Natasha should remember what it would do to my uncle if something were to happen to her. Even if she didn't care about how Zina felt, she should at least consider my uncle, for whom she was now like a daughter.

In the stairway Natasha released my hand, and we descended to the back of the building and the parking lot. Outside, she turned and spoke what might have been her first words in weeks.

— I can't stand looking at her. I want to scratch out my eyes. In Moscow I never had to see her. Now she's always there.

We wound our way out of the parking lot and toward the subdivisions leading back to my house. On the way I decided to stop at Rufus's and pick up an eighth for one of our regular heads. I walked ahead and Natasha trailed along, more interested in the uniform lawns and houses than the specifics of where we were going. Aside from the odd Filipina nanny wheeling a little white kid, the streets were empty. The sun was neither bright nor hot, and the outdoors felt conveniently like the indoors, God's thermostat set to "suburban basement."

— In Moscow everyone lives in apartments. The only time you see houses like this is in the country, where people have their dachas.

— Three years ago this was the country.

We found Rufus on his backyard deck, listening to Led Zeppelin, eating an omelet. Although he was alone, the table was set for four, with a complete set of linen napkins and matching cutlery. Rufus didn't seem at all surprised to see us. That was part of his persona; Rufus never appeared surprised about anything. At twenty he had already accomplished more than most men twice his age. It was rumored that, aside from dealing, Rufus was also a partner in a used-car lot/body shop and various other ventures. Nobody who knew him had ever seen him sleep.

Rufus insisted on cooking us breakfast. Natasha and I sat at the kitchen counter as he explained that even when he ate alone, he liked to set a full table. The mere act of setting extra places prevented him from receding into solipsism. It also made for good karma, so that even when he was not expecting guests there existed tangible evidence announcing that he was open to the possibility. While Rufus spoke, Natasha's eyes roamed around the house. Taking in the spotless kitchen, the copper cookware, the living room with matching leather sofas, the abstract art on the walls. Other than the contents of the basement refrigerator, the house gave no indication that it was owned and inhabited by a drug dealer barely out of his teens. This was no accident. Rufus believed that it helped his business. His clients were all middle-class suburban kids, and despite his bohemian inclinations a nice house in the suburbs was the perfect location. It kept him local, and it meant that for his customers a visit to their dealer felt just like coming home.

Back on the deck I explained to Rufus about Natasha, leaving out certain details I didn't think he needed to know. As Rufus and I talked, Natasha sat contentedly with her omelet and orange juice. Since leaving my uncle's apartment, her attitude toward everything had taken the form of a certain benign detachment. She was calibrated somewhere between resignation and joy.

I noticed Rufus looking at her.

— Did I mention she was fourteen?

— My interest, I assure you, is purely anthropological.

— The anthropology of jailbait.

— She's an intense little chick.

— She's Russian. We're born intense.

— With all due respect, Berman, you and her aren't even the same species.

To get her attention, Rufus leaned across the table and tapped Natasha on the arm. She looked up from her food and returned Rufus's smile. He asked me to translate for him. His own family, he said, could be traced back to Russia. He wanted to know what Russia was like now. What it was really like. Natasha shrugged.

— Russia is shit, but people enjoy themselves.

After that first day, Natasha started coming to our house regularly. I no longer went to pick her up but waited instead for her arrival. Through my basement window I could see her as she appeared in our backyard and wandered around inspecting my mother's peonies or the raspberry and red-currant bushes. If I was in a certain mood, I would watch her for a while before going upstairs and opening the sliding glass door in the kitchen.

We spent most of our days in the basement. I read and Natasha studied television English. When I had a delivery to make, she accompanied me. Between reading, television English, and deliveries, I taught Natasha how to get high. I showed her how to roll a joint, to light a pipe, or, in a pinch, where to cut the holes in a Gatorade bottle. In exchange, Natasha taught me other things. Many of these things had nothing to do with sex.

After our days in the basement, we would listen for my mother to arrive home from work. To avoid some serious unpleasantness, I made a habit of setting my alarm for 5:00 P.M. If we weren't sleeping, the alarm simply reminded us to open a window or get dressed. By the time my mother came home, we were usually in the kitchen or out in the backyard. Chores that had been assigned to me were usually done at this time. It pleased my mother to come home and find me, spade in hand, turning over the earth around the berry bushes. Also, once it was established that Natasha much preferred to stay at our house, my mother grew more than accustomed to having her around. Unlike me and my father, Natasha volunteered to help her in the kitchen. The two of them would stand at the sink peeling potatoes or slicing up radishes and cucumbers for salad. I often came in to overhear my mother telling stories about her childhood in postwar Latvia — a land of outhouses, horse-drawn wagons, and friendly neighbors. In Natasha she found a receptive audience. They spoke the same language — Russian girl to Russian girl. Implicit was a commonality of experience. This despite that, in too many ways, Natasha's childhood couldn't have been more different from my mother's if she had been raised by Peruvian cannibals.

No more than two weeks after I picked her up at my uncle's apartment, Natasha had become a fixture at our house. It was a situation that, for different and even perversely conflicting reasons, suited everyone. It solved the Natasha problem for my uncle. It solved the Zina problem for Natasha. It made my mother feel like she was protecting my uncle's last chance at happiness and also satisfying her own latent desire for a daughter. It absolved me from the need to find a job and cast me in a generally favorable light with the rest of my family. And strangely enough, Natasha's incorporation into the household made the things we did in the basement seem less bad. Or not bad at all. What we did in the basement became only a part of who we were.

One day after some but not too many days together, Natasha simply slid out of her jeans and removed her shirt. We were sitting inches apart, each on our own beanbag. Moments before, we had finished smoking a joint and I had gone back to Kafka's diaries. I became aware of what she was doing slower than a sixteen-year-old should have. That she saw me looking changed nothing. On the beanbag, naked, she turned to me and said very simply: *Do you want to?* At sixteen, no expert but no virgin, I lived in a permanent state of *want to.* But for everything I knew, I knew almost nothing. In the middle of the day, Natasha in the basement was the first time I had seen a live naked girl. All the parts available for viewing. Nothing in my previous dimly lit gropings compared. In my teenage life, what was more elusive than a properly illuminated naked girl? The fact that it was Natasha — my nominal cousin, fourteen, strange — no longer mattered. After years of sex as negotiation, I was amazed to discover that it could be as perfunctory as brushing your teeth.

That day was the first of many firsts. With the house to ourselves and no threat of being disturbed, we did everything I had ever dreamed of doing — including some things that hadn't even occurred to me. We showered together, we slept in the same bed, I watched her walk across the room, I watched her pee. These prosaic things, being new, were as exciting as the sex. And for me the sex was as much about the variation as the pleasure. I kept a mental list from position to position, crossing off one accomplishment after another. Nothing was repeated until everything was attempted. That way, in the event I was struck by a bus, I would feel as though I had lived a full life. Most of the things we did Natasha had already done, but she was perfectly happy to oblige.

In our quieter moments, Natasha told me about the men who had taken her picture. She hadn't minded any of it except that they couldn't explain why they liked one thing over another. They had always known exactly how they wanted her to look, but none of them could give her a reason. Why did they prefer her leg raised this way and not that, why squatting from behind or holding her hand in a certain position? Some of the positions had been practically identical, yet they had insisted on them. The only explanation they offered was that it looked good or that it was sexy. And yet she never felt that way about men. She never cared how they looked or what side she was viewing them from.

— You don't care how I look?

— You look how you look. If you bent over, it wouldn't make any difference to me.

I bent over.

— That doesn't make any difference?

— It looks stupid. But what if I bend over? Does it look stupid?

— No, it looks good.

— Why is that?

— It just does.

— You can't explain it?

I thought it had to do with the forbidden. The attraction to the forbidden in the forbidden. The forbiddenest. But it still wasn't much of an answer.

At the same time that things with Natasha were improving, my mother started to hear the first rumblings of trouble in my uncle's marriage. My grandparents, who had always been accustomed to visiting my uncle frequently, were informed that maybe they shouldn't come over quite so often. Their habit of arriving unannounced was aggravating Zina, who insisted that she had too much to worry about without always having to accommodate my grandparents. My grandmother, although hurt, naturally made excuses for both my uncle and Zina. We were a close family, she said, but not all people can be expected to be the same way. Also, with time, as Zina became more comfortable, she was certain that she would feel differently. In any case, as long as my uncle was happy she was prepared to respect Zina's wishes. My uncle, for his part, said nothing. The signals were mixed. There was what my grandmother said, but my mother also knew that he and Zina took a weekend trip together to Niagara-on-the-Lake and another to Quebec City. After Quebec City my uncle sported a new leather jacket and a gray Stetson. Whatever was happening between them, he wasn't complaining.

I heard all of these things through my mother, but I also heard other things from Natasha. I now knew more about my uncle's life than I ever had, and certainly more than anyone else in my family. I knew, for instance, that he now spent as many nights on the living room couch as he did in the bedroom. I knew that Zina was racking up long-distance bills to Moscow, calling Natasha's father, a drunk who had effectively abandoned them years ago. She called in the mornings as soon as my uncle left for work and made various and emphatic promises. Natasha had seen her father only infrequently as a child and was perfectly content to go the rest of her life without seeing him again. She could say the same thing about her mother. Essentially, since the age of eight she had been on her own. Going to school, coming home, cooking her own dinners, running around with friends. Zina, when not at work, had been chasing after Natasha's father or bringing random men into the apartment. As much as possible Natasha avoided her.

When Natasha was twelve, a friend told her about a man who had paid ten dollars for some pictures of her. The girl had gone and taken a shower in the man's bathroom, and he had not only paid her but also bought her dinner. He had promised her the same again if she could bring a friend. Ten dollars each for taking a shower. Natasha remembered thinking that the man had to be an idiot. She went, took her shower, and collected her ten dollars. There wasn't much to it, and it wasn't as boring as hanging out at her friend's apartment. And ten dollars was ten dollars. Zina hardly gave her anything, so it was good to have some of her own money.

After that man was another, who took pictures of her and some friends in the forest. He had them climb birch trees and lie down in a meadow. He asked some of the girls to hold hands and kiss each other. Another man took some photos of her in her school uniform. None of these men touched her, but she told me she wouldn't have cared if they had. They were nice, and, if anything, she felt sorry for them.

All of this led eventually to a Soviet director who had gone from working at the Moscow studios to making pornographic movies for Western businessmen. The man had a dacha on the outskirts of the city and would send a car around to pick up Natasha and her friends. Some of these friends were girls, some boys. They would spend the day at the dacha eating, drinking, having a good time. At some point the director would shoot some movies of them. Aside from teenagers there were also older women. On the first day, Natasha watched the women have sex. She understood that doing it or not doing it was not a serious consideration. In the end, everyone did it. If not in movies, then somewhere else, and it made absolutely no difference one way or the other. The only thing about having sex at the dacha was that it was much more pleasant. The house was beautiful, and there was a large lawn and a forest. There was also a *banya* and a Jacuzzi. The filming itself didn't even take very long. The rest of the time they just relaxed. She was never asked to do anything she didn't want to do, and she never saw anyone else do something that she wouldn't have done herself. Even though she and her friends knew they wouldn't be at the dacha if it weren't for the movies, the sex never felt as though it were the focus. The director and the other men became their friends. They treated them very well. And if they wanted to sleep with the girls, the girls could see no reason why not. At the end of the day everyone got twenty-five dollars.

Natasha didn't have any of the pictures or movies. It wasn't like she was a model; she didn't keep a portfolio to show prospective photographers. In such endeavors, previous experience was not a virtue. And without having pictures around, there was no risk of Zina's finding out. Not that she thought Zina would care, but she suspected her mother would want the money. When Zina did finally find out, much as Natasha expected, she told Natasha that if she was going to be a whore, she could at least help out with the rent.

I carried all this information around like a prize. It was my connection to a larger darker world. At Rufus's parties it allowed me to feel superior to the other stoner acolytes comparing Nietzsche to Bob Marley. I took Natasha to these parties, and she stood quietly listening to our incoherent and impassioned conversations. Later she would surprise me with just how much she had understood. By midsummer, if called upon, Natasha could answer basic questions and had learned enough to know when to tell someone to fuck off. My friends liked more than anything to hear Natasha say *fuck off* in her crisp Moscow accent. In crude canine fashion, they accepted Natasha as one of their own.

We coasted this way into August, when Zina appeared in our backyard one evening during dinner. The way she looked, it was clear that something horrible was about to happen. My mother opened the sliding door, and Zina burst into our kitchen and inaccurately described what Natasha and I had been doing. Then screams, sobbing, and hysterics. I watched as my father wrenched Natasha's teeth from her mother's bloody hand. Zina let fly a torrent of invective, most of which I couldn't understand. But I understood enough to know that what was happening in the kitchen was nothing compared with what was to come. Zina threatened to call the police, to place an ad in the Russian newspaper, to personally knock on all of our neighbors' doors. Natasha thrashed in my father's grip and freed herself enough to lunge unsuccessfully for a bread knife. She shrieked that her mother was a liar. I sat in my chair, nauseated, contemplating lies and escape.

After my father bandaged Zina's hand, she waited outside while my mother talked with Natasha and me, fumbling for the proper way to pose the question. It was hard to believe that what Zina was saying was true, but why would she make something like this up. Natasha said that it was because her mother hated her and never wanted her to be happy. She was jealous that Natasha was happy with us and wanted to ruin it, just as she had dragged Natasha from Moscow even though she hadn't wanted to go. Zina hated her and wanted to ruin her life, that was all. When my mother turned to me, I denied everything. Unless Zina produced pictures or video, I wasn't admitting a thing. I was terrified but I wasn't a moron.

When it became obvious that we had reached an impasse, my mother called my uncle. He came to our house in a state of perturbation that was remarkable even for him. He sat down between my mother and Zina on the living room couch. I was beside my father, who was in his armchair, and Natasha stood rigidly with her back against the door. My uncle confessed that he didn't know what was happening. Everything had been fine. What situation doesn't have problems, but on the whole he was content. The only explanation was that all of this might have had to do with a fight between Zina and Natasha over a phone bill. There had been a very expensive bill to Russia, almost six hundred dollars, which Zina had said were calls to her mother. He could understand that while getting used to a new life Zina would want to talk to her mother. Also, her mother was alone in Moscow and missed her. It was only natural that there would be calls. That there were so many was unfortunately a financial and not a personal problem. If it was within his means, he would be happy if Zina talked to her mother as much as she liked. But as it was, he had suggested that she try to be more careful about the amount of time she spent on the phone. They talked about it and she said she understood. It was then that Natasha had accused Zina of lying to him. This started a fight. But at no point did he hear anything about me and Natasha. He was certain it wasn't true and was just something between a mother and daughter. Everyone was still getting used to things, and it would be a mistake to make too much of it. In a day or so everyone would calm down and it would be forgotten.

That night my uncle, Zina, and Natasha slept at our house. Natasha in the guest room, Zina on the downstairs couch, and my uncle on the floor beside her. Zina refused to leave the house without Natasha, and Natasha refused to leave with Zina. I was relegated to my basement. In the morning, however, much as my uncle had suggested, Natasha calmed down. She showed no indication of the previous night's hysterics. Without resistance she agreed to return home with Zina and my uncle. Forgoing breakfast, the three of them walked out the door, neither looking at nor touching one another. As we watched them go, my mother announced that she had now seen enough craziness to last a lifetime. Whatever the truth, she knew one thing for certain: Natasha and I were kaput.

But the next day I still expected her. I was alone in my basement, she was with Zina — I couldn't understand why she didn't come. Our afternoons could still be ours. My mother's verdict didn't have to be obeyed between nine and five. Had the situation been reversed, I would not have disappointed her.

After several interminable hours, I gave up and headed for Rufus's. A pool company's van was parked outside, and I followed the sound of voices into the backyard, where I found Rufus with the pool men discussing possible dimensions of a possible pool. Rufus invited me to contribute to the deliberations. If the price was right, they could start digging tomorrow. I had never known Rufus to be much of a swimmer; on nights when some of the other stoners and I would hop the fences of neighborhood pools, he rarely participated.

— Do you even swim?

— Berman, nobody swims in these things. They're for floating. Fill them up with plastic inflatables and free-associate. Gentle swaying stimulates the brainpan.

I watched the pool guys pacing off most of his yard.

— Why not start with a hammock and work your way up?

— Sometimes I'm out here and I need to take a leak. The weather's nice. I want to stay out, but I need to pee. Just for that the pool would be worth the investment.

— You could pee on the bushes.

— I'm a suburban homeowner, there's a social contract. Pissing in the pool is fine, but whipping out your dick and irrigating the shrubbery is bad news. It's all about property value.

I settled back on the deck and waited for the pool guys to leave. I had no deliveries to make that morning, and I had neglected to bring along the books I was supposed to return. I was there without any veneer of pretext. After escorting the pool guys back to their van, Rufus joined me on the deck.

— Where's the girl?

— With her mother.

— I thought she hated her mother.

— She does.

— So what are you doing here? Go liberate her.

— It's forbidden.

— You're sixteen, everything is forbidden. The world expects you to disobey.

— I've been accused of unnatural acts.

— Society was founded on unnatural acts. Read the Bible. You start with Adam and Eve. After that, if somebody doesn't boink a sibling, it's end of story.

— You mind if I use that argument with my mother?

Rufus got up and looked out across his yard.

— What do you think about a hot tub?

— Instead of the pool?

— With the pool. Do everything in mosaic tile. Give it a real Greek feel. Put up some Doric columns. Get a little fountain. Eat grapes. Play Socrates.

He descended from the deck and walked to the corner of his yard and struck a pose that was either Socrates or the fountain. Our conversation was over.

From Rufus's I walked to my uncle's building and lurked until one old man was buzzed in by another old man. Eleven flights later I was in the hallway, passing the smells of other apartments. With one or two exceptions all the doorposts had mezuzahs, just like the hallways above and below. Everyone conveniently assembled for UJA solicitors and neo-Nazis.

I knocked and Zina opened the door. She was wearing the same blue housedress. She blocked the doorway. I had prepared myself for the worst, but she seemed pleased to see me.

— I wanted to apologize to you myself. I don't blame you for what happened. It wasn't your fault. She has turned grown men inside out, and you're just a boy. It was crazy to expect anything else. I know how weak men are. I am to blame. The life in Russia was like a disease to children. Natasha is a very sick girl.

Behind Zina I noticed a movement. Over her shoulder I could see Natasha at the far end of the apartment, leaning against the couch. When I caught her eyes, they reflected nothing, no less remote than the first time I saw her at the airport. I couldn't discern if she was looking at me or the back of Zina's head. Sensing Natasha's presence, Zina turned to look at her daughter. When she looked back at me, her turning was a motion that included the closing of the door.

— It will be best for everybody if you didn't see Natasha anymore.

Late that night, after a day spent despairing over the black void that was the remainder of my summer and my life in general, I heard a knock on my basement window. By the sound of the knock I knew it was Natasha. I looked out and saw her squatting like a Vietnamese peasant in front of the window. In the dark it was hard to see her face. Upstairs in the kitchen I opened the sliding glass door and went into the yard. She was hugging her knees at the base of our pine tree; her suitcase, the same one I had seen at the airport, was lying beside her. When I got close enough, I could see that she had been crying. I joined her on the grass. Already, after only one day apart and remembering the way she had looked at me over Zina's shoulder, I didn't feel as though I could touch her.

— You listened to her lies. Why did you listen to her lies?

— What was I supposed to do?

— You could have knocked her down. You could have broken down the door.

— And what then?

— I don't know. Something. Something else would have happened. But you left me alone with her.

— You looked right at me. Why didn't you say anything?

— But I already told you everything. You saw how she tried to ruin my life and your life, and how she was killing your uncle. You knew all of this, but you didn't do anything. You're like your uncle. You want people to make decisions for you.

Natasha picked at the grass. Tears welled up in her eyes. She let them fall. I got up and picked up her suitcase. It felt empty. I made a move toward the house.

— What are you doing?

— Taking it inside.

— I can't go inside. I can't stay here. I have to leave.

— You have to leave tonight?

— Do you want to come with me?

— Where?

— Florida. One of the businessmen who came to the dacha lives there. He is very rich. He promised that if I ever came to Florida, he would give me a job. He'll give you one too.

— We have to decide this tonight?

— Yes. I can't stay here and I can't go home. There is no more home. My mother has left your uncle. I can't live with her and I can't stay with him. I have nowhere to go.

— What do you mean your mother left my uncle?

— I forced them to decide.

I put the suitcase back down.

— She made him sleep on the couch again. I went out to the living room. At first he was asleep, but when he woke up and understood what was happening, he didn't stop me. He knew whose mouth it was. And then she heard and came out of the bedroom. He needed me to do it that way or he would never have gotten away from her. I wasn't going to let her ruin his life. I wasn't going to let her win.

Strangely, my first thought was about my grandmother. My next thought was that my uncle would kill himself.

— He let her insult him, embarrass him, steal his money. But he wouldn't leave her. He was a coward. So I gave him a coward's reason to leave. It's funny, other men would have felt the opposite way. They would have taken it as a reason to stay and would have spent the next two years fucking me.

I helped Natasha down into the basement and promised her that I would wake her before my parents got up. I gave her my bed and slept on the floor. When the alarm rang, I dug out all the money I had and gave it to her. It amounted to a little more than a hundred dollars. I watched her drag her suitcase down our street, heading toward the bus station and Florida.

When my parents woke up, the phones were already ringing. My uncle had arrived on my grandparents' doorstep at seven in the morning. His marriage was over. As to why the separation had to be so drastic, why he couldn't stay in the apartment until he found a new place, my uncle was vague. They could no longer live together. Nobody in my family asked about Natasha or even knew that she was gone. As far as the family was concerned, once my uncle severed his relationship with Zina, she and Natasha ceased to exist.

For days afterward I stayed in my basement. I had no interest in going out, making deliveries, checking messages. I was compromised by everything I knew. I knew things about my uncle that a sixteen-year-old nephew should not have known. And when my mother invited him to our house for dinner — in an effort to bolster his spirits — I sat across the table from him and tried to suppress the feeling of an awkward bond. It wasn't the sort of bond I wanted to share with my forty-four-year-old uncle, especially under the circumstances. But everything he did during dinner — talking, eating, drinking — reminded me that he had been with Natasha. The mouth he spoke with, the hands he ate with, his physical self, were the same mouth, hands, self that had been with her.

During dinner he avoided the subject of Zina and Natasha entirely. It was the only thing on everyone's mind, and so, characteristically, it was the only thing nobody mentioned. Instead, my uncle gave a very long and detailed history of the Israeli-Palestinian conflict. Arafat, Rabin, Ben-Gurion, Balfour, Begin, Nasser, Sadat. I wondered what kept him going. What life offered him. Why he didn't kill himself. Watching him, listening to him talk, I realized that there was nothing I could do for him.

The following morning I ended my self-imposed seclusion and took the familiar walk to Rufus's. There were books to read and whatever else the rest of my summer still had to offer. At Rufus's house guys with wheelbarrows were carting dirt out from the yard and shoveling it into a truck. Another crew shouldered ten-foot-long Doric columns in the opposite direction. The strains of Bizet's *Carmen* wafted through the air. The neighborhood had never seen anything like it.

In the backyard I spotted most of my friends. Guys that had never held down a real job, guys like me who spent their days in basements reading, smoking, and engaging in self-abuse. They were fanned out across Rufus's yard, straining, digging, smoothing, lifting, side by side with the workmen around a massive hole bordered by a plastic orange fence. They looked very happy, intimately involved.

Up on the deck, with one of the pool guys, Rufus was hunched over a blueprint as though it were a battle plan. I mounted the steps and stood behind Rufus and waited for him to acknowledge me. Over his shoulder I could see the plan: columns, trees, a fountain, the hot tub. When he finally saw me, his face for an instant assumed an expression I had never seen before. Later I recognized it as pity.

— Berman, what's the matter, you don't return calls anymore?

He rose and had me follow him down into the yard. I felt the onset of dread. It was then that I realized that none of my friends had spoken to me. The yard was busy, but not so busy that they wouldn't have seen me. I had, after all, seen them. The sum of these impressions began to register. I knew that whatever it was, it was very bad, and that I was trapped and incapable of avoiding the damage. I sensed all of this as I descended from the deck and heard the screen door open. Using her hip, Natasha slid it closed. She was carrying a tray with a pitcher of water and multicolored plastic glasses. Rufus watched me for a reaction, and then took me gently by the shoulder out to the front of the house.

— Berman, this is why I asked you to call. I wanted to tell you on the phone, but it wasn't exactly the sort of thing I could leave on an answering machine.

Another team of landscapers approached us with a Doric column. I felt a compulsion to stick out my foot and trip them. To start a brawl, draw blood, break bones.

— She doesn't want to see you. I'm sorry about this, Berman. It's just the way it is.

I made way for the column.

— How much do those things weigh?

— Not as much as you'd think. They're masonry and plaster, not marble. If they were marble, I'd need slaves.

— I thought she was going to Florida.

— Come on, Berman, she's a fucking kid. How is she supposed to get to Florida? She barely speaks English. Either she's here or she's on the street.

— Right.

— She thinks you betrayed her. She's very principled. Anyway, she'll be safe here.

— That's one way to look at it.

— I hope you're not mad. It's not personal.

— I still have some of your books and maybe a few grams of weed.

— That's cool. Don't sweat it. Consider them yours.

— What a great deal for me.

— That's a shitty attitude, Berman. You're smarter than that.

— I'm a fucking genius.

— Take care of yourself, Berman.

I lingered in front of Rufus's house after he left and watched the wheelbarrows come and go. I waited for the workmen to bring in the last of the columns and then walked home. In another country, under another code, it would have been my duty to return to Rufus's with a gun. But in the suburbs, at the end of my sixteenth summer, this was not an option. Instead, I resorted to a form of civilized murder. By the time I reached my street everyone in Rufus's yard was dead. Rufus, Natasha, my stoner friends. I would never see them again. By the time I got home I had already crafted a new identity. I would switch schools, change my wardrobe, move to another city. Later I would avenge myself with beautiful women, learn martial arts, and cultivate exotic experiences. I saw my future clearly. I had it all planned out. And yet, standing in our backyard, drawn by a strange impulse, I crouched and peered through the window into my basement. I had never seen it from this perspective. I saw what Natasha must have seen every time she came to the house. In the full light of summer, I looked into darkness. It was the end of my subterranean life.

TIM PRATT

Hart and Boot

FROM POLYPHONY

THE MAN'S HEAD AND TORSO EMERGED from a hole in the ground, just a few feet from the rock where Pearl Hart sat smoking her last cigarette. His appearance surprised her, and she cussed him at some length. The man stared at her during the outpouring of profanity, his mild face smeared with dirt, his body still half-submerged. Pearl stopped cussing and squinted at him in the fading sunlight. He didn't have on a shirt, and Pearl, being Pearl, wondered immediately if he was wearing pants.

"Who the hell are you?" she demanded. She'd been sitting for hours here on the outskirts of a Kansas mining town, waiting for dark, so she could find a bar and a man to buy her drinks. She was in a foul mood lately, as her plans for a life of riotous adventure had thus far come to nothing. She'd fled a teenage marriage in Canada after seeing a Wild West show, complete with savage Indians and lady sharpshooters, and come west to seek her fortune among such fierce characters. Her career as an outlaw was not going well so far. The problem, of course, was men. The problem was *always* men, and the fact that she enjoyed many male qualities didn't change that fact. Seeing a man now, uninvited and interrupting her brooding, made her angry enough to spit in a sidewinder's eye. "What're you doing in the ground?"

"I'm not sure," the man said.

Pearl couldn't place his accent. New England, maybe? "What the hell's that mean? How'd you end up in a damn hole without knowing how you got there?"

He considered that for a moment, then said, "You swear a lot, for a woman."

Pearl dropped the remains of her cigarette to the ground. "I swear a lot for anybody. Are you a miner or something?" She couldn't think of any other reason a man would be underground, popping up like a prairie dog — and even that didn't make much sense, not when you thought past the surface.

"A miner?" He chewed his lip. "Could be."

"You have any money?" Pearl said. She didn't have any more bullets, but she could hit him on the head with her gun, if he had something worth stealing.

"I don't think so."

She sighed. "Get out of that hole. I'm getting a crick in my neck, looking down at you."

He climbed out and stood before her, covered in dirt from head to toe, naked except for a pair of better-than-average boots. Hardly standard uniform for a miner, but she didn't get flustered. She'd seen her share of naked men during her eighteen years on earth, and she had to admit he was one of the nicest she'd seen, dirt and all, with those broad shoulders. Back in Canada (after seeing the Wild West show, but before deciding to leave her husband) she'd had several dreams about a tall, faceless man coming toward her bed, naked except for cowboy boots.

Apart from the dirt, and the lack of a bed, and her not being asleep and all, this was just like the dream.

She finally looked at his face. He seemed uncomfortable, like a man afraid of making a fool of himself, half-afraid he already has. "Nice boots," she said. "What'd you say your name was?"

"Uh." He looked down at his feet, then back at her face. "Boot?"

"I'll just call you John," she said. This could work out. A handsome man, big enough to look threatening, and clearly addlebrained. Just what she needed. "John Boot. I'm Pearl Hart." She stood and extended her hand. After a moment's hesitation, he shook. Soft hands, like a baby's. No way he was a miner. That was all right. Whatever he was, he'd have a new trade soon enough. He'd be a stagecoach robber, just like in the Wild West show.

"Not on my account, honey," she said, dropping a hand below his waist and smiling when he gasped, "but we ought to find you some clothes. If I lured a fella about your size out behind a bar, you think you could hit him on the head hard enough to knock him out?"

"I suppose so, Pearl," he said, as her experienced hand moved up and down on him. "I'll do whatever you want, as long as you keep doing that."

Hart and Boot robbed their way west. Pearl had tried to hold up a stagecoach once on her own, without success. She'd stepped into the road, gun in hand, and shouted for the driver to stop. He slowed down, peered at her from his high seat, and burst out laughing. He snapped the reins and the horses nearly ran Pearl down, forcing her out of the road. A woman poked her head out the window as the stage passed, her face doughy, her mouth gaping. Pearl shot at her, irritated. The recoil stung her hand, and she missed by a mile.

Clearly, she was not a natural lady sharpshooter. She needed a man, the right *kind* of man, one who could be tough and do the necessary, but *also* do as he was told, a man for the look of the thing, so people would take her seriously, and it would be best if he was a man she liked to fuck. She didn't believe such a man existed, except in her dreams.

Until she met John Boot.

They had a simple, and, to Pearl's mind, amusing method of robbing coaches. Pearl would stand weeping and wailing in the road wearing a tore-up dirty dress. There wasn't a stagecoach driver in the West who'd drive past a woman in need, and when they stopped, John Boot would emerge from cover, guns in hand. Pearl would pull her own weapons, and they'd relieve the coach of baggage, money, and mail. John Boot was always very polite, but what with Pearl's cussing, the bewildered victims seldom noticed.

Despite her insistence that John Boot always pull out, Pearl got pregnant once during those wild months. She didn't even realize she'd caught pregnant until the miscarriage. After she'd passed it all she just kicked dirt over the mess, glad to have avoided motherhood. John Boot wept when he found out about it, though, and Pearl, disturbed, left him to his tears. John Boot had depths she didn't care to explore. He mostly did whatever she told him and didn't argue back, which was all she wanted, but it was hard to think of him in terms of his simple usefulness when he cried.

One night after Pearl came back from pissing behind a rock she found John Boot staring up at the stars. Pearl sat with him, drunk a touch on whiskey, feeling good. She liked the stars, the big Western sky, the first man in her life who wasn't more trouble than he was worth.

"We have to stop robbing coaches," Boot said.

This display of personal opinion irritated Pearl. "Why's that?"

"They're on to us anyway," he said, not looking at her. "There's not a coach left that'll stop for a woman in distress anymore."

"Hasn't failed us yet."

"Next time." He paused. "I know. They'll come in shooting, next time."

Pearl considered. John Boot didn't talk much. Most men talked all the time and didn't know shit. Maybe with John Boot the reverse was true. "Damn," she said at last. "Well, it couldn't last forever. But we don't have to *stop,* just change our style."

After that they robbed coaches in the traditional manner, stepping from cover with guns drawn. That worked pretty well.

One night in Arizona, Pearl had trouble sleeping. Seemed like every way she rolled a rock stuck in her back or side, and the coyotes kept howling, and the big moon made everything too bright. She figured a good roll with John Boot might tire her out, so she went to wake him up. No man liked getting roused in the middle of the night, but when they got sex in return, they kept their complaints to a minimum.

Pearl didn't believe in ghosts, but when she saw John Boot lying on his bedroll, she thought he'd died and become one. He held his familiar shape, but she could see the ground right through him, as if he were made of smoke and starlight.

Pearl didn't faint away. She said, "John Boot, stop this goddamn nonsense *now!*"

His solidity returned as he opened his eyes. "Pearl," he said blearily. "What —"

"You're going like a ghost on me, John Boot, and I don't appreciate it."

His eyes took on a familiar pained, guarded look — the expression of a dog being scolded for reasons far beyond its comprehension. "Sorry, Pearl," he said, which was about the only consistently safe response in their conversations.

"I *need* you," she said.

"And I need you, Pearl." He sat up. "More than you know. Sometimes, when you aren't paying attention to me, or you're not nearby, I get so tired, and everything gets dim, kind of smoky . . ."

He shook his head. "I don't understand it. It's like I'm not even strong enough to be real on my own. I want to stay for you, I think I have to, but I get so damn *tired.*"

John Boot almost never cussed. Pearl took his hand. "Don't you dare go away from me, John Boot."

"Do you love me, Pearl?" he asked, looking at her hand in his.

Most men, she'd have said yes just to keep them quiet. But after these past months, she owed John Boot more than that. "I don't know that I love you, but I wouldn't want you gone."

He nodded. "How long do you intend to live like this?"

"As long as it's fun," she said.

"When it stops being fun, Pearl . . . will you let me go? Let me be tired, and just . . . see what happens to me then?"

Pearl sighed. "Help me get these clothes off, John Boot. We'll figure this out later. All this talking makes me want to do something else."

He smiled, and a little of the sadness and weariness receded from his eyes.

The next day a posse caught up with them, and once Pearl and John Boot were relieved of their weapons it became clear that they were being charged with stagecoach robberies and murders. Someone was killing lone travelers in the area, and Hart and Boot were convenient to take the blame for that, though they had nothing to do with it. Pearl declared their innocence of all crimes, but she'd taken a pearl-handled gun in the last robbery, a distinctive weapon, and when the posse found that, it settled all questions in their minds.

Pearl and John Boot never robbed another coach, and neither did anyone else. Stagecoaches and stagecoach robbers, like lady outlaws and wild Indians, were dying breeds. Hart and Boot were the last of their kind.

The lovers were taken to Pima County jail in Florence, Arizona, a depressingly dusty place with no accommodations for women. For propriety's sake the authorities decided to leave John Boot in Florence and take Pearl to a county jail in Tucson. She argued against that course with a blue streak of profanity, but they took her away all the same, and Pearl was separated from John Boot for the first time since he'd crawled out of the ground in Kansas.

Pearl sat in her cell, looking at the rough wooden partition that divided the "women's quarters" from the other half of the cell. She was wishing for a cigarette and thinking about John Boot. What if he just went to smoke and starlight again, and disappeared?

She wanted him with her, wanted him fiercely, and around midnight a knifepoint poked through the thin wooden partition. Pearl watched with interest as the knife made a ragged circular opening, and a familiar head poked through.

"John Boot," she said, not without admiration. "How'd you get out? And how'd you get here all the way from Florence?"

"I'm not sure," he said. "You wanted me, and I came . . . but it made me awfully tired. Can we go?"

Pearl crawled through the hole. The adjoining cell was unoccupied, the door unlocked, and they walked out together as if the had every right in the world to leave. *We can be caught but we can't be kept,* she thought, elated, as they stepped into the starry night.

They stole horses and rode farther southwest, because they hadn't been that way yet.

A week later they blundered into a posse in New Mexico. The men were looking for cattle rustlers, but they settled for Hart and Boot. Pearl offered the men sexual favors in exchange for freedom and called them every nasty name she could think of when they refused. John Boot just stood unresisting, as if the strength had been sapped out of him, as if he'd seen all this coming and knew how it would end.

The lovers were taken back to Florence (Pearl was beginning to hate that place), where they were put on trial immediately. The officers didn't want to keep them overnight and give them a chance to escape again.

The judge, a bald man with pince-nez glasses, sentenced John Boot to thirty years in the Arizona Territorial Penitentiary, a place famed for its snakepit of a dungeon, tiny cells, and ruthless guards. John Boot listened to the sentence with his usual calm, nodding to show he understood.

Then the judge looked at Pearl and frowned, clearly undecided about how to deal with her.

I'm young, she thought, *and a woman, so he thinks I got railroaded into this, that I'm John Boot's bedwarmer, a little girl led astray.*

Pearl couldn't abide that. "What the hell are you waiting for, you silly old bastard?" she asked.

John Boot winced. The judge reddened, then said, "I sentence you to five years in the same place!" He banged his gavel, and Pearl blew him a kiss.

She'd never been to prison before. She figured she wouldn't like it, but she didn't expect to be there for very long.

She was right on the first count, but sadly wrong on the second.

Pearl and John Boot weren't separated during the long ride through the desert, and Pearl vented her fury at him as they bounced along in the back of the wagon, under armed guard. "Thirty years he gave you, and me five. They think five years will knock the piss and wildcat out of me?"

"How do you stay so energetic all the time?" John Boot asked. "You've got enough strength of will for any two people. I'm surprised fire and lightning don't come shooting out your ears sometimes!"

Pearl rode silently for a long time, thinking on that. "You reckon that's how you came to be?" she asked, looking down at her knees. "Some of that fire and lightning I've got too much of spilled out, and made you?"

They'd never really talked about this before, about where John Boot came from, where he might someday return, and Pearl looked up in irritation when he didn't reply.

He was sleeping, head leaning back against the side of the cart.

Pearl sighed. At least she couldn't see the boards through his head this time. He hadn't gone to smoke and starlight. She let him be.

Pearl and John Boot climbed out of the wagon and stood in the rocky prison yard. The landscape outside was ugly, just flat desert and the dark water of the Colorado River, but the prison impressed her. Pearl had never seen a building so big. It seemed more a natural part of the landscape than something man-made. Like a palace for a scorpion queen.

"Put out that cigarette," the warden snapped. His wife stared at Pearl sternly. The warden looked tough, Pearl thought, and his stringy wife in her colorless dress looked even tougher.

Pearl flashed a smile. She took a last drag off her cigarette and flicked it away.

John Boot looked from Pearl to the warden to the warden's wife like a man watching a snake stalking a rat.

"Welcome to the Arizona Territorial Penitentiary," the warden said.

His boots aren't nearly as nice as John's, Pearl thought.

"I hear you two are escape artists," the warden said. "Well, you can forget about that nonsense here." He began to pace, hands knotted behind him. "Back the way you came there's fifty miles of desert crawling with scorpions, snakes, and Indians. The Indians get a reward for bringing back escapees, fifty dollars a head, and we don't care how banged up the prisoners get on the way. They'd love to catch a woman out there, Hart. We'd get you back, but you wouldn't be the same, and I truly don't want that to happen to you, no matter how bad you are."

"I bet I could teach them Indians a few things," Pearl said.

The warden paused in his pacing, then resumed. "Keep your tongue in your mouth, girl. Besides the desert, there's two branches of the Colorado River bordering this prison, moving fast enough that you can't swim across. Then there's the charming town of Yuma." He pointed west. "You try to go that way, and the folks in town will shoot you. They're not real friendly." He turned smartly on his boot heel and paced the other way. "That's not real important, though, because you won't get outside. The cells are carved into solid granite, so you can't cut your way out with a pocketknife." He pointed to a tower at one corner of the wall. "That's a Gatling gun on a turret up there — it can sweep the whole yard. There was an attempted prison break not long ago, and my *wife* manned the gun. Cut those convicts down."

"Ladylike," Pearl said. "Mighty Christian, too."

The wife stiffened and crossed her arms.

"I'm not happy about having you here, Hart," the warden said, putting his face close to hers, exhaling meat-and-tobacco-laden breath. "I had to tear out six bunks to make a ladies-only cell for you, and we had to hire a seamstress to make a special uniform."

"Shit, you dumb bastard," she said. "I'll sleep anywhere, and I'd just as soon go naked as wear whatever burlap sack you've got for me."

John Boot groaned.

"We're gonna clean that backtalk out of you, Hart," the warden said. He turned to the guards. "Get this man to his cell," he said, pointing at John Boot. "My wife and I will escort Miss Hart to her quarters."

The guards led John Boot away. The warden later wrote that he looked distinctly relieved to be leaving his lover.

Pearl went with the warden and his wife through an archway into a cramped corridor. Iron bars filled every opening, and the low ceiling made her want to duck, even though her head cleared it by a good margin. The hall smelled like sweat and urine.

"Did you enjoy shooting those boys, Mrs. Warden? Feeling that big gun jump and buck in your hands?"

"That's enough, Hart," the warden said. "Get in." He pointed to an open cell door. Pearl could see the boltholes on the wall where the bunks had been removed. A curtain hung from the ceiling, blocking the open-pit latrine from view. She'd expected open-faced cells, like at the county jail, but these cells had real doors.

"Cozy," Pearl said, and sauntered in. Men hollered unintelligibly down the corridor.

"We're going to make every effort to guard your modesty," the warden said. "You'll never be alone with a man. My wife or a female attendant will accompany me and the guards if we ever need to see you privately."

"Doesn't sound like much fun," Pearl said. "Maybe just one man alone with me every couple days? You could hold a lottery, maybe." She showed her teeth.

The warden shut the door without a word.

Pearl sat on the bunk for a while, thinking. The cell was tiny, with a narrow window set high in one rock wall. She'd roast all day and freeze all night, she knew. John Boot had better get her out soon.

She got bored, and after a while she went to the door, looking out the iron grille set in the wood. "Hey, boys!" she yelled. "I'm your new neighbor, Pearl!" Hoots and whistles came down the hall. "I bet you get lonely in here! How'd you like to pass some time with me?" She went on to talk as dirty as she knew how, which was considerable. She wondered if John Boot was in earshot. He liked it when she talked like this, though he always blushed.

The men howled like coyotes, and the guards came shouting.

Pearl sat down on the bunk again. She'd wait until the men quieted down, then start yelling again. That should get under the warden's skin and pass the time until John Boot came to set her free.

Pearl woke when John Boot touched her shoulder. She sat up, brushing her hair away from her face. John Boot looked tense and dusty.

"Are we on our way, then?" Pearl asked.

He shook his head, sitting down beside her. "I don't think I can get us out, Pearl."

"What do you mean? You got into my cell, so you can get us out."

"I can get myself out, sure." He laughed forlornly. "Walls don't take much notice of me, sometimes. But you're different. Back in Tucson I had to cut you an opening." He thumped his fist on the granite wall. "I can't do that here."

"You could steal keys," Pearl said, thinking furiously. "Take a guard prisoner, and . . ." She trailed off. There was the Gatling gun to think of, and fifty miles of desert, if they somehow did make it out. "What are we going to do?"

"You've only got five years," he said, "and you being a woman, if you behaved yourself —"

"No! They ain't winning. Or if they do win, I'll make them miserable, so they can't enjoy it. You keep looking, John Boot. Every place has holes. You find one we can slip out of, hear?"

"I'll try Pearl, but . . ." He shook his head. "Don't expect too much."

"Long as you're here," Pearl said, unbuttoning her shirt.

"No," he said. "It's tiring, Pearl, going in and out like this. It's not hard to get dim, but it's hard to come *back.* Look at me." He held up his hand. It shook like a coach bouncing down a bumpy road.

"You're about as much good as bloomers in a whorehouse, John Boot," she said. "Go on back to bed, then." She watched him, curious to see how he moved in and out of impossible places.

He stood, then cleared his throat. "I don't think I can go with you watching me. I always feel more . . . all together . . . when you're paying close attention to me."

Pearl turned away. "I thought only ladies were supposed to be modest." She listened closely but heard nothing except the distant coughs and moans of the other prisoners. She turned, and John Boot was gone, passed through her cell walls like a ghost.

Hell, she thought, *now I'm up, I won't be able to fall back asleep.* She took a deep breath, then loosed a stream of curses at the top of her lungs. The prisoners down the hall shouted back, angrily, and soon cacophony filled the granite depths of the prison.

After listening to that for a while, Pearl slept like a babe.

Pearl gave up on John Boot after about a month, but she didn't figure out a better idea for two years. The boredom nearly crushed her, sometimes, but the time passed. She got to see John Boot a lot, at least — he came to her almost every night, and seemed weaker every time.

"The warden was in here the other day," she said one night. John Boot sat against the wall, tired after his latest half-hearted search for an escape route. "Telling me what a model prisoner you are, how you never spit on the guards at bed check or raise a fuss in the middle of the night. They said you're practically rehabilitated and that you'd want me to behave myself." She punched her thin mattress. "They still think I'm a helpless innocent, led astray by *your* wicked ways, even though I've done my damnedest to show them otherwise. Stupid bastards."

John Boot nodded. He'd heard all this before.

Pearl, sitting on the edge of her bunk, leaned toward him. "I'm tired of being here, John Boot. Two years, and there's only so much hell I can raise from inside a stone box. We have to leave this place."

"I don't see how —"

"Listen a minute. All my life I've hated being a woman — well, not hated *being* one, but hated the way people treated me and expected me to act. It's about time I used that against the bastards, don't you think?"

John Boot looked interested now. He hadn't heard this before. "What do you mean?"

She crossed her legs. "I mean it's time for you to leave, John Boot. Go ghost on me, fade away, get as tired as you want. I think if you hadn't been coming to see me every night, you'd have turned to smoke a long time ago."

His face betrayed equal parts confusion and hope. "But why? How will my leaving help?"

She told him what she had in mind.

"That might work," he said. "But if it doesn't . . ."

"Then I'll figure out something else. Don't waste time, all right? I'm not up for a sentimental goodbye."

He put his hand on her knee. "One last?"

She considered. Why not? "Just be sure to pull out. I don't want to start my free life with a swelled-up belly."

After, he lay against her in the narrow bunk. "I'm a little nervous now," he said. "I'll miss you."

She stretched her arms over her head, comfortable. "I wouldn't think it. You've seemed pretty eager to get away."

"Well . . . in a way. Don't you ever want to go to sleep and never have to wake up again?"

"No," she said truthfully. "I'll sleep plenty when I'm dead."

He was quiet for a moment, and then said, "I don't think I have a choice. About loving you."

Pearl touched his hair, letting her usual defenses slip a little. "I'll miss you, too, John Boot. You're the only man I could ever stand for more than a night at a time. But it's time I let you go."

"Don't look," he said, getting out of bed.

She closed her eyes.

"Goodbye, Pearl," he said, his voice faint. He went away.

It took two days for anyone to notice that John Boot was gone — he'd been so unassuming that they overlooked his empty cell at the first bed check. When the warden and his wife came to tell Pearl that John Boot had escaped, she made a big show of breaking down and crying, saying, "He told me to stay strong, that we'd walk out of here together, that as long as I didn't give in to you he wouldn't leave me!" Weeping with her face in her hands, she could glimpse the warden and his wife through her fingers. They exchanged sympathetic looks — they believed it, the stupid bastards, they still believed that John Boot was the cause of Pearl's bad behavior.

Pearl's behavior changed completely after that. In the following weeks she began wearing a dress, and having polite conversation with the warden's wife, and even started writing poetry, the sappiest, most flowery stuff she could, all about babies and sunlight and flowers. The warden's wife loved it, her tough exterior softening. "Pearl," she said once, "I feel like you and I are much the same, underneath it all." It was all Pearl could do to keep from laughing — talk like this, from the woman who'd once gunned down a yard full of convicts! That was no stranger than a stagecoach robber writing poems, maybe — Black Bart aside, of course — but with Pearl it was an *act.*

She missed John Boot a little, but if his leaving could help get her get out of prison, it was worth it. The warden told Pearl that, with John Boot's influence lifted, she was blossoming into a fine young woman. Two months after John Boot "escaped," the warden and his wife came to visit Pearl again, both of them smiling like cowboys in a whorehouse. "The governor's coming to inspect the prison soon, Pearl," the warden said. "I've talked to him about your case, discussed the possibility of giving you a pardon and an early release . . . and he wants to meet with you."

"That would be just fine," Pearl said demurely, thinking, *Hot damn! About time!*

The governor came into her cell, middle-aged and serious. He wore a nice gray suit and boots with swirling patterns in the leather. The warden and his wife introduced him to Pearl, then stood off to the side, beaming at their new favorite prisoner. The governor looked at them, raised an eyebrow, and said, "Could I have a little time alone with Miss Hart, to discuss her situation?" The warden and his wife practically fell over themselves getting out the door. The governor stood up and closed the cell door. "A little privacy," he said.

"Sir, I'm so glad you decided to meet with me," Pearl began. She'd been practicing this speech for days. It had loads of respect, repentance, and a fair bit about Jesus. If it didn't get her a pardon, nothing would.

"Yes, well," he said, interrupting her. He took a pocket watch from his vest, looked at it, and frowned. Then he looked Pearl up and down, and grunted. "How bad do you want a pardon, girl?"

Pearl kept smiling, though she didn't like that look in his eyes. "Very much, Governor, I've learned my lesson, I —"

"Listen, little girl, that's enough talking. I don't care how sorry you are for what you've done. You're in the worst goddamn place in the whole desert, of course you're sorry, even a rattlesnake would repent his sinful ways if he got locked up here. Now I don't have a whole lot of *time.* There's one way for you to get a pardon, and it doesn't have anything to do with talking, if you see what I mean."

Pearl stared at him, her eyes narrowed.

He looked at his watch again. "Look, you can just bend over your bunk there, you don't even need to take off your dress, I'll just lift it up."

"You go to hell, you bastard," Pearl said, crossing her arms. If he tried to touch her, she'd put a hurt on him like he'd never felt before. She almost hoped he did touch her. The governor was just like all the others, like her husband, like all the men before she'd met John Boot. Boot seemed like just about the only good man in the whole world, and she'd pretty much had to make him up out of her own mind, hadn't she?

The governor went white in the face, then red. "You're going to rot here, Miss Hart. You could've given me five minutes of your time, done what you've probably done with hundreds of filthy men, and been free. But instead —"

"I may've done it with filthy men," Pearl said, "but I've never done it yet with a nasty old pig like you."

The governor rapped on the door, and a guard came to let him out. He left without a word. The warden and his wife bustled in soon after and asked how it went. Pearl thought about telling them, but what was the use?

"It went just fine," she said.

That night, for the first time in years, Pearl cried.

Pearl dreamed of lying in her old bedroom in Canada, giving birth. The baby slid out painlessly, crying, and she picked it up, unsure how to hold it, wrinkling her nose in distaste. The baby looked like a miniature version of the governor, with piercing eyes and grim lines around his mouth. The baby's tongue slid out, over its lips, and Pearl hurled the thing away in disgust. It hit the knotty pine wall and bounced. When it landed, its face had changed, and John Boot's eyes regarded her sadly.

Pearl sat up in the dark of her cell, shivering, but not because the dream disturbed her. She shivered with excitement, because she saw a possibility, a chance at a way out.

She lay back down and thought fondly of John Boot, her wonderful John Boot, her lover, her companion, calling to him in her mind.

Nothing happened, except for time passing, and Pearl's frustration rising. Finally she fell asleep again, fists clenched tight enough to leave nail marks in her palms.

"Pearl," John Boot said.

She opened her eyes, sitting up. It was still dark, but Pearl felt like dawn was near. John Boot was on the floor — no, *in* the floor, half in a hole, just like the first time she'd met him. "Am I dreaming?" she asked.

"No, I'm really here. You felt . . . very angry, Pearl. It pulled me back."

Maybe that's where I went wrong, she thought. *I tried to think sweet thoughts and call him that way, and he didn't feel a thing, but when I got mad, like I was the* first *time, here he comes.* "Pulled you back from where?"

"Someplace where I was sleeping, sort of."

Pearl knelt on the hard granite floor and extended her hand. He took it warily, as if expecting her to try and break his fingers. "I'm not mad at you, John Boot," she said. She wondered about the hole. It would no doubt close up when she wasn't paying attention, as modest in its way as John Boot was himself.

"Then what's wrong?" he asked, letting her help him out of the hole. "Did your plan work, are you getting a pardon?" He sat cross-legged on the floor, naked again, except for his fine boots.

She hesitated. She planned to use John Boot, no two ways about it. Pearl seldom shrank from saying hurtful things, but she hadn't ever hurt John Boot on purpose, and he'd done a lot for her. A little lie to spare his feelings wouldn't do any harm now.

"That's right, I'm getting pardoned," she said. "The governor was very impressed with me. I'm just angry that I have to wait for the order to go through, that I'm stuck here for a few days more . . . and that I'm going to be alone out there, without you."

He lowered his head. "You want me to come back?"

"I wouldn't ask for that." She put her hand on his bare knee. "But . . . I want something special to remember you by."

"What?"

"Sleep with me, John Boot. And don't pull out this time. I want to have your baby. We'll do it as many times as we have to, tonight, tomorrow, as long as it takes."

"You mean it, Pearl?" he said, taking her hand. "Really?"

"Yes." She got on the bed. "I want your baby in the worst way."

He came to her.

A little later, lying tight against him in the narrow bed, she said, "Let's go again. We've got enough time before bed check."

"We can if you want," he said sleepily. "But we don't have to."

"Why?"

"Because it took."

She pushed herself up on her elbow and looked at him. "What do you mean?"

"The baby. It took. You're kindled." He looked into her eyes. "I can feel it. I felt it the other time, too, when you . . . lost it. I wish . . ." He shrugged. "But it's all right now."

"Oh, John Boot. You've made me so happy."

"I should go."

"Wait until dawn? I want to see your face in the morning light one more time."

He held her. When the sun came, he kissed her cheek. "I have to go."

She nodded, then looked away, to give him his privacy.

"No," he said, touching her cheek. "You can look, this time."

She watched. He dissolved like the remnant of a dream, first his warmth fading, then his skin turning to smoke, until finally he disappeared all the way, leaving Pearl with nothing in her arms but emptiness, and a tiny spark of life in her belly.

Pearl waited two months, still behaving herself. Each time she saw the warden, she made a point of anxiously asking if he'd heard from the governor. They hadn't, and the warden's wife clucked her tongue and said everything would work out. Pearl had no doubt about that.

After two months, Pearl asked to see a nurse. The woman examined her, and Pearl told her she'd missed two months in a row. The nurse blushed but didn't ask probing questions. She went to report her findings to the warden.

Pearl's pregnancy created a difficult situation. As far as anyone knew, only one man had been alone with Pearl during her years of incarceration, and that man was the governor. He would say he hadn't slept with Pearl, of course, but she would say otherwise, and publicity like that wouldn't do anybody any good. She knew the governor would take the obvious way out and avoid the scandal.

She didn't have to wait long.

"In light of your delicate circumstances," the warden said two days later, not meeting her eyes, "the governor has decided to grant you a pardon."

"It's about damn time," Pearl said.

On the day of her release a guard gave her a ride to the nearest train station. Pearl looked at the desert where she'd had her adventures, at the harsh ground that had birthed John Boot. She laced her hands over her belly, content.

There were a lot of reporters at the train station. They'd gotten wind of her plans. Pearl had decided that life as an outlaw was all well and good, but it demanded too much sleeping rough and missing meals. She had a baby to think about, now. Originally she'd planned to get rid of the baby at the earliest opportunity, but she was having second thoughts.

Pearl had a job all lined up as a traveling lecturer. A lady outlaw with risqué stories could really pack a room, and it wouldn't be nearly so strenuous as sharpshooting in a Wild West show. She wasn't much good with a gun anyway.

She waved to the reporters as she boarded the train. They only knew she'd been pardoned, not why. They shouted questions, but she didn't pay much attention. Her mind was on other things.

One question got through to her. "Pearl!" the reporter shouted. "Are you going to meet up with John Boot?"

They still thought she needed a man, after all this time. Would that ever change? "You're a stupid bastard," she replied mildly, and followed the porter to her compartment.

RISHI REDDI

Justice Shiva Ram Murthy

FROM HARVARD REVIEW

IT IS A POINT OF DISCIPLINE that Manmohan and I meet always on Thursday afternoons to take luncheon together. This is our routine now and it began soon after my arrival in the U.S. five months back: every Thursday without fail I walk from my son-in-law's home and Manu comes from his son's house and we meet in front of the old church in Copley Square. Of course for me the walking is not so hard as it is for Manu — daily I walk at least forty-five minutes for my exercise. Since I was a young man in law college in India I have been doing that and see, even fifty years later I am still hale and hearty, whereas Manu is a bit lazy, has a slight paunch, and experiences some difficulty climbing steps. Always he was like that even when we were small boys. I try to tell him but he will not listen. What to do if others do not know what is good for them?

You must know that on Christmas Day, when my story begins, I had been living in the U.S. for three months. Already I had opened my own bank account, obtained a law library card, and successfully settled the living arrangements with my daughter and American son-in-law. He is a good fellow, despite having only superficial knowledge of our language and traditions; it was my poor wife, who is no more, who had trouble with the marriage initially. Also I had contacted Manu, with whom I had kept in touch all these years, and we began our present custom of taking luncheon together at an Indian establishment on Boylston Street in the Back Bay area.

That Christmas Day, Manu and I were to meet as usual, and every bit of the city was covered with snow and ice. I had seen snow once before, in Darjeeling in 1968, but I had forgotten how one's foot will slide on it. By the luncheon hour the snow was no longer falling — still, I was surprised to see Manu wearing just a sweater and gloves, waiting for me on the park bench. Even now he does that sometimes. He thinks that he is sitting on Abid Road in Hyderabad as we did when we were youngsters, watching the crowd during the hot season.

"Judge sahib, you are using a cane now, eh?" Manu called to me as I approached. Still he addresses me with the old Urdu term. Of course he tries to intimidate me by speaking English only — but it does not work. I am very comfortable with English. All of the courts in India are operated in that language only.

"I am required to use the cane, Manu. Not out of necessity, mind you. My grandchildren gave it to me as a present for their Christmas holiday. Their feelings would be very much hurt if I left it behind."

He is a short man, much shorter than I am, so I have to look down at him when we speak. But then I leaned the cane on the bench and remained standing while he sat, just so he would know I was speaking the truth.

"Are you not cold?" I asked.

"Not at all," he said, looking casually at the old Trinity Church, making no move to get up even though snow was blowing straight in our faces. "So you are celebrating Christmas these days, is it?"

"Are you teasing me or what, Manmohan? You know I do not like to follow these Western customs. But what else can one do when one is a foreigner in America and one's daughter has insisted on marrying a local fellow?" I picked up the cane again. "*Challo.* Are you not feeling hungry?"

"Okay, okay, Judge sahib." He got up from the bench and swung his arms back and forth like a monkey getting ready for exercise.

I looked at him but said nothing. Sometimes he likes to irritate me for no reason. We have many differences, Manu and I. He has lived in the U.S. since he was fifty-nine years; I did not move here until I was seventy. I am very well traveled, having visited all over India, north south east west. He has been only to Bombay and Madras. I have my head full of hair, he is almost bald. I am a lawyer by training, he is only an engineer. Perhaps that is why I have a slightly more developed moral sense, I do not know.

I am not finding fault with Manu. We have many things in common, or we should not be friendly at all. We are the same age, we are both Murthys of the Brahmin caste, and grew up in the same section of Mozamjahi Market in the old days, when it was still a very nice neighborhood of Hyderabad. We have the misfortune to be widowers and now we both live with our respective children. We are even closely related; my father's own brother married to Manu's mother's cousin-sister. We both came from orthodox families. As boys we learned the *slokas* every day and did not take food in non-Brahmin houses and were strict vegetarians. That is why we always like to eat our own Indian food.

"Raga Restaurant won't be open today," Manu said. "We must find somewhere else to eat."

"Why? It is a Hindu establishment."

"It is an *Indian* establishment, Judge sahib," Manu said. "It will be closed."

"We'll see, we'll see, Manu. You are not an expert on everything in America."

But when we reached the restaurant, no light was there in the building, and the chairs were turned upside down on the tables.

"As I thought," Manu said.

"Most unusual," I said, and bent forward to see if anyone was there inside. I did not want him to realize how disappointed I was. A Christmas tree was placed just beside the hostess stand, decorated with Kashmiri ornaments. A wooden statue of Lord Ganesha stood in the window, looking back at us, as if he too were remembering the April sun and palm trees and mango fruits of his motherland.

"*Challo,* what is there?" Manu slapped me on the back. "We will go and look for some other place."

"But why would any other hotel be open?"

"If you can walk just a little in this snow, we will find another restaurant — unless you're feeling uncomfortable in the cold?"

"What are you talking? I can walk even if we go to the Himalayas and come back."

We went off and I placed my cane carefully, so as not to put it here and there if I saw some ice. But it began growing quite windy and the snow blew from the street into our faces, so I bent down my head and adjusted my scarf around my ears. The large toe in my left foot was paining me because of the cold. Occasionally, a car crept past on the snow-covered street, but no taxis were there at all. At last, a light showed through the window of a small eating place. A sign said: BOYLSTON BURRITO, MEXICAN FOOD AND FUN.

"Manmohan," I said, "let us go in here."

"But that is a fast-food type of place — you won't like it."

"Not true not true. It looks quite fine," I said, thinking only that I had lost all the sensation in my toes and then my fingers were also feeling odd. "And see — it is Mexican. It will be quite good and spicy."

"I know," Manu said. "I come here often."

Inside, a warm gust of air blew from the overhead vent. A cardboard Santa Claus, almost two meters tall, smiled at us stupidly from the corner. The floor was wet with water from the melted snow. Only a young man and girl were sitting and eating together, and another girl, about twenty-five years of age, was standing behind the counter.

Manu gave his order immediately. "Number three special."

"What is that? What is number three special?" I asked him.

"Taco salad."

"Why do you get that salad, *baba?* People here think it is vegetarian food but it is nothing but grass."

"It tastes fine to me," Manu said.

"I suppose there are beans in it?"

"It has beans, lettuce, tomato, peppers, and cheese in a bowl that is eatable. It is written there — number three special." He pointed at the menu board on the wall behind the clerk.

I did not want to tell him that I could not see the small lettering clearly. I had not visited the eye doctor, although my daughter had been insisting on it. I was getting tired of her constant worry about me. Everything in U.S. had been tiring to me in the past three weeks — the people, the weather, the food. Thank God my wife did not have to go through this experience also. She may not have been able to adjust as well as I had been doing.

"I would like the bean and cheese burrito, please," I said. There was a large picture of the meal on the board with its name written underneath. It looked like a rolled-up roti.

The girl behind the counter looked at me. "I'm sorry, sir?" she asked, leaning forward. She raised her eyebrows in the strange way Americans do, which has nothing to do with being sorry at all.

"The burrito — bean and cheese burrito," I said.

"Don't speak so fast, Judge sahib," Manu said in Hindi. "Do you think she can understand when you speak like that?"

"She should be understanding me," I replied to him, purposefully in English. "Nothing is wrong with my language."

He waved his hand in the air and turned around to select a table for us.

I looked at her. She was smiling, but not in a kindly way. "Bean and cheese burrito, please," I said. "With rice and Coca-Cola to drink."

"Special number four is a better deal. It'll save you some money." She was chewing her gum very loudly and was looking so impatient — like a state chief minister at a village function. "And we only have Pepsi."

"Yes, yes, number four then."

"What drink?" she asked.

"I said — Coca-Cola."

She handed me a cup. "You can get your Pepsi at the machine," she said, pointing.

I filled the cup and collected my food and sat down, putting my heavy coat and scarf on the adjacent seat. "Can you believe her arrogance?" I asked Manu. "I prefer our Hotel Raga. They are so polite there — not at all like this rude place."

"Raga is a real restaurant, Judge sahib, this is just a fast-food place. She has trouble with our Indian accent, that's all. One cannot get upset over every little thing."

"Nonsense. Everybody should be understanding English. It is the common language."

"And they don't say 'hotel' here. They say 'restaurant.' It is 'Raga Restaurant,' not 'Hotel Raga.'"

I ignored him. "Everyone in the city is so rude, actually. I do not know why Kirti's husband insists on living in the middle of this city with cars and lorries and noise noise noise everywhere. Just like the Old City neighborhoods in Hyderabad that have become so dirty. What is wrong with those nice new homes in the outskirts with the backyards and gardens and things? Everything is clean there. Then we don't have to put up with these people and walking everywhere. Mind you, I don't object to walking. The only time I drove in India was to travel back and forth from High Court to home. Otherwise, no matter where I went, it was by walking only."

Manu was cutting his salad with a knife. "But see how much freedom there is in walking," he said. "Would you learn to drive in America just to come and have lunch with me every week?"

"Why not?" I asked, swallowing my first bite. It tasted a bit unusual. How I wished I was eating that *navrattan* vegetable curry at Hotel Raga.

"It would become too inconvenient," he insisted. "Probably you would not learn how to drive at all."

I got impatient. "In the sixty-five years we have been acquainted, Manu, still you do not know me. I am a very very independent fellow. Do you remember, even when the other judges were having a driver I drove myself?" I took another bite and swallowed it without even chewing properly.

"I don't know, Judge sahib. It's not so easy to drive in the U.S., you have to follow the rules here."

"What rules? In America there are always these rules those rules here rules there rules. They should be followed. But nobody is following them here any more than in India."

"How can you say that, Judge sahib? Here people drive correctly by staying within the white lines. In India nobody pays attention to those white lines. They're just a decorative item."

I was no longer listening to him. The burrito was tasting quite funny to me, and I examined the stuffing inside. It was dark and crumbling into small pieces. I showed it to Manu, who quickly identified it as beef! He began to put some of his salad onto my plate, to share with me, claiming it was too much for him.

"Clearly I told her *bean,* Manmohan. She knew that I wanted bean." I felt as if some infection was spreading from the back of my throat to my stomach.

"It's okay, Judge sahib —"

"It is not okay, Manmohan," I said. "Everything in the U.S. is not just okay, okay, okay." I got up and walked to the counter and held the plate out to the girl.

"What is this?"

"I'm sorry?" the girl said, raising her eyebrows again. Such a disrespectful expression.

"This — luncheon that you ordered for me — what is it?"

"That's special number four —"

"Does it have beef in it?"

"Ahhh . . . it's a beef burrito, yes."

"But I ordered a bean and cheese burrito."

"You told me you wanted special number four."

"No. *You* told *me* that I wanted special number four —"

"Huh?"

"Judge sahib," Manu said, catching onto my sleeve, "let's go from here. There must be some other open restaurant."

"You gave me the number four special when I told you I wanted a bean burrito," I said to the girl.

"What? Sir, I asked you whether you wanted the special because it would save you some money. If you —"

"Can you not hear correctly? I told you I wanted bean, not beef."

Manu told me later that as I pronounced these words, a little bit of saliva came from my mouth and landed on the girl's sleeve. I do not agree. I think the girl just finally realized how wrong she was. But it is true that at this point, her behavior turned quite bad, her expression became agitated, and she began to talk in a big voice.

"Look, if you want a refund, I'll give you your five dollars back. It's Christmas, and I don't need to be treated so rudely."

"Judge sahib, let's leave."

I pulled my arm out of Manu's grasp. "I don't know what you need and what you don't need, young lady. That is not my concern. But it is a basic teaching of my religion not to eat beef."

"Challo," Manu said, "put on your overcoat." He was already wearing his gloves.

"Give me your name, miss," I said.

"Roxanna Edmond."

"And who is the manager? I would like to speak to him."

"I *am* the manager," she said, pointing to her nametag. "It says right here."

"You should be ashamed of yourself," I said. Now Manu was taking my arm and leading me away, almost by force. "You should be ashamed." I pointed the finger of my free hand at her.

"What am I supposed to be ashamed about?" she said. "Learn to be a gentleman, sir. In this country, men act like gentlemen."

I just stared at her as if I were Lord Shiva opening his third eye. How dare she say that to me, as if I didn't have a right to be here? Did she know that my only daughter had lived here for fifteen years, was the wife of an American and a full professor at a very prestigious college? Where else would I be staying after my wife died?

When we were alone on the sidewalk outside, Manu handed me my coat.

"Can you believe that *avarra?*" I said, patting down my hair. "What does she mean by that? In this country, men act like gentlemen?"

"Let it go, friend, let it go. She's just stupid. She doesn't know anything."

We walked together without speaking. I was so angry that for some time I did not even realize that I had water in my eyes, which were paining from the cold wind. I am glad that Manu did not notice, because maybe he would think I was weeping. Can you imagine? A former Hyderabadi High Court Justice crying like a small boy on the streets of Boston?

On Boylston Street we saw a car collide with a small lorry. Manu thought the accident was the lorry driver's fault and was feeling sorry for the young man who was driving the car. But I saw clearly that he had carelessly gone through the full danger red light. That too on a snowy street when he should be driving with much caution. We stood inside the glass doors of a warm apartment building and observed as a police constable talked with the drivers and the car was towed away. I got some satisfaction from pointing out to Manu that this was yet another example of Americans not following rules. But still I could not forget that burrito girl's insult to me.

We reached my son-in-law's street about fifteen minutes later. "Manmohan, you must consult with your son and give me the name of a solicitor."

"Why?"

"I am considering quite seriously of suing that restaurant."

"Arrey babree!" He held me by the shoulder. "You are going too far. Don't lose your self-respect out of such a small thing."

Manu refuses to take a stand about some matters, even when they are quite important. He even found fault with me for protesting against the Nizam during the police action years ago. That is where we differ, he and I. I have certain values. Sometimes I think Manu has none.

"Are you going to consult with your son? Or shall I ask someone else?"

He kept quiet. Probably he was wondering whom else I would ask. I was wondering that too. He knew quite well that I could not ask Kirti, who would make a big fuss and inquire why I wanted to go through the work of suing someone. She thinks that I should sit calmly like a statue in her husband's living room eating *gulab jamun* and never undertake anything unpleasant.

"I'll talk with him and let you know," Manu said without looking at me.

"When?"

"When? When?" He threw his hands up in the air. "As soon as realistically possible. But let it go, *baba.* Let it go, friend."

"That I will not do," I answered. "And I would appreciate it if you could ask him for the reference without revealing my business to him."

The snow had started falling again, and the gusts were blowing as if we were standing at the highest point of Kanya Kumari and the winds from three oceans were fighting with each other. Only when we reached my son-in-law's front step did I realize what I had done. "My cane! I left it at that dirty place!" I struck my forehead with the palm of my hand. "Now I must return and collect it." Fully I intended to do so. But I could not turn to go. Did I have to meet that girl again — with her gum chewing and her arrogant smile? I looked at Manmohan. My faithful friend closed his eyes.

"You stay here, Judge sahib. I will go and get it." Then he turned and left me, shaking his head.

The next day my daughter and son-in-law took my grandsons to the Museum of Science because they had no school during the winter holidays. I did not feel like being at the museum with so many children screaming and shouting, so I thought it better I should stay at home. My two favorite science fiction television programs were shown during the afternoon. Americans are so imaginative about technology and advances in engineering, even in their fantasy shows. After the programs were finished, I turned off the television, sat in my favorite chair, and rang up Manu.

"Do you have the solicitor's name?" I asked, as soon as he picked up the telephone.

"Yes, yes," he said, sounding irritated. "My son wanted to know everything — what for do I need a lawyer, what is happening, et cetera, et cetera. It was not easy."

"You did not tell him, did you?"

"No. But I don't know why it's a secret."

"It is not a secret, Manmohan."

"Then why couldn't I tell him? He thought it very strange of me. My own son thought I was hiding something awful."

"Must everyone know my affairs? He is your own son, but must he know everything?"

"Don't get upset, Judge sahib."

"I thought in America they respect privacy, individual rights, religion — dignity — dignity most of all."

"What does dignity have to do with it? It would be more dignified if you didn't sue the restaurant."

"You do not know anything about dignity, Manmohan. Tell me, would you not be feeling bad if you were in my position?"

He kept quiet for a moment. I thought maybe I had changed his mind. "Aaaaah, now I understand," he said. "You are ashamed, is it? Yes, that's it, Judge sahib. You are ashamed."

"What do you mean, ashamed?"

"Okay, humiliated then. You feel humiliated. But there is no need for that. These mistakes happen to all of us when we are new to the country. I know so many stories —"

"What are you talking, Manmohan? I speak English very very well, ask anyone in our community, and the beef was hidden inside the burrito, even an American could have thought it was a bean burrito only. Just give me the solicitor's information. End of discussion. Case closed."

"As you wish," he sighed. "One moment. I'll get it."

Then I heard a key in the front lock and Kirti appeared at the door with my younger grandson standing behind her. He was wearing his heavy coat and his gloves, and his eyes, peeking out between his hat and muffler, were red and tired.

"Returned so quickly?"

"It's just me, Poppa," Kirti said, unzipping my grandson's coat. "I brought Vinay back because he wasn't feeling well. Scott and Chandu are still out." She led Vinay to his bedroom.

I nodded as if all was fine but was feeling most bothered. It appeared that I was destined to have everyone know about my affairs.

Manu finally gave the solicitor's name and number. But as I was jotting it down Kirti returned to the room and was looking quite curiously at me.

"Okay, fine, I will call them for you," I said into the receiver, in an effort to preserve my privacy. "No problem, Manu. I will do you this favor once."

By now Manu was quite irritated with me. "I don't know, *baba.* You do what you like and you conduct your business as you like. Sameer has already made an appointment. Second January, two o'clock." He rang off.

"No need to thank me," I said, and also hung up.

By this time Kirti had gone to the kitchen. "Poppa, what is happening?" she called out. "Is something wrong?"

"Why? Why should something be wrong? Only thing wrong is Vinay. How is he feeling?"

"A slight fever, that's all. He's in bed and I'm warming some soup for him." She leaned her head around the kitchen door, and her long hair fell around her face in a way that reminded me of her mother. "Is Manu Uncle asking you to do something you don't want to do?"

"Nothing, nothing. Just a small favor. He is my close friend, after all. Sixty-five years we have known each other."

"Since you were small boys growing up in Mozamjahi Market," she said.

"Since we were small boys growing up in Mozamjahi Market," I repeated. I closed my eyes for a moment, thinking about all that had happened since then. "Sixty-five years," I said again, and turned on the television to watch the afternoon news, but still I could sense she was looking at me as if I had done something wrong. So immediately I got up and went to her.

"I am not intimidated by living here, Kirti."

"I know, Poppa."

"I can conduct myself as a gentleman."

"No question. You always have."

"I would appreciate it if you could make that appointment with the ophthalmologist for me," I said, returning to my favorite chair. "I would like to go for an eye exam."

One week later, after much discussion, Manu agreed to go with me to the solicitor's office. He tried to say that he had no interest in coming and that he would not be contributing to the discussion at all. I pointed out that I would give his name to the lawyer as a witness and he would be contacting him anyway. He might as well cut short the process and come in the first instance only. So, on second January, after Manu returned my cane to me and we uncharacteristically took our lunch on Friday, not Thursday, at Hotel Raga, we caught the underground train to the Financial District.

It was obvious that Manu's son-in-law had referred us to a very good firm. The office was on the twenty-first floor and one full window, from floor to ceiling, gave a view of the harbor with its sailboats and tankers and coast guard motorboats. We sat on smooth black leather chairs and watched the solicitors and barristers in their suits and ties and polished shoes. They were quite serious. They walked quickly and spoke in soft voices. The younger men looked at their elders with respect and even opened the doors for them as they came in and out. I was reminded of my own youthful days of focused discipline, arguing over the legal effect of a word or sentence, fighting for a worthy client. Definitely I approved of Manu's son's choice. Only a marble floor was needed. They had only the wooden type that these locals like so much.

Manu was sitting in his chair like a small boy in the school principal's office. Sometimes he bent to one side, sometimes he bent to the other. He would not look at anyone or anything in the room, then he checked his watch, as if he did not want to be there at all. It was very irritating to me, as I was under tension. He told me to stop tapping my cane on the floor, as if I was irritating to him! It was our good fortune that we waited only a few minutes when a young girl greeted us.

"Mr. Murthy, and Mr. —"

"Yes, I am Justice Shiva Ram Murthy," I said, standing. "I have the appointment today. This is Mr. Murali Manmohan Murthy."

"I'm Sarah, Kelly Golden's assistant. Nice to meet you both. Please follow me," she said. We had waited only ten minutes. That made me think that Kelly Golden could not be a good attorney, though he worked in a posh firm. If truly he was well respected, he should have kept us sitting at least thirty minutes.

We walked down a long corridor and turned into an office. A woman sat behind the desk and stood up as we entered. "Hello," she said, shaking my hand. "I'm Kelly Golden. Sorry to be a little late. Good to meet you — Mr. Murthy?"

I was confused. But only for a moment. After all, I am a modern-thinking man, and there are lady lawyers in India also. "I am Justice Shiva Ram Murthy. This is Mr. Murali Manmohan Murthy," I said calmly.

"Sameer's father — how very nice to meet you." She smiled most graciously. "I have known Sameer for years. Please, have a seat." We sat down in the comfortable upholstered chairs. Kelly Golden's window gave the same view of Boston Harbor that we enjoyed in the waiting room. Perhaps she was well respected after all.

"How interesting — you are a judge," she said to me.

"I retired ten years ago. For twenty-two years I sat on the Hyderabad High Court back home in India. Before that I had my own practice."

"You must miss working in the law." Her gleaming brown hair reflected the sunlight nicely, and I thought her eyes were quite remarkable.

"I very much miss the intellectual challenge," I said.

"When did you move to Boston?"

"Only three months back. But you see, I would not have left Hyderabad at all if my daughter did not need my assistance here." Manu looked at me, but I ignored him.

"I'm sure she's very appreciative," Kelly Golden said.

"It is our Indian way. Family is most important."

"I learned a lot about Indian culture from Sameer, you know," she said, addressing Manu. "We were at MIT together. He'd tell us about you and his mother and life as a boy in India."

Manu waved his hand in the air and smiled a bit shyly. "I hope he did not bore you too much."

"It was fascinating. He talked about Hyderabad all the time. He used to help me study for our physics exams." She smiled. Even though she must have been forty years, she was a pretty girl.

"Oh, he's always willing to help if he thinks someone knows less than him," Manu said lightly. "In my case, Sameer thinks that a lot."

Kelly Golden caught the joke and laughed. "But for me, Sameer's help was truly needed," she said.

"I doubt that," Manu said. "Probably he just wanted to talk with a good-looking classmate."

"And I see where he gets his charm from!"

Now Manu laughed too.

What was all this laughing laughing? Didn't we have some serious business to discuss without Manu acting inappropriately with a woman much younger to him? I tapped my cane against the floor and waited for them to stop their silliness.

"Please give my best to him and Priya," Kelly Golden said to Manu before turning back to me. "Now, Sameer said that you both had something to talk with me about." She took a pen and paper pad out of her desk drawer and placed them in front of her. "I suggested to him that we could talk on the phone —"

"No no," I said. "Very much I wanted to come and discuss matters with you in person."

"What can I help you with?"

I breathed in deeply, then breathed out. "It was an incident that happened on Christmas Day. Every Thursday, we — myself and Mr. Murthy — take our luncheon together. But last Thursday it was the Christmas holiday. Hotel Raga, where we usually take our meal, wasn't open. So we walked to another place. A Mexican fast-food establishment."

"I'm quite familiar with the situation," Kelly Golden said. "I'm Jewish, so I'm often looking for something to do on Christmas Day myself. For my family, it's usually Chinese take-out and a movie."

"Then you must be knowing how I felt that day!" I leaned forward in my chair and told her about special number four and how the girl manager had rudely put forward an order of beef and cheese burrito, even after I had requested a bean and cheese burrito. Manu was being very quiet. "You thought the girl manager was very arrogant, also, isn't it, Manmohan?" I asked.

Manu cleared his throat and addressed Kelly Golden. "I wasn't there, that's the problem — I was already sitting down to eat my food."

"But you could see her," I asked, "that expression on her face, correct?"

Manu turned toward me, blinked his eyes, and said nothing. I looked back at him, waiting. He was incredible. First, he made an appointment with a lady lawyer, then he was flirting with her like a Westerner, then he was refusing to support me in my position. I was about to address him with an appropriate Hindi curse when Kelly Golden spoke.

"Why don't you tell me exactly what happened after you ordered?" she said, picking up her pen.

I gave a deep sigh and closed my eyes and cleared my thoughts of the traitor who was sitting next to me. A disciplined mind is quite capable of doing these things. Then I told, from A to Zed, exactly what happened on Christmas. When I completed the story I put a piece of paper with Roxanna Edmond's name in front of Kelly Golden.

She didn't look at it. She stopped writing on the notepad. "You don't eat beef," she said.

"It is against the customs of my faith to eat beef," I said.

"I'm aware of that."

"I have never, never eaten beef in my life, before this incident. It has never passed my lips. I am a Brahmin, you see."

"It's true," Manu said, "he has never eaten beef as far as I know."

I glanced at him from the corner of my eye. Why was he talking now?

"Not only beef," I said, ignoring him. "I am completely vegetarian. No meat of any kind or eggs. It is the doctrine of Ahimsa. Nonviolence toward any living thing. Even he is the same." I pointed toward Manu with my chin.

"What happened to you after the visit to the restaurant?" she asked. "Any perceivable effects?"

"Perceivable effects?" I asked.

"You might have had an emotional reaction. Did you have increased conflict at home? Any strained relationships? Any outward signs of distress?"

"I live with my daughter and my son-in-law. But I did not tell them about it."

She leaned back in her chair and looked at me for a moment. "What were you hoping to have happen in this case, Justice Murthy?"

"I am thinking to sue the restaurant, of course."

She nodded her head slowly but said nothing. Did she have no sympathy for my position?

"I can understand how you feel, Justice Murthy, but I don't think we would have a successful lawsuit in this situation. The law requires that there be some tangible, perceivable effects of the wrong you suffered. I can see that you were quite upset and harmed by the incident. Your friend can see that you were quite upset. But the law won't recognize it. I would suggest, instead, that you write a letter of formal complaint to the owner and the franchise. It's quite probable that the manager would be disciplined. That would address the real issue as well — the rudeness and insensitivity of this particular employee."

"You will not bring the case?" I said, not quite believing her.

"It would be frivolous to bring suit. Surely you would think so if you were sitting in judgment on this case under Massachusetts law."

I shook my head. "This — is — an — important — Hindu — practice." I tapped the floor with my cane at each word.

Manu put his hand on my arm. "Don't become so angry, Judge sahib," he said.

"I suppose you don't follow any dietary laws?" I said to Kelly Golden. "You are not a religious person?"

She raised her eyebrows, just like the girl at the fast-food counter. "I'm not sure what my habits have to do with the situation, Mr. Murthy." Her face turned a bit red.

"Justice Murthy," I corrected.

"Justice Murthy. Under our legal system, there must be some definite suffering of an emotional or physical type. We could file the case — but it would get thrown out, and I might even get sanctioned. Merely eating a type of meat because of a cashier's carelessness will not get you any money."

I gazed through the window at the harbor. In the cold glare of the Boston sun on the sea, my old life disappeared: the dark chambers of the Hyderabad High Court; my wife sitting in the shade of our banyan tree; myself as a young man, holding baby Kirti's hand as we walk to the vegetable stand behind our home. Shadows in a seventy-year-old mind.

"Definitely this is not about money," I muttered, closing my eyes. "It is the principle of it all." There was nothing more to be said. Kelly Golden and myself could not understand each other. I was standing up to take my leave, but because I am a polite man — a gentleman — I said, "Thank you for meeting with me today." Manu said goodbye and followed behind me.

In the lift I could not speak to him.

"Sorry, Judge sahib."

I kept quiet.

"From the beginning, I did not feel that it was the correct thing to do."

Again, I said nothing.

"*Arrey*, I tried to tell you, didn't I?" he said more loudly. "I tried to say that I did not want to be involved?"

"You are a traitor."

"No —"

"And you are no better than those people — that burrito girl and the lady lawyer. Don't walk with me, traitor, from now on I have no association with you." Quickly I walked across the lobby and outside to the street. He followed.

"Even if I agreed with you, she didn't think you had a case."

"Any solicitor with some thinking power could make a case. You should have heard the arguments that came before me back at home!" My words came as vapor in the cold air. "All I must do is find a respectable solicitor."

"Shiva Ram!" Manu said, catching up to me.

"Not to worry. I have no need of your help. I see what type of help you give. If a mere clerk insults your religious customs, you do not care. If she tells your lifelong friend that he does not belong in this country, it is no concern of yours."

He caught hold of my arm and stopped me. "I am concerned, Shiva Ram. The clerk was a stupid girl. She insulted you, that's right, but her insult is a different matter from whether you eat beef. You can't fix the insult by suing the restaurant about her mistake. It won't teach her anything. Sometimes that is how things are in this country."

"You are a coward."

His face grew red and his eyes were as wide as a sapota fruit. "And you are a big daring fellow. That is why you go insulting ladies who don't agree with you."

"My whole life I have felt that you are a coward. Now finally I am saying it. You have never had the courage to follow your own beliefs. Even when we were boys you were always following whatever I did, feeling jealous of me."

"That's what you think, is it?"

"Yes."

"All of these years that is how you have regarded our friendship?"

"Without question."

"Then let me tell you, Shiva Ram, that I have been eating meat for years. Not just meat, but beef, since the second day that I came to this country. I haven't told you because it would have disturbed you too much. Now what do you say?"

Silently I stared at him: his bald, coconut-shaped head, his skin, two shades lighter than it was during our young days in the Indian sun, the lines that had spread themselves around his eyes and mouth. At that moment, no one was there in the world that I hated more. I felt like giving a slap to him, right there on his face. But I could not degrade myself in that way. "You are an idiot," I said, and walked off. He did not follow me, thank God, because I might have been forced into some action that later I would have regretted.

After some days, while I was still searching for a good solicitor, I wrote a very strong letter to the proprietor of the hotel Boylston Burrito, who sent a reply saying that he was quite sorry about the incident and had taken care of the manager's attitude and put her in her place. The letter was so obliging, so polite, I thought perhaps there are some well-mannered people living in the U.S. after all. I took great pains to respond in a gracious manner and drafted many versions of my reply. "Considering the appropriate actions you have taken," I wrote to the Boylston Burrito proprietor, "the event has been forgiven and forgotten. Please do not worry. I will not be bringing a lawsuit against you or your establishment." Even in the old days my fellow judges criticized me for being too compassionate.

When I walked to the post office, I noticed the first green buds on the trees. The snow was melting so fast, a small river was flowing on the side of every road, just like during the monsoon back at home. The local people on the streets were smiling again.

Three weeks after the Kelly Golden meeting I felt sorry for Manu and rang up to invite him to take luncheon with me. Of course he did not apologize, but we went to Hotel Raga and ate *navrattan* vegetable curry and *palak paneer,* and my favorite waiter served us. America is a lonely place, after all, and I did not wish to isolate Manu without any friends, without anyone to understand him and keep him company, no matter how much he had given up our customs. We Indians must stick together.

GEORGE SAUNDERS

Bohemians

FROM THE NEW YORKER

IN A LOVELY URBAN COINCIDENCE, the last two houses on our block were both occupied by widows who had lost their husbands in Eastern European pogroms. Dad called them the Bohemians. He called anyone white with an accent a Bohemian. Whenever he saw one of the Bohemians, he greeted her by mispronouncing the Czech word for "door." Neither Bohemian was Czech, but both were polite, so when Dad said "door" to them they answered cordially, as if he weren't perennially schlockered.

Mrs. Poltoi, the stouter Bohemian, had spent the war in a crawlspace, splitting a daily potato with five cousins. Consequently she was bitter and claustrophobic and loved food. If you ate something while standing near her, she stared at it going into your mouth. She wore only black. She said the Catholic Church was a jeweled harlot drinking the blood of the poor. She said America was a spoiled child ignorant of grief. When our ball rolled onto her property, she seized it and waddled into her backyard and pitched it into the quarry.

Mrs. Hopanlitski, on the other hand, was thin and joyfully made pipe-cleaner animals. When I brought home one of her crude dogs in top hats, Mom said, "Take over your Mold-A-Hero. To her, it will seem like the toy of a king." To Mom, the camps, massacres, and railroad sidings of twenty years before were as unreal as covered wagons. When Mrs. H. claimed her family had once owned serfs, Mom's attention wandered. She had a tract house in mind. No way was she getting one. We were renting a remodeled garage behind the Giancarlos, and Dad was basically drinking up the sporting goods store. His NFL helmets were years out of date. I'd stop by after school and find the store closed and Dad getting sloshed among the fake legs with Bennie Delmonico at Prosthetics World.

Using the Mold-A-Hero, I cast Mrs. H. a plastic Lafayette, and she said she'd keep it forever on her sill. Within a week, she'd given it to Elizabeth the Raccoon. I didn't mind. Raccoon, an only child like me, had nothing. The Kletz brothers called her Raccoon for the bags she had under her eyes from never sleeping. Her parents fought nonstop. They fought over breakfast. They fought in the yard in their underwear. At dusk they stood on their porch whacking each other with lengths of weather stripping. Raccoon practically had spinal curvature from spending so much time slumped over with misery. When the Kletz brothers called her Raccoon, she indulged them by rubbing her hands together ferally. The nickname was the most attention she'd ever had. Sometimes she'd wish to be hit by a car so she could come back as a true raccoon and track down the Kletzes and give them rabies.

"Never wish harm on yourself or others," Mrs. H. said. "You are a lovely child." Her English was flat and clear, almost like ours.

"Raccoon, you mean," Raccoon said. "A lovely raccoon."

"A lovely child of God," Mrs. H. said.

"Yeah, right," Raccoon said. "Tell again about the prince."

So Mrs. H. told again how she'd stood rapt in her yard watching an actual prince powder his birthmark to invisibility. She remembered the smell of burning compost from the fields and men in colorful leggings dragging a gutted boar across a wooden bridge. This was before she was forced to become a human pack animal in the Carpathians, carrying the personal belongings of cruel officers. At night, they chained her to a tree. Sometimes they burned her calves with a machine-gun barrel for fun. Which was why she always wore knee socks. After three years, she'd come home to find her babies in tiny graves. They were, she would say, short-lived but wonderful gifts. She did not now begrudge God for taking them. A falling star is brief, but isn't one nonetheless glad to have seen it? Her grace made us hate Mrs. Poltoi all the more. What was eating a sixth of a potato every day compared to being chained to a tree? What was being crammed in with a bunch of your cousins compared to having your kids killed?

The summer I was ten, Raccoon and I, already borderline rejects due to our mutually unraveling households, were joined by Art Siminiak, who had recently made the mistake of inviting the Kletzes in for lemonade. There was no lemonade. Instead, there was Art's mom and a sailor from Great Lakes passed out naked across the paper-drive stacks on the Siminiaks' sun porch.

This new, three-way friendship consisted of slumping in gangways, playing gloveless catch with a Wiffle, trailing hopefully behind kids whose homes could be entered without fear of fiasco.

Over on Mozart lived Eddie the Vacant. Eddie was seventeen, huge, and simple. He could crush a walnut in his bare hand, but first you had to put it there and tell him to do it. Once he'd pinned a VACANT sign to his shirt and walked around the neighborhood that way, and the name had stuck. Eddie claimed to see birds. Different birds appeared on different days of the week. Also, there was a Halloween bird and a Christmas bird.

One day, as Eddie hobbled by, we asked what kind of birds he was seeing.

"Party birds," he said. "They got big streamers coming out they butts."

"You having a party?" said Art. "You having a homo party?"

"I gone have a birthday party," said Eddie, blinking shyly.

"Your dad know?" Raccoon said.

"No, he don't yet," said Eddie.

His plans for the party were private and illogical. We peppered him with questions, hoping to get him to further embarrass himself. The party would be held in his garage. As far as the junk car in there, he would push it out by hand. As far as the oil on the floor, he would soak it up using Handi Wipes. As far as music, he would play a trumpet.

"What are you going to play the trumpet with?" said Art. "Your asshole?"

"No, I not gone play it with that," Eddie said. "I just gone use my lips, okay?"

As far as girls, there would be girls; he knew many girls, from his job managing the Drake Hotel, he said. As far as food, there would be food, including pudding dumplings.

"You're the manager of the Drake Hotel," Raccoon said.

"Hey, I know how to get the money for pudding dumplings!" Eddie said.

Then he rang Poltoi's bell and asked for a contribution. She said for what. He said for him. She said to what end. He looked at her blankly and asked for a contribution. She asked him to leave the porch. He asked for a contribution. Somewhere, he'd got the idea that, when asking for a contribution, one angled to sit on the couch. He started in, and she pushed him back with a thick forearm. Down the front steps he went, ringing the iron bannister with his massive head.

He got up and staggered away, a little blood on his scalp.

"Learn to leave people be!" Poltoi shouted after him.

Ten minutes later, Eddie Sr. stood on Poltoi's porch, a hulking effeminate tailor too cowed to use his bulk for anything but butting open the jamming door at his shop.

"Since when has it become the sport to knock unfortunates down stairs?" he asked.

"He was not listen," she said. "I tell him no. He try to come inside."

"With all respect," he said, "it is in my son's nature to perhaps be not so responsive."

"Someone so unresponse, keep him indoors," she said. "He is big as a man. And I am old lady."

"Never has Eddie presented a danger to anyone," Eddie Sr. said.

"I know my rights," she said. "Next time, I call police."

But, having been pushed down the stairs, Eddie the Vacant couldn't seem to stay away.

"Off this porch," Poltoi said through the screen when he showed up the next day, offering her an empty cold-cream jar for three dollars.

"We gone have so many snacks," he said. "And if I drink a alcohol drink, then watch out. Because I ain't allowed. I dance too fast."

He was trying the doorknob now, showing how fast he would dance if alcohol was served.

"Please, off this porch!" she shouted.

"Please, off this porch!" he shouted back, doubling at the waist in wacky laughter.

Poltoi called the cops. Normally, Lieutenant Brusci would have asked Eddie what bird was in effect that day and given him a ride home in his squad. But this was during the One City fiasco. To cut graft, cops were being yanked off their regular beats and replaced by cops from other parts of town. A couple of Armenians from South Shore showed up and dragged Eddie off the porch in a club lock so tight he claimed the birds he was seeing were beakless.

"I'll give you a beak, Frankenstein," said one of the Armenians, tightening the choke hold.

Eddie entered the squad with all the fluidity of a hat rack. Art and Raccoon and I ran over to Eddie Sr.'s tailor shop, above the Marquee, which had sunk to porn. When Eddie Sr. saw us, he stopped his Singer by kicking out the plug. From downstairs came a series of erotic moans.

Eddie Sr. rushed to the hospital with his Purple Heart and some photos of Eddie as a grinning, wet-chinned kid on a pony. He found Eddie handcuffed to a bed, with an IV drip and a smashed face. Apparently, he'd bitten one of the Armenians. Bail was set at three hundred. The tailor shop made zilch. Eddie Sr.'s fabrics were a lexicon of yesteryear. Dust coated a bright-yellow sign that read ZIPPERS REPAIRED IN JIFFY.

"Jail for that kid, I admit, don't make total sense," the judge said. "Three months in the Anston. Best I can do."

The Anston Center for Youth was a red brick former forge now yarded in barbed wire. After their shifts, the guards held loud, hooting orgies kitty-corner at Zem's Lamplighter. Skinny immigrant women arrived at Zem's in station wagons and emerged hours later adjusting their stockings. From all over Chicago kids were sent to the Anston, kids who'd only ever been praised for the level of beatings they gave and received and their willingness to carve themselves up. One Anston kid had famously hired another kid to run over his foot. Another had killed his mother's lover with a can opener. A third had sliced open his own eyelid with a pop-top on a dare.

Eddie the Vacant disappeared into the Anston in January and came out in March.

To welcome him home, Eddie Sr. had the neighborhood kids over. Eddie the Vacant looked so bad even the Kletzes didn't joke about how bad he looked. His nose was off center and a scald mark ran from ear to chin. When you got too close, his hands shot up. When the cake was served, he dropped his plate, shouting, "Leave a guy alone!"

Our natural meanness now found a purpose. Led by the Kletzes, we cut through Poltoi's hose, bashed out her basement windows with ball-peens, pushed her little shopping cart over the edge of the quarry, and watched it end-over-end into the former Slag Ravine.

Then it was spring and the quarry got busy. When the noon blast went off, our windows rattled. The three-o'clock blast was even bigger. Raccoon and Art and I made a fort from the cardboard shipping containers the Cline frames came in. One day, while pretending the three-o'clock blast was atomic, we saw Eddie the Vacant bounding toward our fort through the weeds, like some lover in a commercial, only fatter and falling occasionally.

His trauma had made us kinder toward him.

"Eddie," Art said. "You tell your dad where you're at?"

"It no big problem," Eddie said. "I was gone leave my dad a note."

"But did you?" said Art.

"I'll leave him a note when I get back," said Eddie. "I gone come in with you now."

"No room," said Raccoon. "You're too huge."

"That a good one!" said Eddie, crowding in.

Down in the quarry were the sad cats, the slumping watchman's shack, the piles of reddish, discarded dynamite wrappings that occasionally rose erratically up the hillside like startled birds.

Along the quarryside trail came Mrs. Poltoi, dragging a new shopping cart.

"Look at that pig," said Raccoon. "Eddie, that's the pig that put you away."

"What did they do to you in there, Ed?" said Art. "Did they mess with you?"

"No, they didn't," said Eddie. "I just a say to them, 'Leave a guy alone!' I mean, sometime they did, okay? Sometime that one guy say, 'Hey, Eddie, pull your thing! We gone watch you.'"

"Okay, okay," said Art.

At dusk, the three of us would go to Mrs. H.'s porch. She'd bring out cookies and urge forgiveness. It wasn't Poltoi's fault her heart was small, she told us. She, Mrs. H., had seen a great number of things, and seeing so many things had enlarged her heart. Once, she had seen Göring. Once, she had seen Einstein. Once, during the war, she had seen a whole city block, formerly thick with furriers, bombed black overnight. In the morning, charred bodies had crawled along the street, begging for mercy. One such body had grabbed her by the ankle, and she recognized it as Bergen, a friend of her father's.

"What did you do?" said Raccoon.

"Not important now," said Mrs. H., gulping back tears, looking off into the quarry.

Then disaster. Dad got a check for shoulder pads for all six district football teams and, trying to work things out with Mom, decided to take her on a cruise to Jamaica. Nobody in our neighborhood had ever been on a cruise. Nobody had even been to Wisconsin. The disaster was, I was staying with Poltoi. Ours was a liquor household, where you could ask a question over and over in utter sincerity and never get a straight answer. I asked and asked, "Why her?" And was told and told, "It will be an adventure."

I asked, "Why not Grammy?"

I was told, "Grammy don't feel well."

I asked, "Why not Hopanlitski?"

Dad did this like snort.

"Like that's gonna happen," said Mom.

"Why not, why not?" I kept asking.

"Because shut up," they kept answering.

Just after Easter, over I went, with my little green suitcase.

I was a night panicker and occasional bed-wetter. I'd wake drenched and panting. Had they told her? I doubted it. Then I knew they hadn't, from the look on her face the first night, when I peed myself and woke up screaming.

"What's this?" she said.

"Pee," I said, humiliated beyond any ability to lie.

"Ach, well," she said. "Who don't? This also used to be me. Pee pee pee. I used to dream of a fish who cursed me."

She changed the sheets gently, with no petulance — a new one on me. Often Ma, still half asleep, popped me with the wet sheet, saying when at last I had a wife, she herself could finally get some freaking sleep.

Then the bed was ready, and Poltoi made a sweeping gesture, like, Please.

I got in.

She stayed standing there.

"You know," she said. "I know they say things. About me, what I done to that boy. But I had a bad time in the past with a big stupid boy. You don't gotta know. But I did like I did that day for good reason. I was scared at him, due to something what happened for real to me."

She stood in the half-light, looking down at her feet.

"Do you get?" she said. "Do you? Can you get it, what I am saying?"

"I think so," I said.

"Tell to him," she said. "Tell to him sorry, explain about it, tell your friends also. If you please. You have a good brain. That is why I am saying to you."

Something in me rose to this. I'd never heard it before but I believed it: I had a good brain. I could be trusted to effect a change.

Next day was Saturday. She made soup. We played a game using three slivers of soap. We made placemats out of colored strips of paper, and she let me teach her my spelling words.

Around noon, the doorbell rang. At the door stood Mrs. H.

"Everything okay?" she said, poking her head in.

"Yes, fine," said Poltoi. "I did not eat him yet."

"Is everything really fine?" Mrs. H. said to me. "You can say."

"It's fine," I said.

"You can say," she said fiercely.

Then she gave Poltoi a look that seemed to say, Hurt him and you will deal with me.

"You silly woman," said Poltoi. "You are going now."

Mrs. H. went.

We resumed our spelling. It was tense in a quiet-house way. Things ticked. When Poltoi missed a word, she pinched her own hand, but not hard. It was like symbolic pinching. Once when she pinched, she looked at me looking at her, and we laughed.

Then we were quiet again.

"That lady?" she finally said. "She like to lie. Maybe you don't know. She say she is come from where I come from?"

"Yes," I said.

"She is lie," she said. "She act so sweet and everything but she lie. She been born in Skokie. Live here all her life, in America. Why you think she talk so good?"

All week, Poltoi made sausage, noodles, potato pancakes; we ate like pigs. She had tea and cakes ready when I came home from school. At night, if necessary, she dried me off, moved me to her bed, changed the sheets, put me back, with never an unkind word.

"Will pass, will pass," she'd hum.

Mom and Dad came home tanned, with a sailor cap for me, and, in a burst of post-vacation honesty, confirmed it: Mrs. H. was a liar. A liar and a kook. Nothing she said was true. She'd been a cashier at Goldblatt's but had been caught stealing. When caught stealing, she'd claimed to be with the Main Office. When a guy from the Main Office came down, she'd claimed to be with the FBI. Then she'd produced a letter from Lady Bird Johnson, but in her own handwriting, with "Johnson" spelled "Jonsen."

I told the other kids what I knew, and in time they came to believe it, even the Kletzes.

And, once we believed it, we couldn't imagine we hadn't seen it all along.

Another spring came, once again birds nested in bushes on the sides of the quarry. A thrown rock excited a thrilling upward explosion. Thin rivers originated in our swampy backyards, and we sailed boats made of flattened shoeboxes, Twinkie wrappers, crimped tinfoil. Raccoon glued together three balsa-wood planes and placed on this boat a turd from her dog, Svengooli, and, as Svengooli's turd went over a little waterfall and disappeared into the quarry, we cheered.

Contributors' Notes

NATHANIEL BELLOWS is the author of the novel *On This Day* (HarperCollins 2003). His poems have been published in *The New York Times Book Review, The New Republic, Ploughshares, The Paris Review, The Yale Review,* and many other magazines. He lives in New York City.

▪ In "First Four Measures," I wanted to write about two versions of loneliness, from two different perspectives — young and old — and how, in some cases, both can be quite similar and even quite compatible. The tenuous friendship between the young boy and his elderly house sitter is forged and ultimately tested by the boy's piano lessons — a fraught endeavor of self-expression and personal pride, further complicated by his unconventional teacher.

DAVID BEZMOZGIS's first book, *Natasha and Other Stories,* was published in 2004. His work has appeared in *Harper's Magazine, The New Yorker, Zoetrope All-Story,* and *The Walrus.* He is the recipient of the Commonwealth Writers' Prize for Best First Book (Caribbean/Canada) and the Reform Judaism Prize for Jewish Fiction.

▪ I wrote "Natasha" when I stalled in the midst of another story. I typically do not give myself license to depart from a story unless I have finished it, but in this instance I was badly stuck. The story I had been writing, like all the stories I had been writing over a period of several years, dealt with the same family of Soviet Jews and were told through the voice of the same protagonist. All of the stories originated from some aspect of personal experience. To write them I would excavate my own and my family's history, sifting for some anecdote or incident that seemed substantial enough to sustain a story. When I stalled with the other story, I had already written stories about this family in which the protagonist, Mark, is a boy and also a young man. I hadn't written any in which he was a teenager. My goal for the story cycle was to chart the arc of a family of Soviet Jewish immigrants, and I knew that to realize the arc I needed a story that took place at the midpoint. But the story is also the product of other considerations. I wanted to write something about a version of teenage life as I knew it; I had never written a story about sex and I wanted to do that; and I wanted to write a story about betrayal.

"Natasha" itself was inspired by two incidents:

When I was a teenager, a relative married a woman from Moscow. She, like Zina, came to Toronto with a child. The marriage failed. The essential difference between the real and fictional accounts was that in reality the woman arrived with a son and not a daughter.

Years later, when I was living in Los Angeles, I met a Russian man who was having a difficult time adjusting to his American life. He talked nostalgically about Moscow and about a trip he had recently taken there. He told me about a friend of his, a former director at the prestigious Moscow Studio, who had reinvented himself as a pornographer. The scene he described at the man's dacha stayed with me, and I had been waiting for the chance to use it.

TOM BISSELL was born in Escanaba, Michigan, in 1974. After graduating from Michigan State University, he taught English in Uzbekistan as a Peace Corps volunteer and then worked for W. W. Norton and Henry Holt as a book editor. He is the author of *Chasing the Sea,* a travel narrative; *God Lives in St. Petersburg,* a short story collection; and (with Jeff Alexander) *Speak, Commentary,* a collection of fake DVD commentaries. He is a contributing editor for *Harper's Magazine* and a regular contributor to *The Believer.* His work has appeared in *The Pushcart Prize Anthology XXIX, The Best American Travel Writing 2003,* and *The Best American Science Writing 2004,* among other publications. He is currently working on a nonfiction book about Vietnam, teaches in Bennington College's low-residency MFA program, and lives in New York City.

▪ In December 2001 I went to Afghanistan to cover the U.S. invasion for *Men's Journal.* Although I had never before reported on war, I had traveled around Central Asia a good deal and believed my experience in and knowledge of the region would allow me a better-than-average understanding of what was unfolding. This turned out to be spectacularly mistaken. My trip into Afghanistan lasted five extremely tense but paradoxically uneventful days, and when I got out I was glad to be gone. My brief career as a war reporter more or less unmade me. The piece I was contracted to write was supposed to be six thousand words. I turned in (and I believe this may be a record) a 228-page first draft that was many months late. Not surprisingly, *Men's Journal* opted not to publish my story, and I realized that perhaps war reporting was beyond my ken.

To experience, even briefly, a nation upon which war is being waged is undeniably exciting. It is also terrifying and profoundly sobering, particularly if one's own nation happens to be involved. This is all by way of saying that, for the uninitiated, war's tiniest details fascinate and compel. Hence my 228 pages. But not a few of the journalists I met in Afghanistan — fine reporters all — seemed to me strangely unmoved by many of the war's smaller actualities. They had a job to do. How, I found myself wondering, were these men and women able to achieve such personal equilibrium within the larger insanity of war? I decided that, when the time came, I would try to put some of the details within those 228 pages toward a short story about a journalist for whom the emotional weather of war had become commonplace.

Months later, I awoke in the middle of the night and wrote the last few paragraphs of "Death Defier" in a kind of trance. They seemed to me then, and still seem today, a very dark gift from a hugely troubled world. The rest of the story came quickly; I may have written it in less than a week. "Death Defier" upset and unnerved me as I wrote it — and I am not typically a fiction writer who finds himself moved by the plight of people he has created. But I did not want the end I had already written to occur. I, too, wanted to defy death.

CHARLES D'AMBROSIO is the author of *The Point and Other Stories; Orphans,* a collection of essays; and *The Dead Fish Museum,* to be published in April 2006. He lives in Portland, Oregon.

▪ I suppose *Scheme* is about two people who find themselves at the end of their ability to generate meaning, and for me the quiet allegory, the drama of the act of writing the story, is located in my evolving attitude toward those two characters, Kirsten and Lance. The story existed in a fragmentary way — a girl who was cold and in need of new clothes, a boy who had a weakness for sweets and an easy way with deceit — but it was essentially broken and in pieces, a hopeless remnant. Secretly I sided with Lance's safe dirty realism, his stock confidence-man shtick, his belief in nothing beyond himself, but there didn't seem to be much future in it. I had a feel for Kirsten's pain, but I didn't want to follow her into her life, into the scrying or clairvoyance and her vague desire for her true mother, and because of that I couldn't move the narrative forward. The impulse was there but I personally don't practice that stuff, all that spooky business Kirsten believes in, and I was stalled until *McSweeney's* offered me the chance to submit work for the anthology *Astonishing Stories.*

Somehow working within the universe of permissions granted by the idea of genre helped me, just enough. In stories of the paranormal, the world is uniquely available to the wounded, and certain of those conventions gave me the courage to imagine this woman, about whom, in actual life, I would have had deep and probably intransigent doubts. Working through various drafts with *The New Yorker* brought me full circle, convincing me of the story's continuing realism, its tensile strength. This story represents for me an uneasy alliance between forms, played out on the border between genres, just as the two characters, one plunged in mystery, the other rootedly profane, forge a fragile arrangement between themselves.

CORY DOCTOROW (craphound.com) is European affairs coordinator for the Electronic Frontier Foundation (eff.org), a member-supported nonprofit group that works to uphold civil liberties values in technology law, policy, and standards. He represents EFF's interests at various standards bodies and consortia and at the UN World Intellectual Property Organization. Doctorow is also a prolific writer who appears on the mastheads at *Wired, Make,* and *Popular Science* magazines and whose science fiction novels have won the Campbell, Sunburst, and Locus Awards. His novel *Down and Out in the Magic Kingdom* is a finalist for this year's Nebula Award. He is the coeditor of the popular weblog Boing Boing (boingboing.net). Born in Canada, he now lives in London, England.

▪ Last year, Ray Bradbury pitched a fit because Michael Moore had "stolen" the title *Fahrenheit 9/11* from Bradbury's classic novel *Fahrenheit 451*. It was a comically silly position for a noted champion of free expression to take, and I decided to try my hand at writing a bunch of stories that would deconstruct the politics behind classic SF stories, taking on their titles. This one is a piss-take on Orson Scott Card's *Ender's Game,* taking its inspiration from today's headlines (there are indeed some sleazy game operators who hire sweatshop workers to undertake repetitive crafting tasks in-game). The next one is *I, Robot,* and there are others under way. Living in London for the past year, I thought I'd take a crack at U.K. idiom, too.

EDWARD P. JONES is the author of the novel *The Known World,* which has received the National Book Critics Circle Award and the Pulitzer Prize, and of *Lost in the City: Stories.*

▪ "Old Boys, Old Girls" began with the main character in "Young Lions," a story in *Lost in the City.* In the latter story, Caesar is a thief, not quite twenty-five, and growing into a not very nice man. Now, with "Old Boys," we have that fully formed man — a prisoner who has murdered two human beings.

DENNIS LEHANE is the author of seven novels, including *Mystic River* and *Shutter Island.* He lives in Boston, where he is currently writing a novel about, among other things, World War I, the great influenza outbreak of 1918, the Boston police strike of 1919, and the Tulsa race riot of 1921. The only thing he's sure of is that it won't be short.

▪ I'd had the first line of "Until Gwen" bouncing around in my head for a few years when John Harvey asked me to write a story for a British anthology called *Men from Boys.* The only requirement was that it have something to do with fathers and sons. The deadline was maybe a week off, at best, when I finally tried writing it. I was going through a lot of personal turmoil at the time, and I've never been the kind of writer who can write directly about my own life, but I think I do okay when I approach it obliquely. So I took a notepad out onto my front porch, which is surrounded by a hundred-year-old wisteria, and this rainstorm hit, a huge one, bending trees, clattering all over the street and the roof. But the wisteria kept anything from hitting me. I wrote the first draft that night, on my porch, in this crazy storm. It was supposed to be a comic story — that first line, hell, the whole first scene, is pretty absurd — but page by page it kept getting darker and darker until it ended up being arguably the darkest thing I've ever written. The writing of it, though — that whole storm-within/storm-without, mad-scientist vibe — was one of my favorite creative experiences.

J. Robert Lennon is the author of four novels, including *The Light of Falling Stars* and *Mailman,* and a collection of one hundred stories, *Pieces for the Left Hand.* He also recently released a CD of a hundred very short songs, also called *Pieces for the Left Hand,* under his musical alias, Inverse Room. The CD is available at www.jrobertlennon.com.

▪ When my older son, Owen, was a baby, I would struggle to find something productive to do with the hour or so that he slept each afternoon. These pieces are the result. They originally bore no particular relationship to one another, but eventually certain themes began to emerge, and a consistent narrator, who turned out not to be me. There are a hundred stories in all, and I have come to think of the resulting book not as a collection of a hundred stories but as a novel about a guy who writes a hundred stories, with the stories themselves being the only text. Many thanks to *Granta* for taking a chance with these.

Kelly Link is a graduate of Columbia University and received her MFA in Creative Writing from the University of North Carolina at Greensboro. She is the author of two collections of short stories, *Stranger Things Happen* and *Magic for Beginners,* and was the editor of the anthology *Trampoline.* Link and her partner, Gavin J. Grant, have produced the twice-yearly zine *Lady Churchill's Rosebud Wristlet* for almost ten years. They publish books as Small Beer Press and coedit the fantasy half of *The Year's Best Fantasy and Horror* (St. Martin's) with Ellen Datlow. Link's short stories have been published in *Conjunctions, McSweeney's Mammoth Treasury of Thrilling Tales, Asimov's Science Fiction,* and *The Vintage Book of Amnesia.* She lives in Northampton, Massachusetts.

▪ I wrote and rewrote "Stone Animals" for over a year, while living in an apartment in Brooklyn. I knew the first sentence and I knew the ending, which always seemed both terrifying and ridiculous to me. It was the middle that stayed a muddle for a very long time. I don't think I ever would have finished it but for the intervention of two writers, John Kessel and Richard Butner, organizers of Sycamore Hill, a workshop and retreat that meets every other year. Everyone has to bring a finished story, and so I finished my story. Then I went home and rewrote it a few more times. Some stories seem easier to write, and I'm both grateful and also suspicious when this happens. Other stories — like "Stone Animals" — aren't easy in any way, and this also makes me suspicious. The one part of writing this story that was purely satisfying was getting to make up the names of various colors of paints. I became suspicious of this, too, eventually.

"Stone Animals" owes a debt especially to the short stories of the late Joan Aiken. I've always loved ghost stories, weird tales, true (and untrue) stories of haunted houses. Sometimes I think all good short stories function as ghost stories, in which the people, themes, events that grip an individual writer occur again and again like a haunting. Readers, too, can be haunted by stories. As for this story, something about painting and repainting the rooms of a newly purchased house, now that I think about it, seems like a writerly metaphor. (Or perhaps a re-writerly metaphor.) Like ghost stories, and like the act of writing — and rewriting and rewriting and rewriting — the work is as much about concealment as it is about revelation.

THOMAS MCGUANE was born in Michigan and educated at Michigan State University, Yale, and Stanford, where he held the Wallace Stegner Fellowship in writing. He has lived in Montana since 1968.

▪ "Old Friends" was written in my usual long-way-around-the-Horn style. I first imagined an annoying visit interrupting the protagonist's tranquility, a concept that yielded an underrealized story, if it was a story at all, lacking as it did any sense of precedent between the players. Subsequent drafts brought it to its present state where I would hope a reader would sense the weight of personal histories bearing upon a very small piece of time.

DAVID MEANS was born and raised in Kalamazoo, Michigan. He is the author of three story collections, including *Assorted Fire Events,* which won the Los Angeles Times Book Prize and is forthcoming in a new edition from Perennial. His most recent book, *The Secret Goldfish,* was published by HarperCollins. He lives in Nyack, New York, and teaches at Vassar College.

▪ My children had a goldfish — similar in many respects to the one in the story — who seemed to live on and on, growing larger and requiring a transfer to larger living spaces with better filtering equipment. His death was a classic one, providing that moment when they had to confront that essential, primal truth of loss as we dug the grave in the yard and scraped around for a proper tombstone. Perhaps that was the impetus for the story, as was a small section off the Merritt Parkway, a bit of land and then a house back through the trees that used to catch my eye. I wrote the first draft of the story quickly, on a cold winter day, during two sittings, with a short break to go to the bookstore and buy a book on the Greek philosophers. I sat and read a short section on the philosophy of Heraclitus ("The world is an ever-living fire, kindled in measures and in measures going out") and then went back to finish the story. As I wrote, I moved deeper and deeper into the heroine's plight and then, without intending to do so, I found myself moving into fish's point of view, going over to his side, with the deepest sympathy. The story went through many revisions — and a couple of public readings, including one in Galway, Ireland — before I revised it, in a number of small ways, into its present form.

ALICE MUNRO was born in Wingham, Ontario, on July 10, 1931, and educated in the Wingham public schools and the University of Western Ontario. In 1951 she married James Munro, then lived in Vancouver and Victoria for twenty years. She bore three daughters, divorced, married Gerry Fremlin, and has lived for the past thirty years in Clinton, Ontario, twenty miles from where she grew up. She has, she says, "been writing hopefully since I was around eighteen years old."

▪ "Silence" is the final story in a trilogy in which the first story deals with a girl's finding her place — her man — in the world, the second with her relationship with her parents, her leaving them, and the third with her life with — and then without — her child, her coming to be alone. I don't think it is a sad story, particularly. Or all about loss. There is some gain.

JOYCE CAROL OATES is the author most recently of the novel *Missing Mom* and the story collection *The Female of the Species.* She lives in Princeton, New Jersey, where she is on the faculty of Princeton University and has been a member, since 1978, of the American Academy of Arts and Letters.

▪ "The Cousins," part fiction and part family history, is an imagining, decades later, of my father's mother's life as a woman without a personal, familial, or ethnic identity. My grandmother's parents, German Jews, immigrated to America in the late 1890s, changed their name from Morgenstern to Morningstar, and never acknowledged their Jewish roots. As in the short story, my grandmother's father was a gravedigger who came to a violent self-inflicted end. Rebecca makes a gesture my grandmother never did, establishing contact with a Morgenstern cousin who has, in a very different way, repudiated her Jewish background. Yet the two women were born cousins and the bond is indissoluble.

ALIX OHLIN grew up in Montreal and currently lives in Easton, Pennsylvania, where she teaches at Lafayette College. Her short stories have appeared in *Five Points, Shenandoah, Best New American Voices 2004*, and other publications. Her first novel is *The Missing Person.*

▪ When I was a child, I used to walk around my neighborhood and associate certain noises of the world with images. For example, I used to see the sound of a fire siren as a large red keyhole in the sky. Twenty years later, I suddenly remembered this habit — which had long ago disappeared from my life — and thought, boy, that's incredibly weird. The story began from there. It went on to absorb other childhood memories, including years of piano instruction. Sadly, I wasn't nearly the enthusiastic student that Kevin is, and came unprepared to many a lesson. It was no doubt an aggravation to my highly dedicated piano teacher, Dorothy Gillis, to whom I would like now, however belatedly, to apologize.

TOM PERROTTA is the author of five works of fiction, including the novels *Little Children* and *Election* and the story collection *Bad Haircut.* He lives outside Boston.

▪ Several years ago, I had an idea for a story about a home-plate umpire who finds himself unable to make an important call — i.e., he honestly doesn't know if the crucial pitch is a ball or strike, and he refuses to guess, thereby throwing the whole game into doubt. As often happens with story ideas, I scribbled it on a piece of paper and then did nothing with it for a long time. More recently, I had an idea for a story about a brawl that breaks out at a Little League baseball game. I was thinking about ways to tell it, and I remembered my umpire, who was still wandering around in that sad limbo of characters who have not yet found their stories. I had a good time writing "The Smile on Happy Chang's Face" — it was a pleasure to describe a baseball game in minute detail, from the perspective of a troubled umpire — and I was delighted to see it published in *Post Road,* a very cool literary magazine.

TIM PRATT is a poet and fiction writer living in Oakland, California, where he coedits *Flytrap,* a small literary journal, with his partner, Heather Shaw. His stories have appeared in *Lady Churchill's Rosebud Wristlet, The Third Alternative,* and other publications. His collection, *Little Gods,* appeared in 2003, and his first novel, *The Strange Adventures of Rangergirl,* will be coming out in December 2005.

▪ A few years ago I was doing research on the history and legends of the Old West, gathering material for my first novel, when I came across the story of Pearl Hart, the "robber queen" who in 1898 took part in the last stagecoach robbery in U.S. history. Intrigued, I studied further, and found various contradictory and incomplete versions of her story, most of which suggested more questions than they answered. None of the histories seemed to agree on Boot's first name, on the motivation for Pearl's life of crime, or even on the date of her death, which was given variously as being in the 1920s or the 1950s. "Hart and Boot" is my reconsideration of Pearl's exploits as a magical secret history, with John Boot as a sort of tulpa (a being created and sustained by the power of imagination). I took some small liberties with other historical facts, but the essential elements — the crimes, Pearl's imprisonment, her mysterious pregnancy, Boot's equally mysterious escape — are accurate, as far as I know. Above all I tried to stay true to Pearl's spirit.

RISHI REDDI was born in Hyderabad, India, and grew up in England and the United States. Her short stories have appeared in *Harvard Review, The Louisville Review,* and *Prairie Schooner,* and her English translation of Telugu short fiction has appeared in *Partisan Review.* She practiced environmental law in Boston for ten years, representing the state and federal government, before she began to write fiction seriously. "Justice Shiva Ram Murthy" is from the collection *Karma and Other Stories.* She is currently working on her first novel and lives in Brookline, Massachusetts, with her husband, Alexi Lownie.

▪ Several years ago I read a newspaper article about a recent Hindu immigrant from India who sued a fast-food restaurant for serving him a meal containing beef. The judge ended up throwing the case out of court. I was intrigued and wanted to write about a character who would be motivated to file such a suit. As the story evolved, it also came to be about the status of Indian English, spoken on the subcontinent since the arrival of the British in the early 1600s. I'm embarrassed to say that during my childhood, my friends and I had some fun mimicking our parents' Indian accents, but as an adult I realized that the English language is as much at home on the subcontinent as it is in the United States. So I wanted a South Indian speaker's first-person voice, with unique syntax and expression, to be given legitimacy by appearing on the page.

GEORGE SAUNDERS is the author of two short story collections (*Pastoralia* and *CivilWarLand in Bad Decline*) and the children's book *The Very Persistent Gappers of Frip,* with art by Lane Smith. A novella-length fable (*The*

Brief and Frightening Reign of Phil) and a third collection of stories (*The Red Bow*) are forthcoming. He teaches in the creative writing program at Syracuse University.

▪ I started "Bohemians" in 1994 and got stuck in 1995. There the story sat, stalled at what is now Paragraph 58, through the O.J. case, the rest of the Clinton administration, the Bush election, a change of jobs, the astonishing recession of my hairline, etc., etc., victim of Writer's Error 4A: "Knowing Too Well What You Are Doing." I was sure the story was about The Lack of Relation Between Hardship and Moral Virtue. The story was going to show, rather suavely I hoped, that someone who had Suffered Greatly (Mrs. H.) could *actually be a kinder person* than someone (Mrs. Poltoi) who had suffered much less! The fact that this idea would be totally obvious to anyone who had ever actually lived in the world did not stop me from periodically brushing off the story, failing, and putting it away again. Finally I noticed that every time I got to Paragraph 8 ("So Mrs. H. told again how she'd stood rapt in her yard . . .") I got nauseated. It's not uncommon for me to feel nauseated after reading one of my paragraphs, but this was a special kind of nausea, related to how overwritten this paragraph was, how full of a youngish writer's desire to invoke exotica about a part of the world he had never been to. It sounded like Isaac Babel on stupid pills, as if Babel had also taken some dishonesty pills, then decided to write about an Omaha, Nebraska, he had invented in his mind in order to serve a secret moral purpose, then taken some inefficiency pills. Suddenly, after eight years of becoming nauseated after reading this paragraph, a light went on: it wasn't I who was a dishonest posturing braggart, it was *the character.* And in this way the story came to be about something entirely different from what I thought it had been about all those years, thank God, and could finally be finished.

LYNNE SHARON SCHWARTZ's latest book is the novel *The Writing on the Wall.* Some of her earlier books are the novels *Rough Strife* (nominated for a National Book Award), *Leaving Brooklyn* (nominated for a PEN/Faulkner Award), *Disturbances in the Field,* and *In the Family Way;* three short story collections, most recently *Referred Pain;* a collection of poems, *In Solitary;* and the memoir *Ruined by Reading.* She has also published several translations from Italian, among them *A Place to Live: Selected Essays of Natalia Ginzburg,* and *Smoke over Birkenau,* by Liana Millu, which won the 1991 PEN Renato Poggioli Award for Translation. Ms. Schwartz has taught at many university writing programs here and abroad, and lives in New York City.

▪ "A Taste of Dust" came from a story a friend told me about meeting her ex-husband *en famille* after a bitter and long-past divorce. At that point in her life she was able to talk about the ex-husband's furtive nostalgia and yearning quite calmly, even with some wry amusement. Her story fascinated me and I always wanted to write about it, so at last, after years of hoarding it in the back of my mind, I did. Of course I changed the situation, the nature of the characters, the family setup, the emotional tone, indeed virtually everything, as one does when writing fiction. Or at least as I do. Otherwise it wouldn't seem truly mine. What made the fictionalized version of interest to me, in the end, was the turn that comes in the final paragraph — which has nothing to do with my friend's real-life account. Without that final turn, the story might be simply ordinary and predictable. With it, everything that precedes it suddenly shifts into a new configuration. That turn still surprises me, and I hope it surprises readers too.

JOY WILLIAMS's most recent collection of stories is *Honored Guest*, published in 2004.

▪ I don't know. How do these things happen? For the writer, explaining is a dangerous business. Evoking the literal corrupts. All of these characters exist now, though the story would never have existed if the Girls had dogs instead of cats. When cats enter a story, the gates of Hell yawn wide. Redemption in general is at risk.

100 Other Distinguished Stories of 2004

SELECTED BY KATRINA KENISON

ADICHE, CHIMAMANDA NGOZI
Ghosts. *Zoetrope,* Vol. 8, No. 4.
A Private Experience. *The Virginia Quarterly Review,* Vol. 80, No. 3.

ADRIAN, CHRIS
A Child's Book of Sickness and Death. *McSweeney's,* No. 14.

ALARCON, DANIEL
Lima, Peru, July 28, 1979. *The Virginia Quarterly Review,* Vol. 80, No. 3.

ALEXANDER, ANDREW
The Rat. *The Sun,* September.

ALLISON, WILL
What You Have Left. *One Story,* No. 47.

ALMOND, STEVE
In Hoboken When I Was Young. *Ninth Letter,* Spring/Summer.

ALSUM, BENJAMIN
Happy. *Esquire,* December.

ANSHAW, CAROL
Touch and Go. *Tin House,* Vol. 21.

BEATTIE, ANN
Apologies for a Journey Not Taken. *Ninth Letter,* Vol. 1, No. 2.
The Rabbit Hole as Likely Explanation. *The New Yorker,* April 12.

BLOOM, AMY
I Love to See You Coming, I Hate to See You Go. *Tin House,* Vol. 19.

BOYLE, T. CORAGHESSAN
Chicxulub. *The New Yorker,* March 1.

BROWN, JASON
The Lake. *TriQuarterly Review,* No. 117.

BUDNITZ, JUDY
Miracle. *The New Yorker,* July 12 and 19.

CANTOR, RACHEL
Slave for a Day. *The New England Review,* Vol. 24, No. 4.

CARLSON, RON
Introduction to Speech. *Harper's Magazine,* December.

CHETKOVICH, KATHRYN
The Hour of Everything. *Tin House,* Vol. 18.

CLARK, GEORGE MAKANA
The Wide Boys. *Transition,* No. 95.

CLARKE, BROCK
The Reason Was Us. *The Georgia Review*, Vol. LVIII, No. 1.

COOKE, CAROLYN
Isle of Wigs. *The Idaho Review*, Vol. VI.

DAVIES, PETER HO
The New Corporal. *The Virginia Quarterly Review*, Vol. 80, No. 3.

DIXON, STEPHEN
Phone Rings Six. *The Idaho Review*, Vol. VI.

DOCTOROW, E. L.
Child, Dead, in the Rose Garden. *The Virginia Quarterly Review*, No. 80.

EISENBERG, DEBORAH
Twilight of the Superheroes. *Final Edition*, Vol. 1, No. 1.
Window. *Tin House*, Vol. 19.

EMSHWILLER, CAROL
The Assassin. *Ninth Letter*, Vol. 1, No. 2.
My General. *Argosy*, May/June.

ERDRICH, LOUISE
The Plague of Doves. *The New Yorker*, June 28.

FIRST, JOSHUA
In Turnaround. *Conjunctions*, No. 42.

FORD, RICHARD
The Shore. *The New Yorker*, August 2.

FOX, PAULA
The Broad Estates of Death. *Harper's Magazine*, April.

FROEB, IAN DAVID
The Cosmonaut. *Zoetrope*, Vol. 8, No. 3.

FULTON, JOHN
Hunters. *The Southern Review*, Vol. 40, No. 4.

GATES, DAVID
Round on Both Ends and High in the Middle. *Ploughshares*, Vol. 39, Nos. 2 and 3.

GREER, ANDREW SEAN
The Islanders. *The New Yorker*, May 17.

GURGANUS, ALAN
My Heart Is a Snake Farm. *The New Yorker*, November 22.

HAIGH, JENNIFER
The Bottom of Things. *The Virginia Quarterly Review*, Vol. 80, No. 3.

HARMON, JOSHUA
Rope. *TriQuarterly Review*, No. 118.

HARRISON, JIM
Father Daughter. *The New Yorker*, March 29.

HARVEY, MILES
The Drought. *Ploughshares*, Vol. 39, Nos. 2 and 3.

HELMS, BETH
Collusions. *Bomb*, No. 88.

HEMON, ALEKSANDAR
Szmura's Room. *The New Yorker*, June 14 and 21.

HILL, INGRID
Castelgandolfo. *The Southern Review*, Vol. 40, No. 2.

HOLLADAY, CARY
The Green Children. *Black Warrior Review*, Vol. 30, No. 2.

JONES, EDWARD P.
Adam Robinson. *The New Yorker*, December 20 and 27.

KENNEDY, JENNY
A History of Everything, Including You. *Glimmer Train Stories*, Fall, No. 52.

KLIMASEWISKI, MARSHALL N.
The Third House. *Tin House*, Vol. 21.

KOHLER, SHEILA
Violence. *The Antioch Review*, Vol. 62, No. 3.

LAHIRI, JHUMPA
Hell-Heaven. *The New Yorker*, May 24.

LAPCHAROENSAP, RATTAWUT
At the Café Lovely. *Zoetrope*, Vol. 8, No. 3.
Farangs. *Granta*, No. 84.
LASALLE, PETER
A Late Afternoon Swim. *Tin House*, Vol. 19.
LEE, ANDREA
La Ragazza. *The New Yorker*, February 16 and 23.
LEE, CHANG-RAE
Daisy. *The New Yorker*, January 12.
LENNON, J. ROBERT
Ecstasy. *Granta*, No. 87.
LETHEM, JONATHAN
Super Goat Man. *The New Yorker*, April 5.
LI, YIYUN
Persimmons. *The Paris Review*, No. 171.
The Princess of Nebraska. *Ploughshares*, Vol. 30, No. 4.

MCCOLLUM, MALINDA
The Fifth Wall. *The Paris Review*, No. 171.
Good Monks. *McSweeney's*, Fall.
MCDERMOTT, MORGAN
Clutch. *Swink*, Vol. 1, No. 1.
MCNALLY, T. M.
The Gateway. *Conjunctions*, Vol. 43.
MILLHAUSER, STEVEN
The Room in the Attic. *Tin House*, Vol. 20.
MONTEMARANO, NICHOLAS
The November Fifteen. *Esquire*, September.
MOODY, RICK
Savasana. *The Paris Review*, No. 169.
She Forgot. *Conjunctions*, No. 43.
MOZINA, ANDY
The Women Were Leaving the Men. *Tin House*, Vol. 21.
MUNRO, ALICE
Chance. *The New Yorker*, June 14 and 21.
Passion. *The New Yorker*, March 22.
Soon. *The New Yorker*, June 14 and 21.

NARYANAN, VIVEK
My Father, the Perfect Man. *The Agni Review*, No. 59.
NELSON, ANTONYA
Eminent Domain. *The New Yorker*, January 26.

OATES, JOYCE CAROL
Fat Man My Love. *Conjunctions*, Vol. 42.
Spider Boy. *The New Yorker*, September 20.
OHLIN, ALIX
The Tennis Partner. *One Story*, No. 38.
OSCHNER, GINA
The Fractious South. *The New Yorker*, August 23.

PEARLMAN, EDITH
The Coat. *The Idaho Review*, Vol. VI.
PROULX, ANNIE
Man Crawling out of Trees. *The New Yorker*, July 26.
The Wamsutter Wolf. *The Paris Review*, No. 171.

RABOTEAU, EMILY
The Eye of Horus. *Story Quarterly*, Vol. 40.
READ, BONNA NEWMAN
The Cheese Test. *Zyzzyva*, Vol. XX, No. 3.
REICH, TOVA
Forbidden City. *Conjunctions*, Vol. 43.
ROBINSON, ROXANA
Blind Man. *Daedalus*, Summer.
ROW, JESS
The Train to Lo Wu. *Ploughshares*, Vol. 30, No. 4.

SAUNDERS, GEORGE
Adams. *The New Yorker*, August 9 and 16.
SAYLES, JOHN
Cruisers. *Zoetrope*, Vol. 8, No. 3.

SCHAEFFER, SUSAN FROMBERG
Wolves. *Prairie Schooner,* Vol. 78, No. 3.

SCOTT, JOANNA
Across from the Shannonso. *The Cincinnati Review,* Vol. 1, No. 1.

SERBER, NATALIE
A Whole Weekend of My Life. *The Bellingham Review,* Vol. XXVII, No. 54.

SINGLETON, GEORGE
The Novels of Ray Carver. *Ninth Letter,* Vol. 1, No. 2.

STRAIGHT, SUSAN
Bridge Work. *Zoetrope,* Spring.

TOUTONGHI, PAUL
Thomas Hardy's Heart. *One Story,* No. 36.

TREADWAY, JESSICA
Shirley Wants Her Nickel Back. *Ploughshares,* Vol. 30, Nos. 2 and 3.

TRUEBLOOD, VALERIE
The Magic Pebble. *One Story,* No. 35.

UPDIKE, JOHN
Delicate Wives. *The New Yorker,* February 2.
Elsie by Starlight. *The New Yorker,* July 5.

VANDERMEER, JEFF
Three Days in a Border Town. *Polyphony,* No. 4.

VAPNYAR, LARA
Broccoli. *The New Yorker,* January 5.

VAZ, KATHERINE
The Knife Longs for the Ruby. *Ninth Letter,* Spring/Summer.

Editorial Addresses of American and Canadian Magazines Publishing Short Stories

African American Review
St. Louis University
Humanities 317
3800 Lindell Boulevard
St. Louis, MO 63108-2007
$40, Joycelyn Moody

Agni Magazine
Boston University Writing Program
Boston University
236 Bay State Road
Boston, MA 02115
$17, Sven Birkerts

Alabama Literary Review
272 Smith Hall
Troy State University
Troy, AL 36082
$10, Donald Noble

Alaska Quarterly Review
University of Alaska, Anchorage
3211 Providence Drive
Anchorage, AK 99508
$10, Ronald Spatz

Alfred Hitchcock Mystery Magazine
1540 Broadway
New York, NY 10036
$34.97, Cathleen Jordan

Alligator Juniper
Prescott College
220 Grove Avenue
Prescott, AZ 86301
$7.50, Miles Waggener

American Letters and Commentary
850 Park Avenue, Suite 5B
New York, NY 10021
$8, Anna Rabinowitz

American Literary Review
University of North Texas
P.O. Box 311307
Denton, TX 76203-1307
$10, John Tait

Another Chicago Magazine
Left Field Press
3709 North Kenmore
Chicago, IL 60613
$8, Sharon Solwitz

Antioch Review
Antioch University
150 East South College Street
Yellow Springs, OH 45387
$35, Robert S. Fogerty

Argosy
P.O. Box 1421
Taylor, AZ 85939

coppervale@skyboot.com
$49.95, Lou Anders, James Owen

Arkansas Review
Department of English and Philosophy
P.O. Box 1890
Arkansas State University
State University, AR 72467
$20, Tom Williams

Ascent
English Department
Concordia College
901 Eighth Street
Moorhead, MN 56562
$12, W. Scott Olsen

At Length
submissions@atlength.com
$20, Jonathan Farmer

Atlantic Monthly
77 North Washington Street
Boston, MA 02114
$14.95, C. Michael Curtis

Backwards City Review
P.O. Box 41317
Greensboro, NC 27404
$10, Gerry Canavan

Baltimore Review
P.O. Box 410
Riderwood, MD 21139
Barbara Westwood Diehl

Bamboo Ridge
P.O. Box 6176
Honolulu, HI 96839-1781
$35, Eric Chock, Darrell H. Y. Lum

Bayou
Department of English
University of New Orleans
2000 Lakeshore Drive
New Orleans, LA 70148
$10, Joanna Leake

Bellevue Literary Review
Department of Medicine
New York University School of Medicine
550 First Avenue
New York, NY 10016
$12, Danielle Ofri

Bellingham Review
MS-9053
Western Washington University
Bellingham, WA 98225
$14, Brenda Miller

Bellowing Ark
P.O. Box 55564
Shoreline, WA 98155
$18, Robert Ward

Berkshire Review
P.O. Box 105
Richmond, MA 01254-0023
$8.95, Vivan Dorsel

The Best of Carve
P.O. Box 1573
Tallahassee, FL 32302
$15, Melvin Sterne

Black Warrior Review
P.O. Box 862936
Tuscaloosa, AL 35486-0027
$14, Cayenne Sullivan

Blackbird
Department of English
Virginia Commonwealth University
P.O. Box 843082
Richmond, VA 23284-3082
Gregory Donovan and Mary Flinn

Blue Mesa Review
Department of English
University of New Mexico
Albuquerque, NM 87131
Julie Shigekuni

Bomb
New Art Publications
594 Broadway, 10th floor
New York, NY 10012
$18, Betsy Sussler

Boston Review
Building E53-407 MIT

Cambridge, MA 02139
$17, Joshua Cohen, Deborah Chasman

Boulevard
PMB 325
6614 Clayton Road
Richmond Heights, MO 63117
$15, Richard Burgin

Brain, Child: The Magazine for Thinking Mothers
P.O. Box 714
Lexington, VA 24450-0714
$18, Jennifer Niesslein, Stephanie Wilkinson

Briar Cliff Review
3303 Rebecca Street
P.O. Box 2100
Sioux City, IA 51104-2100
$10, Tricia Currans-Sheehan

Bridges
P.O. Box 24839
Eugene, OR 97402
$15, Clare Kinberg

Callaloo
Department of English
Texas A&M University
4227 TAMU
College Station, TX 77843-4227
$40, Charles H. Rowell

Calyx
P.O. Box B
Corvallis, OR 97339
$19.50, Margarita Donnelly and collective

Capilano Review
Capilano College
2055 Purcell Way
North Vancouver
British Columbia V7J 3H5
$25, Sharon Thesen

Carolina Quarterly
Greenlaw Hall CB 3520
University of North Carolina
Chapel Hill, NC 27599-3520
$12, Amy Weldon

Chattahoochee Review
Georgia Perimeter College
2101 Womack Road
Dunwoody, GA 30338-4497
$16, Lawrence Hetrick

Chelsea
P.O. Box 773
Cooper Station
New York, NY 10276
$13, Alfredo de Palchi

Chicago Quarterly Review
517 Sherman Avenue
Evanston, IL 60202
$10, S. Afzal Haider, Jane Lawrence, Lisa McKenzie

Chicago Review
5801 South Kenwood
University of Chicago
Chicago, IL 60637
$18, Erik Steinhoff

Cimarron Review
205 Morrill Hall
Oklahoma State University
Stillwater, OK 74078-0135
$24, E. P. Walkiewicz

The Cincinnati Review
Department of English
McMicken Hall, Room 369
P.O. Box 210069
Cincinnati, OH 45221
$12, Brock Clarke

Colorado Review
Department of English
Colorado State University
Fort Collins, CO 80523
$24, Stephanie G'Schwind

Columbia
2960 Broadway
415 Dodge Hall
Columbia University
New York, NY 10027-6902
$15, S. K. Beringer

Confrontation
English Department
C. W. Post College of Long Island University
Greenvale, NY 11548
$10, Martin Tucker

Conjunctions
21 East 10th Street, Suite 3E
New York, NY 10003
$18, Bradford Morrow

Crab Creek Review
P.O. Box 840
Vashon Island, WA 98070
$10, editorial group

Crab Orchard Review
Department of English
Southern Illinois University at Carbondale
Carbondale, IL 62901
$15, Allison Joseph

Crazyhorse
Department of English
College of Charleston
66 George Street
Charleston, SC 29424
$15, Carol Ann Davis

Crucible
Barton College
P.O. Box 5000
Wilson, NC 27893-7000
Terrence L. Grimes

CutBank
Department of English
University of Montana
Missoula, MT 59812
$12, Elizabeth Conway

Daedalus
136 Irving Street, Suite 100
Cambridge, MA 02138
$33, James Miller

Denver Quarterly
University of Denver
Denver, CO 80208
$20, Bin Ramke

Descant
P.O. Box 314
Station P
Toronto, Ontario M5S 2S8
$25, Karen Mulhallen

Descant
TCU
Box 297270
Fort Worth, TX 76129
$12, Lynn Risser, David Kuhne

Epoch
251 Goldwin Smith Hall
Cornell University
Ithaca, NY 14853-3201
$11, Michael Koch

Esquire
250 West 55th Street
New York, NY 10019
$17.94, Adrienne Miller

Eureka Literary Magazine
Eureka College
300 East College Avenue
Eureka, IL 61530-1500
$15, Loren Logsdon

Event
Douglas College
P.O. Box 2503
New Westminster
British Columbia V3L 5B2
$22, Cathy Stonehouse

Fantasy and Science Fiction
P.O. Box 3447
Hoboken, NJ 07030
$44.89, Gordon Van Gelder

Fiction International
Department of English and Comparative Literature
San Diego State University
San Diego, CA 92182
$12, Harold Jaffe, Larry McCaffery

Fiddlehead
UNB P.O. Box 4400
Fredericton
New Brunswick E3B 5A3
$20, Mark Anthony Jarman

Five Points
Georgia State University
Department of English
University Plaza
Atlanta, GA 30303-3083
$15, David Bottoms

Florida Review
Box 161346
University of Central Florida
Orlando, FL 32816-1346
$15, Jeanne Leiby

Flyway
206 Ross Hall
Department of English
Iowa State University
Ames, IA 50011
$18, Stephen Pett

Folio
Department of Literature
The American University
Washington, DC 20016
$12, Sandra Beasley

The Frostproof Review
P.O. Box 3397
Lake Wales, FL 33859
$15, Kyle Minor

Fugue
Department of English
Brink Hall 200
University of Idaho
Moscow, ID 83844-1102
$14, Ben George, Jeff P. Jones

The Furnace
Historica Bohemian House
3009 Tillman
Detroit, MI 48216
$20, Kelli B. Kavanaugh

Gargoyle
P.O. Box 6216
Arlington, VA 22206-0216
$20, Richard Peabody, Lucinda Ebersole

Georgia Review
University of Georgia
Athens, GA 30602
$24, T. R. Hummer

Gettysburg Review
Gettysburg College
Gettysburg, PA 17325-1491
$24, Peter Stitt

Gingko Tree Review
Drury University
900 North Benton Avenue
Springfield, MO 65802
$10, Randall Fuller

Glimmer Train Stories
710 Southwest Madison Street, Suite 504
Portland, OR 97205
$34, Susan Burmeister-Brown, Linda Swanson-Davies

Gobshite Quarterly
P.O. Box 11346
Portland, OR 97205
$16, R. V. Branham

GQ
4 Times Square, 9th floor
New York, NY 10036
$19.97, Walter Kirn

Grain
Box 1154
Regina, Saskatchewan S4P 3B4
$26.95, Kent Bruyneel

Granta
1755 Broadway, 5th floor
New York, NY 10019-3780
$39.95, Ian Jack

Greensboro Review
134 McIver Building
P.O. Box 26170
University of North Carolina
Greensboro, NC 27412
$10, Jim Clark

Gulf Coast
Department of English
University of Houston
4800 Calhoun Road
Houston, TX 77204-3012
$14, Mark Doty

Gulf Stream
English Department
Florida International University
Biscayne Bay Campus
3000 NE 151st Street
North Miami, FL 33181
$15, John Dufresne, Cindy Chinelly

Harper's Magazine
666 Broadway
New York, NY 10012
$16, Lewis Lapham

Harpur Palate
Department of English
Binghamton University
P.O. Box 6000
Binghamton, NY 13902
$16, Letitia Moffitt, Doris Umbers

Harvard Review
Poetry Room
Harvard College Library
Cambridge, MA 02138
$16, Christina Thompson

Hawaii Review
Department of English
University of Hawaii
1733 Donaghho Road
Honolulu, HI 96822
$20, Jonathan Padua

Hayden's Ferry Review
Box 871502
Arizona State University
Tempe, AZ 85287-1502
$14, Salima Keegan

Hobart / Monkeybicycle
23-55 38th Street
Astoria, NY 11105
Aaron Burch

Hotel Amerika
Department of English
Ellis Hall
Ohio University
Athens, OH 45701
$18, David Lazar

Hudson Review
684 Park Avenue
New York, NY 10021
$24, Paula Deitz

Idaho Review
Boise State University
1910 University Drive
Boise, ID 83725
$9.95, Mitch Wieland

Image
Center for Religious Humanism
3307 Third Avenue West
Seattle, WA 98119
$36, Gregory Wolfe

Indiana Review
Ballantine Hall 465
1020 East Kirkwood Avenue
Bloomington, IN 47405-7103
$14, David J. Daniels

Indy Men's Magazine
8500 Keystone Crossing, Suite 100
Indianapolis, IN 46240
Lou Harry

InkPot
Lit Pot Press, Inc.
3909 Reche Road, Suite 132
Fallbrook, CA 92028
$30, Beverly Jackson, Carol Peters

Iowa Review
Department of English
University of Iowa
308 EPB
Iowa City, IA 52242
$20, David Hamilton

Iris
University of Virginia Women's Center
P.O. Box 800588

Charlottesville, VA 22908
$9, Gina Welch

Italian Americana
University of Rhode Island
Providence Campus
80 Washington Street
Providence, RI 02903
$20, Carol Bonomo Albright

Jabberwock Review
Department of English
Drawer E
Mississippi State University
Mississippi State, MS 39762
$12, Joy Murphy

The James White Review
Lambda Literary Foundation
P.O. Box 73910
Washington, DC 20056-3910
Patrick Merla

Jewish Currents
22 East 17th Street
New York, NY 10003
$20, editorial board

The Journal
Department of English
Ohio State University
164 West Seventeenth Avenue
Columbus, OH 43210
$12, Kathy Fagan, Michelle Herman

Kalliope
Florida Community College
3939 Roosevelt Boulevard
Jacksonville, FL 32205
$12.50, Mary Sue Koeppel

Kenyon Review
Kenyon College
Gambier, OH 43022
$25, David H. Lynn

Lady Churchill's Rosebud Wristlet
Small Beer Press
176 Prospect Avenue
Northampton, MA 01060
$20, Kelly Link

Lake Effect
Penn State Erie
5091 Station Road
Erie, PA 16563-1501
$6, George Looney

Land-Grant College Review
P.O. Box 1164
New York, NY 10159
$18, Tara Wray

The Literary Review
Fairleigh Dickinson University
285 Madison Avenue
Madison, NJ 07940
$18, Rene Steinke

Louisiana Literature
LSU 10792
Southeastern Louisiana University
Hammond, LA 70402
$12, Jack B. Bedell

Louisville Review
Spalding University
851 South Fourth Street
Louisville, KY 40203
$14, Sena Jeter Naslund

Lynx Eye
ScribbleFest Literary Group
542 Mitchell Drive
Los Osnos, CA 93402
$25, Pam McCully, Kathryn Morrison

Manoa
English Department
University of Hawaii
Honolulu, HI 96822
$22, Frank Stewart

Massachusetts Review
South College
Box 37140
University of Massachusetts
Amherst, MA 01003
$22, David Lenson, Ellen Dore Watson

Matrix
1455 de Maisonneuve Boulevard West
Suite LB-514-8

Montreal, Quebec H3G IM8
$21, R.E.N. Allen

McSweeney's
826 Valencia Street
San Francisco, CA 94110
$36, Dave Eggers

Meridian
Department of English
P.O. Box 400145
University of Virginia
Charlottesville, VA 22904-4145
$10, Caitlin Johnson

Michigan Quarterly Review
3032 Rackham Building
915 East Washington Street
University of Michigan
Ann Arbor, MI 48109
$25, Laurence Goldstein

Mid-American Review
Department of English
Bowling Green State University
Bowling Green, OH 43403
$12, Michael Czyzniejewski

Midnight Mind
P.O. Box 146912
Chicago, IL 60614
$12, Brett Van Emst

Minnesota Monthly
600 US Trust Building
730 Second Avenue South
Minneapolis, MN 55402
Jeff Johnson

Minnesota Review
Department of English
University of Missouri, Columbia
107 Tate Hall
Columbia, MO 65211
$30, Jeffrey Williams

Mississippi Review
University of Southern Mississippi
Southern Station, Box 5144
Hattiesburg, MS 39406-5144
$15, Frederick Barthelme

Missouri Review
1507 Hillcrest Hall
University of Missouri
Columbia, MO 65211
$22, Speer Morgan

Ms.
433 South Beverly Drive
Beverly Hills, CA 90212
$45, Amy Bloom

n + 1
Park West Finance Station
P.O. Box 20688
New York, NY 10025
$16, Allison Lorentzen

Natural Bridge
Department of English
University of Missouri, St. Louis
8001 Natural Bridge Road
St. Louis, MO 63121-4499
$15, Jason Rizos

Nebraska Review
Writers Workshop
WFAB 212
University of Nebraska at Omaha
Omaha, NE 68182-0324
$15, James Reed

New England Review
Middlebury College
Middlebury, VT 05753
$25, Stephen Donadio

New Letters
University of Missouri
5100 Rockhill Road
Kansas City, MO 64110
$17, Robert Stewart

New Orleans Review
P.O. Box 195
Loyola University
New Orleans, LA 70118
$12, Christopher Chambers

New Orphic Review
706 Mill Street
Nelson, British Columbia V1L 4S5
$25, Ernest Hekkanen

New Quarterly
English Language Proficiency Programme
Saint Jerome's University
200 University Avenue West
Waterloo, Ontario N2L 3G3
$36, Kim Jernigan

The New Renaissance
26 Heath Road, Suite 11
Arlington, MA 02474
$13.50, Louise T. Reynolds

New York Stories
English Department
La Guardia Community College
31-10 Thomson Avenue
Long Island City, NY 11101
$13.40, Daniel Caplice Lynch

The New Yorker
4 Times Square
New York, NY 10036
$46, Deborah Treisman

NFG
Sheppard Centre
P.O. Box 43112
Toronto, Ontario M2N 6N1
Canada
$20, Shar O'Brien

Night Train
85 Orchard Street
Somerville, MA 02144
$17.95, Rod Siino, Rusty Barnes

Nimrod International Journal
Arts and Humanities Council of Tulsa
600 South College Avenue
Tulsa, OK 74104
$17.50, Francine Ringold

Ninth Letter
Department of English
University of Illinois
608 South Wright Street
Urbana, IL 61801
$19.95, Jodee Rubins

Noon
1369 Madison Avenue
PMB 298
New York, NY 10128
$9, Diane Williams

North American Review
University of Northern Iowa
1222 West 27th Street
Cedar Falls, IA 50614
$22, Grant Tracy

North Carolina Literary Review
Department of English
2201 Bate Building
East Carolina University
Greenville, NC 27858-4353
Margaret Bauer

North Dakota Quarterly
University of North Dakota
P.O. Box 8237
Grand Forks, ND 58202
$25, Robert Lewis

Northwest Review
369 PLC
University of Oregon
Eugene, OR 97403
$22, John Witte

Notre Dame Review
Department of English
356 O'Shag
University of Notre Dame
Notre Dame, IN 46556-5639
$15, John Matthias, William O'Rourke

Oasis
P.O. Box 626
Largo, FL 34649-0626
$20, Neal Storrs

Oklahoma Today
15 North Robinson, Suite 100
P.O. Box 53384
Oklahoma City, OK 73102
$16.95, Louisa McCune

One Story
P.O. Box 1326
New York, NY 10156
$21, Maribeth Batcha, Hannah Tinti

Ontario Review
9 Honey Brook Drive
Princeton, NJ 08540
$16, Raymond J. Smith

onthebus
Bombshelter Press
Los Angeles, CA 90048
$28, Jack Grapes

Open City
225 Lafayette Street, Suite 1114
New York, NY 10012
$32, Thomas Beller, Joanna Yas

Orchid
3096 Williamsburg
P.O. Box 131457
Ann Arbor, MI 48113-1457
$16, Keith Hood, Amy Sumerton

Other Voices
University of Illinois at Chicago
Department of English, M/C 162
601 South Morgan Street
Chicago, IL 60607-7120
$24, Gina Frangello

Oxalis
Stone Ridge Poetry Society
P.O. Box 3993
Kingston, NY 12401
$18, Shirley Powell

Oxford American
201 Donaghey Avenue, Main 107
Conway, AR 72035
$29.95, Marc Smirnoff

Oyez
School of Liberal Studies
Roosevelt University
430 South Michigan Avenue
Chicago, IL 60605

Oyster Boy Review
P.O. Box 77842
San Francisco, CA 94107
$20, Damon Sauve

Pangolin Papers
Turtle Press
P.O. Box 241
Norland, WA 98358
$20, Pat Britt

Paper Street
Paper Street Press
P.O. Box 14786
Pittsburgh, PA 15234
Arlan Hess

Paris Review
541 East 72nd Street
New York, NY 10021
$34, Brigid Hughes

Parting Gifts
3413 Wilshire Drive
Greensboro, NC 27408-2923
Robert Bixby

Passages North
English Department
Northern Michigan University
1401 Presque Isle Avenue
Marquette, MI 49007-5363
$10, Katie Hanson

Penny Dreadful
P.O. Box 719
Radio City Station
New York, NY 10101-0719
$12

Phantasmagoria
English Department
Century Community and Technical College
3300 Century Avenue North
White Bear Lake, MN 55110
$15, Abigail Allen

Phoebe
George Mason University
MSN 2D6
4400 University Drive
Fairfax, VA 22030-4444
$12, Lisa Ampleman

Playboy
Playboy Building
919 North Michigan Avenue

Chicago, IL 60611
$29.97, Christopher Napolitano

Pleiades
Department of English and Philosophy
Central Missouri State University
P.O. Box 800
Warrensburg, MO 64093
$12, Susan Steinberg

Ploughshares
Emerson College
120 Boylston Street
Boston, MA 02116
$22, Don Lee

Poem Memoir Story
Department of English
University of Alabama at Birmingham
217 Humanities Building
900 South 13th Street
Birmingham, AL 35294-1260
$7, Linda Frost

Porcupine
P.O. Box 259
Cedarburg, WI 53012
$15.95, editorial group

Post Road
P.O. Box 400951
Cambridge, MA 02420
$18, Mary Cotton

Potomac Review
Montgomery College
51 Mannakee Street
Rockville, MD 20850
$20, Eli Flam

Prairie Fire
423-100 Arthur Street
Winnipeg, Manitoba R3B 1H3
$25, Andris Taskans

Prairie Schooner
201 Andrews Hall
University of Nebraska
Lincoln, NE 68588-0334
$26, Hilda Raz

Primavera
P.O. Box 37-7547
Chicago, IL 60637
Editorial group

Prism International
Department of Creative Writing
University of British Columbia
Buchanan E-462
Vancouver, British Columbia V6T 1W5
$22, Catharine Chen

Provincetown Arts
650 Commercial Street
Provincetown, MA 02657
$10, Christopher Busa

Puerto del Sol
MSCC 3E
New Mexico State University
P.O. Box 30001
Las Cruces, NM 88003
$10, Kevin McIlvoy

Quarterly West
2055 South Central Campus Drive
Department of English/LNCO 3500
University of Utah
Salt Lake City, Utah 84112
$14, David Hawkins

Red Rock Review
English Department, J2A
Community College of Southern Nevada
3200 East Cheyenne Avenue
North Las Vegas, NV 89030
$9.50, Richard Logsdon

Red Wheelbarrow
De Anza College
21250 Stevens Creek Boulevard
Cupertino, CA 95014-5702
$5, Randolph Splitter

Republic of Letters
120 Cushing Avenue
Boston, MA 02125-2033
$35, Keith Botsford

River City
Department of English

University of Memphis
Memphis, TN 38152
$12, Tom Carlson

River Oak Review
River Oak Arts
P.O. Box 3127
Oak Park, IL 60303
$12, Mary Lee MacDonald

River Styx
Big River Association
634 North Grand Boulevard, 12th floor
St. Louis, MO 63103-1002
$20, Richard Newman

Room of One's Own
P.O. Box 46160
Station D
Vancouver, British Columbia V6J 5G5
$22, Patricia Robitaille

Rosebud
P.O. Box 459
Cambridge, WI 53523
$18, Roderick Clark

Salmagundi
Skidmore College
Saratoga Springs, NY 12866
$20, Robert Boyers

Salon.com
41 East 11th Street, 11th Floor
New York, NY 10003
Joan Walsh

Salt Hill
English Department
Syracuse University
Syracuse, NY 13244
$15, Ellen Litman

Santa Monica Review
1900 Pico Boulevard
Santa Monica, CA 90405
$12, Andrew Tonkovich

Sewanee Review
University of the South
Sewanee, TN 37375-4009
$24, George Core

Shenandoah
Mattingly House
2 Lee Avenue
Washington and Lee University
Lexington, VA 24450-0303
$22, R. T. Smith, Lynn Leech

Slow Trains Literary Journal
Samba Mountain Press
P.O. Box 4741
Englewood, CO 80155
$14.95, Susannah Indigo

So to Speak: A Feminist Journal of Language
4400 University Drive
George Mason University
Fairfax, VA 22030
$12, Nancy Pearson

Songs of Innocence
Pendragon Publications
P.O. Box 719
Radio City Station
New York, NY 10101-0719
$12, Michael M. Pendragon

Sonora Review
Department of English
University of Arizona
Tucson, AZ 85721
$12, Kristi Maxwell, Carol Test

South Dakota Review
University of South Dakota
P.O. Box 111 University Exchange
Vermilion, SD 57069
$15, Brian Bedard

The Southeast Review
Department of English
Florida State University
Tallahassee, FL 32306
$10, Edward Tarkington

Southern Exposure
P.O. Box 531
Durham, NC 27702
$24, Chris Kromm

Southern Humanities Review
9088 Haley Center
Auburn University
Auburn, AL 36849
$15, Dan R. Latimer, Virginia M. Kouidis

The Southern Review
43 Allen Hall
Louisiana State University
Baton Rouge, LA 70803

Southwest Review
Southern Methodist University
P.O. Box 4374
Dallas, TX 75275
$24, Willard Spiegelman

Spire
532 LaGuardia Place, Suite 298
New York, NY 10012
$18

Story Quarterly
431 Sheridan Road
Kenilworth, IL 60043-1220
$12, M.M.M. Hayes

StorySouth
898 Chelsea Avenue
Bexley, OH 43209
Jason Sanford

Sun
107 North Roberson Street
Chapel Hill, NC 27516
$34, Sy Safransky

Swink
244 Fifth Avenue, No. 2722
New York, NY 10001
$16, *Leelila Strogov*

Sycamore Review
Department of English
500 Oval Drive
Purdue University
West Lafayette, IN 47907
$12, Sean M. Conrey

Talking River Review
Division of Literature and Languages
Lewis-Clark State College
500 Eighth Avenue
Lewiston, ID 83501
$14, editorial board

Tampa Review
University of Tampa
401 West Kennedy Boulevard
Tampa, FL 33606-1490
$15, Richard Mathews

Third Coast
Department of English
Western Michigan University
Kalamazoo, MI 49008-5092
$11, Glenn Deutsch

Threepenny Review
P.O. Box 9131
Berkeley, CA 94709
$16, Wendy Lesser

Timber Creek Review
8969 UNCG Station
Greensboro, NC 27413
$15, John Freiermuth

Tin House
P.O. Box 10500
Portland, OR 97296-0500
$39.80, Rob Spillman

Transition
69 Dunster Street
Harvard University
Cambridge, MA 02138
$28, Kwame Anthony Appiah, Henry Louis Gates, Jr., Michael Vazquez

TriQuarterly
2020 Ridge Avenue
Northwestern University
Evanston, IL 60208
$24, Susan Firestone Hahn

Twenty Pounds of Headlights
17410 Guernewood Lane
Guerneville, CA 95446
Daniel Coshnear

The Vanderbilt Review
Vanderbilt University

Station B
Box 357016
Nashville, TN 37235-7016
$10, rotating

Virginia Quarterly Review
One West Range
P.O. Box 400223
Charlottesville, VA 22903
$18, Ted Genoways

War, Literature, and the Arts
Department of English and Fine Arts
2354 Fairchild Drive, Suite 6D45
USAF Academy, CO 80840-6242
$10, Donald Anderson

Wascana Review
English Department
University of Regina
Regina, Saskatchewan S4S 0A2
$10, Marcel DeCoste

Washington Square
Creative Writing Program
New York University
19 University Place, 2nd floor
New York, NY 10003-4556
$6, James Pritchard

Watchword
P.O. Box 5755
Berkeley, CA 94705
Kasia Newman, Liz Lisle

Weber Studies
Weber State University
1214 University Circle
Ogden, UT 84408-1214
$20, Brad Roghaar

West Branch
Bucknell Hall
Bucknell University
Lewisburg, PA 17837
$10, Paula Closson Buck

Western Humanities Review
University of Utah
255 South Central Campus Drive
Room 3500
Salt Lake City, UT 84112
$16, Barry Weller

Willow Springs
Eastern Washington University
705 West First Avenue
Spokane, WA 99201
$13, Samuel Ligon

Windsor Review
Department of English
University of Windsor
Windsor, Ontario N9B 3P4
$29.95, Alistair MacLeod

Writers' Forum
University of Colorado
P.O. Box 7150
Colorado Springs, CO 80933-7150
$8.95, Alexander Blackburn

The Yale Review
P.O. Box 208243
New Haven, CT 06520-8243
$27, J. D. McClatchy

Yankee
Yankee Publishing, Inc.
Dublin, NH 03444
$22, Michael Carlton

Zoetrope
The Sentinel Building
916 Kearney Street
San Francisco, CA 94133
$19.95, Michael Ray

Zyzzyva
P.O. Box 590069
San Francisco, CA 94109
$28, Howard Junker

THE B·E·S·T AMERICAN SERIES®

THE BEST AMERICAN SHORT STORIES® 2005

Michael Chabon, guest editor, Katrina Kenison, series editor. "Story for story, readers can't beat the *Best American Short Stories* series" (*Chicago Tribune*). This year's most beloved short fiction anthology is edited by the Pulitzer Prize–winning novelist Michael Chabon and features stories by Tom Perrotta, Alice Munro, Edward P. Jones, Joyce Carol Oates, and Thomas McGuane, among others.

0-618-42705-8 PA $14.00 / 0-618-42349-4 CL $27.50

THE BEST AMERICAN ESSAYS® 2005

Susan Orlean, guest editor, Robert Atwan, series editor. Since 1986, *The Best American Essays* has gathered the best nonfiction writing of the year and established itself as the premier anthology of its kind. Edited by the best-selling writer Susan Orlean, this year's volume features writing by Roger Angell, Jonathan Franzen, David Sedaris, Andrea Barrett, and others.

0-618-35713-0 PA $14.00 / 0-618-35712-2 CL $27.50

THE BEST AMERICAN MYSTERY STORIES™ 2005

Joyce Carol Oates, guest editor, Otto Penzler, series editor. This perennially popular anthology is sure to appeal to crime fiction fans of every variety. This year's volume is edited by the National Book Award winner Joyce Carol Oates and offers stories by Scott Turow, Dennis Lehane, Louise Erdrich, George V. Higgins, and others.

0-618-51745-6 PA $14.00 / 0-618-51744-8 CL $27.50

THE BEST AMERICAN SPORTS WRITING™ 2005

Mike Lupica, guest editor, Glenn Stout, series editor. "An ongoing centerpiece for all sports collections" (*Booklist*), this series has garnered wide acclaim for its extraordinary sports writing and topnotch editors. Mike Lupica, the *New York Daily News* columnist and best-selling author, continues that tradition with pieces by Michael Lewis, Gary Smith, Bill Plaschke, Pat Jordan, L. Jon Wertheim, and others.

0-618-47020-4 PA $14.00 / 0-618-47019-0 CL $27.50

THE BEST AMERICAN TRAVEL WRITING 2005

Jamaica Kincaid, guest editor, Jason Wilson, series editor. Edited by the renowned novelist and travel writer Jamaica Kincaid, *The Best American Travel Writing 2005* captures the traveler's wandering spirit and ever-present quest for adventure. Giving new life to armchair journeys this year are Tom Bissell, Ian Frazier, Simon Winchester, John McPhee, and many others.

0-618-36952-X PA $14.00 / 0-618-36951-1 CL $27.50

THE B·E·S·T AMERICAN SERIES®

THE BEST AMERICAN SCIENCE AND NATURE WRITING 2005

Jonathan Weiner, guest editor, Tim Folger, series editor. This year's edition presents another "eclectic, provocative collection" (*Entertainment Weekly*). Edited by Jonathan Weiner, the author of *The Beak of the Finch* and *Time, Love, Memory,* it features work by Oliver Sacks, Natalie Angier, Malcolm Gladwell, Sherwin B. Nuland, and others.

0-618-27343-3 PA $14.00 / 0-618-27341-7 CL $27.50

THE BEST AMERICAN RECIPES 2005–2006

Edited by Fran McCullough and Molly Stevens. "Give this book to any cook who is looking for the newest, latest recipes and the stories behind them" (*Chicago Tribune*). Offering the very best of what America is cooking, as well as the latest trends, time-saving tips, and techniques, this year's edition includes a foreword by celebrated chef Mario Batali.

0-618-57478-6 CL $26.00

THE BEST AMERICAN NONREQUIRED READING 2005

Edited by Dave Eggers, Introduction by Beck. In this genre-busting volume, best-selling author Dave Eggers draws the finest, most interesting, and least expected fiction, nonfiction, humor, alternative comics, and more from publications large, small, and on-line. With an introduction by the Grammy Award–winning musician Beck, this year's volume features writing by Jhumpa Lahiri, George Saunders, Aimee Bender, Stephen Elliott, and others.

0-618-57048-9 PA $14.00 / 0-618-57047-0 CL $27.50

THE BEST AMERICAN SPIRITUAL WRITING 2005

Edited by Philip Zaleski, Introduction by Barry Lopez. Featuring an introduction by the National Book Award winner Barry Lopez, *The Best American Spiritual Writing 2005* brings the year's finest writing about faith and spirituality to all readers. This year's volume gathers pieces from diverse faiths and denominations and includes writing by Natalie Goldberg, Harvey Cox, W. S. Merwin, Patricia Hampl, and others.

0-618-58643-1 PA $14.00 / 0-618-58642-3 CL $27.50

HOUGHTON MIFFLIN COMPANY www.houghtonmifflinbooks.com